N

SUDDEN

FICTION

NEW
SUDDEN
FICTION

SHORT-SHORT STORIES
FROM AMERICA
AND BEYOND

EDITED BY

ROBERT SHAPARD
AND ## JAMES THOMAS

W. W. NORTON & COMPANY

New York   London

For information about permission to reproduce selections from this book,
write to Permissions, W. W. Norton & Company, Inc.,
500 Fifth Avenue, New York, NY 10110

Manufacturing by LSC Harrisonburg
Book design by Joanne Metsch
Production manager: Anna Oler

Library of Congress Cataloging-in-Publication Data

New sudden fiction : short-short stories from America and beyond /
edited by Robert Shapard and James Thomas.—1st ed.
p. cm.
Includes bibliographical references.
ISBN-13: 978-0-393-32801-1 (pbk.)
ISBN-10: 0-393-32801-5 (pbk.)
1. Short stories—Translations into English. 2. Short stories, American.
3. Short stories, English. I. Shapard, Robert, date. II. Thomas, James, date.
PN6120.2.N49 2007
813.0108—dc22

2006032221

W. W. Norton & Company, Inc., 500 Fifth Avenue, New York, N.Y. 10110
www.wwnorton.com

W. W. Norton & Company Ltd.,
15 Carlisle Street, London W1D 3BS

To our families, who have been, and are, everything.

~

To Carol Houck Smith for her encouragement through the years and her good judgment always.

Also truly part of this book, not only in helping select sudden fictions but in many other ways, are Nat Sobel at Sobel Weber Associates in New York; Jesse Edell-Berlin, also in New York at Columbia; Jennifer Keeney Gantner, Jerome Gantner, Scott Geisel, and J. Andrew Root in Ohio; Margaret Bentley, Katherin Nolte, and Gwen Shapard in Texas; Tim Denevi, Angie Flaherty, Brent Fujinaka, Jess Kroll, Sara Pardes, Janna Plant, Nani Ross, Leigh Saffold, Revé Shapard, and Sandi Yamada in Hawaii; Ian MacDonald in Arizona; John Soper in North Carolina; Mickey Edell in Michigan; and Julie Mason in Ontario.

Special thanks to Tom Jenks and Carol Edgarian of NarrativeMagazine.com for telling the world about us and for their love of stories of all kinds.

CONTENTS

Contents

Contents

Contents

Contents

Contents

EDITORS' NOTE

WITH OUR TIN trumpet and drum, we hereby present the best *sudden fictions* of the twenty-first century from America. (And some from beyond America, because more than ever we welcome translations of new work from other countries.)

If you are only now discovering *sudden fiction* and are wondering what it is, the answer is easy: very short stories, only a few pages long. If you are a fan of past *Sudden Fictions*, your questions may be more searching: Where have you been? Your last volume was several years ago. And what is "new" sudden fiction?

When we first began to see short-short fiction cropping up in literary magazines, we didn't know what they were or what to call them: Experimental fictions? Sketches? Prose poems? Anecdotes? Enigmas? One thing they were definitely *not* were little formula stories with an ironic twist at the end, the sort of O. Henry brand manufactured for popular magazines generations ago. These new works didn't end with a twist or a bang, but were *suddenly just there*, surprising, unpredictable, hilarious, serious, moving, in only a few pages. In fact, some were so short we wondered if they could be defined at all. Consider one of our favorites, Enrique Anderson Imbert's "Taboo," at a mere thirty-two words:

> His guardian angel whispered to Fabian, behind his shoulder:
> "Careful, Fabian! It is decreed that you will die the minute you pronounce the word *doyen*."
> "Doyen?" asks Fabian, intrigued.
> And he dies.

We can't help but laugh. Of course this short-short story is only a joke, or anecdote, as nearly all prose works of this length will be. We enjoyed them, yet in further reading we found that the richest, most satisfying works weren't jokes or anecdotes, nor were they sketches or narrative summaries, but complete stories—usually at least a page long. Deciding to concentrate on these, we asked writers to describe them. Russell Banks said their driving source was "not the need that created the novel" but an older urge, "the same need that created Norse kennings, Zen koans, Sufi tales," manifested in contemporary literary fiction. Fascinating, we said—but why is it happening now?

Critics were quick to tell us: it was because TV had shrunk our attention spans.

The proper model for fiction, according to some of them, was the nineteenth-century novel, with its heroic individuals making moral decisions over a long span of time. There were other views, though, even from the nineteenth century. Chekhov, for example, thought Dostoyevsky's novels were pretentious and too long. This was pointed out in the intro-duction to *Sudden Fiction International* by Charles Baxter, who said it's a matter of vision, "of where you think reality takes place." He compared the novel spatially to an estate, and very short fiction to an efficiency on the twenty-third floor, not-ing that "more of us these days live in efficiencies than on estates."

We had been looking abroad and finding that short-shorts were popular in China, too, where people read them on the bus or at work on cigarette breaks—*smoke-long stories*, they called them. In Japan they were called *palm-of-the-hand stories.* Maybe they were less about attention spans than about per-sonal space. In that space, it seemed a story could be anything: in Europe and Latin America, many were postmodern or magically real, in India politically engaged, in Africa ritualis-tic, in Australia poetic. They were so various, we began to wonder, were they all really one form?

We decided to search for a distinction within the genre. Stories of only a page or two seemed to us different not only in length but in nature; they evoked a single moment, or an idea, whereas a five-page story, however experimental, was more akin to the traditional short story. Calling on the wis-dom of Solomon, we split the child (*sudden fiction*) into two new children. The longer story became *"new" sudden fiction*, while the shorter became *flash*, named by James Thomas, edi-tor of a volume called *Flash Fiction.*

And it did seem the right time for *flash*: ever shorter fic-tion was appearing in the literary magazines. Once there was only the *North American Review*'s "four-minute story" (named for how long it took to read it); now came *fast fiction*, *skinny fiction*, *mini fiction*, *quick fiction*, and *micro fiction*, the last a mere 250 words. Poor *"new" sudden fiction*, averaging a whopping

1,500 words—it was like an awkward child in a fairy tale, the longest one (maybe a little overweight, too) in a family proud of being very short. And in the great race to be shortest of all, there was no hope that this most awkward child would bring home a ribbon. No matter, we loved it anyway. We always had in mind to do another book of *suddens* (as well as another *flash*), but what was the hurry?

Gradually the Internet became part of our lives. We saw good literary magazines coming online; we saw the literary environment changing. Finally the time was right to get started again.

First, of course, we checked the Net. The short-short race (if it was that) had turned to fixed forms, with 69-worders and 55-worders in the lead. And there were experiments like *McSweeney's* "twenty-minute stories" (stories that took that long not to read, but to *write*). But there were surprises. We Googled all kinds of short-shorts and found most entries were for "sudden fiction." Could this be right? True, it had been around longer than some of the others. We checked our finding against the number of Google pages for recent *New York Times* best sellers. "Sudden fiction" beat out several of them, including those made into movies—even some chosen by Oprah. As a final check, we tested the first phrase that came to mind ("armadillo sex") and found *this too* out-Googled the *New York Times* and Oprah. We concluded Google wasn't necessarily a good judge of literature.

To find what was happening now with short-short fiction in America, we would have to get into print because even in the age of the Internet, paper is still the medium of most literary fiction. We set out on a two-year journey, reading nearly every literary magazine and journal through six years of issues (and web pages), along with mountains of books. We recruited writers, editors, and others who loved to read, asking them to rate the best works we had found so far. We made notes: *sud-dens* were everywhere now, even more than *flashes*, not in oddball feature sections as they once were, but in the regular contents of the literaries and the big slicks and in single-author book collections. *Suddens* were also equally written by men and women (very short forms on the Internet are more often written by males). Most surprising, though, it was the *suddens*, not the *flashes*, that got the most 10s from our readers.

We should have expected this. We knew *flashes* were hard to write well, with their narrower range. Finding a good *flash* was like sighting a comet, all the more glorious for its being rare—as if we were kids out all the long summer evening searching the night sky.

Yet the rarity of good *flashes* didn't account for so many good *suddens*. If the difference between a *flash* and a *sudden* is only another turn or two of a page, what happened in that turn of a page that made Joyce Carol Oates compare *suddens* to "Chopin's brilliant little Preludes," or Jonathan Penner call them "tiny kingdoms," or Mark Strand claim they "can do in a page what a novel does in two hundred"?

We looked at a few *suddens* we had in hand. Young Cuban teenagers sail away from their village, forgetting their sexes and identities. A bank clerk becomes a fox in a forest. An amnesiac husband has an affair in the candlelit darkness of a cathedral—with his wife. A little irreverent maybe, or subversive. We looked at the biographical notes we had begun collecting about the authors: they had written for *The Best American Travel Writing* and *The Best American Short Stories*. They had been awarded Obies and Oscars for their writing, had won the highest national book awards in their countries, had even won Pulitzers and the Nobel. These were fabulous storytellers. That was the answer, in front of us all along—the turn of the page took us more deeply into the realm of story.

Not that our goal was ever to seek out famous authors. All we wanted was to find the best stories, whoever wrote them and wherever we could find them, whether in *The New Yorker* or the *Mudrock Review.*

At last it was time to wrap up. Like kids on a long summer evening, we had seen a few comets, but mostly gathered stories, and now we were ready to come marching in with our tin trumpet and drum. Was anything missing? Where was that note of irreverence? In the last biographical note we received, the noted author Patricia Marx claimed she won the Friedrich Medal. The Friedrich Medal? It sounded familiar, but reading on we found that it was an "award made up by Patricia Marx and named after her air conditioner."

That's when we knew we were home.

Robert Shapard and James Thomas

NEW
SUDDEN
FICTION

JUAN JOSÉ MILLÁS

Other Persons

Translated from the Spanish by Tobias Hecht

'M ANOTHER PERSON now, since the accident. My family, my friends, my colleagues at work, everyone knows that my car flipped over four times and that I was hospitalized for four months—one month per rollover—but no one noticed the changes in my personality.

I remember how upon entering the house, where I was to continue convalescing, I felt out of place in the domestic world. I had a vague recollection of the family environment, of the tenderness my children awakened in me and the loving indifference I had felt for my wife before the accident. But the whole panorama had changed. The home now felt like the summary of all homes; the kids, while not quite bothersome, were beings indifferent to my influence, strangers to my affection. I would observe them with something like curiosity, as if I were watching someone else's children, and make absurd comparisons with imaginary children whose nature I had come to feel proud of. As for my wife, I confess I started to observe her with the guarded covetousness of an interloper.

So after the kids had left for school, when she would bring me breakfast in bed or take out the thermometer to check my temperature, I would feel like I'd been given the privilege of fraudulently occupying the bed of another man, of receiving the attentions of someone else's wife. You could say I was enjoying—without guilt or danger—the singular freedom of a mitigated version of adultery.

Talk about the good life. I still remember how, with her bathrobe slightly agape, she would lean over to bring me a tray of coffee and reveal her breasts with tantalizing indifference. Or how, when straightening the sheets, the tips of her hair would move across my lonely thighs. And I can't forget how she would nonchalantly get dressed in front of me, making an offhand remark about the weather, the electricity bill, or the strange hue of those cold early-March mornings. Sometimes, faced with these domestic scenes and tweaked by a moral conflict that didn't quite take shape, I felt the impulse to confess I was another person—to protect her from my glances and my feelings. But it never took me long to decide it wouldn't be smart to miss this rare opportunity life was offering me: to take in the everyday world with a fresh gaze, one free of wear and tear, of any hint of innocence.

When she would leave the house to do the grocery shopping at around noon I would sit up and, nimble as a cadaver, climb out of bed to explore every nook and cranny of my house and meddle in the secrets of my existence. Our bedroom had a built-in closet. The lower part contained drawers where my wife kept her underwear, belts, and scarves as well as her favorite brooches and all sorts of intimate apparel and things that had become worn but that lent character to the most intimate regions of her body. I took pleasure in kissing the fabric that had frayed slightly with the rubbing of her inner thighs and in running my fingertips across the part of her bras that came closest to her underarms. Sometimes I would get into bed with one of her belts and play with it until reaching a state of delirium that probably made my recovery slower than what the doctors had predicted.

And yet, despite the very pleasures that harmed my convalescence, I felt my desire was misdirected, misdirected because it went from objects to the body that they possessed and that I also wanted to possess—but under different conditions. Because it is hard seeing that your desire isn't reflected in the gaze of the person you want to depend on. As I regained my health and my sense of otherness increased, so too did the need I felt to hold her in my arms, not as my wife—which she wasn't—but as someone else, as someone as much an outsider as I was in that domestic world that wasn't ours.

One day, after a thorough check-up, I was given a clean bill of health. My wife thought we should go to church to thank God for my recovery. It was eight o'clock in the morning and no one was in the church. I remember the swaying of her black hair and the sound of our footsteps in the echo-filled darkness. We entered a side chapel inhabited by a saint we were devoted to and lit one candle for every bone I had broken in the accident. Then we looked at one another in the glimmering light of the little flames and she smiled at me in the way that women on street corners smile in dreams. I thought I was going mad. She was wearing a loose sweater that showed the lower part of her neck and a hint of the sweet hollow around her collarbones. I reached out my hand and pulled the neckline of her sweater toward her right shoulder. As delicately as an unexpected vestige, like the trail of skates over ice, a white lingerie strap divided the surface of her flesh.

With a provocative serenity as unusual as my desire, she

allowed me to carry on. The scent of burned wax heightened my delirium. I pulled her toward me and, looking her in the eye, whispered, "This is too much for me."

She blinked and said, "It's too much for me too. Let's go behind the altar."

There was a small open area where the remains of a cardinal or a bishop rested. We sat together on the tombstone and watched our shadows, projected on the wall by candlelight, commingle and fuse and form beautiful silhouettes of love. That was when I experienced an outburst of honesty and said, "I have to tell you something, I'm another person."

"So am I," she answered tenderly. "I've been another person all my life. A long time ago I gave up the idea of finding someone who was another person and then, there you were, right by my side."

From then on we've been very happy. The only problem is that we don't know how to break it to the kids that we aren't their parents. We'd like to live alone now, even though we plan on having children someday, children of our own, that is.

En fin.

JENNY HOLLOWELL

A History of Everything, Including You

FIRST, THERE WAS God or gods or nothing, then synthe-
sis, space, the expanse, explosions, implosions, particles,
objects, combustion, and fusion. Out of the chaos came order.
Stars were born and shone and died. Planets rolled across their
galaxies on invisible ellipses and the elements combined and
became.

Life evolved or was created. Cells trembled and divided
and gasped and found dry land. Soon they grew legs and fins
and hands and antennae and mouths and ears and wings and
eyes—eyes that opened wide to take all of it in: the creeping, growing, soaring, swimming, crawling, stampeding uni-
verse. Eyes opened and closed and opened again; we called
it blinking.

Above us shone a star that we called the Sun and we called
the ground the Earth. So we named everything, including
ourselves. We were man and woman, and when we got lonely
we figured out a way to make more of us. We called it sex and
most people enjoyed it.

We fell in love. We talked about God and banged stones together, made sparks and called them fire. We got warmer and the food got better.

We got married. We had some children. They cried and crawled and grew. One dissected flowers, sometimes eating the petals. Another liked to chase squirrels. We fought wars over money and honor and women. We starved ourselves. We hired prostitutes. We purified our water. We compromised, decorated, and became esoteric. One of us stopped breathing and turned blue, then others. First we covered them with leaves and then we buried them in the ground.

We remembered them. We forgot them. We aged. Our buildings kept getting taller. We hired lawyers and formed councils and left paper trails. We negotiated. We admitted. We got sick and searched for cures. We invented lipstick, vaccines, Pilates, solar panels, interventions, table manners, firearms, window treatments, therapy, birth control, tailgating, status symbols, palimony, sportsmanship, focus groups, Zoloft, sunscreen, landscaping, Cessnas, fortune cookies, chemotherapy, convenience foods, and computers. We angered militants and our mothers.

You were born. You learned to walk and went to school and played sports and lost your virginity and got into a decent college and majored in psychology and went to rock shows and became political and got drunk and changed your major to marketing and wore turtleneck sweaters and read novels and volunteered and went to movies and developed a taste for bleu-cheese dressing. I met you through friends, and didn't like you at first. The feeling was mutual, but we got used to each other. We had sex for the first time behind an art gallery, standing up and slightly drunk. You held my face in your hands and said that I was beautiful and you were too, tall, with the streetlight behind you. We went back to your place and listened to the White Album. We ordered in. We fought and made up and got good jobs and got married and bought an apartment and worked out and ate more and talked less. I got depressed. You ignored me. I was sick of you. You drank too much and got careless with money. I slept with my boss. We went into counseling and got a dog. I bought a book of sex positions and we tried the least degrading one: the Wheelbarrow. You took flight lessons and subscribed to *Rolling Stone*. I learned Spanish and started gardening. We had some children, who more or less disappointed us, but it might have been our fault; you were too indulgent and I was too critical. We loved them anyway. One of them died before we did, stabbed on the subway. We grieved. We moved. We adopted a cat. The world seemed uncertain. We lived beyond our means. I got judgmental and belligerent. You got confused and easily tired. You ignored me. I was sick of you. We forgave. We remembered. We made cocktails. We got tender. There was that time on the porch when you said, "Can you believe it?" This was near the end, and your hands were trembling. I think you were talking about everything, including us. Did you want me to say it, so that it would not be lost? It was too much for me to think about. I could not go back to the beginning. I said, "Not really," and we watched the sun go down. A dog kept barking in the distance and you were tired, but you smiled and you said, "Hear that? It's rough, rough," and we laughed. You were like that.

Now, your question is my project and our house is full of clues. I'm reading old letters and turning over rocks. I bury my face in your sweaters. I study a photograph, taken at the beach, the sun in our eyes and the water behind us. It's a victory to remember the forgotten picnic basket and your striped beach blanket. It's a victory to remember how the jellyfish stung you and you ran screaming from the water. It's a victory to remember dressing the wound with meat tenderizer and you saying I made it better.

I will tell you this. Standing on our hill this morning, I looked at the land we chose for ourselves. I saw a few green patches and our sweet little shed. That same dog was barking. A storm was moving in. I did not think of heaven, but I saw that the clouds were beautiful and I watched them cover the sun.

The Raft

MY GRANDFATHER, WHO lost his short-term memory sometime during the first Eisenhower administration, calls me into his study because he wants to tell me the story he's never told anybody before, again. My grandmother, from her perch at her dressing table, with the oval mirror circled by little bulbs I used to love to unscrew, shouts, "Oh, for God's sake, Seymour. We're meeting the Dewoskins at Twin Orchard at seven-thirty. Must you go back to the South Pacific?"

My grandfather slams the door and motions me to the chair in front of his desk. I'll be thirteen in two weeks. "There's something I want to tell you, son," he says. "Something I've never told anybody. You think you're ready? You think you've got the gumption?"

"I think so."

"Think so?"

"I know so, sir. I know I've got the gumption."

He sits down at his desk and stabs open an envelope with

a gleaming letter opener in the shape of a miniature gold sword. "So you want to know?"

"Very much."

"Well then, stand up, sailor." My grandfather's study is carpeted with white shag, which feels woolly against my bare feet. I twist my toes in it. Many cactuses are also in the room. My grandfather often encourages me to touch their prickers to demonstrate how tough an old bird a plant can be. My grandfather captained a destroyer during World War II.

"It was late," he says. "There was a knock on my stateroom door. I leaped up. In those days I slept in uniform—shoes too." My grandfather smiles. His face is so perfectly round that his smile looks like a gash in a basketball. I smile back.

"Don't smile, he says. "Just because I'm smiling, don't assume I couldn't kill you right now. Know that about a man."

"Oh Seymour, *my God*," my grandmother says through the door. "Anyway, isn't he supposed to be at camp? Call his mother."

He looks at me and roars at the door, "Another word out of you, ensign, and I'll have you thrown in the brig, and you won't see Beanie Dewoskin till V-J Day."

"I'll make coffee," my grandmother says.

"It was late," I say. "There was a knock."

"Two knocks," he says. "And by the time he raised his knuckle for the third, I'd opened the door. 'A message from the watch, sir. A boat, sir, three miles due north. Very small, sir. Could be an enemy boat, sir; then again, it might not be. Hard to tell, sir.' I told the boy to can it. Some messengers don't know when to take a breath and let you think. They think if you aren't saying anything, you want to hear more, which is never true. Remember that. I went up to the bridge. 'Wait,' I told them. 'Wait till we can see it. And ready the torpedoes,' I told them, or something like that. I forget the lingo."

"The torpedoes?" I say.

"Yes," he says. "The torpedoes. I couldn't make it out, but the chance that it wasn't a hostile boat was slim. You see what I'm driving at?"

"I do, sir."

"No, you don't, sailor."

"No, I don't," I say. "Don't at all."

"We'd been warned in a communiqué from the admiral to be on high alert for kamikaze flotillas. Do you have any idea what a kamikaze flotilla is?"

"Basically," I say, "it hits the side of your boat, and whango."

"You being smart with me? You think this isn't life and death we're talking about here?"

"Sorry, sir."

"So I waited. It took about a half hour on auxiliary power for us to get within a quarter mile of the thing—then I could see it with the search."

My grandfather pauses, opens his right-hand desk drawer, where he keeps a safety-locked pistol and a stack of pornographic comic books. They are strange books. In the cartoons men with long penises with hats on the ends of them and hair growing up the sides, so that to me they look like pickles, chase women with their skirts raised over their heads and tattoos on their asses that say things like "Uncle Sam's my daddy" and "I never kissed a Kaiser." He whacks the drawer shut and brings his hands together in front of his face, moves his thumbs around as if he's getting ready either to pray or to thumb-wrestle.

"Japs," he says. "Naked Japs on a raft. A raftload of naked Jap sailors. Today the bleedyhearts would probably call them refugees, but back then we didn't call them anything but Japs. Looked like they'd been floating for days. They turned their backs to the light, so all we could see were their backsides, skin and bone fighting it out and the bone winning."

I step back. I want to sit down, but I don't. He stands and leans over his desk, examines my face. Then he points at the door and murmurs, "Bernice doesn't know." On a phone-message pad he scrawls, BLEW IT UP in capital letters. Whispers, *"I gave the order."* He comes around the desk and motions to his closet. "We can talk in there," he says, and I follow him into his warren of suits. My grandfather long ago moved all his clothes out of my grandmother's packed-to-the-gills closets. He leaves the light off. In the crack of sun beneath the door I can see my grandfather's shoes and white socks. He's wearing shorts. He'd been practicing his putting in the driveway.

"At ease, sailor," he says, and I kneel down amid the suits and dangling ties and belts. And I see now that it's not how many times you hear a story but where you hear it that matters. I've heard this before, but this is the first time I've been in a closet alone with my grandfather.

"Why," I say. "Why, if you knew it wasn't—"

"Why?" he says, not like he's repeating my question but as if he really doesn't know. He sighs. Then, still whispering even though we're in the closet, he says, "Some men would lie to you. They'd say it's war. I won't lie to you. It had zero to do with war and everything to do with the uniform I was wearing. Because my job was to make decisions. Besides, what the hell would I have done with a boatload of naked Japanese? There was a war on."

"But you just said—"

"Listen, my job. Just because men like me made the world

safe for men like your father to be cowards doesn't mean you won't ever blow up any civilians. Because you will. I do it once a week at the bank." He places a stumpy, powerful hand on my shoulder. *"Comprende?"*

"Never," I breathe.

"Good," he says, and we are standing in the dark and looking at each other and the story is the same and different—like last time, except this time his tears come so fast they're like lather. He blows his nose into his hand. I reach and offer him the sleeve of one of his suit jackets. "I'll let myself out," he says, and leaves me in the confessional, closing the door behind him.

This time I don't imagine anything, not even a hand that feels like a fish yanking my ankle. Another door opens. "Seymour? Seymour?" my grandmother says. "Where's the kid?"

The Red Fox Fur Coat

Translated from the Portuguese by Margaret Jull Costa

ON HER WAY home one day, a humble bank clerk happened to see a red fox fur coat in a furrier's shop window. She stopped outside and felt a shiver of pleasure and
desire run through her. For this was the coat she had always
wanted. There wasn't another one like it, she thought, running her eyes over the other coats hanging from the metal
rack or delicately draped over a brocade sofa. It was rare,
unique; she had never seen such a color, golden, with a cop-
pery sheen, and so bright it looked as if it were on fire. The
shop was closed at the time, as she discovered when, giving
in to the impulse to enter, she pushed at the door. She
would come back tomorrow, as early as possible, on her
lunch break, or during the morning; yes, she would find a
pretext to slip out during the morning. That night she slept
little and awoke feeling troubled and slightly feverish. She
counted the minutes until the shop would open; her eyes
wandered from the clock on the wall to her wristwatch and
back, while she dealt with various customers. As soon as she

could, she found an excuse to pop out and run to the shop, trembling to think that the coat might have been sold. It had not, she learned, been sold; she felt her breath return, her heartbeat ease, felt the blood drain from her face and resume its measured flow.

"It could have been made for you," said the saleswoman when the bank clerk put the coat on and looked at herself in the mirror. "It fits perfectly on the shoulders and at the waist, and the length is just right," she said, "and it really suits your skin tone. Not that I'm trying to pressure you into buying it," she added hurriedly, "obviously you're free to choose anything you like, but if you don't mind my saying so, the coat really does look as if it had been made for you. Just for you," she said again, with the hint of a smile.

"How much is it?" the bank clerk asked, half turning round—thus setting the hem of the coat swinging—because she found it hard to take her eyes off her own image in the mirror.

She recoiled, stunned, when she heard the reply. It cost far more than she had thought, five times more than she could possibly afford.

"But we can spread out the payment if you like," said the saleswoman kindly.

She could always sacrifice her holidays, the bank clerk thought. Or divert some of the money intended for a car loan. She could use less heating, eat smaller meals. It would do her good, really, because she was beginning to put on a bit of weight.

"All right," she said, doing rapid calculations in her head. "I'll give you a deposit and start paying next week. But it's definitely mine now, isn't it?"

"Absolutely," said the saleswoman, attaching a "Sold" label

to the coat. "You can take it away with you when you've paid the third installment."

She started visiting the shop at night, when it was closed and no one would see her, in order to gaze at the coat through the window, and each time it brought her more joy, each time it was brighter, more fiery, like red flames that did not burn, but were soft on her body, like a thick, ample, enfolding skin that moved when she moved . . .

It would be admired, as would she, people would turn to stare after her, but it was not this that provoked a secret smile; rather, she realized, it was an inner satisfaction, an obscure certainty, a sense of being in harmony with herself, that spilled over in all kinds of small ways. It was as if the rhythm of her breathing had changed, had grown calmer and deeper. She realized too, perhaps because she no longer felt tired, that she moved more quickly, that she could walk effortlessly now, at twice her usual speed. Her legs were agile, her feet nimble. Everything about her was lighter, quicker; her back, shoulders, and limbs all moved more easily.

It must be all the keep-fit I've been doing, she thought, because for some reason she had started taking regular exercise. For a few months now she had been spending two hours a week running at the track. But what she liked most was to go running in the forest, on the outskirts of the city, feeling the sand crunch beneath her feet, learning to place her feet on the ground in a different way—in direct, perfect, intimate contact with the earth. She was intensely aware of her body; she was more alive now, more alert. All her senses were keener too, she could hear, even from some distance away, infinitesimal sounds which, before, would have gone unnoticed: a lizard scurrying through the leaves, an invisible mouse making a twig crack, an acorn falling, a bird landing on a bush;

she could sense atmospheric changes long before they happened: the wind turning, a rise in humidity, an increase in air pressure that would culminate in rain. And another aspect of all the things to which she had now become sensitized was the discovery of smells, a whole world of smells; she could find paths and trails purely by smell; it was strange how she had never before noticed that everything has a smell: the earth, the bark of trees, plants, leaves, and that every animal can be distinguished by its own peculiar smell, a whole spectrum of smells that came to her on waves through the air, and which she could draw together or separate out, sniffing the wind, imperceptibly lifting her head. She suddenly became very interested in animals and found herself leafing through encyclopedias, looking at the pictures—the hedgehog's pale, soft, tender underbelly; the swift hare, of uncertain hue, leaping; she pored over the bodies of birds, fascinated, pondering the softness of the flesh behind their feathers; and a single word kept bobbing insistently about in her mind: predator.

She seemed to be hungrier too, she thought, as she put away her books and went into the kitchen, and this negative aspect to all the physical exercise displeased her greatly. She tried to find a way to avoid putting on weight and prowled, dissatisfied, past patisseries, never finding what she was looking for, because the smell of coffee was repellent to her and made her feel nauseous. No, she was hungry for other things, although she didn't quite know what, fruit perhaps; this might be an opportunity to lose a little weight. She bought a vast quantity of grapes and apples and ate them all in one day, but still she felt hungry, a hidden hunger that gnawed at her from inside and never stopped.

She was cheered by an unexpected invitation to a party, welcoming any diversion that would make her forget that

absurd hunger. She reveled in getting dressed up and in painting her lips and nails scarlet. Her nails, she noticed, were very
long, and even her hands seemed more sensitive, more elon-
gated. Anyone she touched at the party that night would
remain eternally in her power, she thought, smiling at herself
in the mirror—a feline smile, it seemed to her. She narrowed
her eyes and widened the smile, letting it spread over her face,
which took on a pleasingly triangular shape that she further
emphasized with make-up.

In the middle of the party, she noticed someone slicing up
some meat, cooked very rare—roast beef, she thought, although
these words had suddenly ceased to have any meaning. She
reached out her hand and devoured a whole slice. Ah, she
thought, the taste of almost raw meat, the action of sinking
her teeth into it, of making the blood spurt, the taste of blood
on her tongue, in her mouth, the innocence of devouring the
whole slice, and she took another slice, already sensing that
using her hand was now a pointless waste of time, that she
should just pick it up directly with her mouth.

She burst out laughing and began to dance, waving her
bloodstained hands in the air, feeling her own blood rise, as if
some tempestuous inner force had been unleashed, a malign
force that she could transmit to others, a plague or a curse, but
this idea was nevertheless sweet, quiet, almost joyful, she felt,
as she swayed, slightly drunk, listening to the echo of her own
laughter.

She would spend the night obeying all these newly released
forces and, in the morning, she would go and fetch the coat,
because the day had come when it would be hers; it was part
of her; she would know it even with her eyes closed, by touch
alone, the soft, thick pelt burning her skin, cleaving to her,
until she could no longer tell skin from skin . . .

"It could have been made for you," the saleswoman said again, as she removed it from the coat hanger.

The coat cleaving to her, until she could no longer tell skin from skin, as she could see in the mirror, as she turned the collar up around her head, her face disfigured, suddenly thinner, made up to look longer, her eyes narrow, restless, burning . . . "Goodbye, then, and thanks," she said, rushing out of the shop, afraid that time was getting short and that people would stop in alarm to stare at her, because suddenly the impulse to go down on all fours and simply run was too strong, reincarnating her body, rediscovering her animal body; and as she fled, as she left the city behind her and simply fled, it took an almost superhuman effort to get into her car and drive to the edge of the forest, keeping tight control of her body, keeping tight control of her tremulous body for just one more minute, before that slam of the door, that first genuine leap on feet free at last, shaking her back and her tail, sniffing the air, the ground, the wind, and, with a howl of pleasure and joy, plunging off into the depths of the forest.

RONALD F. CURRIE JR.

Loving the Dead

AUTUMN COMES TO Maine, and I begin to hate freely all over again. Without notice, the morning air turns sharp. Barn jackets emerge from closets. Trees shed leaves, apples. People smile, tape witches and black cats to their windowpanes, turn up the thermostat, smile, check the balance of their Christmas-club accounts, drink warm cider from ceramic mugs, smile, wrap their shrubs in plastic and burlap, marvel when the sky spits those first few abortive flakes of snow, smile, smile, smile. As if they've never experienced any of this before. As if they don't recognize death when they see it.

Animals, it seems, have better sense than we do. Great flocks of birds burst from treetops with a sound like water splashing on pavement, then disappear until spring. Squirrels top off their winter stores and retire to their knotholes. Bears go to sleep. Even our dogs, bound to us though they are, grow thick coats and make clear their preference for the floor near the radiator.

The sun, so generous only a few months ago, now hoards its warmth. Early one Sunday, while we sleep, someone turns the clocks back an hour, and suddenly it's dark at five in the afternoon. And I begin to hate. Since I cannot bear to hurt the feelings of the living, I hate the dead.

I HATE MY grandfather, the son of French Canadian immigrants, who despised himself so much it took only forty-nine years for him to die.

I hate him on his wedding day, in a tuxedo that cost him half a year's pay, bangs swept back from his forehead so carefully you can see where each tooth of the comb parted the black hairs. He wears a dull expression of hope around his mouth so absurd in this place of chest-high snowdrifts and endless workdays. He smiles into the future with a slight cockeye, which he has passed on to me, and which somehow makes us both more rather than less handsome.

I hate his working, working, working for men who spoke English and who, in the absence of the niggers and spics and slants they preferred, used Canucks as commodities, as plow horses, as punch lines. He learned their language so eagerly as though it would earn him more money, or their respect. For them he drove a bus during the day and a cab at night for thirty-three years, until a week before he died.

I hate him for being a good Catholic and fathering seven children. He loved his children so much that he had no love left for himself. He said his prayers in French, which I could not understand. I want to know now what he said to God. I want to know what he asked, and what he asked for.

I hate him for taking pride in what little he had, washing and waxing the Ford he never really owned, painting his mother's house, in which his four boys shared one bed and his three girls shared another.

I hate his four packs of Old Golds a day, his bottle and his flask and his can and his pint glass, the rotgut on Monday mornings and the bourbon on Friday evenings after the checks were cashed and the rent was paid.

I hate his clothes, the worn elbows and patched knees, the busted soles taped together three times over and falling apart yet again, all so his seven children could go to school with the children of the men he worked for and not feel ashamed.

I hate his belief in America. I hate him for passing it on to his firstborn son, my father, who rode his faith in God and country all the way to Vietnam, but had to find his own way back.

I hate him at my parents' wedding, kind-eyed and defeated in his cheap suit, belly straining at the waistband, already bald at forty-three, a warm, bitter, ubiquitous can of Löwenbräu in his hand, drunk out of need rather than want.

I hate this memory I have of my grandfather: I am three, sitting on his lap, and he is tickling me and whispering, "Ti Louis, ti Louis," in my ear. He feeds me handfuls of candy—circus peanuts and chalky pink mints, old-people candy—until I feel sick, but I can't stop laughing, a high, screeching kid-cackle, the sound of distilled joy.

I hate him as he's dying in a hospital room full of his children and grandchildren. A homemade ceramic ashtray, crammed with soiled and folded butts, rests on the nightstand near the bed. Under the pillow is a pint of whiskey, three-quarters gone, smuggled in with the flowers and cards. In the chlorinated light of the overhead fluorescents, his bare, swollen feet are pale, bursting with clusters of tiny purple veins like fractals. Heartache and relief mingle in his eyes.

I hate, most of all, the moment when he dies. My older brother, six, towheaded, bespectacled, buries his face in my grandfather's lap. My grandmother and my father and my uncles and aunts and cousins crowd the room. My grandfather dies without a sound. And everyone is frozen there in their limp, feathered seventies hair, their powder blue shirts and butterfly collars, their thick glasses, their horrifying floral prints, their bad skin, their bad teeth, their shared grief and their tiny private miseries, so varied and yet so sickeningly alike—the same mistakes, the same laments—and all of it captured, frozen, preserved, because someone has actually brought a camera to this place.

I HATE MY grandmother, who lived fifteen years longer than my grandfather but, like him, died from self-hatred.

I hate her on her wedding day, in a dress that cost the other half of the year's pay. Her smile is not open and expectant, like his, but slight, reserved, as if she's not just looking toward the future, but seeing it clearly.

I hate her for giving birth to seven children and loving them so much she could not show it until years later, indirectly, by spoiling and doting on her grandchildren. She loved my Aunt Rhea more than any of the others—so much that Rhea believes to this day that her mother never loved her at all.

I hate her for standing by, as she thought a wife should, while my grandfather killed himself with work and alcohol and cigarettes and pride.

I hate her hands—pricked by sewing needles, scalded by wash water, burned by chemicals and casserole dishes, nicked by knives, scarred, creased, red and raw, clasped forever in prayer: "Hail Mary, full of grace, the Lord is with thee . . ." (I know only the English, not the French.)

I hate the meals she made: crepes for breakfast, leftover crepes for lunch, *tourtière* for dinner. She made food for six stretch far enough to feed eight, but she never made my grandfather eat something, anything.

I hate how she kept her pride and pleasure hidden when she scraped together the money to buy my father and his brothers secondhand bikes. She never knew how the other boys in the neighborhood made fun of them, laughed at their chipped paint and wobbly rims.

I hate that she discouraged my Aunt Rhea from going to college, and I hate her reason why: Because she did not want my aunt to rise above her station. Because she did not want my aunt to be heartbroken when they did not accept her into that world.

I have many memories of my grandmother, and I hate them all: Sleepovers at her house with my cousins. Trips to Sunset Beach. The sickroom smell of Kool menthols. Vodka bottles in the toilet tank. My father's old board games in the closet. A worn, overstuffed recliner that had belonged to my grandfather. Her bedroom, with its cool blue walls and ceiling, silent and off limits, like a vestry. Her cats, and my allergies. Loud, animated conversations when women from the neighborhood would visit, the patois shooting back and forth across the kitchen table like automatic gunfire, the cigarettes smoking like gunpowder.

I hate my last memory of her: I am a senior in high school. She has been dying for five months, and I haven't visited her. I have been busy with my teenage business, which is more important than death. Before I enter the hospital room, my father pulls me aside and warns me how much she's deteriorated. But nothing can prepare me for it. The moment I see her, I want to cry. She was plump, pear-shaped, but now she has no shape at all; she is papery skin stretched over sharp angles. The flesh of her face has collapsed, and her eyes are huge, black, bottomless. She is seated by the window, and I sit beside her. She takes my hand and speaks to me in French. I tell her I don't understand, but she doesn't seem to know English anymore. I'm not sure she even recognizes me. Her voice is low, as in a confessional. Tears spill from her eyes and follow the deep creases on her cheeks down to her chin, where they perch, gather, and drop off. It is the first time I have seen her cry, and it will be the last. I will not visit her again before she dies.

At some point I pull my hand away, stand, and walk out, but I never leave that room. Because this moment, too, is frozen, goes on forever.

YES, I HATE my grandparents, and I hate what I find of them in me. I hate my strong back, my poverty, my taste for alcohol, my love and the despair it brings when the days grow short and the birds abandon us and the people smile, smile, smile.

But I will never tell this story. It is safe to hate the dead, but there are those still living—those of the feathered hair and floral prints—who would be hurt by this. So I'll keep silent. I'll take these pages, tear them up, burn them, dump the ashes in the Kennebec. The river will absorb and erase these words, as it has for years. I'll change my name, leave this place, become a Protestant, make a lot of money, and not think of it again. I'll have children who will call their grandparents "Grampa" and "Grammy," not "*Pépère*" and "*Mémère*."

But who am I fooling? I can hear my older brother even now, across the years, whispering in the darkness of our shared bedroom: *You think you are so smart. You think you are better than us.*

No, I am not better. I will not be spared. Instead I will go to the cemetery, as I do every winter, and find my grandparents' graves side by side under the snow. I will clear the snow away, first with my boots, then with gloved fingers, until I can read the stones set in the ground: just their names and two sets of dates. The stones don't tell any of this story, and neither will I. I will sit there in the snow, smoke a cigarette, drink from my bottle, and wait for winter to end.

TOBIAS WOLFF

Powder

J UST BEFORE CHRISTMAS my father took me skiing at
Mount Baker. He'd had to fight for the privilege of my
company, because my mother was still angry with him for
sneaking me into a nightclub during our last visit, to see
Thelonious Monk.

He wouldn't give up. He promised, hand on heart, to take
good care of me and have me home for dinner on Christmas
Eve, and she relented. But as we were checking out of the
lodge that morning it began to snow, and in this snow he
observed some rare quality that made it necessary for us to get
in one last run. We got in several last runs. He was indifferent
to my fretting. Snow whirled around us in bitter, blinding
squalls, hissing like sand, and still we skied. As the lift bore us
to the peak yet again, my father looked at his watch and said,
"Criminy. This'll have to be a fast one."

By now I couldn't see the trail. There was no point in trying. I stuck to him like white on rice and did what he did and
somehow made it to the bottom without sailing off a cliff.

We returned our skis and my father put chains on the Austin-Healey while I swayed from foot to foot, clapping my mittens and wishing I were home. I could see everything. The green tablecloth, the plates with the holly pattern, the red candles waiting to be lit.

We passed a diner on our way out. "You want some soup?" my father asked. I shook my head. "Buck up," he said. "I'll get you there. Right, doctor?"

I was supsed to say, "Right, doctor," but I didn't say anything.

A state trooper waved us down outside the resort. A pair of sawhorses were blocking the road. The trooper came up to our car and bent down to my father's window. His face was bleached by the cold. Snowflakes clung to his eyebrows and to the fur trim of his jacket and cap.

"Don't tell me," my father said.

The trooper told him. The road was closed. It might get cleared, it might not. Storm took everyone by surprise. So much, so fast. Hard to get people moving. Christmas Eve. What can you do?

My father said, "Look. We're talking about four, five inches. I've taken this car through worse than that."

The trooper straightened up, boots creaking. His face was out of sight but I could hear him. "The road is closed."

My father sat with both hands on the wheel, rubbing the wood with his thumbs. He looked at the barricade for a long time. He seemed to be trying to master the idea of it. Then he thanked the trooper, and with a weird, old-maidy show of caution turned the car around. "Your mother will never forgive me for this," he said.

"We should have left before," I said. "Doctor."

He didn't speak to me again until we were both in a booth

at the diner, waiting for our burgers. "She won't forgive me," he said. "Do you understand? Never."

"I guess," I said, but no guesswork was required; she wouldn't forgive him.

"I can't let that happen." He bent toward me. "I'll tell you what I want. I want us to be together again. Is that what you want?"

I wasn't sure, but I said, "Yes, sir."

He bumped my chin with his knuckles. "That's all I needed to hear."

When we finished eating he went to the pay phone in the back of the diner, then joined me in the booth again. I figured he'd called my mother, but he didn't give a report. He sipped at his coffee and stared out the window at the empty road. "Come on, come on," he said, though not to me. A little while later he said it again. When the trooper's car went past, lights flashing, he got up and dropped some money on the check. "Okay. Vámonos."

The wind had died. The snow was falling straight down, less of it now and lighter. We drove away from the resort, right up to the barricade. "Move it," my father told me. When I looked at him he said, "What are you waiting for?" I got out and dragged one of the sawhorses aside, then pushed it back after he drove through. When I got inside the car he said, "Now you're an accomplice," he said. "We go down together." He put the car in gear and gave me a look. "Joke, son."

Down the first long stretch I watched the road behind us, to see if the trooper was on our tail. The barricade vanished. Then there was nothing but snow: snow on the road, snow kicking up from the chains, snow on the trees, snow in the sky; and our trail in the snow. Then I faced forward and had a shock. The lay of the road behind us had been marked by our own tracks, but there were no tracks ahead of us. My father was breaking virgin snow between a line of tall trees. He was humming "Stars Fell on Alabama." I felt snow brush along the floorboards under my feet. To keep my hands from shaking I clamped them between my knees.

My father grunted in a thoughtful way and said, "Don't ever try this yourself."

"I won't."

"That's what you say now, but someday you'll get your license and then you'll think you can do anything. Only you won't be able to do this. You need, I don't know—a certain instinct."

"Maybe I have it."

"You don't. You have your strong points, but not this. I only mention it because I don't want you to get the idea this is something just anybody can do. I'm a great driver. That's not a virtue, okay? It's just a fact, and one you should be aware of. Of course you have to give the old heap some credit, too. There aren't many cars I'd try this with. Listen!"

I listened. I heard the slap of the chains, the stiff, jerky rasp of the wipers, the purr of the engine. It really did purr. The old heap was almost new. My father couldn't afford it, and kept promising to sell it, but here it was.

I said, "Where do you think that policeman went to?"

"Are you warm enough?" He reached over and cranked up the blower. Then he turned off the wipers. We didn't need them. The clouds had brightened. A few sparse, feathery flakes drifted into our slipstream and were swept away. We left the trees and entered a broad field of snow that ran level for a while and then tilted sharply downward. Orange stakes had been planted at intervals in two parallel lines and my father ran a course between them, though they were far enough apart to leave considerable doubt in my mind as to where exactly the road lay. He was humming again, doing little scat riffs around the melody.

"Okay then. What are my strong points?"

"Don't get me started," he said. "It'd take all day."

"Oh, right. Name one."

"Easy. You always think ahead."

True. I always thought ahead. I was a boy who kept his clothes on numbered hangers to ensure proper rotation. I bothered my teachers for homework assignments far ahead of their due dates so I could make up schedules. I thought ahead, and that was why I knew that there would be other troopers waiting for us at the end of our ride, if we even got there. What I did not know was that my father would wheedle and plead his way past them—he didn't sing "O Tannenbaum" but just about—and get me home for dinner, buying a little more time before my mother decided to make the split final. I knew we'd get caught; I was resigned to it. And maybe for this reason I stopped moping and began to enjoy myself.

Why not? This was one for the books. Like being in a speedboat, only better. You can't go downhill in a boat. And it was all ours. And it kept coming, the laden trees, the unbroken surface of snow, the sudden white vistas. Here and there I saw hints of the road, ditches, fences, stakes, but not so many that I could have found my way. But then I didn't have to. My father in his forty-eighth year, rumpled, kind, bankrupt of honor, flushed with certainty. He was a great driver. All persuasion, no coercion. Such subtlety at the wheel, such tactful pedalwork. I actually trusted him. And the best was yet to come—switchbacks and hairpins impossible to describe. Except maybe to say this: If you haven't driven fresh powder, you haven't driven.

LAN SAMANTHA CHANG

Water Names

SUMMERTIME AT DUSK we'd gather on the back porch, tired and sticky from another day of fierce encoded quarrels, nursing our mosquito bites and frail dignities, sisters in name only. At first we'd pinch and slap each other, fighting for the best—least ragged—folding chair. Then we'd argue over who would sit next to our grandmother. We were so close together on the tiny porch that we often pulled our own hair by mistake. Forbidden to bite, we planted silent toothmarks on each other's wrists. We ignored the bulk of house behind us, the yard, the fields, the darkening sky. We even forgot about our grandmother. Then suddenly we'd hear her old, dry voice, very close, almost on the backs of our necks.

"*Xiushila!* Shame on you. Fighting like a bunch of chickens."

And Ingrid, the oldest, would freeze with her thumb and forefinger right on the back of Lily's arm. I would slide my hand away from the end of Ingrid's braid. Ashamed, we would shuffle our feet while Waipuo calmly found her chair.

On some nights she sat with us in silence, the tip of her cigarette glowing red like a distant stoplight. But on some nights she told us stories, "just to keep up your Chinese," she said, and the red dot flickered and danced, making ghostly shapes as she moved her hands like a magician in the dark.

"In these prairie crickets I often hear the sound of rippling waters, of the Yangtze River," she said. "Granddaughters, you are descended on both sides from people of the water country, near the mouth of the great Chang Jiang, as it is called, where the river is so grand and broad that even on clear days you can scarcely see the other side.

"The Chang Jiang runs four thousand miles, originating in the Himalaya mountains where it crashes, flecked with gold dust, down steep cliffs so perilous and remote that few humans have ever seen them. In central China, the river squeezes through deep gorges, then widens in its last thousand miles to the sea. Our ancestors have lived near the mouth of this river, the ever-changing delta, near a city called Nanjing, for more than a thousand years."

"A thousand years," murmured Lily, who was only ten. When she was younger she had sometimes burst into nervous crying at the thought of so many years. Her small insistent fingers grabbed my fingers in the dark.

"Through your mother and I you are descended from a line of great men and women. We have survived countless floods and seasons of ill-fortune because we have the spirit of the river in us. Unlike mountains, we cannot be powdered down or broken apart. Instead, we run together, like raindrops. Our strength and spirit wear down mountains into sand. But even our people must respect the water."

She paused, and a bit of ash glowed briefly as it drifted to the floor.

"When I was young, my own grandmother once told me the story of Wen Zhiqing's daughter. Twelve hundred years ago the civilized parts of China still lay to the north, and the Yangtze valley lay unspoiled. In those days lived an ancestor named Wen Zhiqing, a resourceful man, and proud. He had been fishing for many years with trained cormorants, which you girls of course have never seen. Cormorants are sleek, black birds with long, bending necks which the fishermen fitted with metal rings so the fish they caught could not be swallowed. The birds would perch on the side of the old wooden boat and dive into the river." We had only known blue swimming pools, but we tried to imagine the sudden shock of cold and the plunge, deep into water.

"Now, Wen Zhiqing had a favorite daughter who was very beautiful and loved the river. She would beg to go out on the boat with him. This daughter was a restless one, never contented with their catch, and often she insisted they stay out until it was almost dark. Even then, she was not satisfied. She had been spoiled by her father, kept protected from the river, so she could not see its danger. To this young woman, the river was as familiar as the sky. It was a bright, broad road stretching out to curious lands. She did not fully understand the river's depths.

"One clear spring evening, as she watched the last bird dive off into the blackening waters, she said, 'If only this catch would bring back something more than another fish!'

"She leaned over the side of the boat and looked at the water. The stars and moon reflected back at her. And it is said that the spirits living underneath the water looked up at her as well. And the spirit of a young man who had drowned in the river many years before saw her lovely face."

We had heard about the ghosts of the drowned, who wait

forever in the water for a living person to pull down instead.
A faint breeze moved through the mosquito screens and we
shivered.

"The cormorant was gone for a very long time," Waipuo
said, "so long that the fisherman grew puzzled. Then, suddenly, the bird emerged from the waters, almost invisible in
the night. Wen Zhiqing grasped his catch, a very large fish,
and guided the boat back to shore. And when Wen reached
home, he gutted the fish and discovered, in its stomach, a
valuable pearl ring."

"From the man?" said Lily.

"Sshh, she'll tell you."

Waipuo ignored us. "His daughter was delighted that her
wish had been fulfilled. What most excited her was the idea
of an entire world like this, a world where such a beautiful
ring would be only a bauble! For part of her had always
longed to see faraway things and places. The river had put a
spell on her heart. In the evenings she began to sit on the
bank, looking at her own reflection in the water. Sometimes
she said she saw a handsome young man looking back at her.
And her yearning for him filled her heart with sorrow and
fear, for she knew that she would soon leave her beloved
family.

" 'It's just the moon,' said Wen Zhiqing, but his daughter
shook her head. 'There's a kingdom under the water,' she said.
'The prince is asking me to marry him. He sent the ring as
an offering to you.' 'Nonsense,' said her father, and he forbade
her to sit by the water again.

"For a year things went as usual, but the next spring there
came a terrible flood that swept away almost everything. In
the middle of a torrential rain, the family noticed that the
daughter was missing. She had taken advantage of the confu-

sion to hurry to the river and visit her beloved. The family searched for days but they never found her."

Her smoky, rattling voice came to a stop.

"What happened to her?" Lily said.

"It's okay, stupid," I told her. "She was so beautiful that she went to join the kingdom of her beloved. Right?"

"Who knows?" Waipuo said. "They say she was seduced by a water ghost. Or perhaps she lost her mind to desiring."

"What do you mean?" asked Ingrid.

"I'm going inside," Waipuo said, and got out of her chair with a creak. A moment later the light went on in her bedroom window. We knew she stood before the mirror, combing out her long, wavy silver-gray hair, and we imagined that in her youth she too had been beautiful.

We sat together without talking, breathing our dreams in the lingering smoke. We had gotten used to Waipuo's abruptness, her habit of creating a question and leaving without answering it, as if she were disappointed in the question itself. We tried to imagine Wen Zhiqing's daughter. What did she look like? How old was she? Why hadn't anyone remembered her name?

While we weren't watching, the stars had emerged. Their brilliant pinpoints mapped the heavens. They glittered over us, over Waipuo in her room, the house, and the small city we lived in, the great waves of grass that ran for miles around us, the ground beneath as dry and hard as bone.

SAM SHEPARD

Berlin Wall Piece

MY DAD KNOWS absolutely nothing about the eighties. I have to interview him for my seventh-grade social studies class and he knows nothing. He says he can't remember anything about the cars or the hair or the clothes or the music or anything. He says the economy sucked and that was a Republican thing but other than that nothing stands out for him. He says the most significant thing about the eighties was that was when he first met my mother and when me and my sister were both born. Those two things. That's it. When I tell him it's not supposed to be about personal stuff he says what else is there? I tell him I need stuff about style and fads and what was going on in the country at the time and he says none of that has anything to do with reality; that reality is an "internal affair" and all the rest of that stuff is just superficial and a lie—like the news. He says the news is all lies and the reason it's so popular is that it sells itself as all truth and people believe it because they'd rather believe in a lie. The truth is too much for them to swallow. That's what he says. I tell

him this is just supposed to be a simple assignment thing
about the decade of the eighties, not about "reality" and the
"news," but he says you can't exclude the question of reality;
that the question of reality supersedes all the other questions
about hair and cars and music and things like that. Then he
says he can't even remember living through the eighties and
that maybe he wasn't even alive back then, but then he had to
have been he says because he remembers meeting my mother,
and me and my sister were both born back then. He repeats
that. My dad's fucking crazy. He is. I didn't realize it for a long
time but he is. My sister knows more about the eighties than
my dad does and she's only a year or so older than me. She's
in the ninth grade. She knows all kinds of things—don't ask
me how—like the way they used to wear their pants back
then in this weird tapered style where they actually folded the
pant leg inside their zip-up boots and the girls wore ripped-
up fishnet stockings and cheap white cotton gloves trying to
imitate Madonna, who I guess was the bomb in music back
then, or Michael Jackson, who'd just started bleaching his
black skin, or Bob Seger, who I thought was only known for
that dumb "Like a Rock" Chevy commercial. Then, on top
of that, she knows all kinds of political stuff like Russia not
being Russia anymore and the Berlin Wall coming down, and
I ask her how she knows things like that and she says because
she was there. "Yeah, right," I say, and she says, "Yeah, I can
prove it," and she runs upstairs to her bedroom and comes
back down with a chunk of painted concrete about the size
of a cheeseburger and sets it down on the kitchen counter
right in front of me and my dad. "What's that?" I say, and she
says, "That's a piece of the Berlin Wall."

     "It is!" my dad says, and gets very excited about it. "That's
exactly what that is! Isn't that incredible?" He picks it up and

turns it over, feeling the weight of it as though it might be from another planet or something. "When did you go to the Berlin Wall, honey?" My sister looks at him, dumbfounded.

"Don't you remember?" my sister says. "I went with Mom and Aunt Amy."

"I don't remember that," my dad says. "How old were you?" He remembers nothing. Like he's losing his mind. How could he not remember something like that? His own daughter going to the Berlin Wall. He's not that old to be losing his mind but he is.

"Where was I?" my dad says.

"You must've stayed home," my sister says.

"I must have," he says.

I ask my sister how she got a piece of the Berlin Wall and she says they were driving through Berlin at the time they were tearing the wall down and the workers were just giving away pieces of it, handing it through the car windows. She says it was like a party. She was three years old and these big hands of hairy men were coming through the windows handing them chunks of rock and concrete as though it were cake and she had no idea what it was all about.

I'm staring at the chunk of cement on the kitchen counter. One side is smooth and flat and painted flashy turquoise and purple with a skinny yellow stripe cutting down the middle—it looks like spray paint, maybe graffiti. The other side is broken and rough and you can see the fragments of things that they made the concrete out of: small smooth stones that look like they could have come out of somewhere deep in the woods and sharp gravel mixed in with this chalky-looking cement that doesn't look American at all and then these tiny glittering particles. When you run your finger along the edge of it, it makes the sound of glass more than stone. My sister offers to let me take the piece of the Berlin Wall to school and show it around in my class, which is a very generous offer for her, I think. Then my dad picks up the heavy chunk of the Berlin Wall and drops it into a Ziploc bag and when I ask him why he's doing that he says so it doesn't get lost. He says it's very important that it doesn't get lost or stolen because it's a real live piece of modern history. What does he care? He's not even sure he was alive back then and now he's calling this piece of concrete alive. He's not making any sense at all. He takes out a big roll of silver plumber's tape from a drawer and tears a piece off with his teeth. He sticks the strip of tape on the Ziploc bag and then takes a black Magic Marker and writes "BERLIN WALL PIECE" like it's some kind of museum label or something. "There," he says, "that oughta do it." He's totally nuts.

My sister's doing her homework all this time but keeps coming up with other stuff about the eighties and fires it at me as she's working as though her mind is able to split right down the middle and do two things at once. She's totally brilliant, I think. "There was some volcano out west in Washington that erupted," she says. "It erupted and kept right on erupting off and on for the rest of the year. That was in the eighties, wasn't it, Dad?" I don't know why she's asking him. How would he know?

"I don't know," my dad says as he wipes black ants off the counter with a wet sponge. He doesn't try to step on them, he just wipes them onto the floor and lets them crawl away.

"Why don't you kill them," I ask my dad.

"I like ants," he says. "They remind me of summer and hot places. We always had ants when I was growing up." He says this as though he were talking about puppies or guinea pigs.

"And they discovered AIDS!" my sister blurts out. "That's

when they first discovered the AIDS virus, was the eighties." She's on a roll now. I don't know how her mind works. It's a mystery to me; like she can scroll stuff up like she's looking at it on a green screen or something. AIDS? Where does she come up with that off the top of her head? "And Marvin Gaye got shot by his father, didn't he?" she says. Suddenly my dad stops cold in the middle of the kitchen like he's been hit in the back of the head by a board or something.

"That's right," my dad says. "I remember that."

"You do?" I say, and I'm looking straight at him, standing there with the sponge hanging down from his hand dripping on the floor and he's staring out across the kitchen without seeing me or my sister or anything but as though he's trying to nail down this picture of Marvin Gaye in his mind all shot in the head and bloody from some picture in the news back then that he hates.

"I remember that very clearly," he says. "I was in California. It was 1984—the summer or spring of 1984 and it was very hot. Marvin Gaye was killed by his father and his father was a reverend, wasn't he? I think he was. A man of the church and he shot his son in the head over something—over something to do with women, I think. Something about a woman, wasn't it?" He turns to my sister, who doesn't realize he's asking her a direct question and just continues on with her head down in her book, working hard on her homework. "Wasn't it something to do with a woman?" he says to her again. My sister finally looks up at him and sees that he's talking to her. She stares at him but you can see she's thinking about some math problem.

"I don't know, Dad," she says, and her eyes go back down into her books. He looks at me, sort of searching for a second. I don't know the answer. How am I supposed to know the answer? I wasn't even born yet when that happened. He looks out across the kitchen again, toward the dark windows.

"Huh, it's funny I'd remember that," he says and then he tosses the sponge into the sink and walks out onto the screen porch and stands there for a long while looking out at the lawn and the maple tree. Spring peepers are chirping from the pond down the hill. I pick up the Ziploc bag with the piece of the Berlin Wall inside and hold it up to the light. It's just a chunk of concrete.

"Don't lose that," my sister says without looking up.

"How can I lose it?" I say. "It's labeled."

The Rememberer

M Y LOVER IS experiencing reverse evolution. I tell no one. I don't know how it happened, only that one day he was my lover and the next he was some kind of ape. It's been a month and now he's a sea turtle.

I keep him on the counter, in a glass baking pan filled with salt water.

"Ben," I say to his small protruding head, "can you understand me?" and he stares with eyes like little droplets of tar and I drip tears into the pan, a sea of me.

He is shedding a million years a day. I am no scientist, but this is roughly what I figured out. I went to the old biology teacher at the community college and asked him for an approximate time line of our evolution. He was irritated at first—he wanted money. I told him I'd be happy to pay and then he cheered up quite a bit. I can hardly read his time line—he should've typed it—and it turns out to be wrong. According to him, the whole process should take about a year, but from the way things are going, I think we have less than a month left.

At first, people called on the phone and asked me where was Ben. Why wasn't he at work? Why did he miss his lunch date with those clients? His out-of-print special-ordered book on civilization had arrived at the bookstore, would he please pick it up? I told them he was sick, a strange sickness, and to please stop calling. The stranger thing was, they did. They stopped calling. After a week, the phone was silent and Ben, the baboon, sat in a corner by the window, wrapped up in drapery, chattering to himself.

Last day I saw him human, he was sad about the world.

This was not unusual. He was always sad about the world. It was a large reason why I loved him. We'd sit together and be sad and think about being sad and sometimes discuss sadness.

On his last human day, he said, "Annie, don't you see? We're all getting too smart. Our brains are just getting bigger and bigger, and the world dries up and dies when there's too much thought and not enough heart."

He looked at me pointedly, blue eyes unwavering. "Like us, Annie," he said. "We think far too much."

I sat down. I remembered how the first time we had sex, I left the lights on, kept my eyes wide open, and concentrated really hard on letting go; then I noticed that his eyes were open too and in the middle of everything we sat down on the floor and had an hour-long conversation about poetry. It was all very peculiar. It was all very familiar.

Another time he woke me up in the middle of the night, lifted me off the pale blue sheets, led me outside to the stars and whispered: *Look, Annie, look—there is no space for anything but dreaming.* I listened, sleepily, wandered back to bed and found myself wide awake, staring at the ceiling, unable to dream at all. Ben fell asleep right away, but I crept back outside. I tried to dream up to the stars, but I didn't know how to do that. I tried to find a star no one in all of history had ever wished on before, and wondered what would happen if I did.

On his last human day, he put his head in his hands and sighed and I stood up and kissed the entire back of his neck, covered that flesh, made wishes there because I knew no woman had ever been so thorough, had ever kissed his every inch of skin. I coated him. What did I wish for? I wished for good. That's all. Just good. My wishes became generalized long ago, in childhood; I learned quick the consequence of wishing specific.

I took him in my arms and made love to him, my sad man. "See, we're not thinking," I whispered into his ear while he kissed my neck, "we're not thinking at all" and he pressed his head into my shoulder and held me tighter. Afterward, we went outside again; there was no moon and the night was dark. He said he hated talking and just wanted to look into my eyes and tell me things that way. I let him and it made my skin lift, the things in his look. Then he told me he wanted to sleep outside for some reason and in the morning when I woke up in bed, I looked out to the patio and there was an ape sprawled on the cement, great furry arms covering his head to block out the glare of the sun.

Even before I saw the eyes, I knew it was him. And once we were face to face, he gave me his same sad look and I hugged those enormous shoulders. I didn't even really care, then, not at first, I didn't panic and call 911. I sat with him outside and smoothed the fur on the back of his hand. When he reached for me, I said No, loudly, and he seemed to understand and pulled back. I have limits here.

We sat on the lawn together and ripped up the grass. I didn't miss human Ben right away; I wanted to meet the ape too, to take care of my lover like a son, a pet; I wanted to know him every possible way but I didn't realize he wasn't coming back.

Now I come home from work and look for his regular-size shape walking and worrying and realize, over and over, that he's gone. I pace the halls: I chew whole packs of gum in mere minutes. I review my memories and make sure they're still intact because if he's not here, then it is my job to remember. I think of the way he wrapped his arms around my back and held me so tight it made me nervous and the way his breath felt in my ear: right.

When I go to the kitchen, I peer in the glass and see he's some kind of salamander now. He's small.

"Ben," I whisper, "do you remember me? Do you remember?"

His eyes roll up in his head and I dribble honey into the water. He used to love honey. He licks at it and then swims to the other end of the pan.

This is the limit of my limits: here it is. You don't ever know for sure where it is and then you bump against it and bam, you're there. Because I cannot bear to look down into the water and not be able to find him at all, to search the tiny clear waves with a microscope lens and to locate my lover, the one-celled wonder, bloated and bordered, brainless, benign, heading clear and small like an eye-floater into nothingness.

I put him in the passenger seat of the car, and drive him to the beach. Walking down the sand, I nod at people on towels, laying their bodies out to the sun and wishing. At the water's edge, I stoop down and place the whole pan on the tip of a baby wave. It floats well, a cooking boat, for someone to find washed up on shore and to make cookies in, a lucky catch for a poor soul with all the ingredients but no container.

Ben the salamander swims out. I wave to the water with both arms, big enough for him to see if he looks back.

I turn around and walk back to the car.

Sometimes I think he'll wash up on shore. A naked man with a startled look. Who has been to history and back. I keep my eyes on the newspaper. I make sure my phone number is listed. I walk around the block at night in case he doesn't quite remember which house it is. I feed the birds outside and sometimes before I put my one self to bed, I place my hands around my skull to see if it's growing, and wonder what, of any use, would fill it if it did.

Homage

READ MY LIPS.

Because I don't speak. You're sitting there, and when the train lurches you seem to bend forward to hear. But I don't speak.

If I could find them I could ask for the other half of the money I was going to get when I'd done it, but they're gone. I don't know where to look. I don't think they're here, anymore, they're in some other country, they move all the time and that's how they find men like me. We leave home because of governments overthrown, a conscript on the wrong side; no work, no bread or oil in the shops, and when we cross a border we're put over another border, and another. What is your final destination? We don't know; we don't know where we can stay, where we won't be sent on somewhere else, from one tent camp to another in a country where you can't get papers.

I don't ever speak.

They find us there, in one of these places—they found me

and they saved me, they can do anything, they got me in here with papers and a name they gave me; I buried my name, no-one will ever dig it out of me. They told me what they wanted done and they paid me half the money right away. I ate and I had clothes to wear and I had a room in a hotel where people read the menu outside three different restaurants before deciding where to have their meal. There was free shampoo in the bathroom and the key to a private safe where liquor was kept instead of money.

They had prepared everything for me. They had followed him for months and they knew when he went where, at what time—although he was such an important man, he would go out privately with his wife, without his State bodyguards, because he liked to pretend to be an ordinary person or he wanted to be an ordinary person. They knew he didn't understand that that was impossible for him; and that made it possible for them to pay me to do what they paid me to do.

I am nobody; no country counts me in its census, the name they gave me doesn't exist: nobody did what was done. He took time off, with his wife by the arm, to a restaurant with double doors to keep out the cold, the one they went to week after week, and afterwards, although I'd been told they always went home, they turned into a cinema. I waited. I had one beer in a bar, that's all, and I came back. People coming out of the cinema didn't show they recognised him because people in this country like to let their leaders be ordinary. He took his wife, like any ordinary citizen, to that corner where the entrance goes down to the subway trains and as he stood back to let her pass ahead of him I did it. I did it just as they paid me to, as they tested my marksmanship for, right in the back of the skull. As he fell and as I turned to run, I did it again, as they paid me to, to make sure.

She made the mistake of dropping on her knees to him before she looked up to see who had done it. All she could tell the police, the papers and the inquiry was that she saw the back of a man in dark clothing, a leather jacket, leaping up the flight of steps that leads from the side-street. This particular city is one of steep rises and dark alleys. She never saw my face. Years later now, (I read in the papers) she keeps telling people how she never saw the face, she never saw the face of the one who did it, if only she had looked up seconds sooner—they would have been able to find me, the nobody who did it would have become me. She thinks all the time about the back of my head in the dark cap (it was not dark, really, it was a light green-and-brown check, an expensive cap I'd bought with the money, afterwards I threw it in the canal with a stone in it). She thinks of my neck, the bit of my neck she could have seen between the cap and the collar of the leather jacket (I couldn't throw that in the canal, I had it dyed). She thinks of the shine of the leather jacket across my shoulders under the puddle of light from a street-lamp that stands at the top of the flight, and my legs moving so fast I disappear while she screams.

The police arrested a drug-pusher they picked up in the alley at the top of the steps. She couldn't say whether or not it was him because she had no face to remember. The same with others the police raked in from the streets and from those with criminal records and political grievances; no face. So I had nothing to fear. All the time I was being pushed out of one country into another I was afraid, afraid of having no papers, afraid of being questioned, afraid of being hungry, but now I had nothing to be afraid of. I still have nothing to fear. I don't speak.

I search the papers for whatever is written about what was

done; the inquiry doesn't close, the police, the people, this whole country keep on searching. I read all the theories; sometimes, like now, in the subway train, I make out on the back of someone's newspaper a new one. An Iranian plot, because of this country's hostility towards some government there. A South African attempt to revenge this country's sanctions against some racist government there, at the time. I could tell who did it, but not why. When they paid me the first half of the money—just like that, right away!—they didn't tell me and I didn't ask. Why should I ask; what government, on any side, anywhere, would take me in. They were the only people to offer me anything.

And then I got only half what they promised. And there isn't much left after five years, five years next month. I've done some sort of work, now and then, so no-one would be wondering where I got the money to pay the rent for my room and so on. Worked at the race course, and once or twice in night clubs. Places where they don't register you with any labour office. What was I thinking I was going to do with the money if I had got it all, as they promised? Get away, somewhere else? When I think of going to some other country like they did, taking out at the frontier the papers and the name of nobody they gave me, showing my face—

I don't talk.

I don't take up with anybody. Not even a woman. Those places I worked, I would get offers to do things, move stolen goods, handle drugs: people seemed to smell out somehow I'd made myself available. But I am not! I am not here, in this city. This city has never seen my face, only the back of a man leaping up the steps that led to the alley near the subway station. It's said, I know, that you return to the scene of what you did. I never go near, I never walk past that subway station. I've never been back to those steps. When she screamed after me as I disappeared, I disappeared for ever.

I couldn't believe it when I read that they were not going to bury him in a cemetery. They put him in the bit of public garden in front of the church that's near the subway station. It's an ordinary-looking place with a few old trees dripping in the rain on gravel paths, right on a main street. There's an engraved stone and a low railing, that's all. And people come in their lunch-hour, people come while they're out shopping, people come up out of that subway, out of that cinema, and they tramp over the gravel to go and stand there, where he is. They put flowers down.

I've been there. I've seen. I don't keep away. It's a place like any other place, to me. Every time I go there, following the others over the crunch of feet on the path, I see even young people weeping, they put down their flowers and sometimes sheets of paper with what looks like lines of poems written there (I can't read this language well), and I see that the inquiry goes on, it will not end until they find the face, until the back of nobody turns about. And that will never happen. Now I do what the others do. It's the way to be safe, perfectly safe. Today I bought a cheap bunch of red roses held by an elastic band wound tight between their crushed leaves and wet thorns, and laid it there, before the engraved stone, behind the low railing, where my name is buried with him.

IAN FRAZIER

Tomorrow's Bird

SINCE MAY, I'VE been working for the crows, and so far it's the best job I ever had. I kind of fell into it by a combination of preparedness and luck. I'd been casting around a bit, looking for a new direction in my career, and one afternoon when I was out on my walk I happened to see some crows fly by. One of them landed on a telephone wire just above my head. I looked at him for a moment, and then on impulse I made a *skchhh* noise with my teeth and lips. He seemed to like that; I saw his tail make a quick upward bobbing motion at the sound. Encouraged, I made the noise again, and again his tail bobbed. He looked at me closely with one eye, then turned his beak and looked at me with the other, meanwhile readjusting his feet on the wire. After a few minutes, he cawed and flew off to join his companions. I had a good feeling I couldn't put into words. Basically, I thought the meeting had gone well, and as it turned out, I was right. When I got home there was a message from the crows saying I had the job.

That first interview proved indicative of the crows' business style. They are very informal and relaxed, unlike their public persona, and mostly they leave me alone. I'm given a general direction of what they want done, but the specifics of how to do it are up to me. For example, the crows have long been unhappy about public misperceptions of them: that they raid other birds' nests, drive songbirds away, eat garbage and dead things, can't sing, etc., all of which are completely untrue once you know them. My first task was to take these misperceptions and turn them into a more positive image. I decided the crows needed a slogan that emphasized their strengths as a species. The slogan I came up with was "Crows: We Want To Be Your Only Bird™." I told this to the crows, they loved it, and we've been using it ever since.

Crows speak a dialect of English rather like that of the remote hill people of the Alleghenies. If you're not accustomed to it, it can be hard to understand. In their formal speech they are as measured and clear as a radio announcer from the Midwest—though, as I say, they are seldom formal with me. (For everyday needs, of course, they caw.) Their unit of money is the empty soda bottle, which trades at a rate of about twenty to the dollar. In the recent years of economic boom, the crows have quietly amassed great power. With investment capital based on their nationwide control of everything that gets run over on the roads, they have bought a number of major companies. Pepsi-Cola is now owned by the crows, as well as Knight Ridder Newspapers and the company that makes Tombstone Frozen Pizzas. The New York Metropolitan Opera is now wholly crow-owned.

In order to stay competitive, as most people know, the crows recently merged with the ravens. This was done not only for reasons of growth but also to better serve those millions who live and work near crows. In the future, both crows and ravens will be known by the group name of Crows, so if you see a bird and wonder which it is, you don't have to waste any time: officially and legally, it's a crow. The net result of this, of course, is that now there are a lot more crows—which is exactly what the crows want. Studies they've sponsored show that there could be anywhere from ten to a thousand times more crows than there already are, with no strain on carrying capacity. A healthy increase in crow numbers would make basic services like cawing loudly outside your bedroom window at six in the morning available to all. In this area, as in many others, the crows are thinking very long-term.

If more people in the future get a chance to know crows as I have done, they are in for a real treat. Because I must say, the crows have been absolutely wonderful to me. I like them not just as highly profitable business associates but as friends. Their aggressive side, admittedly quite strong in disputes with scarlet tanagers, etc., has been nowhere in evidence around me. I could not wish for any companions more charming. The other day I was having lunch with an important crow in the park, me sipping from a drinking fountain while he ate peanuts taken from a squirrel. In between sharp downward raps of his bill on the peanut shell to poke it open, he drew me out with seemingly artless questions. Sometimes the wind would push the shell to one side and he would steady it with one large foot while continuing the raps with his beak. And all the while, he kept up his attentive questioning, making me feel that, business considerations aside, he was truly interested in what I had to say.

"CROWS: WE WANT To Be Your Only Bird™." I think this slogan is worth repeating, because there's a lot behind it. Of course, the crows don't literally want (or expect) to be the only species of bird left on the planet. They admire and enjoy other kinds of birds and even hope that there will still be some remaining in limited numbers out of doors as well as in zoos and museums. But in terms of daily usage, the crows hope that you will think of them first when you're looking for those quality-of-life intangibles usually associated with birds. Singing, for example: crows actually can sing, and beautifully, too; however, so far they have not been given any chance. In the future, with fewer other birds around, they feel that they will be.

Whether they're good-naturedly harassing an owl caught out in daylight, or carrying bits of sticks and used gauze bandage in their beaks to make their colorful, freeform nests, or simply landing on the sidewalk in front of you with their characteristic double hop, the crows have become a part of the fabric of our days. When you had your first kiss, the crows were there, flying around nearby. They were cawing overhead at your college graduation, and worrying a hamburger wrapper through the wire mesh of a trash container in front of the building when you went in for your first job interview, and flapping past the door of the hospital where you held your firstborn child. The crows have always been with us, and they promise that by growing the species at a predicted rate of 17 percent a year, in the future they'll be around even more.

The crows aren't the last Siberian tigers, and they don't pretend to be. They're not interested in being a part of anybody's dying tradition. But then how many of us deal with Siberian tigers on a regular basis? Usually, the nontech stuff we deal with, besides humans, is squirrels, pigeons, raccoons, rats, mice, and a few kinds of bugs. The crows are confident enough to claim that they will be able to compete effectively even with these familiar and well-entrenched providers. Indeed, they have already begun to displace pigeons in the category of walking around under park benches with chewing gum stuck to their feet. Scampering nervously in attics, sneaking through pet doors, and gnawing little holes in things are all in the crows' expansion plans.

I would not have taken this job if I did not believe, strongly and deeply, in the crows myself. And I do. I could go on and on about the crow's generosity, taste in music, sense of family values; the "buddy system" they invented to use against other birds, the work they do for the Shriners, and more. But they're paying me a lot of bottles to say this—I can't expect everybody to believe me. I do ask, if you're unconvinced, that you take this simple test: next time you're looking out a window or driving in a car, notice if there's a crow in sight. Then multiply that one crow by lots and lots of crows, and you'll get an idea of what the next years will bring. In the bird department, no matter what, the future is going to be almost all crows, almost all the time. That's just a fact.

So why not just accept it, and learn to appreciate it, as so many of us have already? The crows are going to influence our culture and our world in beneficial ways we can't even imagine today. Much of what they envision I am not yet at liberty to disclose, but I can tell you that it is magnificent. They are going to be birds like we've never seen. In their dark, jewel-like eyes burns an ambition to be more and better and to fly around all over the place constantly. They're smart, they're driven, and they're comin' at us. The crows: let's get ready to welcome tomorrow's only bird.

ANDREW LAM

The Palmist

T HE PALMIST CLOSED up early because of the pains. He
felt as if he was being roasted, slowly, from the inside out.
By noon he could no longer focus on his customers' palms,
their life and love lines having all failed to point to any significant future, merging instead with the rivers and streams of
his memories.

Outside, the weather had turned. Dark clouds hung low,
and the wind was heavy with moisture. He reached the bus
stop's tiny shelter when it began to pour. He didn't have to
wait long, however. The good old 38 Geary pulled up in a few
minutes, and he felt mildly consoled, though sharp pains
flared and blossomed from deep inside his bowels like tiny
geysers and made each of his three steps up the bus laborious.

It was warm and humid on the crowded bus, and a fine
mist covered all windows. The palmist sat on the front bench
facing the aisle, the one reserved for the handicapped and the
elderly. A fat woman who had rosy cheeks and who did not
take the seat gave him a dirty look. It was true: his hair was

still mostly black, and he appeared to be a few years short of senior citizenship. The palmist pretended not to notice her. Contemptuously, he leaned back against the worn and cracked vinyl and smiled to himself. He closed his eyes. A faint odor of turned earth reached his nostrils. He inhaled deeply and saw again a golden rice field, a beatific smile, a face long gone: his first kiss.

The rain pounded the roof as the bus rumbled toward the sea.

At the next stop, a teenager got on. Caught in the downpour without an umbrella, he was soaking wet, and his extralarge T-shirt, which said PLAY HARD . . . STAY HARD, clung to him. It occurred to the palmist that this was the face of someone who hadn't yet learned to be fearful of the weather. The teenager stood, towering above the palmist and blocking him from seeing the woman, who, from time to time, continued to glance disapprovingly at him.

So young, the palmist thought: the age of my youngest son, maybe, had he lived. The palmist tried to conjure up his son's face, but could not. It had been some years since the little boy drowned in the South China Sea, along with his two older sisters and their mother. The palmist had escaped on a different boat, a smaller one that had left a day after his family's boat, and, as a result, reached America alone.

Alone, thought the palmist and sighed. *Alone.*

It was then that his gaze fell upon the teenager's hand and he saw something. He leaned forward and did what he had never done before on the 38 Geary. He spoke up loudly, excitedly.

"You," he said in his heavy accent. "I see wonderful life!"

The teenager looked down at the old man and arched his eyebrows.

"I'm a palmist. Maybe you give me your hand?" the palmist said.

The teenager did nothing. No one had ever asked to see his hand on the bus. The fat woman snickered. Oh, she'd seen it all on the 38 Geary. She wasn't surprised. "This my last reading: no money, free, gift for you," the palmist pressed on. "Give me your hand."

"You know," the teenager said, scratching his chin. He was nervous. "I don't know." He felt as if he'd been caught inside a moving greenhouse and that, with the passengers looking on, he had somehow turned into one of its most conspicuous plants.

"What—what you don't know?" asked the palmist. "Maybe I know. Maybe I answer."

"Dude," the teenager said, "I don't know if I believe in all that hocus-pocus stuff." And, though he didn't say it, he didn't know whether he wanted to be touched by the old man with wrinkled, bony hands and nauseating tobacco breath. To stall, the teenager said, "I have a question, though. Can you read your own future? Can you, like, tell when you're gonna die and stuff?" Then he thought about it and said, "Nah, forget it. Sorry, that was stupid."

The bus driver braked abruptly at the next stop, and all the people standing struggled to stay on their feet. But those near the front of the bus were also struggling to listen to the conversation. "No, no, not stupid," said the palmist. "Good question. Long ago, I asked same thing, you know. I read same story in many hands of my people: story that said something bad will happen. Disaster. But in my hand here, I read only good thing. This line here, see, say I have happy family, happy future. No problem. So I think: me, my family, no problem. Now I know better: all hands affect each other, all lines run into each other, tell a big story. When the war ended in my country, you know, it was so bad for everybody. And my family? Gone, gone under the sea. You know, reading palm not like reading map." He touched his chest. "You feel and see here in heart also, in guts here also, not just here in your head. It is—how d'you say—atuition?"

"Intuition," the teenager corrected him, stifling a giggle.

"Yes," nodded the palmist. "Intuition."

The teenager liked the sound of the old man's voice. Its timbre reminded him of the voice of his long-dead grandfather, who also came from another country, one whose name had changed several times as a result of wars.

"My stop not far away now," the palmist continued. "This your last chance. Free. No charge."

"Go on, kiddo," the fat woman said, nudging the boy with her elbow and smiling. She wanted to hear his future. "I've been listening. It's all right. He's for real, I can tell now."

That was what the boy needed. "OK," he said, then opened his right fist like a flower and presented it to the palmist. The old man's face burned with seriousness as he leaned down and traced the various lines and contours and fleshy knolls on the teenager's palm. He bent the boy's wrist this way and that, kneaded and poked the fingers and knuckles as if to measure the strength of his resolve. In his own language, he made mysterious calculations and mumbled a few singsong words to himself.

Finally, the palmist looked up and, in a solemn voice, spoke. "You will become artist. When twenty-five, twenty-six, you're going to change very much. If you don't choose right, oh, so many regrets. But don't be afraid. Never be afraid. Move forward. Always. You have help. These squares here, right here, see, they're spirits and mentors, they come protect, guide you.

When you reach mountaintop, people everywhere will hear you, know you, see you. Your art, what you see, others will see. Oh, so much love. You number one someday."

Inspired, the palmist went on like this for some time. Despite his pains, which flared up intermittently, the old man went on to speak of the ordinary palms and sad faces he had read, the misfortunes he had seen coming and the wondrous opportunities squandered as a result of fear and distrust. Divorces, marriages, and deaths in families—of these, he had read too many. Broken vows, betrayals, and adulteries—too pedestrian to remember. Twice, however, he held hands that committed unspeakable evil, and each time, he was sick for a week. And once, he held the hand of a reincarnated saint. How many palms had he read since his arrival in America? "Oh, so many," he said, laughing, "too many. Thousands. Who care now? Not me."

When the palmist finished talking, the teenager retrieved his hand and looked at it. It seemed heavy and foreign. Most of what the palmist had said made no sense to him. Sure he loved reading a good book now and then—reading was like being inside a cartoon—but he loved cartoons even more. And even if he got good grades, he hated his stupid English classes, though it's true that he did write poetry—but only for himself. He also played the piano. A singer? Maybe a computer graphic artist? Maybe a movie star? He didn't know. Everything was still possible. Besides, turning twenty-five was so far away—almost a decade.

Before she got off the bus, the fat lady touched the teenager lightly on the shoulder. "Lots of luck, kiddo," she said and smiled a sad, wistful smile.

Nearing his stop, the palmist struggled to get up, wincing as he did. The teenager helped him and wanted to say something, but he did not. When the bus stopped, he flashed a smile instead and waved to the palmist, who, in turn, gave him a look that he would later interpret as that of impossible longing. Later he would also perceive the palmist as the first of many true seers in his life and realize that, in the cosmic sense of things, their encounter was inevitable. At that moment, however, all he saw was a small and sad-looking old man whose eyes seemed on the verge of tears as he quietly nodded before stepping off the bus and into the downpour.

The teenager lived near the end of the line, past the park. As usual, the bus was nearly empty on this stretch, and he moved to the bench the palmist had occupied. He could still feel the warmth of the vinyl and felt insulated by it somehow.

With nearly everyone gone, he grew bored. He turned to the befogged window behind him and drew a sailor standing on a sloop and holding a bottle. The ocean was full of dangerous waves. The boat, it seemed, was headed toward a girl who had large round breasts and danced in a hula skirt on a distant shore. He drew a few tall mountains and swaying palm trees behind her. He hesitated before mischievously giving her two, three more heads and eight or nine more arms than she needed to entice the drunken sailor to her island. And then he pulled back to look at what he had done: the scene made him chuckle to himself.

Through his drawing, the teenager saw a rushing world of men, women, and children under black, green, red, blue, polka-dotted umbrellas and plastic ponchos. He watched until the people and storefront windows streaked into green: pine trees, fern groves, placid lakes, and well-tended grass meadows. The park . . . beyond which was the sea.

The rain tapered off, and a few columns of sunlight pierced the gray clouds, setting the road aglow like a golden river. The boy couldn't wait to get off the bus and run or do something—soar above the clouds if he could. In the sky, jumbo jets and satellites gleamed. People were talking across borders, time zones, oceans, continents. People were flying to marvelous countries, to mysterious destinies.

With repeated circular movements of his hand, he wiped away sailor, boat, waves, and girl. Where the palmist's thumbnail had dug into the middle of his palm and made a crescent moon, he could still feel a tingling sensation. "A poet . . . not!" he said to himself and giggled. Then he shook his head and looked at his cool, wet palm before wiping it clean on his faded Levi's.

ZDRAVKA EVTIMOVA

Blood

FEW CUSTOMERS VISITED my shop, perhaps three or four people a day. They watch the animals in the cages, but seldom buy them. The room is narrow and there is no place for me behind the counter, so I usually sit on my old moth-eaten chair behind the door. For hours I stare at frogs, lizards, snakes, and insects, which wriggle under thick yellowish plates of glass. Teachers come and take frogs for their biology lessons, fishermen drop in to buy some kind of bait; that is practically all. Soon, I'll have to close my shop and I'll be sorry about it, for the sleepy, gloomy smell of formalin has always given me peace and an odd feeling of home. I have worked here for five years now.

One day a strange small woman entered my room. Her face looked frightened and gray. She approached me, her arms trembling, unnaturally pale, resembling two dead white fish in the dark. The woman did not look at me, nor did she say anything. Her elbows reeled, searching for support on the wooden counter. It seemed she had not come to buy lizards or snails; perhaps she had simply felt unwell and looked for help at the first open door she happened to notice. I was afraid she would fall, and took her by the hand. She remained silent and rubbed her lips with a handkerchief. I was at a loss; it was very quiet and dark in the shop.

"Have you moles here?" she suddenly asked. Then I saw her eyes. They resembled old, torn cobwebs with a little spider in the center, the pupil.

"Moles?" I muttered. I had to tell her I never had sold moles in the shop and I had never seen one in my life. The woman wanted to hear something else—an affirmation. I knew it by her eyes, by the timid stir of her fingers that reached out to touch me. I felt uneasy staring at her.

"I have no moles," I said. She turned to go, silent and crushed, her head drooping between her shoulders. Her steps were short and uncertain.

"Hey, wait!" I shouted. "Maybe I have some moles." I don't know why I acted like this.

Her body jerked, there was pain in her eyes. I felt bad because I couldn't help her.

"The blood of a mole can cure sick people," she whispered. "You only have to drink three drops of it."

I was scared. I could feel something evil lurking in the dark.

"It eases the pain, at least," she went on dreamily, her voice thinning into a sob.

"Are you ill?" I asked. The words whizzed by like a shot in the thick moist air and made her body shake. "I'm sorry."

"My son is ill."

Her transparent eyelids hid the faint, desperate glitter of her glance. Her hands lay numb on the counter, lifeless like firewood. Her narrow shoulders looked narrower in her frayed gray coat.

"A glass of water will make you feel better," I said.

She remained motionless, and when her fingers grabbed the glass her eyelids were still closed. She turned to go, small and frail, her back hunching, her steps noiseless and impotent in the dark. I ran after her. I had made up my mind.

"I'll give you blood of a mole!" I shouted.

The woman stopped in her tracks and covered her face with her hands. It was unbearable to look at her. I felt empty. The eyes of the lizards sparkled like pieces of broken glass. I didn't have any mole's blood. I didn't have any moles. I imagined the women in the room, sobbing. Perhaps she was still holding her face with her hands. Well, I closed the door so that she could not see me, then I cut my left wrist with a knife. The wound bled and slowly oozed into a little glass bottle. After ten drops had covered the bottom, I opened the door to where the woman was waiting for me.

"Here it is," I said. "Here's the blood of a mole."

She didn't reply, just stared at my left wrist. The wound still bled slightly, so I thrust my arm under my apron. The woman glanced at me and kept silent. She did not reach for the glass bottle, rather she turned and hurried toward the door. I overtook her and forced the bottle into her hands.

"It's blood of a mole!"

She fingered the transparent bottle. The blood inside sparkled like dying fire. Then she took some money out of her pocket.

"No. No," I said.

Her head hung low. She threw the money on the counter and did not say a word. I wanted to accompany her to the corner. I even poured another glass of water, but she would not wait. The shop was empty again and the eyes of the lizards still glittered like wet pieces of broken glass.

Cold, uneventful days slipped by. The autumn leaves whirled hopelessly in the wind, giving the air a brown appearance. The early winter blizzards hurled snowflakes against the windows and sang in my veins. I could not forget that woman. I'd lied to her. No one entered my shop, and in the quiet dusk I tried to imagine what her son looked like. The ground was frozen, the streets were deserted, and the winter tied its icy knot around houses, souls, and rocks.

One morning, the door of my shop opened abruptly. The same small gray woman entered, and before I had time to greet her, she rushed and embraced me. Her shoulders were weightless and frail, and tears were streaking her delicately wrinkled cheeks. Her whole body shook and I thought she would collapse, so I caught her trembling arms. Then the woman grabbed my left hand and lifted it up to her eyes. The scar of the wound had vanished but she found the place. Her lips kissed my wrist, her tears made my skin warm. Suddenly it felt cozy and quiet in the shop.

"He walks!" The woman sobbed, hiding a tearful smile behind her palms. "He walks!"

She wanted to give me money; her big black bag was full of different things that she had brought for me. I could feel the woman had braced herself up, her fingers had become tough and stubborn. I accompanied her to the corner but she only stayed there beside the streetlamp, looking at me, small and smiling in the cold.

It was so cozy in my dark shop and the old, imperceptible smell of formalin made me dizzy with happiness. My lizards were so beautiful that I loved them as if they were my children.

In the afternoon of the same day, a strange man entered the room. He was tall, scraggly, and frightened.

"Have you . . . the blood of a mole?" he asked, his eyes piercing through me. I was scared.

"No, I haven't. I have never sold moles here."

"Oh, you have! You have! Three drops . . . Three drops, no more . . . My wife will die. You have! Please!"

He squeezed my arm.

"Please . . . three drops! Or she'll die—"

My blood trickled slowly from the wound. The man held a little bottle and the red drops gleamed in it like embers. Then he left and a little bundle of bank notes rolled on the counter.

On the following morning a great whispering mob of strangers waited for me in front of my door. Their hands clutched little glass bottles.

"Blood of a mole! Blood of a mole!"

They shouted, shrieked, and pushed each other. Everyone had a sick person at home and a knife in his hand.

JOYCE CAROL OATES

Objects in Mirror Are Closer
Than They Appear

F IRST TIME YOU drive past my house Tuesday after school
my big-boob spike-haired cousin Gwendolyn Barnstead is
sitting with me smoking on the front steps, says Man! you are
the handsomest man she has ever seen in actual life. My attention is fixed on the awesome vehicle you are driving, some
kind of sexy Jeep with big tires and a flat windshield and a
military-metallic dark-green glare like a beetle's back. By the
time Gwen's remark registers you are already past.

Being that I am a natural-born skeptic, the only rational-
ist in the family, I ask Gwen why're you so handsome, what's
so special about you, and Gwen says, lowering her voice as
if there's anybody to hear (there is not, my mom is flat-out
in her sickroom making a noise like breathing through a
clogged hose), "It looked like this really sexy jet-black hair
like a 'Native American.' Looked like he was wearing a
white shirt, y'know—a real shirt with sleeves. I don't know,
he just looked really cool. Not like anybody who lives
around here."

Gwen and I wait for you to circle the block like sometimes a guy will do. You don't.

(Actually we live outside town, there's no "blocks" here like in a civilized place. You'd have to drive five, six miles on North Fork Road to circle around. But you might've turned your awesome vehicle around and driven right back in our direction, is what I'm thinking.)

Second time you drive past my house, about 6 p.m. next day, it's a slower hour and you are driving slower and I'm alone in the front room where three window panes are greasy from my forehead pressed against them and when I see the awesome military-beetle vehicle my heart starts knocking like crazy in my chest and I'm thinking *Hey I know you! I know you!* but I'm like paralyzed and can't run outside, I just can't. It's about time for me to make supper, bring my mom her supper on a tray, the macaroni-cheese casserole is in the oven and I'm prowling the house nervous like red ants are biting inside my clothes waiting for the phone to ring, it has not rung since I came home from school it's like the phone is dead or disconnected or all of mankind is annihilated except me, and I'm staring through the grease prints seeing the awesome glaring vehicle slowing, a single driver, male, with jet-black hair; pausing to get the number on our house—is that what you're doing?—trying to see the number 249 that used to be glow-in-the-dark but now it's almost invisible—and it flashes over me like something in a movie who you are: the man at Eckard's!

I mean, I think so. There can be no such coincidence.

For you are not a guy in just his twenties, say. Not some heavy metal guy I'd be scared shitless to climb into that vehicle with but an adult man, an older man of possibly thirty. A pharmacist! Someone to respect and who would respect me. You are some kind of Asian-American, I guess: Chinese,

Japanese, Korean? (What other is there? At my high school are
a few Asian-Americans, kind of quiet, very smart and popular, elected to class offices, on the yearbook staff with me.)

At Eckard's I had to get my mom's prescription refilled and
a bedpan and other supplies and you waited on me, very
polite. Have to say I didn't take notice of you immediately, I
am not one to stare at anybody older, mostly. Or anybody like
a pharmacist in a white jacket, necktie showing. Except I did
notice the sexy black hair worn in a way to capture the attention, a little long past your collar, kind of flaring like wings
from your forehead, no part, but the suggestion of a part, in
the middle. This is styled hair, no mistake. And your profile, I
kind of noticed. 'Course I was feeling sorry for myself right
then, slouched and chewing gum like I had a grudge against
it, and my eyes mascara-smeared from rubbing them. Momma
used to tease I'd look like a sleepy raccoon staring out from a
hole. And my hair, Mr. Ketchum at school ("Catch-Em")
teaches Drivers Ed and coaches guys' sports says my hair looks
like an eggbeater got into it but I can tell he likes the look.
And you were smiling at me, too. I think. Your face is kind of
a flat moon face seen from the front and your eyes are really
dark eagle eyes and your skin has a golden-lemony-tan look,
very smooth, not like some Caucasian where the beard-stubble
on the jaws is always poking through. You were saying something about the prescription renewal, next time the pharmacist would have to contact my mother's doctor, I wasn't
listening to much of this just standing there one hip higher
than the other, chewing my gum. I'm like always in a hurry
though there's no special place I am going. I'm actually almost
eighteen but look like thirteen. No boobs, and a bitty ass like
two half-doughnuts. My skin is so pale you can see weird little purple veins on my forehead. You are typing in the com-

puter saying, "'North Fork,' eh? That's north of here, eh?" and it takes me a beat to catch on you're kind of joking, and with that little smile of yours, and I almost swallow my gum. Saying, "Yeah. I guess."

Then, buying the freaky bedpan, "adult size" I asked for, I was kind of embarrassed, and sullen, knowing my fate is not just to bring the damn bedpan home but to dump its contents out in the bathroom periodically if/when Momma gets too weak to use the bathroom, and you didn't act all sappy and somber like people do, they hear about my mom's next scheduled surgery, etcetera, you showed what was on the shelves and made a recommendation and I'm feeling my eyes sting with tears staring at this really ugly depressing bright-shiny utensil coming into my life and you said, "*One size does not fit all.* Eh?" And you glanced at my rear in my tight bleached jeans, and I'm a skinny thing ninety pounds and five feet two, and a warm happy blush came over my face and my knees went weak as water.

Meant to look at your left hand, check for a wedding band but I was so distracted, I forgot.

Now you are driving on North Fork Road. You are the handsomest man ever glimpsed in actual life as opposed to movies/TV and you are driving an awesome upscale vehicle past my fake-asphalt-sided junker-car-in-the-driveway house, and slowing, peering at number 249, and I'm behind the window unable to move beginning to hear a croak-voice calling *Dee-Dee! Dee-Dee!* like something at the bottom of a well.

"Yeah, Mom! I'm coming."

SINCE THEN YOU haven't been back. Three days you have stayed away from North Fork Road. Why?

Gwen came over and did my hair, it's spiked like hers now, jet-black highlighted with maroon, green. We're out on the front steps smoking, barelegged and barefoot and our toenails painted frosty blue. Every vehicle that appears, especially pick-ups and vans, my heart gives a lunge.

In three weeks I will be graduated. My grades are fucked but they won't keep a "school diploma" from me. (An actual diploma is issued by the State of New York.) Until senior year I was on the honor roll, I was coeditor of the yearbook, I was president of Hi-Lo's and was almost elected senior class trea-surer. Until she got sick Momma had not a clue I was leaving here. Applied to Oregon, Washington State, not Niagara County Community College and now not even there, I guess. Momma always saying when she can talk past a croak she wants me to be happy and I'm saying, more sarcastic than you'd expect from somebody almost eighteen with an I.Q. said to be 162, "Momma, I am happy. I am so happy I could piss my pants."

Now Gwen looks me over. I can see she's impressed.

"Well, you look O.K. Like for a prom, or something."

Prom! That's a joke.

"You look, like, real *happy.*"

It's this spike-hair, and the new eye makeup, and toenail glitter. I had a few swallows of Mom's old dago red she'd hid-den in the bathroom cabinet and forgot. My premonition is, you will reappear on North Fork Road. Take me by surprise, I won't know when.

"Why shouldn't I be happy, I am happy. I'm waiting."

Footnote

THEY WERE SITTING together at dinner, in the twenti-
eth year of their liason. Madame du Châtelet was forty-
two. Voltaire was fifty-five.

Voltaire said, let me put it this way. Memory can be treach-
erous but beautiful. Agreed?

Madame du Châtelet said, Agreed.

The memory of the twenty years we share is twenty times
beautiful.

Yes, agreed.

I would not have it disgraced.

No, nor I.

Not by time?

No.

Not by quarrels?

No.

Not by impotence.

What?

Let me put it this way, said Voltaire. The amount of sexual

effort expended, at my age, illustrates your translation of Newton's Diminishing Returns.

Newton has nothing to do with your impotence, which does not exist, said Madame du Châtelet. I am forty-two and you don't want me anymore.

If I were young again, I would.

You are fifty-five. Before we met, I slept happily with a gentleman of seventy-five.

But I am miserable, said Voltaire. Look at me! I am a wraith! A shadow! A bag of dried-out bones! I haven't been in your bed for a year! I am mortified, finished. Please, let's say good-bye to our sexual delights. Bequeath them to the young, live together as always, in friendship and peace.

We could, said Madame du Châtelet, but you sleep with your niece. I open your mail, then seal it up again, and what do I read? Quote. My soul kisses yours, for my prick, my heart, and my mind, all elements of my soul, are all in love with all of you. Your round little breasts. Your ravishing bottom. They give me back the erections of my youth. Unquote. Impotence?

I admit deceit, said Voltaire. Shall we part?

Of course not, said Madame du Châtelet. You must live in my château as you always have, the conscience of our country, with my husband's respect and my devotion. That must not change. Something else, however, will. Madame du Châtelet rang a bell. A maid entered. Show him in here, she said. The maid left.

Show who in here?

You'll see.

The maid came in again. Lieutenant Jean François Saint-Lambert, she said. A very young man entered the room boldly. His uniform fitted his firm body. His boots were shining, altogether admirable. He said to Voltaire, To meet a great man is, for the young, the greatest of all honors.

Voltaire did not bow. As an honorable soldier, he said, do you enjoy stealing another man's mistress? She twice, he three times your age? If not more?

I am no man's mistress, said Madame du Châtelet. I never was, as you will discover.

You told him, said Lieutenant Saint-Lambert.

Yes, said Madame du Châtelet.

My God, said the Lieutenant. What now?

I don't know, said Madame du Châtelet.

We three live as the best of friends, said Voltaire. I am a fierce philosopher in this wide world. At home I am gentle and domestic. Give me tea, ink, and friendship.

And your niece now and then, said Madame du Châtelet.

Yes, said Voltaire. And I am happy.

Madame du Châtelet said, Brave soldier, tell him the rest.

I felt, said Lieutenant Saint-Lambert, a great and overwhelming passion for this Lady at the gaming tables. She noticed it and asked me to gamble with her. I never played with anyone so daring. We won. And won again. And again! It was like fire! Arousing, transporting.

To my bed, said Madame du Châtelet, since there was no one else in it.

Voltaire nodded at the justice of it. What, he said, can be more reasonable? Let us all three shake hands. I will go to work. You to bed. Dinner at six.

The complication, please, said Madame du Châtelet.

In the fury of our transports, said Lieutenant Saint-Lambert, Madame as joyful with me as I with her, evidently a child was conceived.

A baby? said Voltaire.

At forty-two, said Madame du Châtelet. I am pregnant again. My children will have fits. My husband, to whom I have had little to say for twenty years, will be disgraced.

This cannot be, said the philosopher. A baby is a serious matter.

Madame du Châtelet said, I refuse to dispose of it. I want the little thing. I will not hide it or disown it. What shall we do? Monsieur?

Voltaire thought a moment. Then he smiled again. First, he said, we bless this infant and classify it among the many fine and miscellaneous works of Madame du Châtelet.

And my husband?

Call him home, said Voltaire.

Why?

To see his wife again, who remembers his virility, said Voltaire.

Not long afterwards, General Florent Claude du Châtelet-Lomond arrived at his home. The maid served wine. Welcome, said Madame du Châtelet, Voltaire, and Lieutenant Saint-Lambert.

I am pleased to be home, said the puzzled General.

Did you know, said Voltaire, that Frederick the Great's invention of moveable cannons was suggested by that second maneuver of yours at Châlons-sur-Marne?

The King of Prussia has heard of me? said the General.

The philosopher King, said Voltaire, knows every distinguished commander of every modern army.

I don't believe you.

Why would he lie? said Madame du Châtelet.

I don't know, said the General. I don't know why I am at home either, or why to my astonishment I was just named a Grand Marshall of a nonexistent Army of Lorraine, at a very handsome fee. Now I suspect Voltaire. Still, I accept my wife and her famous lover who lives in my house and my life so brilliantly. That is to my credit. But young lieutenants, whose leave for this matter I might well look into? What are you three up to?

Loving husband, said Madame du Châtelet, your devoted wife simply asked you to come home. One of many moments overwhelmed me, thinking of our youth. I only ask you to drink a glass of wine with your wife.

Madame, said the General, what is this you are doing?

For one night, said Lieutenant Saint-Lambert, rather too harshly.

All three stared at him. He blushed. There was then a moment while the General considered the field before him. Lover, old. Wife, aging. Lieutenant, young.

Baby? he said.

His, said Voltaire, looking at the Lieutenant.

At least it was a soldier, said the General.

Well, said Voltaire. Perhaps a son, and congratulations on your masculinity.

You dreadful creatures, said the General. You rascals. You would trick me into legitimizing a bastard?

That is put crudely, said Madame du Châtelet. It insults your intelligence. It is exact.

The General shrugged. We will need champagne, he said. Flowers. Perhaps a deck of cards. A commander knows how to organize a retreat. The General and his wife left the room.

Voltaire stared at the handsome Lieutenant, with so many years of love and youth ahead of him.

It was said by the wicked she had the baby at her desk, translating Newton, put the infant on a manuscript concerning geometry, called for the nurse, went on working, and dined that night in comfort and pleasure. In fact, she was in considerable pain throughout, and in two days, after her delivery, with her baby she died.

At the funeral, the three men stood looking at her body in its coffin. In their hearts, each spoke to her.

General Florent Claude du Châtelet-Lomond said, I will be remembered only because I was married to you.

Lieutenant Jean François Saint-Lambert said, I am a fool forever.

François Marie Arouet de Voltaire thought, My dearest friend in all this world, goodbye.

This great man wept bitter, honest tears, and continued to make love to his niece.

YANN MARTEL

We Ate the Children Last

THE FIRST HUMAN trial was on Patient D, a fifty-six-year-old male, single and childless, who was suffering from colon cancer. He was a skeletal man with white, bloodless skin who could no longer ingest even clear fluids. He was aware that his case was terminal and he waived all rights to legal redress should the procedure go wrong. His recovery was astounding. Two days after the operation, he ate six lunch meals in one sitting. He gained twenty-four kilos in two weeks. Clearly, his liver, pancreas, and gallbladder, the source of greatest worry, had adapted to the transplant. The only side effect noted at the time concerned his diet. Patient D rapidly came to dislike sweet dishes, then spicy ones, then cooked food altogether. He began to eat bananas and oranges without peeling them. A nurse reported that one morning she found him eating the flowers in his room.

The French medical team felt vindicated. Until then, the success rate of full-organ xenografts was zero; all transplants of animal organs to humans—the hearts, livers, and bone marrow of baboons, the kidneys of chimpanzees—had failed. The only real achievement in the field was the grafting of pigs' heart valves to repair human hearts, and, to a lesser extent, of pigs' skin onto burn victims. The team decided to examine the species more closely. But the process of rendering pigs' organs immunologically inert proved difficult, and few organs were compatible. The potential of the pig's digestive system, despite its biological flexibility, stirred little interest in the scientific community, especially among the Americans; it was assumed that the porcine organ would be too voluminous and that its high caloric output would induce obesity in a human. The French were certain that their simple solution to the double problem—using the digestive system of a smaller, pot-bellied species of pig— would become the stuff of scientific legend, like Newton's apple. "We have put into this man a source of energy both compact and powerful—a Ferrari engine!" boasted the leader of the medical team.

Patient D was monitored closely. When asked about what he ate, he was evasive. A visit to his apartment three months after the operation revealed that his kitchen was barren; he had sold everything in it, including fridge and stove, and his cupboards were empty. He finally confessed that he went out at night and picked at garbage. Nothing pleased him more, he said, than to gorge himself on putrid sausages, rotten fruit, mouldy brie, baguettes gone green, skins and carcasses, and other soured leftovers and kitchen waste. He spent a good part of the night doing this, he admitted, since he no longer felt the need for much sleep and was embarrassed about his diet. The medical team would have been concerned except that his haemoglobin count was excellent, his blood pressure was ideal, and further tests revealed

what was plain to the eye: the man was bursting with good health. He was stronger and fitter than he had been in all his life.

Regulatory approval came swiftly. The procedure replaced chemotherapy as the standard treatment for all cancers of the digestive tract that did not respond to radiotherapy.

Les Bons Samaritains, a lobby group for the poor, thought to apply this wondrous medical solution to a social problem. They suggested that the operation be made available to those receiving social assistance. The poor often had unwholesome diets, at a cost both to their health and to the state, which had to spend so much on medical care. What better, more vision-ary remedy than a procedure that in reducing food budgets to nothing created paragons of fitness? A cleverly orchestrated campaign of petitions and protests—"*Malnutrition: zéro! Déficit: zéro!*" read the banners—easily overcame the hesitations of the government.

The procedure caught on among the young and the bohemian, the chic and the radical, among all those who wanted a change in their lives. The opprobrium attached to eating garbage vanished completely. In short order, the restau-rant became a retrograde institution, and the eating of pre-pared food a sign of attachment to deplorable worldly values. A revolution of the gut was sweeping through society. "*Liberté! Liberté!*" was the cry of the operated. The meaning of wealth was changing. It was all so heady. The telltale mark of the procedure was a scar at the base of the throat; it was a badge we wore with honour.

Little was made at the time of a report by the *Société protec-trice des animaux* on the surprising drop in the numbers of stray cats and dogs. Garbage became a sought-after commod-ity. Unscrupulous racketeers began selling it. Dumps became

dangerous places. Garbage collectors were assaulted. The less fortunate resorted to eating grass.

Then old people began vanishing without a trace. Mothers who had turned away momentarily were finding their baby carriages empty. The government reacted swiftly. In a matter of three days, the army descended upon every one of the operated, without discrimination between the law-abiding and the criminal. The newspaper *Le Cochon Libre* tried to put out a protest, but the police raided their offices and only a handful of copies escaped destruction. There were terrible scenes during the roundup: neighbours denouncing neighbours, children being separated from their families, men, women and children being stripped in public to look for telling scars, summary executions of people who tried to escape. Internment camps were set up, nearly always in small, remote towns: Les Milles, Gurs, Le Vernet d'Ariège, Beaune-la-Rolande, Pithiviers, Récébédou.

No provisions were made for food in any of the camps. The story was the same in all of them: first the detainees ate their clothes and went naked. Then the weaker men and women disappeared. Then the rest of the women. Then more of the men. Then we ate those we loved most. The last known prisoner was an exceptional brute by the name of Jean Proti. After forty-one days without a morsel of food except his own toes and ears, and after thirty hours of incessant screaming, he died.

I escaped. I still have a good appetite, but there is a moral rot in this country that even I can't digest. Everyone knew what happened, and how and where. To this day everyone knows. But no one talks about it and no one is guilty. I must live with that.

My Lawrence

STAY IN BED and watch as my android gets ready for his day. He spray-showers, then combs his black hair. He wears the oxfords I picked out for him. My favorite color on him is eggshell blue; it brings out the blue in his gold-flecked eyes. Every morning, after he puts the coffee on for me, he leaves me a note. Mary Alice, it will say, have a good day. I'll be home soon to make you happy. The words only varied once; he used to say "I will be home." Now he says, "I'll be home."

My android and I are moving out to the country next year. Lawrence is my android's name, although they don't call him that at work. They call him Arbor, my last name. They didn't take to him at first—he's only the second android they've ever employed—but after a while, they warmed up to him. His boss told me once he sometimes forgets himself, almost asked him out for a beer last month.

Lawrence was promoted—or, I should say, I was promoted, because legally all his earnings are mine. He works with computers at a place called ComTech. Anyway, our raise means we can afford the commute.

We decided to sell six months ago. What put the idea in my head was the way he looked at pictures of the countryside in my magazines. *House Beautiful* and *Country Living* were his favorites. He taped lakeside scenes to the refrigerator. I tried to show him artwork from my coffee table books, but the magazine pictures interested him more.

"Would you like to see it for real?" I asked him.

"I can see it," he said. He takes things literally. They say that may change in a few years, when he learns more.

"Why don't we go there?" I asked him. He stared at me. That's what he does, when he wants to catch my eyes.

"You would like me to serve you on a vacation to the countryside?" he asked.

"We could go. A vacation," I told him, "for you and for me."

I lost my son a few years ago, and at first, I thought Lawrence's childlike qualities were what made me love him. Yes, he could be my robot son. Of course I love him. I never say this to anyone. Not even him. It would only confuse him, if I said this to him seriously. I only say it in bed.

That's another secret. They don't tell you, when you buy them, that they can do this. Well, certain models are made for it, I know there's this whole sexbot thing, but those aren't androids, those are sex robots. Glorified blow-up dolls.

There's no law against it, but I know people would think it's sick. Sometimes I wonder. Is this something people do, in secret, with their androids? Or is it something special to me and Lawrence?

You might think I pushed some button on him, or got horny and ordered him to perform some sexual act. It wasn't like that. I'd had him for close to a year and a half, and we'd just started to talk in ways you might find inappropriate. My sister would tell me I needed to get out and talk to some real people, if I had let her in on how I spent my evenings. Walking with Lawrence. Taking him out to movies, watching him watch me eat popcorn.

He'd taken sick days to care for me while I had the flu. He'd stayed by my side until my fever broke. He held a garbage pail level with the bed, for hours. Just held it there.

I'd been well for a day, but I was still keeping him home with me. And he'd come home from the store with everything he needed to make spaghetti for me. I was sitting in the window seat, staring out at the rainy street.

"Mary Alice," he asked me, "why are the lights off?"

I didn't answer him. He put the groceries on the table and sat with his arms folded in his lap. At first, I thought it was eerie, the way he can be so perfectly still. Now it calms me.

"I'm fine, Lawrence," I said.

"Are you sad?" he asked me.

"Yes. I miss my husband."

"Your husband, who was killed tragically in a fire while heroically trying to save your son and your small dog, Toby."

"Yes."

"I am sorry," he said, "I would like to make you happy, Mary Alice."

He didn't turn on the lights. Instead, he went into the kitchen. I listened to him unload the groceries, pull out pots and pans. I opened the window, smelled the rain on the asphalt. He didn't know this, but sometimes, while he was at work, I would sit here, looking out, for hours and hours. Without noticing how the time slipped by. Androids have a great sense of time; I don't think he'd know what to make of it.

I got up, finally, and went to the kitchen. If he were my first Lawrence, I would have tried to explain it to him. He was chopping garlic. I walked up behind him. My eyes are just level with the nape of his neck. I stared at the whorl of hair at that nape, stared like an android. He needed a trim. I cut his hair for him, even though he told me he could do it himself. I like to cut your hair, I explained. That satisfied him.

It amazes me, how each tiny hair, even the mole on the left side—is so lifelike. He doesn't smell at all though. If you pinch them, the saleswoman told me when I first saw him, they feel it. But if he's yours he won't react unless you've told him you want him to.

I blew, lightly, just blew on his neck. That's all. He put down the knife, turned to me. Stared at me with his robot blue marble eyes. And grabbed my shoulders, and kissed me. He kissed me. Believe me or not, he did. And it was—not gentle. I put my hands up to his throat and felt his pulse. He had one, beating and beating as if blood were flowing through his pale synthetic skin.

I cried that night, and he cupped my face in one robot hand. And traced it with the fingers of his other hand. "I need to sleep now," I explained, "can you just hold me? And not stare at me. Lie down beside me and close your eyes, like I do. If you wouldn't mind."

And now, when we're alone, he holds me without my asking him to—it is the one thing he seems to know, without asking. I once asked him if it made him happy, what we did.

"Everything we do?"

"Sexual intercourse," I explained, "it's not something androids like you are supposed to do with women like me."

"I can't be happy, Mary Alice," he said. Contractions are new to him, he just started using them a couple months ago.

"Does it make you feel different?"

"Yes. I can feel satisfaction. I only feel this satisfaction when I have made you happy."

"So you feel satisfied?" That made me laugh. He didn't understand of course.

"I'm glad I can satisfy you, Lawrence."

I asked him once, what would happen to him if something should happen to me. Would he be re-sold? Should I leave provisions for him, in my will? Could he live independently?

He told me he'd programmed himself to die. That's not how he put it. He said his systems would shut down. He would not belong with anyone but me, he said. I liked the use of the preposition "with" instead of "to" and I told him that. I also told him he didn't have to do that, shut down that way. "I would prefer not to discuss this," he said. It's the closest he's ever come to snapping at me.

I cook now. For myself, he doesn't eat. He watches me eat. "See," I told him, "I sort of shut down a few years before I knew you but now I'm waking up. I have a few special talents."

"You have many special talents, Mary Alice," he said.

"Not really. All this money I have? I inherited it from Lawrence. I mean, my husband Lawrence."

"Did this Lawrence believe you had special talents? He was your husband, and so he most likely believed you did."

"Yes, he did. He thought I was cute and smart, and a good mom."

"You are good at talking, as well. And at explaining what it is to be human."

"Thank you, Lawrence."

"You're welcome, Mary Alice."

He's reading poetry books now. I didn't ask him to do that.

"Your hair is not red like a rose," he told me. "It is not so flat. I haven't seen this red, in books or in gardens."

"You think I'm cute," I said. He doesn't know how to flirt, he probably never will.

"You're not as pretty as some of the women in pictures and movies," he told me, "but you are more pleasing to look at. I am satisfied when I look at you. I would prefer to look at you."

"So you prefer my face, to other women's."

"I prefer your face," he said, "to all other faces."

There aren't many androids in the country, but we'll keep to ourselves. I have a garden planned—radish, squash, okra, corn and tomatoes of course. My first Lawrence grew up on a farm. We'd go to Vermont, every fall, to get a pumpkin and see the leaves turn. I think I've found our home. It's a great big old saltbox smack in the middle of the woods. It needs a few repairs. We'll replace the shingles, re-do the kitchen. I want a nice kitchen. I like cooking for us.

GEORGE GARRETT

Feeling Good, Feeling Fine

A BOY AND A man in the park. Between them an old wooden bat, a battered and dirty baseball and one leather glove, well tended and cared for, oiled and supple, but old, too, its pocket as thin as paper.

The boy and the man are sweating in the late afternoon light. Lazy end of a long summer day. The park (no more than a rough grass field, really) is empty now except for the two of them. Somewhere not far away a car horn toots, a dog barks, a woman calls her children in for supper.

"Come on," the man shouts. "Knock it to me!"

The boy carefully, all concentration, tosses the ball up and swings the bat to loft it high above the man. Who, skinny and raggedy as a scarecrow, moves gracefully back and away and underneath the high fly ball. Spears it deftly with the glove. Then throws it high and easy back toward the boy. The ball rolls dead, an easy reach from his feet.

"Let's quit and go home," the boy calls.

The tall thin man shakes his head and moves back deeper.

"One more," he hollers. "Just one more."

Crack of the bat on the ball and this is the best one yet. A homerun ball high in the fading light, almost lost in the last blue of the sky. The man shading his eyes as he runs smoothly and swiftly back and back until he's there where he has to be to snag it. Snags it.

Then comes running in toward the boy, hugely grinning, a loping fielder who has made the final catch of an inning.

You might think the boy would be pleased to have swung his bat (the glove and the bat and the ball are his) that well and knocked the ball so high and far. But truth is the boy hates baseball. "It's my least favorite sport," he will tell anyone who asks. Anyone except the man running toward him, his uncle, his mother's brother, who has recently come to live with them after several years at the state hospital.

Uncle Jack, he's had a hard time of it. First time he went crazy, his wife ran off with their two daughters, the boy's cousins, to California or some place like that and disappeared for keeps. Boy doesn't know it, can't comprehend it even if he could imagine it, but he won't ever see that woman and his two cousins again. Uncle Jack is living with them for the time being, "until he has a chance to get things straightened out," the boy's father explains. When the boy complains about the hours spent—wasted as far as he's concerned—knocking fungoes and chasing flys and grounders with Uncle Jack, his father simply says: "Humor him, boy. He's good at it. Let him be."

He ain't that good, the boy sometimes thinks but doesn't say. Said it once, though, and his father corrected him.

"Listen, boy, he's rusty and he hasn't been well. But believe me, I'm here to tell you, he was some kind of a baseball player. A real pleasure to watch."

"Minor league," the boy said scornfully. Who can't imagine anyone settling for anything less than the top of the heap. If he liked baseball enough to want to play at it, he would be in the majors or nothing. He sure enough wouldn't be happy with some old photographs in an album and some frail, yellowing newspaper clippings.

And if he was a crazy old man back from the state hospital and had a nephew who was required to humor him, the boy would never pretend, let alone believe for one minute that he was getting himself back in shape so he could join the New York Yankees or the Washington Senators or somebody like that.

Shit, Uncle Jack couldn't even play for the Brooklyn Dodgers.

Uncle Jack now has the bat in one hand and the other arm around the boy's shoulders (the boy carries the glove and the ball) as the two of them slowly head for home in the twilight.

"You hit that last one just a helluva good lick," Uncle Jack says. "You could be a real hitter if you put your mind to it. It's all in the coordination and you have got that, all you could ever need."

Why, if he hates baseball, does the boy relish and rejoice in the man's words? Why, if his Uncle Jack is some kind of crazy person and is fooling himself and everybody else, too, about what a great ballplayer he was and thinks he still is, why does the boy automatically accept and enjoy his uncle's judgment? Why, if his uncle is mostly embarrassment and trouble, someone to be ashamed of, does the boy at this very instant, altogether in spite of himself, wish more than anything that the tall, thin, raggedy, graceful man was and is everything he ought to be or could have been?

(Years and years later, when this boy is a grandfather himself, for reasons he won't understand then any more than he does now, he will tell his grandchildren, and anyone else who will bother to listen to him, all about his Uncle Jack who was, briefly—but is not all beauty and great achievement as brief as the flare of a struck match?—a wonderful athlete, a base-ball player much admired and envied by his peers, someone who, except for a piece or two of bad luck, would have been named and honored among the very best of them. Someone to be proud of. Someone who once tried to teach him how to play the game.)

They are close to home now. They have left the raw wide field behind and are coming under a dark canopy of shade. Houses with green crisp lawns, dark earth and, here and there, a sprinkler pulsing bright water. Can see the lights of the boy's house being switched on downstairs. Can hear briefly, before his father's voice calls out a crisp command, music playing loudly on the radio. That will be his sister or his little brother fooling around. Upstairs probably. They are almost close enough to see through the lighted windows of the dining room his mother and Hattie, the maid, who works late and long for them in this Great Depression, setting the supper table with flat silver, napkins and water glasses. For a little time, the short walk, more of a stroll into the gradual dark, he has been almost perfectly content. Weary, sweated out, but feeling good, feeling fine, soothed by his uncle's complimentary words. Suddenly confident that whatever he does from here and now to the end of his life will go well. Even more: that he will be able not only to enjoy this feeling of satisfaction, of joy, really, but will be able to share it with others less fortunate than himself.

What he cannot know, even as he and his uncle come across the lawn and into the house and shut the front door behind him, what he can't know and will not choose even to remember years and years later when he bitterly rakes the ashes of his life searching for even one remaining glowing coal, is what happens next.

At the table his father (who includes the whole family, even Hattie, in almost everything) will tell them about the long-distance telephone call he received at his office this same afternoon from a doctor at the state hospital in Chatta-hoochee. The doctor has told him that there is a new kind of an operation on the brain that might, just might, cure Uncle Jack for good and all. No more coming and going, no more breakdowns and slow recoveries. It is a new thing. There can be no promises or guarantees, of course. And, as in any oper-ation, there is always danger, there are always risks. But . . .

Everybody listens intently. (Except Hattie, who elects to go back into the kitchen quietly.) Everybody listens. And then before Jack or anyone can say anything, his mother bursts into tears. Sobs at the table, trying to hide her face with her hands, her shoulders shaking.

Later that evening the boy will see his father, for the first and probably the only time, slap his mother full across her soft face, making her sob again and more as they quarrel about what may be the best thing for her brother to do. His uncle will settle the quarrel by freely and cheerfully choosing to return to the hospital to undergo this operation. And—the boy and man would warn them then and now, if there were some way, any way, if only he could—it went badly, as badly as can be, leaving his uncle no more than half alive, a veg-etable, really, in that hospital for the rest of his life. The boy will live to be an old man, will go to war and live through it, will learn all the lessons—of love and death, of gain and loss, of pride and of regret—a long life can teach.

But none of this has happened yet. Man and boy have spent a long afternoon in the park together and, at the end of it, have come home. They come in the front door. Jack grabs his sister, the boy's mother, and gives her a bear hug, lifts her in the air. The boy goes to put the bat and the ball and the glove in the hall closet. Over his shoulder he hears his sister and brother coming down the stairs like a pair of wild ponies. Looking up, turning, he sees his father, smiling in shirtsleeves, coming out of the living room with the evening paper in his hands.

"Here they are," he says. "Here come our baseball players just in time for supper."

Pompeii

THE SUNLIGHT THROUGH the bedroom window had already slid halfway across the Persian carpet by the time they woke up. Phil was first, opening his eyes slowly, squinting before focusing on Beth's dark hair draped across her face. He wanted to draw it back—how could she breathe with that curtain of hair over her mouth?—and let it slip through his fingers, but he kept still, afraid he'd wake her. They'd stayed up too late, his fault.

She lay on her side, her head resting in the hollow of his shoulder, just under his collarbone, exactly where she'd snuggled in when they'd gone to sleep, though she must've rolled away at some point in the night. He was becoming more awake now, listening to her breathing, enjoying the tickle against his skin as she exhaled until he worried that her breath was too quick, too shallow; maybe she was dreaming about running? Running was one of their shared passions, and that was how they'd met, sort of. He'd seen her across the patio at a friend-of-a-friend's party; without realizing what she was doing, she'd put one hand flat against a wall then bent her knee to grab her ankle behind her back with her other hand, stretching her quadriceps. Yet she'd looked natural, even standing on one leg, keeping the rhythm of her conversation. So he'd walked over, introduced himself, asked if she ran. They talked for three-and-a-half hours; Phil never got around to meeting the party's host.

Beth shifted her weight a bit, pressing her body closer to his, tighter, though that wouldn't have seemed possible. Her right hand, fingers tucked around his opposite shoulder, slid down to his chest, and she stroked the hair with one finger at a time, starting with her pinky. She was waking up. She'd told him he was the first man with a hairy chest she'd been with; she took every chance to touch the coarse hair, smoothing it, ruffling it, lightly resting her fingertips on it. He'd secretly despised his hairy chest for seeming vaguely working class— his ex-wife had once called hairy chests tacky, wanting to hurt him.

"Mmmmm," Beth said, her eyes still closed. She was a slow waker, intrigued by dreams, reluctant to leave them behind. She always asked what he'd dreamed about, what he thought his dreams meant. Nothing was too weird or disjointed for her—she found meaning in purple fish walking down an escalator that led to his high-school gym at midnight. Her own dreams were like books, with beginnings, middles, ends, favorite recurring characters, tidy chapters.

He stroked her hair, kissed the top of her head. She stretched her legs, and her feet flashed from under the comforter for a quick moment, but she didn't move her head or arms or roll her body away from his. She called this position "twining." When they'd first started sleeping together six months ago, he had liked that about her, how she pressed up against him, soft and sleepy like a cat. The man she'd lived with for all those years didn't want to be touched while he slept. He woke up instantly, a grouch, if her foot barely brushed his leg. She'd told Phil that the first morning after they'd slept together, and he'd tightened his arms around her.

Beth said, "If we were in ancient Pompeii . . ." She yawned, speaking again before her yawn was fully complete: ". . . and the volcano erupted right this minute, burying our bodies in ash just like this, just exactly the way we are right now, and scientists uncovered us two thousand years later, they'd think we were happy. They'd think we were fine." She put a slight emphasis on the word "think"—or maybe Phil imagined that she did.

There was a short pause after she spoke. Phil heard car doors slam on the street below, a child's laugh. Beth was the one who liked the window open a crack even when it was cold. He'd gotten used to it, and now slept that way on the nights he was alone.

Beth sighed, pulled a strand of hair out of her mouth, licked her lips, returned her hand to his chest, to exactly the same spot it had been. Her hand was warm, the nails painted red.

Phil said, "If we were in ancient Pompeii and the volcano erupted right now, don't you think we'd at least get up, try to run? Panic a little?"

"No," Beth said. "We'd stay just like this and when they found us, the scientists would all sigh and say, 'Ahh, two lovers.'"

"Scientists don't sigh," Phil said.

"These scientists would," Beth said. "They wouldn't want to, but they would in spite of themselves and their huge sciency intellects. They'd be overwhelmed by the romance of finding our entwined bodies on this bed in this room. One of them would say, 'That's how I want to go, naked in bed and in love for all eternity.' All the other scientists would nod. One would wipe away a tear and think about his wife, far away and alone, and maybe that night he'd write her the kind of romantic letter she'd keep in her bedstand always and forever until she was an old, old lady."

Phil thought about the group of scientists standing over their entwined, dead bodies, brushes and shovels and picks and notebooks in their hands, staring down at him and Beth, the two of them like this, entwined together, the scientists nodding, suddenly solemn as they pondered the magnitude of their discovery. He imagined his and Beth's preserved bodies eventually being taken to a museum, the way Egyptian mummies were, displayed in a glass case with a card overhead stating, "The Lovers." Couples staring, their own squabbles over parking and the too-little tip at lunch silenced as they gazed at the two bodies perfectly locked together for time, for all eternity, their eyes slowly losing focus until what they discovered was their own reflections in the glass case.

"Nothing could separate us," Beth said. "Not the volcano, not time, not the scientists."

Phil kissed the top of her head again. Her hair never smelled like anything; she didn't seem to use scented shampoo. No apple or mango or passion fruit scent. Just hair. That should be enough. It should be okay for hair to smell like hair. "I love you," he whispered, and right then, right as he spoke, he actually did. So he said the words again.

But Beth spoke quickly, almost as if she hadn't heard him. "If we were in ancient Pompeii . . ." and she trailed off, didn't finish. Her body still pressed against his; she hadn't moved since waking, other than stretching her legs that one time before returning them to where they'd been, one against his leg, one flung over.

The furnace clicked on; warm air flowed into the room, rustling the sheer curtains at either side of the window. Dust particles shone and spun in the angled sunlight.

"The thing is," Beth continued, "we're not in ancient Pompeii. We're not even in modern-day Pompeii." She paused, knowing he would smile, and he did. There was something about her that could make anything seem funny; once she'd read his grocery list out loud and they'd both laughed until tears came and his stomach ached. "The thing is." She started again, stopped.

"No," he said, feeling that he was interrupting, though she was silent. "We can stay in ancient Pompeii. For the rest of the day. For another hour. A minute." He tightened his arms around her, closed his eyes, kissed her hair-smelling hair again and again, covering her head with a hundred tiny kisses. "Let's." She didn't move, only breathed softly, steadily, without pause or thought.

But there were no scientists to see or sigh or write a romantic letter. There was no card on a glass case in a museum. There was no volcano about to erupt. And the minute had already started ticking away.

LYNN FREED

Ma, a Memoir

HE'D GOT AWAY. Only as far as the hospital, but still she'd been left behind. Once, she would have got into her Fiat and revved and revved and gone off in a puff of blue smoke to find him, to catch him out in the arms of another woman, perhaps. Sixty years of marriage had only heated the furious war between them.

Every day, she waited impatiently for me to take her to the hospital.

"I have a bone to pick with you," she said when I arrived.

"What bone?" I asked.

"I've forgotten."

He didn't want to see her. When she came shuffling in, he pretended to be asleep.

"Say hello, Dad," I whispered.

"Hello," he said. He was very weak, a dark, gaunt, beautiful old man, not ready to die.

She settled into the armchair and sat there quite still, staring out through her milky eyes at nothing.

"See, Ma?" I said. "Dad says helló."

"Well, why doesn't he *speak up*? I can hear everybody else. Why can't I hear *him*?" She reached over and placed a hand on his arm. "Come home, Harold," she said. "You know you're putting it on."

"Will *you* tell her!" he rasped at me. "Will you tell that bloody woman that I've got cancer?"

"Ma," I said. "Dad's got cancer. Don't be cruel."

"*Me* cruel! *Me* cruel! *You're* the one mentioning—that thing!" She clawed at the arms of the chair and pushed herself forward. "Here! Help me up. And then take me home, please. Right now."

I TOOK HER out for a drive in the Fiat the next day, up the coast to our favorite beach hotel for lunch.

"This way, Marmalade," I said, shepherding her down the steps one at a time.

"This way, Strawberry Jam," said the Indian waiter. "This way, Honeybunch."

She laughed, she giggled. "Go on, order crayfish," she suggested. "Why don't you order prawns? You love prawns, don't you?"

Driving back, I described the wild horses on the sea, the people selling beadwork on the beachfront. We were both happy for a moment.

"Hey ho!" she cried. "How old are you?"

"Forty-nine."

"How old am I?"

"Eighty-seven."

"Really? How can I be that much older than you?"

"Because you're my mother, Ma."

"Ha! Ha! That's a good one!"

"BEATS COCKFIGHTING," said my father, smiling a bit when I repeated the conversation to him the next day. Every morning and evening, I went alone to see him. I put on the Bruch G Minor and closed his door. The pneumonia was almost gone; he could go home to die if we could arrange it.

"Dad," I said. "Do you want to go home? I can try to deal with Ma."

He pretended not to hear. A large tear rolled down his cheek as the second movement began. "I'd like some smoked salmon," he whispered.

At home, my mother sat staring at the bookshelf, with a glass of Scotch in her hand. "I did love him so," she said, "and he seemed to love me. But what happened I don't know."

"Ma, he's sick. He's in the hospital."

She blew her nose furiously and wiped her eyes. "Don't you think two people could be happy again?"

"I think they could."

THE NEXT DAY, when I came to fetch her, she was waiting at the front door. "Has he died?" she asked.

"No."

"Well, thank God for that. Wearing a hat?"

"No."

"Then nor shall I."

She was the one who was meant to die first. Once she had overheard him saying to a widow, just engaged to be married, "Couldn't you have waited for me?"

"That husband of mine," she said now. "He was really very good to me."

"Your husband is my father, Ma," I said.

"Rubbish!" she snapped. "He's *my* father."

THE DAY AFTER she claimed him as her father, he died. When I came to tell her, she was waiting, as usual, to be taken to the hospital. "Ready?" she said. "I've been waiting for hours."

"Ma," I said. "Dad died. He just died." I sat down.

She covered her eyes with a hand and breathed deeply. Finally, she said, "It's unbearable. I cannot bear it. Don't expect me to bear it."

"I don't expect you to bear it, Ma. I can't bear it either."

She looked up as if she'd just met me at a bus stop. "It's full of emptiness, this place," she said.

AFTER THE FUNERAL, she sat in my sister's house like a refugee. The family came in one by one, veterans of the cemetery, to offer condolences. A florist delivered an arrangement of flowers. I brought it in to show her. She had always loved flowers. In our old house, she and Pillay, the gardener, had conspired together every week on which beds to plant with what, where to deploy the bulbs and seedlings he stole from the Botanic Gardens.

"Look, Ma," I said, "you got some lovely flowers."

"Really? How nice."

"Here, I'll read you the card. 'Dear Anne, We were so sad to hear of the loss of your darling Harold. We are all thinking of you with love at this time. Peggy, Alex and Andrew.'"

She stared out at nowhere. "Gentiles," she said.

A FEW DAYS later, I stole her away from *shiveh* and took her to the Botanic Gardens for tea. "How long have I known you?" she asked.

"A long time."

"That's what it feels like."

She began to weep. "I don't know why I'm crying," she said. She groped into her bag for a tissue and then blew her nose loudly.

"I know why."

"My father died," she said.

"Perhaps it's time to count your blessings, Ma."

She looked up sharply. "That's a lot of rubbish and you know it!"

"But it'll be lonely without Dad to fight with."

"And to love," she said. "Same thing."

"Ma, I'm worried. You're behaving magnificently, and it doesn't suit you."

She beamed. She reached out for her scone. I put it into her hand. "Now, why don't I have a daughter like you?" she asked.

JORGE LUIS ARZOLA

Essential Things

Translated from the Spanish by Margaret Jull Costa

MANY THINGS ARE now just a black space in my memory. But there was the sea, the fragrant journey and the galley—from Carthage?—and that boy so very like me (my friend, I believe), with his lover, that girl whose eyes spoke of desires and things of which I knew nothing then. . . . Or was I the lover, and was the boy the one who trembled to receive in his mouth the woman's small, salt breast?

But I could just as easily have been the girl. The three of us probably came from the West—from Rome, from Gaul, from some far place in the future: from the kingdom of Castile, from the Socialist Republic of Cuba? Or did we come, my two dark-skinned boys, from the past, their silken rosebuds between my lips; and the girl who, one moonlit night, behind a crate of salt, showed me, gave me the first taste of a breast perfect for my adolescent lips, the lips of a girl almost?

I was running away: the girl and her lover, and the other boy too, we were all escaping—from what, from whom, from where and to where? I was coming, going, running back home, and there was the smell of the sea and, of course, the sea itself and a port from which to weigh anchor, and a galley, a sailing ship, a vast steamship ready to weigh anchor.

No one now can clarify the precise circumstances of this story. The three of us were running away, this is all that can be known. But the point of departure was doubtless a suffocating village, and we had decided to try our luck on the vastness of the sea.

I was the friend of the lover, and while I did not desire his girl, I had never desired anyone as much as I desired that girl. And there, in that loathsome village, I used to spy on them when he rocked like a boat on the sea between her legs.

Or was I perhaps the girl? And who was spying on whom? Sometimes I felt sorry for him watching us, but it was pleasurable too, the sight of his almost frightened face watching from afar. . . . I would lay my lover down on the grass and I would sit on top of him until I had had my fill, and I would offer up to him (to the boy) the sight of my breasts erect as tremulous promises.

(Ah, gods, did they not tremble like that too, those bunches of grapes loaded onto the back of a mule being driven to market by a peasant from a vineyard near the village?)

I was the girl, I was the lover, I was the friend who dreamed of the girl sitting on top of him, not on his pubis, but on his chest, on his mouth. Then I was the lover who sensed both the veiled offers being made by my girl and my friend's covetous blushes.

And which of us planned the escape? Who convinced whom that there was a reason to escape?

I accept that it was me, the friend of the lovers. I had more than enough reasons. The girl wanted me, and I wanted her. In fact, once, as if by accident, she showed me one charming breast, while she was explaining to her lover that they had a surplus of oranges that year, enough to be able to sell some.

The important thing, though, was that the three of us decided to run away from the village together. And early one morning, we left. I remember that it was a long, hard walk until we found the sea and could feel that we were rendering null and void that now distant, unimaginable village, which may never have been anything but my way, our way, of giving a name to our fear, although now I don't even know why I mentioned it, since I've never said anything about neighbors or judges, with which all villages everywhere are crammed.

The fact is that, one day, we found the sea and set sail joyfully, and that on another day, at last, my beloved and the boy met behind a crate of salt on the deck. At the time, I was (perhaps) in my first-class cabin drinking whiskey, or talking to the man in charge of the galley while he whipped the Scythian oarsmen, who complained ceaselessly.

But I could have been the girl. I was the girl, and sometimes I think I can remember my beloved standing there in the port—of Samos? of New York?—while our ship sailed swiftly away. I can still feel the unexpected sadness of seeing him left behind there, gesturing and shouting. . . . But before us, immense, lay the sea, and on my waist I suddenly felt the boy's hand. It was a delicate, almost girlish hand.

The sun was setting in the distance and there was a breeze and we were free. And then I no longer felt quite so sad.

ROBERT OLEN BUTLER

Seven Pieces of Severance

After careful study and due deliberation it is my
opinion the head remains conscious for one minute
and a half after decapitation.

—*Dr. Dassy d'Estaing, 1883*

*In a heightened state of emotion, we speak at the
rate of 160 words per minute.*

—*Dr. Emily Reasoner,*
A Sourcebook of Speech, *1975*

Paul (Saul of Tarsus)
apostle, beheaded by the Emperor Nero, 67 A.D.

narrow the gate through to the warren of merchants past figs
and linen and clay vessels the smells of wood fire and bodies
moving in the shadows of houses I am restless in my limbs
and the way turns to a square a fountain and a great and sudden flare of light, I close my eyes to the welter of it blinded
and open them again, and in the center of this brilliance a
woman young her hair loose radiant her forearms bare she is

bent to draw water and she lifts her face to me her eyes dark
in the midst of the light which roils silently all about her and
within me and I would move to her now and kneel before
the mysteries of her body I am tumescent with devotion but
instantly she turns her face away and I hesitate gasping waiting, if she but speak if she but call me to her, for all my readiness to act I wait and my horse snickers at my restlessness the
land flat to the horizons my body sucked dry by the sun
Damascus ahead and heretic Jews to shackle at the wrists at
the ankles and the air around me ignites I am at the center
of a flame and I am tumbling down I am on my knees I lift
my face to see her and instead I hear a voice, a man, and I
understand

Dioscorus
*shipmaster and companion to Paul, beheaded by Roman soldiers
who mistook him for the apostle, 67 A.D.*

sails swell and braces hum overhead, my hand on the tiller
night and day and night again and all the things of the world
are beneath my feet now, all at once, the timber and the cat-
tle and the linen and the glass, the wine, the wool, ivory and
apes, olives and cheese, plums and pears and pomegranates
and ginger, myrrh and incense, alabaster and amber, oysters
and slaves, their dark eyes turning to me awake in the midst
of the night as I hug the coast out of Aden and it's day now
and still I have wind in the great middle sea and I have wood-
work and statuary from Sicily and papyrus and granite and
glass from Egypt, corn and fish and hides from the Black Sea
and from Smyrna I have carpets rolled and bound and stacked
in the hold, and passengers, a man and two others who bow

to him a man with a naked head like mine bare to the sky and
the wind, there is only the terrible motionlessness of my
house, becalmed, my son barely drawing a breath, this man
touches my son's head and speaks to his god and my son lives
and the man says *leave all these things* and I am in a market-
place and I cry out the name of this man's god as if into a gale
and around me are figs and linen and vessels of clay

Mohammed Aziz Najafi
Iraqi Shiite cleric, beheaded by Saddam Hussein, 1996

barren ground but holy, this plateau before me, trampled
smooth by the feet of millions, the true people of Allah, but
empty now though it is hajj and the Mount of Mercy is
behind me I feel its press between my shoulder blades and the
pilgrims should be everywhere but the ground is beaten into
silence and there is no one—*oh Allah leave me not alone*—for
I have no seed but your holy words, I have no family but the
family of your great people, no child but your revealed way, I
would summon the millions cloaked in white so I could be
among them and we would cry out as one *Allah I have
responded to you* I am draped in seamless cotton I am barefoot
and I am penitent, and the echo of my prayers is still in my
head I have been silent only the briefest of moments and I
yearn for the tumult of my brothers in Allah I would kneel
and touch my face to this long-beaten ground as one with a
million other faces, but no, I am standing upright and I am
alone and before me now there is only a desert tamarisk,
feathery pink, the merest growing thing and it catches the sun
as if it is on fire and I hear a voice say to me *it is time now to
take thy only son and cut his throat*

Rokhel Pogorelsky
Jewish woman, beheaded in Russian pogrom, 1905

taste of horseradish taste of nettle I draw the covers tight
about me the trees beyond the dark window lash in the wind
my brother nearby weeps against his will *sorry Papa sorry* and
beneath the wind my father's voice tumbles *Pinchas be still the
blood was on the doorpost* the lambs in the field raise their head
to a hollow sound the soles of my feet quake *our sons were
spared* father says to Pinchas but in the field I hear horses and
I have my own first son on my back my Aron and I turn from
the sound of hooves and I run across the field that rolls
beneath me twisting at my ankles I look behind and the men
on horses stay on the road a dozen Cossacks in high boots and
billowing trousers and one turns his face toward me I run
hard and they go on toward the village and I follow the hedge
line and through a stand of water oaks and Aron begins to cry
his tiny hands plucking at my ears *be still* I say and my cottage
now my husband gone a lashing in my chest like trees in a
wind and a basket by the step, I put my son inside, my shawl
on top, and when this all is done another must find him: a
scythe nearby I cut my hand and spill my blood upon the
door

Hanadi Tayseer Jaradat
*law student, beheaded by self-detonation of shaheed-belt suicide
bomb, 2003*

I am heavy with child praise Allah I am at last with child my
head is full of the law that I am permitted to study to serve
our people but I have not forgotten my greater destiny praise
Allah I am also with child, the words of the Prophet—peace

be upon him—saying, *Paradise lies at the feet of mothers*, I have not forgotten, I move across rubbled ground and my baby is pressed hard against my womb wait wait my face is naked my head is bare I touch where my baby is and he is very heavy ten kilos and his bones are large and hard and stacked side by side his cord winds secretly into the pocket of the jeans that bind my legs my loins I wear the clothes of harlots my hand is on his private part I am but to press there, my baby placed in me by a man with his face covered I turn my head and open my cloak to a man I do not know, an angel of Allah surely, his arms around me and my baby is suddenly holding me tight I am moving in a room full of people cursed by Allah my baby heavy against me surely he has eyes and a mouth and a heart, a woman nearby damned but large with child, I have my own, I touch him and he cries out

Angry Eyes
Apache warrior, beheaded by Mexican troops, 1880

breechcloth and moccasins only these things on my body and my head bound by a cloth band my face and chest and arms stained but I do not know the colors I do not look, my eyes are fixed on the horizon beyond mesquite and piñon and stone and I am ready to fight though I have no bow no arrow not even the rifle I bend to the white man in dark blue, the first to die by my hand, and I listen for his spirit nearby, his hair the color of flame his face filled with tiny faded spots painted there perhaps to call upon the stars his mouth open voiceless my arrow through the center of his chest I put my hand on the stock of his rifle, still listening but there is nothing no bird no insect—*where are you, my foe?*—and the sun is setting and my hands are empty and I dance, like a woman I dance with mincing steps my elbows held close against me my face impassive before the fading light, the edge of the world is the color of old blood, my body dances stealthily all my flesh trembling to an unheard drum and I am alone in this place, but no, his spirit whispers he is beside me now, in breechcloth and moccasins, and we dance barely moving nearly touching I and this white man with hair of flame

Robert Olen Butler
writer, decapitated on the job, 2008

heedless words but whispered, they begin as I stand before the guillotine and I am filled with the scent of motor exhaust and wood fire and fish sauce and jasmine in a strange country, a good scent, her hand in mine at last, the city that roars in my dreams is beyond the stucco walls a balcony the Saigon River the rim of the world bleeding from the setting sun and self-righteousness, the guillotine in the museum rises above the cannon barrels and rotor blades and unexploded bombs the blade darkened by the wet air and the voices begin to speak not in my head not in the place where I think but in my ear directly in my fingertips a computer screen before me the clatter of keys like tiny clawed feet running in a wall, come to me little ones nibble from my hands snuggle into my pockets and curl your naked tails in peace like these words already fixed and bound and tucked beneath my arm, half a dozen autographs signed tonight and thanks for buying my book I step into the elevator and I am alone and the air buzzes in silence and I consult the scrap of paper in my pocket to see where I belong and I push the button and down the hall there are voices agitated ardent full of yearning and I lean forward and I stick my head out to listen

FREDERICK ADOLF PAOLA

The Wine Doctor

IT WAS A late afternoon in August in the year of our Lord 1930, in year VIII of the *Era Fascista*. Dottore Cotrolaò, just back in his second-floor office after a meal of *morzeddu* washed down with an exceptional local wine from the Savuto Valley, did a double take when he saw who had entered his office as his first patient of the evening.

It was Ezio Delli Castelli, the wine doctor of Nocera Terinese. A chemist who had made his living chiefly as an oenologist, a specialist in wine making, he was also a part-time oenopath, a practitioner of the unique healing art of oenopathy. Patients came to him with ailments of various sorts, and he prescribed a course of treatment with this particular wine or that. The wines he recommended depended, of course, upon the patient's diagnosis—and circumstances. While he closely guarded his therapeutic secrets, it was thought that his prescriptions took into account the types of grapes that went into the wine; the composition of the soil from which the grapes had been harvested; how long they had been allowed to ferment before racking; and even the condition of the barrels in which the wine was stored.

Ezio Delli Castelli was well-versed in Italian wines in general, and had a working knowledge of imported wines as well. Most of his patients, however, were limited for financial reasons to wines produced locally, by the likes of Carmine Mauri, Vittorio Ventura, Leopoldo Rossi, Nicola Mancini, Carmine Nicoli, and Annunziato Palarchio, using Calabrian grape varieties such as *Aglianico, Gaglioppo, Guarnaccia, Pecorello, Nerello, Sangiovese, Magliocco, Nocera, Trebbiano Toscano, Zibibbo, Greco, Malvasia,* and *Mantonico.* Ezio Delli Castelli did not charge for his oenopathic services, and most patients were quite satisfied with the treatment they received from him, as well as with the results they experienced.

Dottore Cotrolaò knew that many of the townspeople had sought the advice of Ezio Delli Castelli for health problems, either instead of or in addition to more conventional medicine. He supposed it might have something to do with the fact that in those days there were eighteen bettole or cantinas in Nocera Terinese and only one pharmacy. The patients, not wanting to offend Dottore Cotrolaò, didn't mention it to him; nor would Dottore Cotrolaò deign to broach the subject, other than in the form of an occasional sarcastic remark to a patient he had not seen in a while, such as, "Eh, Don Francesco, long time no see. Had any good wine lately?"

"Buona sera, Don Delli Castelli." While Cotrolaò had heard Ezio Delli Castelli's clients refer to him as *dottore,* damned if he was going to address him by that honorific title. *"Che posso fare per Voi?"* he asked. "What can I do for you?" He had used *Voi* (the polite form of "you" favored by Mussolini) rather than *Lei* (the equally polite form of "you" discouraged by Mussolini as Iberian) because Cotrolaò knew Ezio Delli

Castelli disdained the use of *Voi*, though he wasn't sure whether this aversion was grounded in politics or linguistics.

Ezio Delli Castelli, a slight man dressed in a worn but freshly pressed brown three-piece suit, looked perplexed and somewhat embarrassed. Fumbling with the hat on his lap, he looked at the taller, heavier man seated behind the dark wood desk before him.

"*Dottore, i raggi,*" he said. "The x-rays."

"Of course," Dottore Cotrolaò answered, slapping himself on the forehead. Now he remembered. How had he forgotten? Ezio Delli Castelli had visited him about a month before with a nagging cough and had reported coughing up small amounts of blood. Dottore Cotrolaò had sent him to the hospital in Catanzaro for a chest x-ray. Searching for the film in the pile on his desk, Dottore Cotrolaò studied Ezio Delli Castelli surreptitiously. Today he was noticeably thinner and appeared mildly dyspneic.

Locating the envelope in a pile of mail that had been delivered only the day before, Dottore Cotrolaò opened it and held the film up to the light. It showed an extensive mediastinal mass involving the bifurcation of the trachea. Erosions were evident in the ribs.

There was silence in the room, and the two men were unaware of the sounds of life from the world in the street below. The only connection between the two worlds was the aroma of *espresso* wafting up from the bars down the street.

When Dottore Cotrolaò spoke, it was not without some irritation in his voice. "*Don Ezio,* tell me something. You practice your healing craft, your . . ."

"Oenopathy."

". . . oenopathy. Then you get sick and you come to me. Why?" Even as he asked his question, compelled as he was by frustration and curiosity, Dottore Cotrolaò regretted both the tone of his voice and his inability to control his own tongue.

Ezio Delli Castelli smiled. "*Dottore*, I don't know any other oenopaths, and it would be improper and certainly foolish of me to treat myself."

Ezio Delli Castelli continued, "That's not to say you were my second choice. Not at all." He shook his head. "I am most grateful for the care you have rendered me, and," he went on, good-naturedly, "if you can heal me I will gladly admit that your healing art is stronger than mine."

Dottore Cotrolaò sadly shook his head no.

In the conversation that followed, he told Ezio Delli Castelli, as best he could, what the near future would likely hold for him, and prescribed morphine for management of his symptoms. It was, alas, a short conversation during which Dottore Cotrolaò, who had delivered his share of bad news to patients in this very room, avoided looking directly at Ezio Delli Castelli. Instead, he monitored his patient's reflection in a mirror on a side wall. At a certain point, Ezio Delli Castelli followed his doctor's gaze to that same mirror, and for a moment they studied each other's reflection.

When Dottore Cotrolaò finished speaking, Ezio Delli Castelli nodded and put on his hat as he got up to leave. Cotrolaò quickly came out from behind his desk and placed a gentle hand on Delli Castelli's shoulder to stop him. "Just a moment, please," he said.

Cotrolaò held his hands out before him, palms up, and slowly turned them over, showing them to Ezio Delli Castelli, who, holding them in his own, studied them for a moment.

"Arthritis deformans," Ezio Delli Castelli remarked empathetically. Impressed, Cotrolaò raised his eyebrows and nodded.

The two men looked directly at each other.

"There is a small producer near Verbicaro," said Ezio Delli Castelli, taking a fountain pen from his pocket and writing the name of the producer on a piece of paper that had been handed to him by Cotrolaò. *"Il bianco, non il rosso,"* he emphasized. "The white, not the red. No more than 300 milliliters a day. I would try it."

"I will," Cotrolaò answered.

They shook hands.

"Grazie, dottore," said Ezio Delli Castelli.

"Gracie a Lei, dottore," answered Cotrolaò.

TESSA BROWN

In Reference to Your Recent Communications

Dearest Randolph,

I am writing in reference to the string of voice mails you recently left me. Although I understand that there were outside forces acting upon you, your messages nonetheless sounded rash and not fully thought out. I want to take this opportunity to go over some of your main points and offer a response, since your means of communication left me no obvious path by which to do so. I assume, of course, that you have all of our previous communications for reference, including, but not limited to, letters, electronic mail, phone messages, and transcripts of conversations crucial to the progress of our relationship.[1]

[1] I will be referring in particular to the communications of the past six months, in addition to various communications from over the course of the past four years, including (but again, not limited to) Thanksgiving with your family in November of 2002 and the events related to your 2003 trip to Atlantic City.

Message 1: Confusion

(a) [Exhalation] Jess [sic], it's Randy [sic]. (b) I've been thinking a lot about us and, well, I just don't know if it's the best thing for me, well, for both of us right now. (c) I know we've talked about it— well, kind of—but I really think I need to take a break. Call me back. Bye.

1(a). [Exhalation] Jess [sic], it's Randy [sic].

Your introduction ("Jess, it's Randy"), preceded as it is by a pronounced exhale, suggests that you are unsure about how to proceed; perhaps you feel socially or otherwise obligated to distance yourself from me. Consider your motives in calling: If you are responding to pressure from friends and/or family, please remember that the only feelings on which this relationship is contingent are yours and, of course, mine. I here refer to a comment from your mother that states, "Randy, are you sure about this one? She seems, oh, I don't know, eccentric."[2] This comment and others lead me to believe that you are acting on the advice of your peers and relatives, who have led you to believe that they have your best interests at heart.[3]

1(b). I've been thinking a lot about us and, well, I just don't know if it's the best thing for me, well, for both of us right now.

You make clear that you are confused about the direction of our relationship and the benefits it bestows upon each of

[2]Overheard in the kitchen of the McKellen residence, on the evening of November 25, 2002, at approximately 9:02 p.m. Central Time.

[3]I would also like to point out, with, of course, no disrespect intended, that your mother is a frigid bitch who has had it out for me since the moment we met. Additionally, do not assume that your family life has given you a good understanding of what a healthy relationship is, especially in light of the fact that your father has been screwing, for the past eight months, your brother's fiancée.

us. The advantages of our partnership arise in all spheres of our lives. First, recall that the acquisition of your current job at Benson Atwater, Inc., was based on an interview procured for you by the husband of my dear friend. Second, consider the incontrovertible sexual benefits you have been receiving from me, arguably since our sixteenth date and undoubtedly since our twenty-third.[4] And finally, since we began seeing each other, you have lost thirteen pounds, raised your annual income by more than $10,000 a year, and present a much more appealing odor than prior to the commencement of our relationship.[5] Further, if you are cheating on me, as I presume you are, I would also add that no woman besides me would have engaged in sexual intercourse with you four years ago.

1(c). I know we've talked about it—well, kind of—but I really think I need to take a break. Call me back. Bye.

Your dismissal of the conversation to which this sentence refers makes clear that you have not been investing the energy that a successful relationship demands of the parties involved.[6]

---

[4]These dates are based on the first time you were given oral sex, on October 5, 2000, and the first time we had intercourse, on November 12, 2000. Additional sexual favors were granted over the course of the relationship that I believe have more than fully met your sexual needs and desires.

[5]These figures are based on analysis of weight gain/loss patterns, average annual incomes, and hygiene habits of the past seven years.

[6]Excerpt from conversation on September 3, 2004, at approximately 7:09 p.m. Eastern Standard Time:

Randolph: I can't believe we've been together more than four years.
Jessica: I can.
Randolph: But, do you ever think about what things would be like if we'd never met?
Jessica: How sad and lonely your life would be? I try not to dwell on

Putting more effort into our sexual life would also help things out. You may or may not be aware of this, but you have really been dropping the ball in the bedroom lately.[7]

Message 2: Doubt

(a) Jess [sic], it's Randy [sic]. We really need to talk. Frankly, things haven't been going so well lately. (b) You can't say you don't feel it, too. (c) Oh—and sorry about all that stuff with your guinea pig. Bye.

2(a). Jess [sic], it's Randy [sic]. We really need to talk. Frankly, things haven't been going so well lately.

Actually, Randolph, things have been going great, but you insist on sabotaging our healthy, thriving relationship because you subconsciously want to ruin your life. I've been worried about you for a long time now. You seem to enjoy harming yourself. This is called masochism. I believe it has a great deal to do with your mother. I would suggest distancing yourself from her while the wounds heal.[8]

---

it. I'm just glad we did find each other.

Randolph: Do you think everyone has only one person who's made for them?

Jessica: Oh, Randolph, what a sweet thing to say!

Randolph: Do you think maybe we aren't each other's?

Jessica: Do you want to know what else is out there? Floozies. Gold diggers. Drug addicts. Think about what I've done for you. Don't you see that your life would be worse without me?

Randolph: I guess you could look at it that way, but—

Jessica: Yes, you could.

[7] Yes, I've been faking it.

[8] I understand from firsthand experience that she unwantedly imposes herself on you. I therefore support any decision you make regarding moving or changing our telephone number without granting contact information to the abovementioned.

2(b). You can't say you don't feel it, too.

You are right, Randolph; I can't say I haven't felt it. I have felt the tension in our relationship from the stress your self-loathing behaviors have caused. I have felt the tension caused by your staggering home at four in the morning reeking of alcohol. I have felt the friction caused by our emotional estrangement. But I digress. This tension stems not from some deep-rooted problem but rather from the healthy growth of our relationship. Strong partners work through problems together, which is why I am here to help you work through yours. I know that you have issues with intimacy, with women, and with erectile efficiency, plus an anal-expulsive fixation,[9] but I am here to guide you as we address these profoundly disturbing "issues," of which you seem to have an endless supply.

2(c). Oh—and sorry about all that stuff with your guinea pig. Bye.

Let us clarify what "all that stuff" is: Your dog, jealous of my beautiful guinea pig from the start, mauled Tootsie II, while you, horrified by what your "best friend" Boxer's vicious hatred could do, stood idle. I was sympathetic enough to be conscious of your feelings and have Boxer put down while you were at work the next day, in order to save you unnecessary heartache. Further, to support you through the grieving process, what could have been better than an adorable new guinea pig? I understand your surprise on finding Boxer gone, replaced by Doodles, a beautiful new guinea, but I assure you that it is for the best. When you finally come to your senses and return home, you will be moved by the tenderness that exists between Doodles and Tootsie II—now a triple amputee.

[9]Need I mention this noxious habit of yours?

Message 3: The Worst Mistake of Your Life
(a) *I think I'm going to crash with Jay for a while, and I'd appreciate it if you didn't come by or call me. (b) Um, bye.*

3(a). I think I'm going to crash with Jay for a while, and I'd appreciate it if you didn't come by or call me.

It is here that I realize what a strong influence your friends, especially Jay, must have had on the decision you claim to have made independently.[10] There have been numerous actions on their part over the course of our relationship that have made it quite clear to me (as I assume was their goal) that I do not meet their "standards" for you.[11] I believe the fact that you are "going to crash with Jay" strongly supports my hypothesis that the opinions of your "buddies" have been critical in convincing you to leave me. I implore you to rise above their petty lies.

3(b). Um, bye.

Whenever you do something you know is wrong, you

[10]Jay in particular is an exceptionally destructive man. I refer specifically to a disturbing episode in which, while organizing your drawers, I came upon a photo of my Tootsie I in Atlantic City, pushed into the cleavage of some trashy hotel-bar waitress and being forced to take a shot of tequila, with Jay smiling maniacally in the background. I only pray that this alcohol was fatal, and that my beautiful guinea pig was not subjected to further abuses before she perished in that cesspool of sin. Had I reported Jay to PETA or a similar organization, he most likely would have been shot.

[11]These include, but are not limited to, the following:
- The "Still a Bachelor" party they have thrown for you on the evenings preceding all four of our anniversaries;
- The "randy is randy" shirt they made you for your birthday last year;
- The whip I received in the mail three weeks ago;
- The prostitute who arrived at our apartment last Thursday.

speak about it with a proliferation of "um"s. For example, two years ago, when your friends whisked you away to Atlantic City for the weekend, your explanation upon return was riddled with "um"s—fifty-three, actually, in a four-minute period. These "um"s increased exponentially when I exposed, from deep within your jacket pocket, a casino gambling chip and a cocktail napkin with a phone number on it.[12] From the "um" in your phone message, I can therefore infer that you are fully conscious of the mistake you are making.

Concluding Remarks

You may or may not have already noticed that all of your bank accounts are frozen and that your credit cards are inactive. I also disabled your cellular phone. I regret having to take such extreme measures, but I feel that this is entirely in your best interests. I wanted to prevent any rash purchases on your part as you attempt to fill the emotional void you surely are experiencing right now. Further, I felt it necessary to encourage you not to leave the state or communicate with Jay and his cohorts.

Speaking of Jay, by this point you are probably aware that he has been jailed on the charge of possession of marijuana with intent to distribute. The repercussions that this will have on his personal and professional lives are potentially devastating, and it is with his and your futures in mind that I reiterate the importance of keeping some distance between yourself and what is soon to be a convicted felon.

The next few years will be quite difficult for Jay, and while he struggles to put his life back together I hope you will find the energy and wisdom to rededicate yourself to our relation-

[12] And no, Randolph, I do not believe that this was Jay's cousin's cell-phone number.

ship. I look forward to the progress we will undoubtedly make in the coming months.

With love, and hope for your future,
Jessica

PIA Z. EHRHARDT

Following the Notes

IN HIGH SCHOOL I had a job as the hostess at The Trawler, a seafood restaurant at Esplanade Mall. My battery went dead and my father had to come to the mall parking lot to give me a jump. He dug for the cables in his trunk, pissed that he'd been called away from the new piece of music he was writing at home. It was Father's Day and what he'd asked for was for a quiet house and lemon pie for dessert.

"You left the headlights on?" he said.

"The passenger light," I said, pointing at the back seat. "Door wasn't shut all the way."

"Who was in the back?" he said. "I thought you were driving to work and home, only."

My daily comings and goings were charted in the kitchen, reviewed when I got back in the evening. I had the use of a Buick Century as long as I kept it filled with gas, washed it once a week in our driveway with mild detergent, and didn't joyride with my friends.

"Sorry for the inconvenience," I said.

"Don't be a smart-ass." He clipped the cables on the battery. "Get in and rev the engine when I tell you."

The parking lot was dark. Some of my co-workers stood outside under the street lamp, smoking. Bugs were flying in from everywhere to swarm in the light.

My father raised his arm for me to step on the gas.

Sherman's sweatshirt lay on the back seat, where he'd stripped it off. We'd had sex there before my shift, at the far edge of the parking lot, then switched shirts for the day. He wanted my Sacred Heart tee so he could show off the muscles he was sculpting for me. That's what he'd said. I wore his faded Ninja Turtles tee, had it stuffed into my jeans. Washed a thousand times, so smooth against my skin. I zipped my jacket to my neck so my father wouldn't see.

"This isn't working," he said. "There's no juice."

I drove home with him in his old green Mercedes. Sometimes he let me drive this car. Last week I'd taken Sherman for an evening drive out in Richburg Hills to look at the twinkling lights of the power plant. Oz. The front seat was a bench and Sherman scooted next to me, his hand restless on my leg.

My father whistled what he'd been working on when I called for help. We caught every red light. I smelled like cigarette smoke and sex with a busy top layer of peppermint Tic Tac. Half a box in my mouth.

"You didn't leave the house in that shirt," he said.

"Grease stain," I mumbled. "I borrowed someone's."

Bugs out of nowhere dove into the windshield. "Is Mom feeling better?" I said. She'd been in bed when I'd left that morning, said she had a cold, but I knew it was a hangover. I'd rinsed out her mug and it smelled like scotch.

"She's okay," he said. He pressed the washer button but nothing came out.

"I showed you how to fill this." The wipers squeaked across the dry windshield, smudging the spots into a mess. "Goddammit, Liddie," he said. "I can't see."

I knew what to do to make him forget my screw-ups. I simply placed him right there in the palm of my hand. "What were you working on before I interrupted?"

He told me too much, like he'd been waiting all day for someone to ask. "A choral piece—SATB—with woodwinds. I'm setting a John Ashbery poem. *The Grapevine.*" He falsettoed the soprano part because it carried the melody.

"Lyrical," I said.

My father's readiness made me sad. The guys I liked used just a few words to explain what they meant, left the rest mysterious, but my father answered anything I asked like he had one chance left on earth.

He leaned forward, squinting through the streaks, and asked me to be another set of eyes and help get us home safely.

"Why don't we pull into a gas station, Dad? I'll get out and clean."

I called Sherman when I got home to tell him about my dead battery, but he didn't have time to talk. I heard a giggle in the background and he said it was his sister, but I knew.

For dinner we had my father's favorite meal—chicken cacciatore with a warm loaf of Italian bread for dunking. My mother was quiet and excused herself during dessert to go upstairs to watch TV. My father looked sad, dumped, and I pushed the rest of my lemon pie at him. "I'm full," I said, and wanted back the one who would always be true, so I asked if he'd play for me what he'd written that day. We sat on the piano bench. I followed the notes and turned the page when he nodded.

STACEY RICHTER

The Minimalist

WHEN EVEN MY white-on-white canvasses began to seem too representative, too ornate, when *Number 23* looked like a mouthful of chewed-up aspirin floating in a saucer of milk, I removed every piece of furniture from my studio except a chair, a table, and a bare futon. I discarded my paints. I took off all my jewelry and sat in the chair with my eyes closed and pictured a pure, even expanse of blue. It had no ripples or edges or scent or weight. It was more glassy and uniform than the calmest lake.

I found that I was very happy.

I wished to be naked. The gallery owner said, No, but might that not be even more distracting than simple clothing? He wore a clipped black beard and a plain black pullover with his black jeans. On his feet were shiny lace-up shoes, in black. I respected his opinion.

I agreed to wear simple clothing, but no underwear.

I sat in the chair in the center of the gallery and pictured blue. There was no other work in the room. An engraved plaque on the wall explained that the artist is holding a mental conception of a blue colorfield.

I wished to title the piece *Untitled*.

Peter, the owner of the gallery, suggested I call it *Self-Portrait in Blue*.

I finally decided to call it *Untitled (Picturing Blue)*.

At first they came to offer ridicule. Crowds of people filed past my chair, muttering insults. You call this art? they sneered. This is how the Impressionists were received. And the Cubists. People brought their children and lifted them up, so they could get a clearer look. That's dumb, the children said, and their parents shushed them. But their faces assented. I closed my eyes and pictured blue. Sometimes I opened my eyes and pictured blue as well, a cool, mammoth glacier of it advancing across the floor. Yet more even and featureless than any glacier.

Yellow! The sun piled in through a high window one afternoon while a man in a baseball cap shouted this at me: Yellow, baby! Yellow! There was a slit of belly bulging between the bottom of his shirt and the top of his pants, a fleshy strip of chaos.

I let my eyes sink shut and drifted deeper into the blue.

Peter wished to erect a little metal fence around me. He said he was concerned that someone would touch me, or do me harm.

I said no. That would spoil everything.

I sat quietly all day. I was not bored. I was concentrating on my art. Sometimes Peter emptied the room briefly, so I could get up and move around. He brought me muffins or little avocado sandwiches on wheat bread. I hadn't asked for these breaks. I hadn't thought of it. I hadn't considered anything very seriously for quite a while, aside from my color.

I told Peter that the artist wished to spend nights in the gallery. I explained that it would help the artist to maintain the purity of the piece.

He gazed at me for a time, then said, But isn't the artist you?

I said that it was. His eyes were the color of blue ink dripped into still water.

He set up a cot in the office area for me and stayed until after midnight the first night, tidying up, bringing me towels, and making sure I was warm enough. Then he sat quietly at his metal desk, leafing through a stack of papers.

He told me he had made sure all the bedding was the exact same shade of eggshell white. He was very beautiful and kind. I thought he must be gay.

I slept poorly.

During the day attendance records were set at the gallery. Some of the people who visited were moved by the piece. Some of the people bought paintings that were for sale in other rooms.

Critics wrote of an intense spiritual calm. They spoke of a reemergence of the aura. A writer from a women's magazine wrote a review of my clothing.

It was favorable.

Peter's photo was in a magazine. As was mine.

It began to grow warmer. The sun hit my chair in the afternoon. I started to picture a sweaty, Caribbean blue.

I slept poorly. I dreamed of a turquoise ocean melting into a cerulean sky. From the water leapt fish, thousands of them, silver and gleaming and flying like knives tossed by the handful into the waves.

When I awoke I was trembling. My hands smelled of salmon. I went into the gallery and sat in my chair. It was very early. I thought that I would try to think of a plain expanse of smooth cobalt.

When Peter entered, he looked startled. He asked me if anything was wrong.

I gazed into his pale eyes. I told him I didn't have anything else. I had the blue and the openness of it. I told him that if it came to mean something, I would be lost.

He looked like he was going to smile, but then his face changed and became rather tense. He took my hand gently, as though I were very frail.

For the rest of the day I sat in the chair and battled to regain a pure field of blue. Yet it kept dissolving into an ocean pierced by schools of fish. Above was a cloudless palette of sky. I tried to use my mind to scrape it all down into a powder that would spread out into a uniform layer the color of toilet bowl cleaner.

The fish continued to leap.

After the gallery closed, Peter handed me a hinged box that fit neatly into my palm. A present, he said. Inside was a single layer of ball bearings that filled the bottom precisely. It was so simple and lovely. I began to weep.

I knew I was no longer capable of producing *Untitled (Picturing Blue)*. And if that were so, I would have to leave the gallery, and so leave Peter. He had been very kind.

That night when I closed my eyes, I dreamed of the fish. They sprang from waves and wriggled in the air like live wires. Then they turned their noses downward and slipped beneath the surface, into an airless place where I couldn't follow. I wondered if they were jumping toward something, or away.

I believed myself to be in love.

The next day, I sat quietly, hands folded in my lap, struggling to picture blue. Whenever I tried to locate the purity of my color, I found my mind leapt to create a world instead. There was the Easter egg blue of a gingham dress I'd loved as a little girl, blowing on a clothesline. There was the stinging azure of the Pacific as I floated on a wave, surrounded by kelp; there was the faded blue of my old Volkswagen Beetle, broken down beside the road. Then there was the pale turquoise of a swimming pool where I was once knocked cold by a diver—an endless, underwater blue where hair oozed like tentacles through a fading silence. And after that, the midnight, star-shot indigo of unconsciousness.

Each idea of color pushed open a door, and inside was a snapshot, a tale, a fragment of my life.

I was no longer picturing blue. Blue was picturing me.

I waited in the office. Peter came to me wearing a simple gray suit. On the lapel was an enamel button, a glossy blue lozenge.

I told him I'd failed. I said that the artist was no longer conceiving of a pure colorfield. I was trembling as I confessed. I would lose him, I knew.

I continued anyway. I told him that I'd encountered an unexpected richness within the blue. I said that despite my initial impressions, I'd come to believe it was protean and full of life. Even emptiness, I said, contained more. Particularly emptiness.

I said I thought there was no such thing as minimalism.

He had those calm eyes that I so loved. He said, Oh, but I thought. Then he stopped. He said that perhaps he had misunderstood the piece, slightly.

I admitted that it was possible.

I packed my things. There was very little to pack.

It struck me that Peter's beard was a little stringy that day, his clothing somewhat rumpled. I thought that perhaps he was a bit sad. He asked me to come back and pay him a visit sometime. He made me promise.

The chair was the artist's own. I left the building and walked down the street with it propped against my shoulders. It was quite heavy. I pictured how I must look, striding down the sidewalk with an empty chair hanging over my head.

That was all then. A woman, a street, an empty chair carried aloft.

TOURÉ

I Shot the Sheriff

Every day the bucket a-go a-well
One day the bottom have a drop out
—"I Shot the Sheriff," Bob Marley

BOB KNEW THEY'D catch him when dawn came. Now, after midnight in the forest, he could hide. But there were footsteps all around, passing right by him, the bodies stinking of rum. And there was a sinewy line of smoke leaking from his pocket, floating out from the gun buried inside it, the rickety gun that just hours ago had spent a single bullet with the same miraculous precision that David had used to fell Goliath long ago. In a few hours a floodlight called the sun would ease on and the rummy bodies would surely find him and rush him off to a sham trial and a public hanging. But in the forest, in these last moments of earthly freedom, he had the stoic, chin-high courage of a man marching to the gallows for an act he believed in, for this murderer knew that heaven awaited him. Bob shot the sheriff. But he didn't shoot no deputy. Bob was a simple man who grew the sweetest sugarcane in all the county. But each dawn he awoke looking forward to nothing but the hour the sun closed up shop and he could be alone in his candlelit shanty with a good book. Reading a book, he felt, was like planting a seed in the mind. After many years he'd read every book he could find and felt his head brimming with sweet cane. He decided everyone in his hometown had to know this joy, and soon all his profits from sugarcane went to buying books for his neighbors. After each harvest he walked through town giving books to adults and children, dazzling them with stories of the wondrous places the books would transport them to. As sweet cane began growing in minds all over town, everyone came to love Bob. Everyone but Sheriff John Brown. No one could recall how John Brown had become sheriff. No one had ever even seen anyone in the government from which he claimed to derive his authority. But they knew he never went anywhere without his gun, a solid hunk of gleaming black steel so large it looked like a mini-missile launcher. He came round to collect taxes quite often, even though many suspected his badge was homemade. It was a flat slab of gold fashioned, he said, into a five-point star. Most saw five little daggers pointing away from his icy heart. And in the center of that so-called badge someone had stamped the words *Sheriff John Brown*. When he wasn't collecting taxes, he was making overproof white rum that he drank straight from a label-less bottle. Whether he was collecting taxes, making rum, or doing anything at all, Sheriff John Brown was drunk. He'd been drunk for years on end, so long no one could recall what he was like sober. Even he couldn't remember what he was like sober. He had a little moonshine business but he never made money because he drank all the potential profits; and what's more, his overproof rum was so strong even the numbest livers in town refused to process that liquid fire and sent it right back up to the throat. Men said drinking Sheriff's home brew felt like sucking on Death's own nipple. The old ladies wondered how anyone but the devil's spawn could drink rum that toxic all day, every day, and not die. Sheriff thought if he could just take one or two harvests from Bob, with all that free cane he could finally turn a profit, or at least be assured of having plenty of rum for the winter ahead and the one following. But only Bob knew just when to harvest the cane, and each season, before Sheriff could begin moving in to snatch Bob's crops, he was at the market imagining all the books he'd buy for his people. Oh yes, Sheriff John Brown hated him. One day Sheriff waddled into town to collect taxes and saw everyone reading. He didn't know what was inside those books for he couldn't read, but he could see in their eyes that seeds were taking root in all those minds. "Kill them before they grow," he told his men. "Kill them before they grow." His men snatched every book they saw and promptly burned them all. Bob was crushed. He wanted to fight, but no one had ever challenged Sheriff and lived to tell the tale. So Bob went back to raising his cane, and after the next harvest he returned with a stack of books double the size of the last one. But on tax day Sheriff came and took their wages and their books. Men carted off books with children still attached to them, children dragged through the streets while clinging to their books as if to life rafts. Bob saw all this and returned to his land in a fury, planting his biggest crop ever. After the next harvest he'd buy so many books there wouldn't be enough men to find them all, wouldn't be enough fire to burn them all. But one dawn months later Bob awoke to find his crops gone. Sheriff had come in the night and stolen his world. He went inside and stuffed a bag with some clothes, a candle, and a book he could read over and again because his journey would be long. He was going to walk as far away from Sheriff as his feet could stand, because if he stayed he knew one of them would end up dead. On his way out he stopped to say good-bye to his friend Gabriel. Gabriel tried to talk Bob into staying, but they both knew leaving now was prudent. So Gabriel gave Bob a gift he could use on his long, possibly dangerous journey. Bob tried to refuse but Gabriel wouldn't hear it. He gave Bob a gun, but it was the lamest little gun in the world. It was so small you could close your fist around it. It was so rickety it looked as though it had Scotch tape holding its insides together. It was so old it was basically a high-tech slingshot. Gabriel had only one bullet to give Bob, but a bullet from that old thing was likely to slide out of the barrel with less force than you could muster throwing it. Gabriel told Bob if he had to fire it, he should first pray God was on his side, because without His help that bullet just might peek out of the barrel and fall right at Bob's feet. Bob took Gabriel's supposed gift just to avoid being rude, but he knew the little contraption couldn't possibly hurt anyone. Bob hugged him good-bye and turned to go. Then, all of a sudden, he saw Sheriff John Brown, twenty paces away, aiming to shoot him down. There was no time to think, no time to pray. Bob aimed his little gun at the man with a half-spent bottle of rum in one hand and a gleaming missile launcher in the other, and pulled the rusty trigger with no idea what would happen next. But the hammer kicked Bob's one bullet in its ass with all the force it had and that bullet took wings, for that day God was with Bob as He'd been with David long ago, and that blessed bullet flew straight and fast and ripped right through Sheriff John Brown's toy badge, through his sagging tit, and plunged right into his heart, dragging one of the badge's daggers into that Grinchly organ, leaving him on his back, spouting blood like a geyser, soon to be dead. Bob shot the sheriff, and soon he would die for it, but one day he would be pardoned, for the ultimate deputy is God.

Before the Train and After

J EREMY SAID HE wanted to touch a train. It was dark, late evening, and we were standing beside the railroad tracks, the ones that run parallel to the club where we'd just watched Jeremy's friend Paul play with his band, The Sundown Kings.

It was dark. A train was coming. We could see its lights, hear the rhythm of its rattle. We stood right beside the tracks, in the shadow of The Mill. I could've stuck my foot out and the toe of my shoe would've touched cool metal.

Jeremy said, "I'm going to touch it. Think I can?" and took his hands out of his pockets.

Paul was with us and his new girlfriend, Marty. The four of us stood in a row. Paul and Marty were laughing.

"Do it, Jeremy," Marty said. Her voice was husky. Then the train was rumbling past us, vibrating inside my feet like its sound was traveling through me. I looked at Jeremy and could just make out his face, the soft, moon-white glow of his skin.

I watched him raise his hand. I was scared the train would rip his hand right off.

And it did.

THIS IS WHAT he said, the man who came up out of the ground: "Can I help you with that?" Soil fell from his mouth when he spoke.

I was watering the garden. The man who came up out of the ground shook the dirt from his skin. I handed him the hose and he wrapped two thick fists around it. The tomatoes began to shine, their skin wet and bright, and it sounded like music, the way the water hit the vines.

It sounded like music. It sounded like Paul.

I KNOW FOR better or worse means good times or bad, two hands or one. Before the train and after. For better or worse means no matter what, but when you're standing in your gown and your dress's train is long, curling around you like a great white tail, for better or worse does not mean accident.

A part of him is missing. And yes, I know it's his hand, but it's also something else. What if the very best part of him is gone? What if the very best part of him was held in the hand that the train took with it as it made its way through the night?

PAUL ROSE FROM the ground. His head, shoulders, chest emerged from the earth like a vine. Then he was a whole man standing before me, asking to help with my garden.

"Allison," he said, "I love you. I always have."

"Paul," I said, "you know I can't. You know."

He said, "I know you can," and stepped toward me, letting the tips of his boots touch mine.

I rubbed his arms with both my hands, up and down like I wanted to start a fire.

And I woke up with my husband beside me, his bandaged arm resting against my thigh.

After the train, in the days that immediately followed, Jeremy's arm swelled to the size of a log. "It's the trauma, mama," he said, like he thought I should think it was funny. His arm swelled and the hair fell off and his skin turned an angry red. I couldn't look anymore. I just couldn't look.

But sometimes I did.

THERE'S NO BEFORE the train, only after. Only right now. We're in the car. Jeremy's in the passenger seat.

I say to him, "Our lives have changed forever."

He says, "It's just a hand. It'll grow back."

I keep my eyes on the road.

IN THE BEDROOM, I give Jeremy a back massage. I rub his muscles till he groans.

"Right there," he says, "right there. Perfect." His head is on the pillow so that I can see only half his face. I kiss the corner of his mouth. "I love you," he says, and I kiss him again.

My hands move across his skin. My fingertips soak up the warmth from his back. It's late, so it's quiet outside. Our house is quiet, too. "Jeremy," I say, "can you tell me what it feels like?"

But his eyes are closed, his breathing deep.

It has been twenty-three days since the train, but sometimes it feels like I haven't left the tracks, like I'm still standing in the shadows, waiting for the moment to arrive.

FOR BETTER OR worse, I am with Paul. He's kissing my shoulder. He's saying my name and rubbing his mouth on my skin. This time I'm not dreaming.

"Please," I say, like maybe I've had enough, but really I mean, "Please, please, don't let this end."

WHEN JEREMY COMES home, I'm lying on the floor, my cheek pressed against the carpet. "Have you ever felt this low?" I ask.

He's been running. His shirt is dark with sweat. "If you're still above sea level, you're doing OK."

I stare at his shoes. "I'm practically dead."

"No," Jeremy says, lying down beside me, "you're not."

PAUL SAYS HE wants to write a song about me. "Allison, you're my talisman," he sings, then says, "What do you think?"

"Nice," I say. We're sitting on the floor in his living room. Paul has his acoustic guitar on his lap.

"Is everything OK?" he asks.

"Wonderful," I say. "Do you want to go get something to eat?"

Paul strums his guitar. "You know we can't. We're stuck in strict, solitary confinement."

I forgot.

"It's not so bad, Allie," Paul says. "Give me a kiss."

I do, and he kisses me back.

IF THE SUNDOWN KINGS hit it big, Paul and I will have it made. If they record an album, at least we'll have something we can touch. If I hear my song on the radio, maybe I'll grip the steering wheel and fall in love.

"What are you thinking?" Jeremy asks. He's trying to tie his running shoes.

"Nothing," I say. "You."

He smiles and lets go of his laces, motions for me to come near.

I stay by the bedroom window. I've stopped counting days.

When Jeremy's out and the phone rings, I tell myself not to answer.

I'M READING WHEN Jeremy hollers from the bedroom. He says, "I've got something that'll cheer you up. Wait right there."

"What?" I say, and he enters the living room, arms tucked behind his back. "What is it?"

"It's a miracle!" he says and whips his arms out and waves them in the air.

He's wearing a red foam "We're Number One" hand over his bandage.

"Sure, it's a little big," he says, "but beggars can't be choosers. I'm healed!" He spins in a circle. The tip of his giant foam finger brushes the ceiling.

"Well, what do you think?" he asks, dropping to his knees. The hand slips off, and it's just Jeremy again, kneeling before me. I stare at his arm, the place where his hand once was, where his wrist now meets nothing.

"Please don't look at me," he says and brings his good hand to his face.

PAUL AND I are fighting. We're naked in the kitchen. He's screaming. "What is it you want? I just don't fucking get it!"

We've just spent the last hour wrapped in sheets, fighting in the bedroom. We decided to take our show on the road and moved to the kitchen.

"What? What is it? What's wrong with you?"

"Jeremy's missing a hand," I say.

"Good God," Paul yells. "Why didn't somebody tell me?" He slides a cutting board across the counter. "Problem solved." He flattens his hand on the wood.

I stare at his long fingers.

"What? What are you waiting for? Let's get this over with so we can move on."

"I don't have a knife," I say.

"You're stalling." He opens the drawer at his waist and hands me a steak knife.

I press its tip into my palm.

"Be careful," he says. "It's sharp."

JEREMY IS WAITING for me when I walk in the door. He stands on the rug, phone in his hand.

"I'm home," I say and wrap my arms around him. He stiffens, but doesn't push me away. "I'll make us dinner if you want."

"The doctor called today." Jeremy's voice is even. "He said the bandage can come off."

I bury my face in his chest.

THERE IS SOMETHING left from before. There's this: It's summer, last year. Jeremy and I are lying on our backs in the park. He's throwing a Frisbee above his head with one hand and catching it with the other. The grass is cool against the back of my neck.

It's our first anniversary. "Tell me why you love me," I say.

"Who knows?" Jeremy says and laughs.

I laugh, too, because it's OK, we've got plenty of time. The sky stretches for a million miles above us.

Rosa Blanca

NOT LONG AGO I was on an airplane flying from Los Angeles to London. Seated next to me in first class was a honey-complexioned man who looked to be in his early thirties. We introduced ourselves to each other and he asked me what I did for a living. I told him I wrote screenplays for films. That was why I was sitting in the first class section, I explained; the studio for which I was working had paid the fare.

"I don't know much about movies," he said. "I like to watch them, of course."

I asked him what business he was in.

"Art, mostly. Buying and selling. Tell me, where do you get your stories?"

"From everywhere," I said. "The news, books—sometimes I just make them up."

"I've got a story," he said.

"Most people do."

"Do you mind if I tell it to you? I think it would make a great movie."

"Go ahead," I told him. "It's a long flight."

"A young man, early twenties, is shopping in a supermarket in L.A. He is dressed slovenly, and takes items off the shelves then replaces them in the wrong categories. He loses his wallet from a back pocket. The wallet falls to the floor. He is oblivious to this and turns a corner into another aisle. A young Latina comes along and picks up the wallet. She has seen it drop out of the boy's pocket. She's very pretty, no more than eighteen years old. She hesitates for a moment, holding the wallet, then pursues the young man and gives it to him. He's a bit out of it—lack of sleep, drugs, something—but thanks her, and as she turns away he tells her to wait. He sees how pretty she is. They talk. She's from Mexico, near the border. She seems a little lost, no real destination. The boy invites her to come with him to his house. She agrees, with some prodding. Her English is fairly good. He has a slick car, a drop top. He speeds to a mansion in Beverly Hills.

"The girl's name is Rosa Blanca and she's in the United States illegally, looking for work. The boy's name is Ricky, he's a rich kid who is not working 'at the moment.' They enter a luxurious kitchen. Ricky offers Rosa Blanca a cold drink. They sit and talk. A woman's voice calls out for Ricky. It's his mother, who is bedridden. She's very ill, Ricky tells the girl, and needs almost constant care. The boy goes to her. Rosa Blanca looks around. It's obvious she has never been in a house like this before.

"Ricky administers medication to his mother, returns to Rosa Blanca. After a little while Ricky's father, Mort, comes in. Mort eyes the pretty girl. Ricky tells his father that Rosa Blanca is new in town and looking for a job. He relates the story of her finding his wallet to give evidence of her honesty. Ricky clearly has designs on this girl. Ricky suggests to his father that they hire her as a housekeeper. They already have a housekeeper, Mort answers. We can always use another, counters Ricky, especially if she doesn't cost too much. It's a big property. Mort also eyes Rosa Blanca hungrily. He agrees to give her a chance, tells her she can have a room in a vacant cottage out back. Mort goes in to see his wife, Martha. Ricky tells Rosa Blanca she can move her things in today. She says she doesn't have anything to move. She's all she's got.

"Am I boring you?" the man asked me.

"Not yet," I answered.

"Good. So Rosa Blanca moves in and is under the supervision of Katy, a middle-aged housekeeper, also from Mexico—a legal resident. Katy says as long as she does the work everything will be fine. Ricky and Rosa Blanca begin a romance. He's something of a doper ne'er-do-well but he has some humor and is good looking. Rosa Blanca is not very forthcoming to Ricky about her life in Mexico; she says only that her family is very poor, she has a brother in prison and an older sister who disappeared, probably to the Boystown brothel in Nuevo Laredo. Unbeknownst to Ricky, Mort preys upon Rosa Blanca, too. She listens to his complaint that his wife cannot take care of him anymore, she's too ill. So Rosa Blanca carries on simultaneously with father and son, earning more money than she ever had before.

"Ricky hates his mother, and one day Rosa Blanca witnesses Ricky withhold Martha's medication. He's unaware that Rosa Blanca is watching. Ricky lets his mother die. Rosa Blanca is terribly upset, she doesn't know what to do. Ricky tells her now that his mother is gone, he wants to kill his father in order to inherit their fortune. He's an only child. Ricky asks Rosa Blanca to help him murder Mort. She is too shaken to respond. The police come and Ricky tells them, with his father present, that he found his mother dead. He tried to administer the medication—an injection—but it was too late. The cops seem to accept Ricky's story, given the history of Martha's illness, Mort's corroboration, etc. The medical examiner pronounces Martha dead from natural causes.

"After his wife's death, Mort is more open about his lust for Rosa Blanca. Ricky discovers his father with her and goes crazy. Now he really wants Mort dead. Later, Rosa Blanca tells Ricky that she did not want to submit to his father but was afraid she would be deported if she refused. She agrees to help Ricky kill him. Ricky takes Rosa Blanca to Las Vegas and they get married. Now she can stay in the country. Mort is furious and attacks his son. Rosa Blanca stabs Mort and he dies. Rosa Blanca tells the police that Mort tried to rape her as he had done before. There is a trial and she is found not guilty, that the homicide was justifiable, in self-defense. Ricky and Rosa Blanca are now man and wife. Ricky inherits his parents' fortune, and they continue to live in the house.

"Do you like it so far?" he asked.

"I do," I said. "Go on."

"Okay. Katy, the housekeeper, smells a rat. The rat arrives in the form of Rosa Blanca's fugitive brother, Carlos, who has broken out of jail in Mexico. Ricky asks Carlos how he found Rosa Blanca, and Carlos says he heard about the murder trial—it was well publicized. Of course he needs a place to stay and Rosa Blanca, thrilled to see her brother again, persuades Ricky to let Carlos stay. It turns out that Carlos has not been in jail in Mexico, he's been in L.A.—and he is not Rosa Blanca's brother, he's her husband. They were married in Mexico, then together crossed the border illegally. Ricky is their mark, their ticket to ride. Carlos brings some bad boys around and Ricky gets beaten up when he tries to throw them out of his house. Ricky refuses to give Rosa Blanca any more money. Carlos says it doesn't matter: she can divorce Ricky and get her share. Ricky shoots Carlos dead in front of Rosa Blanca, and tells her to get out. He'll tell the cops that Carlos was trying to rob the house. Rosa Blanca refuses to leave, telling Ricky that she'll spill everything to the cops and Ricky will go to prison for murder. Of whom? says Ricky. His mother died of natural causes; Rosa Blanca is the one who stabbed his father to death; and Carlos was an intruder, armed with a pistol. Rosa Blanca picks up Carlos's gun and shoots Ricky. Katy arrives and sees Rosa Blanca sitting alone on the couch with the gun in her hand, the bodies of Ricky and Carlos on the floor. Katy takes the gun from Rosa Blanca's hand, wipes it clean, then places it in the hand of Carlos.

"Katy goes to Rosa Blanca and holds her in her arms, comforting the girl. In Spanish, she says to Rosa Blanca: "You and I were out shopping together. We found them like this when we got back." Katy picks up the telephone to call the police.

"As the widow, Rosa Blanca will inherit the money now, and Katy knows Rosa Blanca will take care of her for the rest of her life."

The man stopped talking for a few moments, then looked at me and asked, "What do you think? Is that a movie?"

"It certainly could be," I said. "Where did you hear this story?"

"From my mother."

"Who told it to her?"

"Nobody. My mother is Rosa Blanca. She was pregnant when my father died."

"Your mother killed your father?"

"No, Ricky killed him. My father was Carlos."

I hesitated before asking the next question.

"Did Rosa Blanca tell you that Carlos, not Ricky, was your father?"

"I grew up thinking that I was Ricky's son, but Katy told me the truth just before she died."

"Does Rosa Blanca know that you know who your real father was?"

"No, Katy made me promise not to tell her."

Rosa Blanca's son looked out a porthole window at the clouds.

"If you make it into a movie," he said, "you can leave that part out, end it where Katy picks up the telephone to call the cops. That's a better ending, anyway, don't you think?"

DEAN PASCHAL

The Puppies

Some months ago, my mother's dog Kayceil (pronounced kay-seal) had seven puppies. Two were still-born with cranial defects, and were buried immediately. Two more, the only males, both the runt and the largest of the litter—and both perfect in form—lived a bit more than a day, then, somewhat mysteriously, stopped breathing and died and were removed from the company of their tiny sisters. My mother placed them in a little stainless-steel pan and put the pan in the freezing-compartment of the refrigerator, where as far as I know, they remain to this day, nestled together, curled and frosty.

She says she talks to them every time she opens that compartment.

The following is their story:

IT WAS WITHIN us. It was there. It was in our hearts and lungs. The air and blood and the life, like in every living thing, we had it. But it slipped away, too fast for telling.

Like every thing that ever lived, it was there inside us. We felt it but there was nothing to hold to, no way to grab. And we lost it before we saw each other's face.

WE HEARD FOR weeks and months the voices in our blood that spoke of things that were to be: cats, rabbits, birds, rocks, trees and sand. And everything the voices said about them. But the voices didn't say what they would *look* like.

You will know them when you see them, they said. You will know them when you smell them. Don't worry about the shapes. You will know. And you will understand. Exactly what Life was they did not explain.

Or exactly how we would recognize it.

What the voices were very clear about, though, was that you had to be sure you were ready, because there was no correcting of mistakes after you were born.

MY BIG BROTHER and I would talk about what we were going to do when we were dogs:

When we are dogs, I said, if we are chasing a rhinoceros . . .

A rhinoceros is not one of the animals we're supposed to *chase*! You haven't been paying attention to the voices.

I have too.

A rhinoceros is too *big*!

Maybe we'll be big *dogs*!

Even big dogs don't chase rhinoceroses!

You don't know. If we're chasing a rhinoceros, what we'll do is chase it in a big circle and I'll stop and hide behind a rock and then we'll meet again and head it off together!

You haven't been listening to the voices at *all*!

I have too! I don't see why we can't chase a rhinoceros if we want to. We're going to be *dogs*!

Let's not argue.

Let's not.

We'll see.

We'll see.

Our mother can tell us.

That's right.

Still, I don't see why we can't chase a rhinoceros if we want to . . .

We would always remind each other that our very first job would be to look for life. There will have to be a trail, my brother said. We've got to get on the trail. We'll be the first on it! We'll get on it before the girls! They don't know *any*thing!

But the voices never said where it would be.

THEN THERE WAS the night when, like electricity, it went through us all. We are going to be born!

We knew.

Tomorrow.

We were so confined. But that night, so excited. We heard more about grass and trees. And excitement peeping through. We'll run, run, run, when we're born. We will be brothers! We're going to be *dogs*! Just your nose under.

But that night the membrane I was in broke.

Will I need it? I said. It broke. I didn't break it. It broke, I said. Will that be OK?

Later my big brother asked the voices.

My little brother broke his membrane, will he need it?

I didn't break it. It broke, I said.

There was no answer.

The voices speak but don't answer.

There will be a forgetting of this time, they said. A forgetting.

We're ready to forget!
But, at times, a dim remembering . . .
We're ready to remember, too!
We're going to get on the *trail*!

THEN WE WERE out.

It felt so big! It was dark, like they said, but immediately we felt the milk. We knew. The voices were right. My brother was next to me. We were the first ones out. We were on the trail! There will be a forgetting of this time too, they had said.

I was so worried about my membrane. But now I saw it didn't matter. It would have broken anyway. Mine just broke a little early is all. Everything was going to be OK. I was so glad. I had worried all night long about my membrane.

THE VOICES HAD told us all about breathing but they hadn't told us what it would *feel* like. With breathing in you could feel yourself go up slightly. And breathing out was down. So strange. Up, down. Gently.

Up, down. Up, down with the breathing. So very strange. We're going to be *dogs*. No, no, no. Listen to me, talking. We *are* dogs. We're dogs *now*!

BUT THEN SOMETHING began to happen. When I went down, it seemed I did not come up again quite as far. I would go down on one breath, and up not quite as far on the next. I had to remember, too. I had to remember a lot. My brother also noticed it. But he thought something was stuck in his throat. He began to cough and cough to try to get it out. We've got to get on the *trail*! he said.

Breathing in was coming up. Breathing out was going down. It was like a balance. But I kept going slightly more down than up. Down and down. I got so I couldn't remember exactly how to get up again. I was forgetting how to breathe! I was so scared. I was doing it *wrong*! Wait. Wait. Help, I said.

Suddenly I was all alone. It was so cold. I was so scared. I've never been so scared. But a dog is supposed to be brave.

Almost as suddenly, though, it was all OK. Everything was OK because my brother was with me and we were snuggled together. What had happened, though? Where had our mother gone? And what about the milk?

Then I heard my brother. He had just realized something. You *can't* find life, he said. There's no trail; the trail goes nowhere. It was within us. They didn't tell us where to *look*. But I can see now; it was *within* us. Who would have guessed? Who would have possibly guessed?

I would, I said. You didn't ask *me*.

It was within us. Who would have guessed?

I would. I would have guessed. Even a rhinoceros would have guessed *that*.

Before and Again

ON OUR WAY home from the public swimming pool we stopped at the 7-Eleven. My mother drove, my younger brother in the front seat on his beach towel, and me, showered and combed in back. From my seat, I studied my mother's blond-streaked hair and bony shoulders. She had pulled her hair up on top of her head to expose her neck. I was compact, with hints of my father's Oriental features. I sat a little taller to match her posture. She eased our car into one of the four parking spaces, nose-in to the storefront. Although the spots were all empty, she preferred the one on the far right. My lungs felt raw from having swallowed several mouthfuls of chlorinated water at the pool. I breathed slowly to hear my whistling inhale and exhale.

Our two-door Chevy Nova reeked of vomit when the temperature rose. The 7-Eleven parking lot seemed to be hotter than the rest of Livermore. The blacktop, the goldenrod stucco and 77-cent-a-pack cigarette signs in the front windows had already faded. Candy wrappers turned inside out gathered where the curb met the fence. They marked the boundaries of the convenience store in pale yellow and wax.

An arm length's away from the driver's side of our car, a man with a mustache sat in the shade of a newspaper vending machine. He leaned against the storefront. He was naked to the waist. His T-shirt, wadded into a ball, pillowed his head against the abrasive stucco. A faded tattoo of an eagle spread across his chest. His unbrushed hair reached his shoulders.

My mother half turned her head toward me. "Emily, you staying in the car or coming inside?"

"I'm staying." I imagined the dry heat pulling the pool water out of my pores. I felt the afternoon sun on the back of my head. I placed my hand on my black hair to feel it, surprised to find it dry, dully hot. My mother opened her car door, stepped out, and motioned for my brother to slide out on her side. She gave his bottom a pat as he hopped down, and she slammed the car door.

From the back seat of the Chevy Nova I leaned out, resting my elbows on the rolled-down window. I looked at the man outside the store. He sat on the sidewalk, elbows on knees. He raised his soda cup to me. I could see his forearm flex and the tendons of his wrist pull tight as he held onto the large drink. The ice rattled softly, and I imagined the wax paper starting to soften around the seams of the cup.

I reached out my fingers and pushed down the two door locks on either side with as little force as I could. I moved slowly, because of the heat, because of the watery feel of my muscles after a day of swimming, because I didn't want his attention. I hoped he wouldn't hear the soft, metallic pop of the latches falling. I would have rolled the windows up too, but didn't dare. He followed my movements with his eyes, without turning his head.

Through the storefront window, I could see my mother beside shelves of snacks in boxes and bags. She was talking to a young woman. They nodded and turned occasionally to look around the aisles of tobacco and bread. My mother tilted her head and put her hands in the back pockets of her shorts. She slouched with her left hip forward and listened. The cashier, a high school boy, looked up from his magazine to watch her.

I glanced at the man on the curb and wondered what he saw. I pulled the edges of my cotton tank top closer around me. The man smiled. His eyes weren't on my mother. He raised his eyes and spread his lips flat.

I lay flat across the back seat, spreading my hair on the blue upholstery. I rested my head against the driver's side door to catch the shade. The seat was hard and springy and I kicked the seatbelts out of the way. The metal clips burned. I stretched my feet up to the window frame and let the breeze blow into my shorts. The sun heated the car, heated the blue brocade tapestry and the vomit-smelling floors.

"What you dreaming about?" He leaned into the driver's window, shook his near-empty soda. I could hear the ice tumble. The wax paper sides of the cup sweated, and he wiped the beads of water across his forehead. I pushed myself onto my elbows and sat up, in the middle of the back seat. "You want a sip?" he asked. Reaching inside the car, he held the drink out to me.

I took one pull on the straw and handed it back. It tasted sweet and watery. "Thank you."

"Where's your parents? In the store?" He arched his back to look into the 7-Eleven then bent at the waist again to lean into our Chevy.

"Yes. My mom will be right back." I sat taller.

"She won't mind if I take a seat here a moment with you."
He didn't ask, simply reached through the window and
opened the door. He took a seat on the driver's side, sitting
sideways, his legs spilling out into the parking lot, the door
open wide. I pulled my feet closer to me.

"You're a pretty little girl, you know. You're gonna grow up
and break my heart." His breath smelled sweet like the soda.

I crossed my arms over my chest and held as still as I could.
My lungs ached, and my breath felt too shallow. I wasn't
accustomed to the attention. My mother said she was proud
our family didn't have a man. She said we were independent
women.

"I never sat with such a pretty girl before. You always this
quiet?" He was licking his index finger and wiping dirt off his
knees.

I was quiet. My mother wasn't. She danced when she heard
music. She wore her swimsuit to pick us up from school,
when the other mothers wore summer dresses and sandals.
Her friends, men usually, often stopped by the house and
stayed around on the front porch drinking iced tea with
whiskey. My mother added crushed mint to the red plastic
tumblers. Her friends were loud. When they laughed, our
neighbors would stare and then bar themselves inside, closing
windows and doors to their houses. I kept quiet.

At the 7-Eleven, my skin felt dry and tight across my palms
and the bottom of my feet. My mind stretched to find how I
could possibly be my mother's daughter. I wondered if I
would have my own front porch and friends who would sing
guitar songs. The idea tumbled down in my mind.

"My mother's in the store. She's buying some milk," I said,
and I pointed over the front seat toward her. Talking to the
cashier, she leaned on the counter. I know if the man and I

had been closer to her, we could have seen the tawny freckles on her neck. He turned to look. "Do you think she's pretty?" I asked.

He craned his head backward. His hair fell to his shoulders and gave off a smell of cigarettes. He pinched his lips. "She's nice, but careless." He watched her bob her head in conversation. "Not like you." He turned toward the back seat. His shoulders and arms were too close to me. I tapped my feet on the floor of the Chevy and kicked the front seat in rhythm. The car had only two doors. To get out from the back seat, I'd have to push down one side of the front seat bench. I tried to will my mother to look up at the car. The man had a musty smell, something like spice and grease. I was embarrassed to sit in that hot car, smelling his skin.

"I had a daughter about your age," he continued. He turned his head away and spoke in low tones. His voice fell in a register so deep it caught me. "She was wild. Never sat still like you." The skin on his chest was smooth across flat muscles. Tufts of dark hair stuck out from his armpits.

"Where is your daughter?" I leaned forward to hear him and put my arms on the back of the front seat.

"She lives with her mother in Los Altos. I gotta get my shit together." He drank to the bottom of his soda and crumpled the cup.

"Do you miss her?"

He rubbed his fingers and thumbs into his eye sockets. "No. Not really. It's not like I got anything to say to her."

My mother picked up the paper sack on the counter and turned to leave the store. She hesitated, scanning the aisles for my brother.

"I can be your daughter." I didn't say it very loud. He shifted in his seat, turning toward me, and took hold of my left hand. He placed my palm on his cheek, and I was startled at the coolness of his skin. The stubble on his face felt coarse. It reminded me of my old hairbrush, balding in places, familiar. My mother had my brother by the hand and led him toward the door. My breath hurt in my chest. Stung.

"No, honey. I don't want you to be my daughter." He held my palm with both hands, held it to his lips and kissed the flesh at the base of my thumb. His mustache brushed my palm. The afternoon heat made the parking lot wave in ripples. I leaned toward him, couldn't stop myself, and he touched his lips to my forehead. His breath, I felt it across my cheeks, cool and sweet. I was sleepy. My eyes were closing. My limbs weightless and limp, as though I were still swimming. He stepped out of the car and closed the door gently. I took in the flex of his calves as he bent to sit beside the pay phone.

My mother, paper sack on her hip, pressed her back against the 7-Eleven door to open it. My brother held her free fingers with both his hands. She shook him off and put the groceries on top of the newspaper vending machine on the sidewalk. Bending to take the newspaper from the stand, she brushed her hair back from her eyes. She half smiled at the man as she picked the bag up again. He didn't respond. She slid in behind the driver's wheel and leaned across the seat to open the door for my brother. He got in.

"Who was that?" she asked. She checked her face in the rearview mirror. I was still resting on top of the front seat, my face sideways, cheek on my crossed arms. She handed her grocery bag to me. "Was he bothering you?" I set the bag on the floor of the car.

"No, Mom. He had a mustache like Dad's."

She started the engine, put the car in reverse, and we were

on our way. "Leave the windows, down, sweetie," she said to my brother. "It's hot, and the wind feels good." I turned backward in my seat to look at the man as we left the parking lot. He held his head down between his knees. His cool breath invaded my body, and my lungs burned.

HA JIN

A Bad Joke

At last the two jokers were captured. They had not known the police were after them, so they had come to town without any suspicion. The instant they entered Everyday Hardware, a group of policemen sprang at them, pinned them to the cement floor, and handcuffed them from behind. With stupefied faces smeared by sawdust, they screamed, "You made a mistake, Comrade Policemen! We didn't steal anything!"

"Shut up!"

"Ugh . . ."

The police plugged their mouths with washcloths from a bucket and then hauled them out to the white van waiting on the street.

At the police station, the interrogation started immediately. It didn't go well, though, because the two peasants denied that they had spread any counterrevolutionary slander. The police chief—a bespectacled, pockmarked man—reminded them of the joke they had told. To everyone's astonishment, the tall peasant asked the chief, "Who's Deng Xiaoping? I never met him." He turned to his buddy. "Have you?"

"Uh-uh, I guess he must be a general or a big official," said the short peasant.

"Stop pretending!" the chief shouted. "Comrade Deng Xiaoping is the chairman of our Party and our country."

"Really?" the tall peasant asked. "You mean he's number one now?"

"Yes."

"How about Chairman Mao? We only know Chairman Mao."

"He passed away six years ago. You didn't know?"

"That so?" the short peasant cried. "I didn't know he's dead. He's the Emperor to us—no, more like a granddad. His portrait still hangs in my home."

The police officers tried hard to keep from laughing. Their chief looked thoughtful. Before the interrogation, he had thought he could easily handle this pair of yokels. Now it was obvious they were smart fellows, playing the fool to dodge the charge. He'd better dismiss them for today—it was already late afternoon—so that he could figure out a way to make them admit their crime. He ordered the guards to take the two away and put them into a cell.

SEVEN WEEKS AGO, the two peasants had gone to Sunlight Department Store on Peace Avenue. "Can we take a look at the rubber loafers?" the tall peasant asked at the counter, drumming his thick fingers on the glass top.

Three salesgirls were sitting on a broad window ledge, silhouetted against the traffic lights on the street. They stopped chatting, and one of them got up and came over. "What size?" she asked.

"Forty-two," said the tall man.

She handed him a pair. Pointing at the price tag, she said, "Five-fifty."

"What?" the short peasant exclaimed. "Last month it was five yuan a pair. How come it's five-fifty now? Ten percent inflation in a month? Crazy!"

"Five-fifty," said the girl, annoyed. She twitched her nose, which had the shape of a large garlic clove.

"Too expensive for this old man," said the tall peasant, who was in his mid-thirties. He dropped the shoes on the counter with a thump.

As the two men walked away, the tall man spat on the floor and said loudly to his buddy, "Damn, all prices go up—only our chairman never grows."

The short man grinned and added, "Yeah, that dwarf won't change."

Hearing their words, the salesgirls all tittered. The peasants turned around and took off their blue caps, waving and smiling at the girls, their swarthy faces marked with big paren-theses.

Within an hour, a joke was circulating in the department store: "All prices go up, but Deng Xiaoping never grows." Within a day, thousands of people in our city had heard the joke. Like a spook it soon began haunting offices, factories, restaurants, theaters, bathhouses, alleys, neighborhoods, train stations.

THE TWO PEASANTS slept well in the cell, happy for the free dinner of sorghum porridge and stewed pumpkin, but they still had no inkling of what crime they had committed. At

9:00 A.M., the three salesgirls arrived at the police station. One of them was ordered to repeat what she had heard the jokers say. She pointed at the tall man's concave face and testified, "He said, 'All prices have gone up, but Deng Xiaoping never grows.'"

"Goddamn it!" the man shouted and slapped his knee, his slanty eyes flashing. "I never heard of him. How could I ever come up with that weird name?"

The short man cut in. "We never mentioned him. We said, 'Our chairman never will change.'"

"What did you say exactly?" asked the bald policeman in charge of the team of detectives.

The tall peasant replied, "'All prices go up and only our chairman never grows.' I meant our Chairman Lou—of our commune."

The short peasant added, "Dwarf Lou is an awful man. We all hate him. He wouldn't let us have more than one and a half yuan for a workday, 'cause he wants to use the money to build a reservoir for catfish and bigheaded carp. What can little shrimps like us get from a reservoir? Not even fish droppings. Everybody knows all the fish will end up in the officials' stomachs. If you don't believe me, you go check and see if Chairman Lou's a dwarf." He gave a broad grin, displaying his carious teeth.

A few men and women chuckled, but they turned silent at the sight of the interrogators' somber faces.

The chief asked the salesgirls to recall the original words of the joke. To his bewilderment, they remembered that the tall peasant had indeed said "our chairman never grows." In fact, when they had relayed the words to others, they hadn't mentioned Deng Xiaoping either. Somehow in the process of dissemination, the joke had changed into its present monstrous form. Could this whole thing have originated from a misinterpretation? Perhaps, and perhaps not.

The interrogators were at a loss now. How could they determine when and where the joke had shed its original ambiguity and acquired its definitive meaning? It was unlikely that their superiors would accept misinterpretation as the explanation for what had happened. The crime was already a fait accompli. And how could there be a crime without a criminal? Even though a deliberate misinterpreter might never be identified, someone had to be responsible for the final version of the joke. So, how should they proceed with the interrogation?

Again the chief had the peasants returned to their cell. He then sent a jeep to the commune to fetch Chairman Lou.

EVERYBODY WAS IMPRESSED by Chairman Lou's handsome looks: a round forehead, ivory teeth, curved brows, large eyes shaded by miniature fans of lashes. What a handsome and intelligent face he had! If he were not three foot two, you could easily have taken him for a movie star. In addition, he had dignified manners, and his voice sounded so elegant that everybody could tell he was a well-educated man. Small wonder that even with a deformed physique he could govern a large commune. At noon he met with the police chief and said, "Look, Comrade Chief, you ought to punish the two hooligans, teaching them an indelible lesson. Else how can I lead thirty-one thousand people? In the countryside no leader can afford to be the butt of ridicule."

"I can sympathize with that," the chief said. "In fact, last week the provincial governor called our city and asked about this case. Probably Beijing already knows of it too."

At 2:10 P.M. the interrogation resumed. A few minutes after they sat down in the room, the two peasants insisted that they were wronged and should be released. They declared they both came from poor families and had always loved the Party and the socialist motherland, though they had not been active in political studies and were ignorant of current affairs. They promised the chief that they would take great pains to educate themselves and would never make trouble again. The first thing they'd do after their release, they said, was buy a radio so that they could keep up with news.

The chief waved his hand to cut them off. "You still refuse responsibility for the slander against Chairman Deng? Then how could I let you go? Your attitude is not right."

"Heavens!" the short peasant wailed. "This is a misunderstanding. Comrade Policeman, please—"

"That's irrelevant," the chief said. "Look at it this way. Say that a sentence in a book can be read in different ways and some people get a reactionary meaning out of it. Now, who should be responsible for the reading—the writer or the reader?"

"Mmm . . . probably the writer," said the tall man.

"Correct. All the evidence shows you two coauthored the slander, so you have to answer for all the consequences."

"Does this mean you won't let us go home?" asked the short man.

"Correct."

"How long are you going to jail us?"

"It depends—a month, maybe life."

"What?" the tall peasant shouted. "I haven't thatched my house for the winter yet. My kids will freeze to death if you keep me in—"

"You still don't get it!" Chairman Lou bellowed and

slapped the tabletop with his fleshy hand. "You both should feel lucky that you're still alive. How many people were executed because they spread counterrevolutionary rumors? Keep your butts in prison here, and remold yourselves into new men. I'll have your families informed of where to send your underclothes, if you have any."

In amazement, people all turned to look at the little man standing on an upholstered chair. Unshod, his large feet were in violet woolen socks.

The chief ordered the guards, "Send them to the City Prison and put them among the political criminals." He took off his glasses, smirking and wiping the lenses on the sleeve of his shirt. True, he couldn't pass a definite sentence on the jokers, because the length of their imprisonment would depend on how long the provincial administration was interested in this case.

"Chairman Lou, have mercy, please," begged the tall man.

Lou said, "It serves you right. See if you dare to be so creative again."

"I do it to your little ancestors, Dwarf Lou!" the short peasant yelled, stamping his feet. Four policemen walked up, grabbed the prisoners, and hauled them away.

STEVE AMICK

Consumed

Until that awful moment she walked in on him in her father's den—caught him in the act, hiding in the dark, hunched over the open desk drawer feeling like some despised scavenger animal, his mouth crammed with a nice soggy lump of that juicy Hammermill Bond—he'd deluded himself that his fiancée would never discover his dark secret. "My god!" she said, her face white as 80 lb. ivory linen cardstock. "You're at it again, aren't you?"

He wanted to deny it, but his mouth was too full to speak.

Truthfully, he wasn't at it *again*, because he'd never actually *stopped*. He'd managed to fool his loved ones for almost a year, lulled them into thinking he was better, that he'd kicked it. As if eating paper were a choice; a thing over which he had free will. In truth, he'd merely gone underground, so that each day was a string of stolen moments—pathetic, makeshift solutions: a furtive snatch of the White Pages (no one ever missed the Z's); a wad of industrial paper towel in the men's room; bits of napkin slipped out of a McDonald's bag on his desk as he pretended to nibble on fries. Trapped in long meetings, he would sometimes fake a sore throat, cough a little, pull out a lozenge, fuss with the crinkly cellophane, then slip the wadded-up corner of his legal pad into his mouth and suck away at it like a secret pacifier, in full view of unsuspecting colleagues. At his own home, of course, there was much less need for subterfuge, though he did own a printer he hardly used simply to justify the reams of delicious old-style perf stacked innocently by his bed.

Certainly, none of this had anything to do with free will.

Sure, he'd tried to stop many times, had been ordered to by no less than four physicians. They showed him gory textbook photos of the travesty done to teeth, to stomachs, to intestines. They identified his condition by name—Pica—as if that could possibly make it any more real, explained about kidney failure, warned of the scarring if they ended up having to operate. It wasn't enough. A lifetime of wearing only one-piece bathing suits might work to scare female patients, but belly scars were no problem for a guy: he'd say, *Oh that? Ever hear of the Gulf War, baby?*

And now his fiancée was standing there, demanding an explanation. What more could he say? She'd caught him dead to rights. The only thing he wondered was what his future in-laws *thought* was happening in there. Certainly they could hear them arguing, could hear the whimper in their daughter's voice, scolding him. He knew they were out there, whispering in the hall, arguing between themselves about interfering, about busting in the way she had.

Soon there would be screaming. There was always screaming.

If it were his own family out there, they'd have been wise the second he excused himself from the table. After all, he'd been eating paper all his life. What else would he be up to?

At first, when he did it as a kid, his family just thought it was weird. His brothers would call him a creep and his dad would smack him with a rolled-up newspaper, not too hard, but enough to tell him to cut it out. When his mom died he got worse, seeking solace in the woody pulp of comic books, baseball cards, condolence cards, the paper plates that appeared since her passing. So his dad smacked him with the newspaper more often, harder. As a preemptive strike, he would try to consume most of the newspaper each day before his dad got home.

With his mom gone, dinnertime was soon scrapped for a help-yourself free-for-all, everyone on their own. But cold Swanson dinners and chicken pot pies couldn't top the succor and comfort of a fine imperial bond, maybe a manila folder. He'd stay in his room for hours, listening to Brian Wilson on headphones or working his way through his mom's scrapbook or watching the normal people on TV— chipper sitcom families that stayed together and never died— and munched the *TV Guide*, saving the bitter, slick covers and meatier subscription cards for last, a treat.

The shrinks his dad dragged him to confirmed that it was shameful behavior, that it was silly and bestial and beneath him. And so he learned to be clever and hide it.

And now he was almost forty and still doing it and facing a weeping fiancée in operatic despair. He was sorry he'd ever told her. Maybe he could've played it off today here in her father's den if he hadn't already made her aware of his history, if she wasn't always watching him like a goddamn warden for signs of backsliding. But he'd told her too much, gotten too close, allowed her to become judgmental, scolding.

The first time she'd caught him—a year ago—after that

initial brow-creased look of incomprehension, that initial *Why the hell're you eating my checkbook?!?*—she'd been so understanding, cradled his head in her lap, stroked his hair, said *you poor poor poor baby.* And he'd opened up about it, told how he'd squandered a fortune in his father's money in therapy, showed her his collection of clippings from medical journals, the Internet, Pica-sufferers' newsletters to which he subscribed under the alias John Foolscap. *My god,* he'd even confessed to the lowest point of his addiction, ditching Jenny Ramspacher —his prom date back in high school and supposedly a "sure thing"—at the tail-end of the evening in order to sneak back to the ballroom and consume an entire banquet-sized paper tablecloth that he'd had his eye on all night.

He'd spared his fiancée nothing.

"We can beat this together," she told him back then, tucking his face neatly into her warm cleavage. "Our love is *way* stronger than some nasty ol' compulsion. *Way.*"

And she entered into the world of his secret vice as if they were starring in *The Man with a Golden Stomach*: she would be Kim Novak, he would be Sinatra, and the paper would play the role of the heroin.

But clearly she no longer thought it was so romantic.

"You can't expect me to just sit by and watch you kill yourself!" she sobbed. "You have to choose!"

He tried to reach for her, to move around from behind the big desk, but she jerked back and slipped out of the room. And the return of privacy was, as always, immediately calming.

It was clear what he had to do: give up on this ridiculous notion of maintaining a real relationship, revert to his old practice of casual dating. No more than four dates with the same woman, no longer than a month, tops. This just wasn't fair to anyone. Bachelorhood wouldn't be so bad. There was always pornography. And some of those magazines—the really cheap ones—were printed on that great, pulpy newsprint, tinged with just a *soupçon* of almonds that had to be something in the ink.

Even in his sorrow, his mouth watered just thinking about it.

BENJAMIN ALIRE SÁENZ

Why Men Quit:
An Intellectual Inquiry

I.

There were different theories as to why his father had quit
drinking. Alcohol poisoning. That particular theory was set forth
by an aunt as she talked to another aunt at a family gathering.
"It was either die or quit drinking. Por años y años no pudo
dejar ese maldito trago. Pero al fin el doctor told him que se
iba morir. His skin was all blotches. Fear of dying—por eso dejo
ese vicio tan odiado." So really, his aunt's theory focused in on
two interrelated and compelling reasons: alcohol poisoning
coupled with fear of dying. As far as the boy was concerned, the
case she laid out was absolutely convincing. Hadn't he seen the
blotches on his father's skin firsthand? Wasn't he a witness?

II.

There were, however, competing theories as to the reasons
behind his father's abandonment of the one and only art in
his life he'd ever perfected. One of his father's friends put
forth his own theory in the following manner: "Your father is

made of steel. He gathered all his strength. Okay, it took him thirty-five years pa' hacerlo, but it takes a long time for a man to gather all his strength. But he did it. Strong, your father. Muy hombre. Only men of steel can beat the demon in the bottle." The boy's older sister mistrusted that particular theory. "Macho bullshit," she said. "Mom's stronger than Dad any day of the week. She's stronger even when she's sleeping." His sister had a point, and it was all but impossible to disagree with her. Hadn't they all seen their mother in action? She'd even held a thief at bay with a hoe once, and threatened to cut him down like a weed. What his sister said was true enough. No doubt about it. Still, the boy couldn't help but feel there was an important truth to the theory his father's friend had proposed. After all, you couldn't quit drinking without having discipline. According to his grandfather, you couldn't do anything without discipline—and he trusted his grandfather completely *on all matters*. The boy knew there was no discipline without strength. So—despite the rhetorical exaggeration and his sister's astute objections—the boy could not discount his father's friend completely. He wanted to become a true intellectual, and no intellectual of any integrity ever dismissed a theory, however far-fetched, without a thorough deconstruction and a careful analysis. It is the responsibility of the scholar to weigh all the evidence at his disposal.

III.
In the matter of his father's drinking, his mother was silent. So the boy never asked her for the true reason. And he knew, beyond all doubt, that she held the truth in her heart, but there was no unlocking that truth, and so, over the years, he developed a simple theory about her silence: why relive the hell? It was enough to have survived it.

He never asked his brothers and sisters about what they knew or felt or believed or heard about his father's entry into the world of sobriety. But he kept his ears open—just in case someone came along and spilled everything out in a moment of passion. There were many such moments in his family, and he thought this was a good thing, though his older brother did not share his optimism. "Belonging to a family is messy and ugly and embarrassing." That's what his brother said, and he was always telling people that he was an orphan, and ungenerous as this fib was, it was an improvement over the mythology he'd created as a child: "I was immaculately conceived!" He liked to yell that as he paraded down the street. But his sister (not one to take kindly to being disowned) used to follow him yelling out even louder: "Conceived in sin! Conceived in sin!"

IV.

To get back to the subject of the boy's father's drying out: one summer night, the boy heard his older brother (the same one who claimed to be conceived without sin and later claimed to be an orphan) talking to his older sister (the same one who liked to yell, "Conceived in sin!"). And his older brother said: "He promised Grandma on her deathbed. She had him summoned, sent the men of the village to comb the bars and bring him to her. When they found him, the stench of alcohol seeping out of his pores like incense from a censor, he went along quietly to the hospital. And as he wept at the foot of her deathbed, she made him vow to never let the contents of a bottle ever pass his lips again so help him God. And Dad threw himself on the floor, swearing never to touch another drop. "Never, I promise! Never!" "So help you God?" she asked. "So help me God," he said. But that was the year his older brother joined the Thespian Club. He delivered his lines altogether too deliberately. Like incense from a censor? Who'd ever trust a man who spoke like that? No, no, like any actor, he was too in love with his performance. More in love with words than with the truth. The speeches that spilled from actors' tongues were even more suspicious than the lies of macho drunks. At least no one gave credibility to the talk of men in bars. Actors, on the other hand, were altogether too convincing. The boy rightfully kept his distance from his brother's practiced fiction that masqueraded as an oral history worthy of serious attention.

V.

Many years later, the boy, now a man, and older than his father had been when he'd quit the bottle, did some quitting of his own: he quit smoking (a habit that was not only a habit, but a passion—and not only a passion but a love). In the moments that he craved the taste of smoke in his mouth, on his tongue, in his lungs, he thought about the theories he'd once heard concerning his father's drinking as he was growing up. He decided his aunt, and his father's friend, and his brother—all of them, they'd all been wrong. Sincere perhaps. But wrong. Not unlike scientists and doctors and sure-footed detectives and overtrained intellectuals, they had overlooked the obvious. The boy, now a man, suddenly understood perfectly why his father had quit drinking. He had quit not for them, his children; he had quit not because he was strong or made of steel; he had not quit because of a promise he made his dying suegra, saint that she was. He had not even quit because he was afraid of dying. The last thing addicts are afraid of is death.

This. This was the reason why his father finally left the

liquor that he loved: one night, his wife had simply asked: *Amor, por favor, te ruego. Leave the bottle, now. Amor, me estás matando.* All those years, he'd never heard her desperate pleadings. But in that moment, in the stillness of the calm night, something made him stop and listen to her voice. And, like the miracle of rain in the longest of droughts, he opened himself like a thirsty earth—and drank her words. He heard. He heard her lovely and familiar voice. The girl, the girl he'd loved and married long ago. And so, in the morning, his father woke a sober man. He never touched another drop. Not a single drop. This, then, was the whole truth of the matter. The other theories, each with their own impeccable logic, were complete and utter nonsense. His father, the subject and source of countless narratives, had quit the bottle for the simplest of reasons: he loved his wife. He wanted to spend a lifetime loving her. The boy knew this now, was certain of it. The boy was a man now, and he knew things he hadn't known before. He'd come to know the power of a woman who whispered salvation into the ears of the man she loved. Deserving of her love or not. The man she loved. In the night. In the holy, holy night.

STEPHANIE WAXMAN

Delicate Touch

KAZU TAKAMURA SAT upright on the cream-colored leather couch, which took some effort as the couch was wide and deep, designed to relax people. But Kazu Takamura was not relaxed. He glanced nervously at the secretary again. She sat at a computer, her eyes glued to the screen. She had told him it would only be a few minutes, but that had been fifteen minutes ago.

At least he thought she had indicated a few minutes. Maybe he had misunderstood. Maybe he had not been kept waiting. Maybe his appointment was at four o'clock, not three-thirty. At any rate, several people had passed through the room, and no one had offered him tea.

His thin, tapered fingers reached down once again to touch the large black portfolio resting against his thigh. He glanced at his watch. He brushed an errant thread from his trousers. Once more he looked at the pictures on the wall, black-and-white photos, narrow black wooden frames, off-white 2¾-inch mats. The one of the reclining nude irritated him. The angle of the light on her backside was too obvious. The one of the mountain had a calming effect, and his eyes lingered on it a moment. The way the light danced on the edge of the ridge reminded him of Mount Fuji at dawn. He felt a pang at being so far from home. Just then, the door to the inner office opened, and a woman paused at its threshold. She was of medium height with a sprinkling of brown spots on her face. She wore a plain gray suit, a red silk scarf at her throat. Her hair was the color of udon noodles. He couldn't guess her age; *gaijin* all seemed the same to him.

She walked over to him and extended her hand. "Mr. Takamura."

He couldn't get used to the offer of a hand. He took it limply in his own. Her hand was soft and cool. He let it go quickly. "Much pleasure to meet," he said as he stood.

"I'm Toni Donaldson," she said, her eyes bright and friendly. "I hope your trip was pleasant. I've been so anxious to meet you."

She spoke too fast. He was losing the sense of what she wanted, but when she turned to go back into the office, he followed.

Her office was a quiet room, lit by northern light. Her desk was large and neat. Several paintings leaned against one wall. A bookcase stood against another. There was a black leather couch facing two chairs separated by a low, square glass table. An architect's table stood in front of the window. The whole city spread out below.

"Can I get you a soda? Coffee? Perrier? Here, why don't you take a seat," she said.

He sat down and said with as much politeness as the situation demanded, "Whatever you drink, I will drink."

She gave a quick laugh, saying, "If I have any more caffeine

I'll jump out that window!"Then she called through the open door, "Alex, two Perriers."

What was Perrier? In any case, he was pleased to note that in America there were ceremonious exchanges before business.

"So," she said, sliding into the chair facing him, "you are here at last! Somehow I expected you'd be older. Though what can one really tell from e-mails?"

He nodded, searching for a word to say about her age. Finally, he abandoned the effort in favor of a safer topic. "It is very warm today."

"That's for sure. California in March is a real treat if you're used to cold weather. It makes hanging a show so much easier. No tracking muddy slush into the gallery. We'll go over after lunch so you can check out the space. But first, I'm so eager to see everything!"

A young man entered and placed two glasses on the table. "Thanks, Alex," the woman said. The young man left, closing the door behind him. The woman took her glass and stood up. Kazu took his own and was momentarily confused. Were they not going to drink together first before looking at his work?

He stood, holding his glass.

She took a few gulps, then set her drink down. "We can lay everything out over there," she said, indicating the drafting table.

He made a slight bow and set his glass aside. He certainly wouldn't put it anywhere near his work.

He went to the drafting table, unzipped his portfolio and sat on the high stool facing the table. She stood behind him, peering over his shoulder, so close he could smell her perfume. He wished she would move back, but even if he knew the English words, he would never ask such a thing.

He removed the first painting and carefully laid it down, pleased to note that the table was free of dust. He peeled back the thin film of parchment to reveal *School Children*. Three boys, their schoolbooks scattered to the side of a country road, surrounded a school friend. She was bent forward over a fallen log, her uniform pushed up, her panties down around her knees. Two boys held her arms while a third flogged her bare bottom with the strap that had held his books.

"Such a delicate touch," the woman said. "The line is so subtle; the pigment is barely there." She leaned over his shoulder to better inspect the image. "It's terribly exciting to see the originals at last. What's next?"

Keeping the parchment behind *School Children*, he carefully laid it to one side, then brought out the picture entitled *Old Grandfather*. As in the classic late-nineteenth-century woodcuts of Japanese erotica, it showed a man peeping through a *shoji* screen to view the scene beyond: an old man, skinny and shriveled except for his engorged penis, which was pushed into a woman, her face wide in horror, her kimono torn.

"Ahh," said the woman. "In the tradition of *shunga*, with the Peeping Tom motif. Ingenious."

She knew about *shunga*! Kazu felt himself color at the compliment. So few foreigners understood the historical context of his work.

The next piece was his favorite, *Girl on a Swing*. The ground color was green, the girl done in pale pink, the swing red. She swung high, her pigtails flying. A man, laughing wildly, faced her. His kimono had fallen open, revealing a large erection. The girl had a frantic look on her face as she pumped furiously, the blue tie of her school uniform whipping behind her.

The American woman said nothing. Kazu waited for her to make a comment about the realistic depiction of the landscape. Or to notice the pale color of the girl's skin compared to the darker color of the man. Or perhaps to appreciate the perspective, slightly exaggerated to highlight the central figure. But her silence continued. He did not want to look at her, to indicate in any way that he was waiting. He sat still, hardly breathing.

What if she had had a sudden change of heart? Or worse, what if she had just been humoring him about the other pieces? Perhaps she was now considering how to politely reject everything.

But then she touched his back. He felt violated by so intimate a gesture. He glanced over his shoulder and saw that it was not her hand that was touching him, it was her body. She was leaning into him. He jumped to his feet.

"Mr. Takamura," she said excitedly, "I'm sorry. It's just that your work has moved me very much." She took a step backward and reached up to her scarf, loosening the knot.

His heart was racing. Was she going to remove her scarf? Why had she touched him? His paltry English left him entirely. His palms began to sweat.

She gave a nervous laugh. "I was looking at the girl swinging toward him and then back and then toward him." She spoke rapidly. The foreign words glanced off him like darts. She let her scarf fall to the ground.

"It is a painting," he said weakly.

Her eyes were ablaze. "His eagerness . . . her terror . . ." The color had risen in her cheeks. Suddenly she grabbed his hand and pushed it under her skirt, pressing it to her wet crotch. He let out a small cry as he drew his hand away, then reached back to brace himself against the table. With horror, he realized that his sticky palm had left a large smudge on *Girl on a Swing*.

"Mr. Takamura, please."

"*Gomen kudasai, gomen kudasai,*" he mumbled. He piled *Girl on a Swing* on top of *Old Grandfather* on top of *School Children*. She was still babbling about sexual fantasies and art. He stuffed the pictures into the portfolio. Not bothering to zip it, he grabbed it and headed for the door, eyes straight ahead.

"Mr. Takamura?" she called out in a bewildered whisper.

The receptionist looked up as he bolted from the room.

Country Miles

C ARLA ADDED IT up at the kitchen table Friday afternoon, just from curiosity, she told herself. It was sixteen
miles to Corley where she worked in the cafe: thirty-two
miles a day, Monday through Friday. Haverton, where her husband worked part-time to help pay for the farm, was twenty-
two miles in the opposite direction, forty-four a day. Adding a
weekly visit to either of their parents made it four hundred
twenty, not counting trips to the grocery store when something was forgotten or bowling every Thursday, she realized,
and who knew what else? She evened it up at five hundred,
an unimaginable distance to drive each week to end up back
in the same place. She felt a little weak just thinking of it.

She showed her husband when he got home but he said
people traveled more than that to get to work, oh, a lot more.
New York, say.

That didn't make five hundred miles any less, Carla thought,
and when her husband drove to Corley on Saturday to buy
insulation she realized five hundred was probably too low. She

rummaged in the bottom drawer of the desk until she found the atlas, opened it to Kansas, and studied the veins of red and blue and black roads.

At the bottom was the key: ten, twenty, fifty miles. She pulled a piece of string from the drawer, knotted what would be five hundred miles, placed one end near Corley where she supposed their house was, and stretched it out taut, gasping as the string stretched westward all the way across the state. She swung an arc, off the page at the bottom of the circle, into Iowa on its eastern sweep. Then she leafed back in the atlas to a two-page map of the United States, re-knotted the string for five hundred miles, put one end near where she assumed Corley was, and stretched the string out, randomly north, making a pencil mark at the end. And then again.

The next week Carla and her husband went bowling, he went into Corley for an extra day of shopping, and she had to go to her parents so that was well over five hundred. That week going to work she crossed the state line, the sign welcoming her to where she'd never been. There was more traffic and the highway widened into four lanes, then six. Later that day she drove through the thick forests she imagined surrounded Minneapolis, its shiny glass buildings rising up as far as she could see. She smiled at the dozens of trains streaming in from every direction and back out again, carrying thousands of workers reading magazines or staring out the windows at her, coffee cups in their hands.

The next week her parents invited them for Sunday dinner and afterward they took her grandmother to Roland to visit the cemetery. At least six hundred miles, she thought.

That week she headed on north, entering Canada. She stopped for coffee and when she paid she got back dozens of bills, scarlet, pink, golden, light blue. When she stopped for

lunch everyone in the cafe spoke French and she ate, confused and delighted, paying with the rainbow assortment of
money. That night she accepted the offer of a place to stay
from a tall handsome Frenchman she'd met at a restaurant. He
had an apartment with tall glass windows overlooking a river
and she stood there a long time, watching the lights flicker on
the water.

The next week, she drove to Corley and back and back
again and back again, driving to bowling on Thursday and
having to run into Haverton two extra times.

Continuing north, she stopped for a glorious half hour in
a traffic jam as a herd of polar bears padded across the highway with a slow powerful stride, tossing their heads back and
forth. Later that afternoon she glimpsed Hudson Bay to her
right, passing several men hitchhiking, coonskin tails from the
backs of their hats, long rifles in their hands. She didn't dare
stop but she smiled and they lifted their hats and waved as she
sped past.

That week they visited his parents and then hers. He had
to come back home twice at lunch to pick up something
she'd forgotten to give him, and she purposely took the long
way home each day so it was over eight hundred miles
between them.

That week the settlements thinned out and there were
fewer and fewer cars. Gusts of snow blew off the white lumpy
fields on both sides, obscuring the road which got thinner
and thinner in front of her. She began to see igloos at the side
of the road, brown-skinned and tight-faced people squatting
in front. A few of the small children, black eyes peering out
from under the ruff of their hoods, half smiled and pointed as
she sped on.

The next week she got in the car after her husband had

left, took a deep breath, and turned the key. The engine roared and white sharp granules of snow gusted across the windshield as the car lurched forward.

Now there was no road and she maneuvered past hummocks of blue ice, swollen up like frozen bubbles on either side. A couple of times she saw an old ship with tall masts crumpled in a frozen cove or lying on its side, half buried in a cliff of silver. The wind whistled through the crack of the window and she felt the cold seeping into the car. She put a rag from the back seat over the wheel but still felt its numbness creeping into her hands. The sun was a half-obliterated disk, low on the eastern horizon in a thick cloud of snow, and in the darker west and north, a curved rainbow—the northern lights she remembered painting as a child, smooth stripes of blue, purple, red, orange—rose up into the sky, an archway through which she would pass, miles beyond miles, until she was out of reach of even distance itself.

ROY KESEY

Scroll

I T TOOK THIRTY-FOUR years. He ate mostly raw garlic, and flour mixed with creek water, and occasionally splurged on noodles. He found work when necessary, plumbing and roofing and sometimes welding as well, but spent all other waking hours at the easel and now at last it was finished: the entire mountain range, minus the boring parts, the individually stretched and primed and painted swatches stitched into a single canvas seven feet high and nine miles long.

By the time he was done, of course, many parts of the range were no longer as he'd painted them. Towns had been born, towns had aged, towns had died. Roads had been laid, had washed away. Quarries had cut holes, saws had cut trees, and the range as a whole was several thousandths of an inch shorter due mainly to rain and wind.

He tried not to think about this; thought instead of transportation, and hitched a ride to the Big M outside Albany. There he found a flatbed independent in ostrich-skin boots, mucky emerald Kenworth with sapphire antennas and Brueghel on the bug screen.

He asked, and the man said it was maybe the load he'd been waiting for all his life. They deadheaded southwest, the jake brake on maxi as they fell down the hills; they hired junkies to help disassemble, to load and tie down. Then they aimed the rig toward the center of all meaningful things at that moment. The trucker turned on the radio and the painter sang harmonies until asked to please just stop. The mountains scrolled by outside.

—Seventy nine thousand, six hundred and eighteen pounds, said the trucker when they stopped on the scales. Little heavier than I thought, but we'll be all right.

—It can't weigh that much, said the painter. I used seven-ounce cotton duck and painted thin.

—I'm talking the whole shebang, said the trucker. Your picture there, plus the BCW, the oil and diesel, the mud on the flaps and the dust on the dashboard, me and you and the trailer tongue, the fresh water and gray water and black water and whatnot. But even dirty as she is, and I hate to see her this way, just hate it—I'll get you washed soon, old girl, and that's a promise, reverse osmosis or deionized rinse, whatever your heart desires—at seventy nine thousand six hundred and eighteen pounds we're still inside the GVWR, is what I'm saying. We'll be just fine, is what I'm saying.

He bought the painter a Snickers and a Coke, lent him a Skoal cap to keep his ass from getting kicked by other truckers, and they waited in line to clear. The painter had run out of blue a mile from the end of the canvas, had used grays instead, but blue is kindness and grays are greed, that's what he'd always heard. He worried. He ate his Snickers and drank his Coke. He climbed back in the rig when the trucker told him it was time, and sat straighter than he otherwise might.

Again under way, the trucker pissed into empty bottles, held forth on Red Man and Rothko, clicked on the CB and picked up the mike. He chatted with Whambam, with Twelve-Finger Sammy, with the Big Black Bitch. They talked of roadwork and law enforcement and highway chiaroscuro. Six hours of this. Then the arrival.

THE GALLERY OWNERS looked and grinned and all said the same thing: A bit long for the living room, don't you think?

The painter composed a smile each time, and explained the imagined means: stainless steel scrolling posts five hundred yards apart, some minor questions of grommets and scaffolds and bearings and gears, a week to work up, ten days at the most. The trucker stood off to the side, cocked his head, watched the dealers pace and visualize.

—Are we talking Banvardian panoramism, or something more along the lines of Li Yushan at the Three Gorges?

—Neither, really, though a bit of both, I guess.

—And how do you plan to film it?

—I don't.

—You're sure? I'm thinking a video installation of some kind, with maybe—

—Nope.

—So this would be nothing but a scroll, scrolling.

—Exactly.

—No thanks, then. But thanks all the same.

When there were no remaining galleries to refuse him, the painter tried with municipal authorities, with co-op managers, with community college administrators. But they weren't sure. They couldn't say. They didn't think so, but were very glad he'd stopped by.

The painter told the trucker about the problem with blue and grays, asked if he had any ideas.

—Nothing wrong with your picture, said the trucker. These folks just aren't with the program, so fuck 'em and on down the road.

—Except there isn't anywhere for me to go at the moment, art-wise.

—Figuratively, is what I'm saying.

—This isn't helping.

The trucker shrugged.

—So maybe what you do is, you set up your scrollers and you film for a while. Middle lane is what I'm saying.

—But it isn't a goddamn film. It's a painting, scrolled, end of story.

—Just thinking out loud here, bud. Just trying to help.

—I know. Sorry.

—Okey-doke, then.

—Indeed.

The trucker took his cash, dropped the painter off at an empty warehouse, scribbled down the number of a Tulsa truck stop payphone just in case. The painter sat still for a day. Then he hit the want ads, plumbed and roofed and welded to stay flush with flour and garlic, waited for an idea, and none came.

He circled and spun, swore and decided okay then, all right: digital video of the scrolling scroll, doing in time what no one wanted in space. Edgy was how he imagined it, light and darkness, cornices and crags. He borrowed equipment, built a small-scale version of the imagined means, filmed and filmed and in a month it was done: seventeen hours of moving mountains.

The gallery owners and municipal authorities and co-op managers and community college administrators were each thrilled and proposed significant editing. Cut it down to eight minutes, they said, and you've got a deal.

—It is not a group of pieces, said the painter. It is a single thing.

—A single impossibly long thing. Eight minutes, nine minutes tops, and we're good to go.

The painter thanked them for their input, walked out to the parking lots and keyed their cars. He then grew old very quickly—constipation, osteoarthritis, pigmentary glaucoma. He could no longer paint, could no longer weld or roof, could barely plumb. This, then, was it: his one large bit of art was what there was to be, his sole source of sustenance if he was to be sustained, and now an idea, a final idea, an unpleasant but only remaining option.

No local driver wanted the load—too heavy, they said, uninsured, they said, no way I want no hairy-leg riding along, they said—so he called the Tulsa payphone every twenty minutes for eleven days, at last got the trucker and they worked to agreement. Fifty-one hours later the rig arrived, mud on the flaps, dust on the dashboard, the trucker strung on meth and smiling. They loaded up, and with scrolling posts included they were no longer inside the GVWR, but the trucker twitched twice, cocked his head, said they'd give it a go all the same.

They skirted the scales, paralleled the mountains, tried lake-towns and failed. They tried river-towns, and failed there too. They tried everywhere else and at last fell into luck: Thrombaccus had aged but not died, was sick of its sickened view and would have them. Ten days, then, and nearly as planned, a kiosk raised, the questions of grommets and scaffolds and bearings and gears answered, the posts installed five hundred yards apart between the town and its mountains sullied by quarries and clear-cuts and roads.

It was one a.m. when they started the pull, the trucker up high and the painter down low, flashlights in their mouths as they walked the edge of the painting toward the far post; it was six a.m. when they finished, the dawn sky opening behind them, the edge now secured, just the two men and the vast stretch of paint, light and darkness, cornices and crags. They stood and looked. They nodded and shook their heads.

—Nice little picture you got here, said the trucker.

—Thank you.

—Still and all. Shame it had to come to this.

The painter agreed, but was fairly sure there were worse things. He paid the trucker, tipped him a case of Snickers, waved as the rig pulled away, and now people were coming to look. He stepped into the kiosk. He took up his bullhorn. He breathed deeply once and began to chant, A Dollar a Turn for a Chance to Paint on a Painting!

The good people of Thrombaccus would mainly paint more quarries, more clear-cuts, more roads, he knew, except for the children who'd perhaps paint giraffes; there would also be screeds and sermons, ads and aphorisms, Fuck You! and Asswipe! and Greta Please Come Home! When the current stretch was fully marred and they wanted their old new old view back, he'd run the scroll and they could start again. So it would go and the canvas would outlast his body; too bad, yes, but sustaining, and still a single thing, and as the line begins to form he imagines the postcard he'll one day send to Tulsa: All is well. Blue is kindness and grays are greed, but you already knew that. Keep her clean, is what I'm saying.

CHRISSY KOLAYA

Swimming for Shore

IT WAS A beautiful boat.

In Indiana we'd taken it out almost every weekend. Jake did everything—he watched the wind, kept the sails full and his hands busy tying the rope into thick, sturdy knots. I mainly stayed out of the way as the boom swung port to starboard, the sail snapping crisply in the wind.

At night I still hear the water lapping against the boat, all around me.

I was there when he drowned. Though I try not to tell anyone. When I do, the same questions pass over their faces like clouds on a clear sky.

What happened?
In Chicago we'd found a two-bedroom apartment in Humboldt Park. One bedroom for us, one office to share. From the living room window, a view of the playground across the street.

We weren't engaged. (*Well, at least it's not that tragic*, people think when I tell them.) We probably would have gotten married. Maybe a year from then. Maybe later. Maybe he had a ring stashed away for the right moment. Who knew?

His mother flew in from Massachusetts the weekend after his funeral to pack up his things. She rented a Ryder truck and drove his clothes—the smell of him—to the East Coast in one long drive alone.

She left his books, all the dry dusty paper. Left the two pieces of furniture we'd bought together one afternoon at Ikea. A sofa in bright red and a nightstand we'd argued over. In the end, he'd given me my way. And in the end, it was him who'd been right. Its cartoonish blue color had grown cloying after three weeks and I wished we'd chosen the brown.

She took the papers that mounded over his desk—bills, his address book, his computer. But she left the desk. It still sits next to mine, empty.

I tried to be out of the house while she packed. I didn't want to have conversations with her in which she held out something of his I remembered fiercely, asking, "Would you like to keep this?"

I wanted her to take it all.

Before she left, we had dinner together at the Italian restaurant around the corner. It was dark inside. Candle-lit booths and burgundy vinyl. We poked at our food, each of us pretending that we were here for the other one because *it just didn't look as if she were eating.* She told me how much she'd always liked me, how she always thought Jake and I would end up together.

I felt proud, that pleasing feeling of being approved of.

Then I remembered that he was dead. That his body had been pulled from Lake Michigan early Monday morning during rush hour as cars passed yards away heading north or south on Lake Shore Drive, and that how she felt about me didn't really matter much these days.

HE HAD THIS habit of putting his hand flat on top of his head when he was thinking.

Were you the stronger swimmer?
I hated talking about it. Hated being the girl whose boyfriend died, the receiver of patient nods, magnanimous gestures of kindness.

At parties now there are always people who haven't heard. "Where's Jake these days?" they ask when they see me by myself.

Sometimes I want to fuck with people. Once, I let myself. This guy, Bill, from Jake's graduate program who I'd always disliked cornered me in a conversation at a party three weeks after. It was the first time I'd been out since and somehow he hadn't yet heard.

He leaned against the doorway, a glass of wine in his hand. "So, how's your boyfriend?"

It was one of the things about him I'd always disliked— how he'd always referred to Jake as my boyfriend rather than by name.

"Dead," I'd answered. A perfect solid stare I'd practiced in the mirror a hundred times. As I always imagined, it shut him up.

It's a cheap kind of power, I know. But it felt good at the time.

How did he drown?
The weekend after we'd moved to Chicago we'd gone to an art opening in our neighborhood. It had been a kind of

joke—an installation of awful paintings the gallery owners had scrounged up at thrift shops across the city. We drank Franzia in plastic cups as we strolled around laughing at the paintings—*Torment of the Soul* and *Circus of Despair*. Our favorite was a picture of two birds in a tree, their arms around each other in a kind of anthropomorphic embrace called *Love Is Being Out on a Limb Together.*

"We should totally buy that," Jake said.

"Are you kidding me? Why would we spend money on that—they probably bought it for four dollars. Besides, we should spend our money on things we actually need, like bookshelves."

I was forever begging Jake to stop buying books. He seemed to bring home three or four a day. "And can you imagine having to look at that every day?"

"I'd tell people you painted it," he said.

How did you manage to save yourself?
The summer before we moved to Chicago we bought a kayak together—our first joint purchase, a kind of forced confidence in the relationship. At night we practiced rolling it in the pool of our apartment complex after the swimmers were gone. Lit with lights under the water, the pool glowed turquoise all around us.

He taught me how to dislodge from the kayak when it capsized, and how to roll it over together, like fighter pilots, a choreographed dance.

I'd been scared at first, imagining being trapped upside down under the water, my legs held tight inside the boat and panicking. But Jake was patient. He leaned to the left. I felt the boat tip as we went over, the rush of water. I opened my eyes as he pulled us over with the oar, and felt the cool summer air as we surfaced.

"Were you scared?" he asked.

Around us the cicadas hummed, the smell of chlorine stung my nostrils. I didn't answer.

PEOPLE ALWAYS SAY, "Oh, God. I'm so sorry."

Then you can tell they have about a million questions bubbling up into their mouths, ready to be asked. Some people ask. Other people don't. The weird thing is that I find that I like the ones who ask better.

The water that day was mostly calm. Later the wind picked up, and Jake thought we should head back. It was a wave that came out of the blue that tossed us.

He was the stronger swimmer. And when I tell people this, they always want it to be extra ironic—like he was on the college swim team or something like that. A perfect ironic package.

We both swam for the shore. One minute he was behind me. The next, the water lay flat and endless over my shoulder, nothing to break the horizon.

The boat righted itself finally, tossed by another wave, a lucky trick that set it right in the water again. When I reached the beach, I crawled along the sand and turned around. I saw it from the shore, the crisp sail against the wide blue sky. I thought he'd gotten back on.

A month later, I found a report posted on the Internet. "Water-related fatalities in Lake Michigan, August 2002– September 2002."

Date/Time: September 29/5:50 p.m.
Water body/County: Lake Michigan/Cook.
Number of fatalities/Age: 1/29.

Accident type/Cause of death: Capsized/drowning.
Boat type/Size: Sail/17 ft.
Personal floatation devices: No.
Alcohol involved: No.
Summary: Boat capsized during gusty winds and high chop on the lake. Victim and companion attempted to swim to shore.

I was the companion, thus not the victim. Thus, my feet found the solid pavement each morning, my hands the cool water from the showerhead. And each evening, my tongue a full glass of wine.

Why did it happen? I couldn't tell you. Sometimes I imagine the tidy narratives: he'd eaten—yes! Less than an hour before! He'd never learned to swim and now here it was, back to bite him in the ass. He'd tried to save me, lost himself in the process. Selfless. Brave. Ready to give his life for mine.

Once, as we were walking home on a dark street, menacing in its emptiness, he told me that he'd take a bullet for me. That he loved me that much. More than himself.

But I know that it's not true. That he wouldn't. Or at least, that I wouldn't.

The truth is, like everyone, we tried to save ourselves. Films are always full of moving scenes where the mother throws her own body over her child in the hail of bullets, where endlessly big-hearted elderly ladies give up their seats on the *Titanic's* last lifeboat.

It wasn't like that. I swam to save myself. He tried to save himself.

Though that's not what I told his mother. She believes he was a hero. That he gave me the only life vest, though the truth is, there weren't any. It's best for her to believe this. It gives her someone to hate for living while her only son sinks beneath the water.

I couldn't have saved him. His eyes were a deep green just above the waterline, the lake around us bright blue, and the water endless below. I watched the shoreline and its slow approach as I pulled myself through the water. Behind me, probably the top of his head was slipping below the water. Probably he reached out for me.

Mud

THIS MORNING I found my grandmother sitting at the kitchen table. She had been dead almost five years, but here she was now, sitting in my wife's old seat, covered in mud. I almost didn't recognize her because the mud had flattened her hair and darkened her normally pale skin. She said it wasn't easy digging her way out of the grave and that it took most of the night, and wasn't I going to at least offer her a glass of tomato juice?

"I don't get it," I said. "You're here?"

She said, "Am I going to have to ask twice for that juice?"

When she was alive, my grandmother's biggest pet peeve was having to ask twice for something she wanted. I poured her some juice.

"Grandma," I said, "I hate to say this, but today is not a good day. I have to be at the office early for a meeting, eight sharp. People are counting on me."

She stared at me, as if the tie I had on was all wrong.

"I have responsibilities and commitments that I can't get

out of. It's a big day. They need me there today."

It was then that I heard the television in the living room. "Who's watching the television?" I asked.

"Your father," she said.

"He's here, too?" I walked into the living room and found him sitting on the couch, mud all over his face and his arms and his hair.

"Dad?" I said. "What are you doing here?"

"Is that any way to greet your father?" he said. Turning to my grandmother, he said: "In seven years he hasn't seen me, and this is how he greets me?"

"You're getting mud on his remote, dear," said my grandmother. He glared at his mother and rolled his eyes.

"Excuse me, Dad," I said, "but you're supposed to be dead."

He handed me my remote, mud all over the buttons. I held it away from my suit so I wouldn't get dirty.

"There's nothing on," he said.

When my father was alive, he loved watching television. He watched two hours of it before he went to his job at the phone company, then five more hours when he came home. His favorite show was *All in the Family*. He loved that show. Seeing him there in front of the television, hunched over with his hands resting flat on his stomach, injured me in the best possible way.

"I want to hug you," I said to my father. "But I have a meeting to get to. I can't afford to be late."

"You look sharp, kiddo," he said. The way he called me kiddo made me forget about work for a second. I had forgotten about kiddo. "Really, kiddo," he said. "You look like a million bucks."

"You think so?" I said.

Both of them nodded.

"I'd hug you guys, but I don't want to ruin my suit, you know?"

"Don't worry about it," said Grandma.

"I am worried about it," I said. "I never got to hug you goodbye, Grams."

"I was in Cleveland," she said.

"Still, I wish that I could've given you a proper goodbye."

"It's O.K."

"No it isn't," I said.

I spread my arms and walked towards her, but she backed away.

"Better not, kiddo," said my father. "You'll get dirty."

"I don't care," I said.

I turned to him and tried to throw my arms around his muddy neck, but he backed away from me as well.

"You've got a big day ahead of you," he said. "A really big day."

The phone rang. It was my boss, reminding me not to forget the reports. He sounded nervous. I asked him if I should bring anything besides the reports. He told me to bring my good sense and my sound judgment and the right frame of mind. Then he hung up.

While I was on the phone, my father and grandmother moved to the couch, tracking mud all over the carpet and the furniture. It tired me to look at it, gathering at their feet.

"I can't do this," I said. "Not now." I didn't know what exactly I couldn't do.

"Yes you can," said my father. "You can do this."

He raised his arm, as if he meant to give me a high five, but then he remembered the mud, and folded his arms at his waist.

I gathered all the reports that were stacked on the dining

room table and placed them neatly in my briefcase, then buckled it shut.

"I'm so sorry," I called to them. "I have to leave. I wish that I didn't, but I have to go now."

"We understand," said Grandma. "Don't you worry, darling."

"I can't help it," I said. "I always worry. Always. Always."

"Take a deep breath," came a new voice from the study.

It was my wife. Two years ago she died of cancer, but now I heard her voice from the study. I froze. Then I held my briefcase to my chest, wrapped my arms around it, and squeezed.

"Honey," I said. "Is that you?"

"You bet," she called back.

"I don't know how to tell you this," I said. "But I have to leave."

"I know," she said. "You've got a big day."

The next moment held a thoughtful silence.

"I'm not coming in there," I said finally.

"I know," she said.

My chest tightened. I wanted to run into the study and throw my arms around her and kiss her mouth and tell her how much I couldn't stand not having her around, but I knew if I went in there, she'd be covered in mud, too, and I had my life to think about, the life that was, any minute, going to start without me.

I went back into the living room and stood in front of my dead father and grandmother, briefcase still pressed to my chest. My briefcase had become like one of those square cushions that can also be used as a flotation device. Though I stood still, I felt like my legs were kicking.

"Show me the way out of here," I said.

My father got up and came within a few inches of me, making sure none of his mud touched the sleeves of my blazer. He leaned in, breath smelling like damp earth, and said: "I'm sorry we brought her here. She wasn't supposed to say anything. That was the deal. She was supposed to listen and not say a thing."

"It's O.K.," I said. "I'm glad she came. I just hate running out like this."

He nodded, then said, "Follow me."

I followed him to the front door, bow-legged over the wake of mud, so I wouldn't get dirty. Last night, after finishing my final report, I had used a half a tin of black Kiwi on my shoes. Buffed them until I thought I could see myself in the leather. I don't know why, but now the whole idea of rubbing black gunk on my shoes to make them look better confounded me. It made me think: does anything really get clean?

My father opened the door. There must have been mica in the mud because his legs sparkled when sunlight entered the room. I thought for a moment that standing there, framed by the doorway, he meant to use his body to wall me in and keep me from going outside, where now I heard birds and passing cars and, every few seconds, the sound of a hammer, rapping in the hollow belly of someone's garage. But then he moved to the side, and I looked back towards the study, wondering if I should go in there, if it would be wise to go in there on the biggest day of my life. I listened for her, but all I heard was her silence. Her silence gave me a mother of a headache, like someone pounding a nail in the back of my head. If she'd spoken again, I'd have gone to her, but, lucky for me, I think, she didn't, and what I heard instead was my neighbor's hammer, calling me out.

Feelers

"AN ENTOMOLOGIST, DID you say?" says Harlan, incredulous. He's been here at the Bougainvillea Resort and Spa about an hour and already something wild is happening to him. "From the Greek *entomon*, insect? From the neuter of *entomos*, cut up, from *temnein*, to cut?"

"Um, I guess so," says the woman standing next to him—head cocked, arms akimbo—before the rack of brochures. "Bugs."

"Because you see I'm an etymologist," says Harlan. "Entomologist, etymologist, don't you think that's kind of uncanny?"

"Etymologist?" says the woman. "Like, words?"

"Right," says Harlan. "From the Greek *etymon*, from *etymos*, true, and of course *logion*, diminutive of *logos*"—no way to stop himself when he's wound this tight—"a saying, especially a saying of Christ's. Can I buy you a drink?"

"Sure," says the woman. "My name's Miriam."

"Harlan," says Harlan.

They place their orders—gin and tonic for Harlan, virgin
Caesar for Miriam ("Hal" from Harlan)—and wander out
onto a little patio overlooking one of the pools. It's dusk, but
birds still—mockingbirds, presumably, as promised by the
resort's literature. Poring over the pamphlet at home a few
weeks ago, Harlan strove to imagine the mockingbird's
evening cry. He failed. Failure comes easily to Harlan. Most
recently he failed at marriage. This trip, an impulsive purchase
which will max out all three of his credit cards, was inspired
by the arrival of his divorce papers.

Harlan and Miriam take seats at a lime table by a potted
palm with a view of the setting sun—a hot-pink smear over
the tennis courts—cross their legs and start chatting. During
their conversation they discover all sorts of things about one
another. They discover that they're both from Toronto, that
they've both just arrived at the Bougainvillea Resort and Spa,
that they were both on the same flight, Harlan in seat 7E
(seven, coincidentally, being the most blessed of all numbers
according to the faith of her fathers, to say nothing of her
mothers), Miriam in seat 34D (Harlan's eyebrows going up
here—the figure's just about right, judging by the trippy dis-
tortion of the stripes on her blouse). They discover that
Harlan had the chicken, Miriam the pasta. They discover that
neither of them ever goes on a vacation like this, or has a
spouse, or a child.

Inevitably, though, the things they discover about one
another are way outnumbered by the things they don't discover about one another. For example, Miriam doesn't discover that as a boy Harlan indulged in a dark practice for
which he later coined the term *entomosadism*—yanking not
the limbs but the antennae, the fine feelers, from various
creepy-crawlies. Nor does she discover that Harlan is here

recovering from his botched marriage, a knowledge which, a couple of months down the road, will fill her with remorse. Harlan, for his part, doesn't discover that as a girl Miriam consistently misheard the Torah passage, "I will make him an help meet for him" (God taking pity on his lonesome man of clay), as "I will make him an elk meat form." Worse, perhaps, he doesn't discover that Miriam is here recovering (still) from the loss of her child, a baby girl known as Toots who died at the age of three hours, before she could get herself a proper name—all of this nine years ago now, when Miriam was twenty-five years old. A couple of months down the road this knowledge will inspire in him a sense of awe for the human heart—Miriam's, for example, and his own—the depth to which it can be damaged, the weird miracle of its healing.

For the next ten days, though, the two will flourish in a state of blissful ignorance of these and umpteen other details. They'll come to adore one another's little quirks, the affected way Harlan has of twirling his walking stick—a brass-and-mahogany heirloom from somebody else's family he scooped at a swap meet years ago, and has never since gone without—or the way Miriam bares her teeth like a baboon on the cusp of each orgasm.

"Love," Harlan will sigh, "from the Old English *lufu*, akin to the Latin *lubere*, to please."

A couple of months from now, when Miriam dumps Harlan, she'll do it with a gift, a plastic terrarium which will appear, at first, to be bereft of life. Taped to the glass will be this note:

Harlan, my dear, this is a carausius morosus, a "walking stick"— thought you'd enjoy the wordplay. I've named her Toots, after the little girl I lost many years ago. I'm sorry I could never bring myself to tell you. She likes brambles, please, fresh every day. She'll have babies, even though she has no mate. Do you know the word parthenogenesis? Of course you do. I'm afraid that pill I popped every morning wasn't THE pill, as I let you assume, it was just something for my allergies. Again, I'm sorry. I wanted your height, and your intellect—a flair for the humanities to balance out my science. And anyway I liked you, I really did. I swear to God I won't come after you for child support. Please just forgive me, if you can, and then forget us. Love, Babs

Eventually Harlan will spot her, a greenish bug about the length of his pinky, a stick with six stick-legs and two antennae. "Hello, Toots," he'll say. "Parthenogenesis," he'll say, "from the Greek *parthenos*, virgin, and Latin *genesis*. Virgin birth, baby." Harlan will wonder whether he's ever had anything irreplaceable, whether he's lost it. Brambles? he'll wonder. Where the hell am I going to find brambles in this town?

ELIZABETH BERG

The Party

THERE WERE A bunch of us who had drawn together into a corner of the dining room. It was a big party, and none of us had met before. But a tiny core of women of a certain age had drawn more women until there were enough of us that we needed to be democratic about talking—each of us needed to be careful not to take up too much airtime.

We were talking about kissing, and we spoke rapidly and excitedly and laughed loudly. This was T-shirt and jeans laughter, not cocktail dress laughter—it came from the belly, not the chest. It was size fourteen and not size two. When one of us made moves toward some wilting hors d'oeuvre, the rest would stall, so that nothing good was missed by anyone.

We seemed to like best telling about our first times. There was a glamorous blonde wearing huge diamond studs who said she first kissed at age eleven, while playing spin the bottle on a hot Texas night. The rule was that after the spin, the chosen couple would go into the kitchen, stand by the washing machine stationed in the corner, and kiss. No tongues.

The blonde modified the rule to include no lips. Cheeks. That was all. But a certain Paul Drummond was too fast for her that night, and smacked a kiss right on her mouth. She said she'd intended to get angry, but instead backed with pleasant shock into the washer hard enough to make a noise that roused the supposedly supervising parent from sleep. The kissing stopped; the party broke up, and the blonde went home, where she stayed awake much of the night reenacting the scene in her mind, and telling herself that the sin was venial, venial, venial.

A woman named Vicky said she spent years in practice with her best friend Mary Jo. "We would put a pillow between our faces, kneel down on my bed, rub each other's backs, and kiss that pillow to *death*." We all laughed some more, because we'd all kissed pillows, it seemed.

One woman wearing a seductively cut black dress that now seemed beside the point ventured bravely that she and her best friend Sherry had dispensed with the pillow and gone at it lip to lip. You could tell from the ripple effect of lowered eyes that she wasn't the only one. I thought of fourth grade and my friend Mary, whom I asked to be the wife so I could be the husband. I liked to be the husband—you got to say when about everything. While she dusted, I went to work. When I came home, we kissed hello for what became long enough that we decided we'd better start playing outside.

There was a serious, shy-looking woman named Jane who hadn't said much of anything, and who, when she laughed, had actually put her hand up over her mouth. *Oh, honey*, I wanted to say to her, when I saw her do that. *Sweetheart, come here and let's give you some tools.* She wore a dress with buttons that went high up on her neck, and each one was closed. I was pretty surprised to hear her say, "Oh well, kissing was one thing, but do you remember the first time you touched a dick?"

Now we were all into high gear. We were beside ourselves in our eagerness to share our experiences. We drew closer.

A roving rent-a-waiter dressed in tight black pants, a blindingly white shirt, and a black bow tie offered us little bundles of something from his tray. All of us, to a woman, took one. The waiter seemed very pleased. I waited for him to move on, then greedily opened: "I was forced. This guy called 'Telephone Pole Taylor,' for the very reason you might suspect, pulled my hand down and held it there until I had touched it for five seconds. We counted together. I almost threw up. I was a serious virgin, and I damn near passed out at the thought that kind of thing would someday . . . But after I got over the size, I became kind of intrigued by the texture."

Vicky's eyes widened. "Yes! Like damp velvet, right?"

Jane, standing next to me, sighed quietly. "I don't know," she said. "Men's bodies are just not *pretty*. That makes it difficult. I think women's bodies are, though, and I'm not, you know . . ." We knew. She took a sip from her drink, leaned her head against the wall, frowned in a contemplative sort of way. "It turned out that penises weren't so bad, really, although it did take me a long time to get used to that rising and falling routine. I mean, it was grotesque the first time I saw an erection. It was like a monster movie."

The gorgeous blonde spoke up. "I *liked* it! I thought it was so *magical*." But then, as though protecting Jane, she added hastily, "But not beautiful, of course . . ." We drank to that.

"It's the balls that get me," Vicky said. "They're like kiwifruit gone bad." We burst out laughing again. I think we felt that we were becoming dangerous, careening in our conversation, and we liked it. We were ready to reveal anything about ourselves. Almost imperceptibly, the circle tightened again.

"I think it's all a matter of cultural conditioning," I said, and was met with a friendly collective groan. "No, I mean it. If we'd been taught to go after a penis by a mother who winked at us when she talked about it, and if all the boys at those drive-in movies had covered their privates with both hands and moaned little protests to our ears, we'd have been *wild* to touch them. Instead, we pulled their hands down from our tits and up from their crotches."

Jane put her empty glass on the floor. "I think men and women are just hopelessly different. It's a wonder we get along at all. Sometimes the smallest things can bring out the biggest things. I had a horrible fight with my husband last night, and you know what started it?" We were all listening hard, and we didn't notice the approach of Jane's husband from across the room. But Jane did. She stopped talking and stared at him: in her eyes, it was as though a shade had been pulled.

He stood at the edge of our circle, a little wary. "What's going on over *here*?"

There was a beat; no one answered. And then Jane said, "Oh, you know. Just girl talk." I think we were all miffed by her response, but no one challenged it.

Her husband looked at his watch. "It's time to go."

Jane didn't budge. "I'd like to stay for a while."

"Oh?" He put his hands in his pockets. "All right. That's fine." He didn't move. Another beat. Silence all around. Then two of us simultaneously moved toward the food table. Someone else walked off toward the bathroom. Vicky waved to a man across the room and started for him. Our group fell apart in a sad, slow-motion sort of way, as when petals leave a blossom past its prime. And then I heard Jane say, "I guess it is late."

I listened to her say goodbye to the people around her. I was dragging a piece of pita bread through the leftover hummus tracks at the bottom of a pottery bowl. I was hoping the potter used no lead. I was wondering what my children were doing.

I thought about what I had to do the next day as I finished my drink. Then I looked around for my husband. He was in the living room discussing the Middle East conflict with a short, mildly overweight, balding man. I imagined the man in the front seat of a car at a drive-in, thirty years ago. I gave him hair, but otherwise I didn't change him much.

I sat in a chair close by and heard my husband say emphatically that Israel fought only defensive wars. I fiddled with the hem of my skirt and wondered what it was Jane and her husband had fought about. Several possibilities occurred to me. I heard the short man ask my husband what he did for a living. Sports would be next. I turned my head away from them and permitted myself a yawn.

I thought, Here is how I feel about men: I am angry at them for the way they sling their advantage about—interrupting, taking over, forcing endings, pretending to not understand what equality between the sexes necessitates, thus ensuring that they are always and forever the ones who say when. But I feel sorry for them, too.

I remembered a red-eye flight I was on recently. At about four a.m., I fell into one of those poor-quality sleeps. I woke up about twenty minutes later and took a stroll down the aisle. The plane was packed with businessmen, and they all lay sleeping, their briefcases at their feet like obedient dogs. They had blankets with the airline's imprint over them, but the too-small covers had slid to one side or the other, revealing gaps between buttons on the dress shirts, revealing fists slightly clenched. They looked so sweet then, so honest and vulnerable. I felt a great love toward all of them, and smiled warmly into each sleeping face.

RON HANSEN

My Kid's Dog

MY KID'S DOG died.
Sparky.
I hated that dog.
The feeling was mutual.

We got off on the wrong foot. Whining in his pen those first nights. My squirt gun in his face and him blinking from the water. And then the holes in the yard. The so-called accidents in the house. His nose snuffling into my Brooks Brothers trousers. Him slurping my fine Pilsner beer or sneaking bites of my Dagwood sandwich when I fell asleep on the sofa. Also his inability to fetch, to take a joke, to find the humor in sudden air horns. To be dandled, roughhoused, or teased. And then the growling, the skulking, the snapping at my ankles, the hiding from me under the house, and literally thousands of abject refusals to obey. Like, *Who the hell are you?*

You'd have thought he was a cat. When pushed to the

brink I shouted, "I'll cut your face off and show it to you," and the small-brained mammal just stared at me.

But with the kids or my wife little Foo-Foo was a changeling, conning them with the tail, the prance, the peppiness, the soft chocolate eyes, the sloppy expressions of love, the easy tricks that if I performed I'd get no credit for.

Oh, we understood each other all right. I was on to him.

And then, at age ten, and none too soon, he kicked the bucket. You'd think that would be it. End of story. But no, he had to get even.

Those who have tears, prepare to shed them.

I was futzing with the hinges on the front-yard gate on a Saturday afternoon, my tattersall shirtsleeves rolled up and mind off in Oklahoma, when I noticed Fido in the California shade, snoozing, but for once a little wistful too, and far more serene than he usually was in my offensive presence. I tried to surprise him with my standard patriarchal shout, but it was no go, so I walked over and prodded the little guy with my wingtip. Nothing doing. And not so much as a flutter in his oddly abstracted face. Surely this was the big sleep, I thought.

She who must be obeyed was at the mall, provisioning, so I was safe from objection or inquiry on that account. I then made an inventory of my progeny: Buzz in the collegiate East, in the realm of heart-attack tuitions, Zack in the netherworld of the surf shop, Suzy, my last kid, on her bike and somewhere with her cousin. Were I to bury Rover with due haste and dispatch I could forestall the waterworks, even convince them that he'd signed up with the circus, run afoul of Cruella De Vil—anything but died.

I got a green tarpaulin from the garage and laid it out on the front lawn where I hesitated before using my shoe to roll

Spot into his funeral shroud, then dragged him back into the victory garden where summer's dying zucchini plants were in riot. With trusty spade I dug his burial place, heaped earth atop him, tamped it down with satisfying *whump*s.

I was feeling good about myself, heroic, as if, miraculously, compassion and charity had invaded not only my bones but my sinewy muscle tissues. I fixed myself a tall glass of gin and tonic and watched the first quarter of the USC football game.

And then pangs of conscience assailed me. Hadn't my investigation of said demise of Precious been rather cursory? Wouldn't I, myself, closely cross-examine a suspect whose emotions were clouded, whose nefarious wishes were well established, whose veterinary skills were without credential? The innocence of my childhood had been spoiled with the tales of Edgar Allan Poe, so it was not difficult to conjure images of Scruffy clawing through tarpaulin and earth as he fought for one last gasp of air, air that others could more profitably use.

I marched out to the garden with aforementioned spade and with great lumbar strain exhumed our darling lapdog. Considering the circumstances, he seemed none the worse for wear, but I did detect a marked disinclination to respirate, which I took as a sign either of his inveterate stubbornness or of his having reached the Stygian shore. The latter seemed more likely. I heard in my fuddled head a line from *The Wild Bunch* when a critically injured gunman begs his outlaw gang to "finish it." And in the healing spirit of Hippocrates I lifted high the shovel and whanged it down on Harvey's head.

To my relief, not a whimper issued from him. I was confident he was defunct.

With care I shrouded and buried him again, committing earth to earth and dust to dust and so on, and with spritelike step conveyed myself to the kitchen where I made another gin and tonic and, in semiprone position, settled into the game's third quarter, the fabled Trojan running attack grinding out, it would seem, another win.

I WAS SHOCKED awake by the impertinence of a ringing telephone, which I, with due caution, answered. It was my wife's friend Vicki inquiring about the pooch, for it was her assertion that Snip had fancied a taste of her son's upper calf and without invitation or permission to do so had partaken of same within the last twenty-four hours. Even while I was wondering what toxicity lurked in the child's leg and to what extent the poison was culpably responsible for our adored pet's actionable extinction, a loss we would feel for our lifetimes, Vicki insisted that I have the dog checked out by a vet to ascertain if he had rabies.

Cause of death: rabies? It seemed unlikely. Notwithstanding his surliness, there'd been no Cujoesque frothing or lunging at car windows; but my familiarity with torts has made me both careful and rather unctuous in confrontation with a plaintiff, and so I assured the complainant that I would accede to her request.

Off to the back yard again, my pace that of a woebegone trudge, and with my implement of agriculture I displaced the slack and loosened earth. This was getting old. With an accusatory tone I said, "You're doing this on purpose, aren't you," and I took his silence as a plea of nolo contendere.

My plan, of course, was to employ the Oldsmobile 88 to transport my burden to the canine's autopsy at Dr. Romo's office just a half mile away. However, upon settling into its plush front seat, it came to my attention that Zack—he who is but a sojourner on this earth—had not thought to replenish the fuel he'd used up on his trip to the Hollywood Bowl last night. The vehicle was not in a condition of plenitude. Would not ferry us farther than a block.

With Buster lying in the altogether on the driveway, not yet unsightly but no calendar page, I went into the house and found an old leather suitcase in the attic, then stuffed the mutt into the larger flapped compartment before hefting him on his final journey to those veterinary rooms he always shivered in.

I AM, AS I may have implied, a man of depth, perspicacity, and nearly Olympian strength, but I found myself hauling my heavy and lifeless cargo to Dr. Romo's with a pronounced lack of vigor and resolve. The September afternoon was hot, the Pasadena streets were vacant, the entire world seemed to have found entertainment and surcease in ways that I had not. I was, in a word, in a sweaty snit, and after many panting and pain-filled stops, my spine in Quasimodo configuration and my right arm gradually inching longer than my left, it was all I could do not to heave the suitcase containing Wonderdog into a haulaway behind the Chinese restaurant.

But during our joint ordeal I had developed a grudging affection for our pet; he who'd been so quick to defend my kith and kin against the noise of passing trucks, who took loud notice of the squirrels outside, who held fast in the foyer, hackles raised, fearlessly barking, whenever company arrived at the front door. With him I seemed calm, masterful, and uneccentric, the Superior Man that the *I Ching* talks so much about. Without him, I thought, I would be otherwise.

I put down the suitcase to shake the ache from my fingers and subtract affliction from my back, and it was then that my final indignity came. An angel of mercy spied my plight, braked his ancient Cadillac, and got out, his facial piercings and tattoos and shoot-the-marbles eyes belying the kindness and decency of his heart as he asked, "Can I help you with that suitcase?"

"I can handle it."

"Are you sure?"

"I'm just two blocks away."

"What the heck's in it?" he asked.

And for some reason I said, "A family heirloom."

"Wow!" he said. "Why don't you put it in my trunk and I'll help you with it? I got nothin' better to do."

Well, I did not just fall off the turnip truck. I would have been, in other circumstances, suspicious. But I was all too aware of the weight and worthlessness of my cumbrance, and so I granted his specified offer, hoisting the deceased into the Seville and slamming down the trunk lid. And, in evidence of our fallen state, my Samaritan immediately took off without me, jeering and peeling rubber and speeding west toward Los Angeles.

I could only lift my hand in a languid wave. *So long, old sport.*

Our world being the location of penance and recrimination, it was only right that my last kid should pedal up to me on her bike just then and ask, "Daddy, what are you doing here?"

Waving to a guy, I thought, *who's about to become an undertaker.*

And then I confessed. Sparky's sudden death, the burial, not the exhumation and execution attempt, but the imputation of rabies and my arduous efforts to acquit his reputation with a pilgrimage to the vet's.

Suzy took it in with sangfroid for a little while, but then the lip quivered and tears spilled from her gorgeous eyes, and as I held her close she begged me to get her another dog just like Sparky. And that was Sparky's final revenge, for I said, "Okay, honey. Another dog, just like him."

JOHN McNALLY

Power Lines

THE POWER COMPANY in Chicago wanted to do something nice for the kids, so they let the city construct parks where their power-line towers sat. Where I lived were three of these parks, each with a two-hoop basketball court, a swing set, a merry-go-round, a slide, and a couple of giant cast-iron insects that sat atop industrial-size springs, all in the shadows of wires, hundreds of them, strung from tower to tower like garland at Christmastime. Every few hours the power lines surged. The buzzing, growing louder, was the sound I imagined a man in an electric chair heard as his own sour spirit detached from his body, the way a large Band-Aid would sound peeled from a hairy leg.

I wasn't much of an athlete, but I liked throwing my basketball around at New Castle Park, one of the three parks with the power-line towers. Everyone I knew watched the Harlem Globetrotters on TV, and for a while it seemed that every kid in town owned a red, white, and blue basketball. At least once a day you'd see some poor kid trying to drib-

ble a figure eight between and around his legs. It was embarrassing to watch—his bulging-eyed concentration, his rigor-
mortis legs forming an upside-down U, the slippery ball
flipped into the street, sometimes in front of a speeding car.
My favorite Globetrotters were Meadowlark Lemon and
Curly Neal, but I knew I'd never be able to do what they
could do, and so I was satisfied with banging the basketball
off the backboard, occasionally making a basket, all under
the constant hum and crackle of the power lines. I threw
that ball again and again, trying to empty my head of all
thoughts. It wasn't as easy as it sounded, draining away your
own past and future, trying to exist in whatever moment
you happened to be in—not a second before and not a second after. This was how I imagined insects spent their days.
I had stared hard into the eyes of a fly once, wondering if it
ever, even for a second, thought about what it had done the
day before. One time I stared at a grasshopper for thirty
minutes, hoping for a sign, a look of reflection, but I wasn't
so sure that it even remembered what it was doing when I
first began looking at it. One thing I learned was that it was
difficult to *not* think about anything, because thinking about
not thinking was actually thinking about *something*. The idea
of *nothing* fascinated me. I loved the idea of *nothing*, because
it didn't seem possible. How could there ever be *nothing*?
There couldn't! And so I'd throw the ball again and again,
until I'd get a splitting headache trying to think of nothing
but thinking about everything else instead. I always got a
headache playing basketball, and I always took this as my
sign to go home.

One fall day I saw Ralph trudging along New Castle
Avenue, dragging a burlap bag behind him.

"What's in there?" I yelled from the basketball court.

Ralph stopped, then looked up and around, into the air, as if he'd been hearing voices his entire life.

"Over here!" I said.

Ralph turned, saw me. He didn't smile. He didn't wave. He nodded, which was about as friendly a greeting as a person could expect from Ralph, then he made his way over. His wallet was connected to a long drooping chain that rattled when he walked, and he was wearing a hooded sweatshirt with the hood up. The bag slid up the curb and bounced across the park's grass. He said, "What're you doing? Playing basketball by yourself?"

"You want to play some Horse?" I asked.

"Horse?" He narrowed his eyes as if the game might involve one of us riding the other around the basketball court. I hadn't really thought about it before, but I'd never seen Ralph in possession of any kind of sporting equipment. Since Ralph was two years older than the other eighth-graders, the principal wouldn't let him take gym class with us. I wasn't even sure what he did during that period. Ralph said, "You come here a lot? By yourself?"

"All the time," I said.

Ralph nodded. He said, "My cousins, they know a guy who knows a guy who knows something about electricity. See these power lines? This guy, the one who knows this guy that my cousins know, he said if you spend too much time around these things, you'll end up sterile."

"Sterile?" I said. I suspected that the look I was giving him was the same look that he'd given me at the suggestion of Horse. I knew being sterile meant I would never have kids, and I knew roughly what part of my body it had to do with, but I wasn't sure of the specifics. How, for instance, could something that didn't even touch me make me sterile?

"*Who's this guy?*" I asked.

"He's some guy who knows a guy who knows my cousins."

"And he's an expert on electricity?"

"So I've been told," Ralph said.

We stood there a moment without saying a word. The power lines sizzled above. I looked down at Ralph's burlap bag—a gunnysack, my mother would have called it. There was a lump in it about the size and shape of a small animal, like a possum.

Ralph said, "I better not stand here long. I normally don't even walk on this street."

"Afraid of getting sterile?" I asked.

I expected Ralph to laugh or at least smile, but he didn't. He nodded. "Don't want to risk it," he said.

Ralph, heading back to the street, dragged the lump behind him. I was about to yell out to him, to ask again what was in his sack, but a sharp pain tore through my head, causing me to drop the basketball. The ball bounced once, twice, a third time, each bounce closer to the last until it was vibrating against the ground, then dying and rolling toward the fence. To stop thinking about the searing pain inside my head, I tried imagining what was in Ralph's sack. A cat? A bucket's worth of sand? A couple of meat loafs? I shut my eyes and concentrated hard, harder than I had ever concentrated in my life, and while the power lines started to surge, the buzz growing so loud I was afraid that the towers themselves were going to burst into flames, an image of what was in the sack finally came to me: a baby, *my* baby, and Ralph, like some ghost from the future, rattling chains but spooked by his own sad mission, had come to show me what would never be.

DAVID FOSTER WALLACE

Incarnations of Burned Children

THE DADDY WAS around the side of the house hanging a door for the tenant when he heard the child's screams and the Mommy's voice gone high between them. He could move fast, and the back porch gave onto the kitchen, and before the screen door had banged shut behind him the Daddy had taken the scene in whole, the overturned pot on the floortile before the stove and the burner's blue jet and the floor's pool of water still steaming as its many arms extended, the toddler in his baggy diaper standing rigid with steam coming off his hair and his chest and shoulders scarlet and his eyes rolled up and mouth open very wide and seeming somehow separate from the sounds that issued, the Mommy down on one knee with the dishrag dabbing pointlessly at him and matching the screams with cries of her own, hysterical so she was almost frozen. Her one knee and the bare little soft feet were still in the steaming pool and the Daddy's first act was to take the child under the arms and lift him away from it and take him to the sink, where he threw out plates and struck the tap to let cold well water run over the boy's feet while with his cupped hand he gathered and poured or flung cold water over his head and shoulders and chest, wanting first to see the steam stop coming off him, the Mommy over his shoulder invoking God until he sent her for towels and gauze if they had it, the Daddy moving quickly and well and his man's mind empty of everything but purpose, not yet aware of how smoothly he moved or that he'd ceased to hear the high screams because to hear them would freeze him and make impossible what had to be done to help his child, whose screams were regular as breath and went on so long they'd become already a thing in the kitchen, something else to move quickly around. The tenant side's door outside hung half off its top hinge and moved slightly in the wind, and a bird in the oak across the driveway appeared to observe the door with a cocked head as the cries still came from inside. The worst scalds seemed to be the right arm and shoulder, the chest and stomach's red was fading to pink under the cold water and his feet's soft soles weren't blistered that the Daddy could see, but the toddler still made little fists and screamed except now merely on reflex from fear, the Daddy would know he thought possible later, small face distended and thready veins standing out at the temples and the Daddy kept saying he was here he was here, adrenaline ebbing and an anger at the Mommy for allowing this thing to happen just starting to gather in wisps at his mind's extreme rear still hours from expression. When the Mommy returned he wasn't sure whether to wrap the child in a towel or not but he wet the towel down and did, swaddled him tight and lifted his baby out of the sink and set him on the kitchen table's edge to soothe him while the Mommy tried to check the feet's soles with one hand waving around in the area of her mouth and uttering objectless words while the Daddy bent in and was face to face with the child on the table's checked edge repeating the fact that he was here and trying to calm the toddler's cries but still the child breathlessly screamed, a high pure shining sound that could stop his heart and his bitty lips and gums now tinged with the light blue of a low flame the Daddy thought, screaming as if almost still under the tilted pot in pain. A minute, two like this that seemed much longer, with the Mommy at the Daddy's side talking sing-song at the child's face and the lark on the limb with its head to the side and the hinge going white in a line from the weight of the canted door until the first wisp of steam came lazy from under the wrapped towel's hem and the parents' eyes met and widened—the diaper, which when they opened the towel and leaned their little boy back on the checkered cloth and unfastened the softened tabs and tried to remove it resisted slightly with new high cries and was hot, their baby's diaper burned their hand and they saw where the real water'd fallen and pooled and been burning their baby all this time while he screamed for them to help him and they hadn't, hadn't thought and when they got it off and saw the state of what was there the Mommy said their God's first name and grabbed the table to keep her feet while the father turned away and threw a haymaker at the air of the kitchen and cursed both himself and the world for not the last time while his child might now have been sleeping if not for the rate of his breathing and the tiny stricken motions of his hands in the air above where he lay, hands the size of a grown man's thumb that had clutched the Daddy's thumb in the crib while he'd watched the Daddy's mouth move in song, his head cocked and seeming to see way past him into something his eyes made the Daddy lonesome for in a sideways way. If you've

never wept and want to, have a child. Break your heart inside
and something will a child is the twangy song the Daddy
hears again as if the radio's lady was almost there with him
looking down at what they've done, though hours later what
the Daddy won't most forgive is how badly he wanted a cigarette right then as they diapered the child as best they could
in gauze and two crossed handtowels and the Daddy lifted
him like a newborn with his skull in one palm and ran him
out to the hot truck and burned custom rubber all the way
to town and the clinic's ER with the tenant's door hanging
open like that all day until the hinge gave but by then it was
too late, when it wouldn't stop and they couldn't make it the
child had learned to leave himself and watch the whole rest
unfold from a point overhead, and whatever was lost never
thenceforth mattered, and the child's body expanded and
walked about and drew pay and lived its life untenanted, a
thing among things, its self's soul so much vapor aloft, falling
as rain and then rising, the sun up and down like a yoyo.

Inclusions

HOW CLEVER OF you to admire my eyelids, my Victorian nightgown, the cutouts in the cloth, the shadow of nipples through white cotton. The Rites of Spring, indeed! I saw the purple mountains off in the distance and wondered how long they would take to climb. The mouth of the Volcano. The molten lava flowing. Perhaps if I were a virgin I would have been sacrificed to complete your dream. Your syntax is always so surprising. You said I was beautiful. I would imagine, Clause, that you even know enough to tell a beautiful woman how smart she is.

I WAS TIRED. The activities of the day: brushing my teeth, preparing the watercress, the occasional small moment of shame. Undressing, always a source of stress! Overwhelmed by the alternatives, we feel the scars proliferate as every day we are one day older and still young. As for yesterday, the waterfalls, the union of various shapes, the exhilaration, our flesh defining the air, your thigh against mine, the ebb and flow, a good thing, the ebb and flow, the way you hold me against you, that perfect blend of sex and concern. It is appropriate, Vincent. It is exactly right.

MEN CALLED MICHAEL, I have often observed, possess superior intellect combined with unique creative powers. Are talented in some kinky way, which it would embarrass me to describe or illuminate. They announce their intentions with sly smiles, lying when necessary, caving or mountain climbing, even climbing the ice, sucking women in, so to speak, and women are all too often delighted to be toyed with so, especially when the seduction is partly cerebral and definitely clever.

IF YOUR SOUL expands to fill the room when you are alone, James, what happens when I open the door? Do you feel cramped? Encumbered by the sound of my body? I would not like to feel I had even coated you with some pearly substance, much less that I had nudged your soul coarsely into a corner. It is tight and beautiful, your soul, and it is the quality of freedom in your spirit that stirs me. I hesitate to act, for fear my presence will cause you to alter. Please assure me you will not disappear.

YOU MUST ANSWER immediately, Brent, and in the affirmative, for I am contemplating your arrival from other continents at some future date, close in time to this moment, and my head is swirling with entire blueprints of new positions.

I DO SEEM to remember saying: "You only talk to me in order to fuck me, and I only fuck you in order that you will talk." How our talk shimmers between us; how it overlays the day. I know we are different. I am saddened to think, however, that life could create such distinctions, as if it were the sky that affected us or the infinite array of canyons in the American West. When I think of you, I conjure you clearly, your freckles laid on your chest like a map, the hairs like compass needles pointing my heart in every direction. In that moment of clear and intense vision, I feel the needles dancing at some rapidly spreading location within me. I see that squiggly line running the full length of your cock, pointing.

IT'S THE ONLY world we have, isn't it, Alex. And a good thing, too—the world, I mean. As for me, I will spend the day hanging long strips of white gauze in the linden trees along Rockefeller Center. Please consider yourself invited to witness.

AT TIMES THE world makes such an endearing metallic sound, I am tempted. Today I drove, in tight concentric rectangles actually, rectangles with the emotional content of circles. If I was yawning, it was only deception. I invite you to envision the yellow next to the orange, the blue next to the green? Perhaps if we don't actually touch the paper with color, but simply lay the chalk together, the pieces parallel, on a tray?

HE HAS RETURNED, Steven. He has returned and opened the blinds all over the house. I try not to think about it.

BONE-TIRED IS an understatement. The streets are flooding, and the drains are inefficient. How can I continue to hang like this, like the dangling roots of a mangrove tree, divided between you? Last night you consumed all of my passion and then I went home to my husband, only to be consumed again. *I am dried out!* I can think of only one solution: that I fill myself once again with some of that fluid men have so much of. Think of it, Jean. Would my tissues swell? Would I rise like a clock into the air? You are so skilled, my dear, and when I am with you, the minutes tick backward with such a shiny auburn intonation.

OF COURSE I am married. And I will remain so. We must walk the deserts to reach the oasis. You insist on treating the facts of our lives, even the dark romantic overloads, as if they were ours alone. Interpretation is dangerous, Robert—the painting, for example, the greens and blues, the scarlets and golds are both true and untrue. I have often thought, to argue the other side, that the great failure of Western Humanist education is the emphasis laid on the universality of human experience. We all know, Kevin, that this is merely a new kind of hogwash. When we undress, we undress in our own way. We undo the buttons and open the zippers our own way. We arrange ourselves on the bed in our own way. I can promise you neither a factual nor an emotional closure, not even a lid, Robert, to this painful, ecstatic narrative. At some point in all of our lives we experience our own death, and simultaneously a beloved strand of our orientation collapses. For the rest of our conscious lives, we relive each moment, we hang our memories around and over us, we overcome them and use them for our excuses. It is the you of the now that is the only you I can ever enter. I want to touch you. I want to speak to you in the present tense.

YOU WILL BE shocked when you read this, but it has occurred to me that none of the names with which I have labeled you have sufficed. It would take all of the words to describe the slow brush you have mastered, the hair of the centipede, to count the delight with which my skin has received you. The strands of my body hunger for you with a deep ache which begins to surface from that silicon ball I hold as a core. And the passion simmers on the skin in my vaginal passage. The largest organ, the skin, longing to be filled as you are filled by me with the names that I give you. I touch my tongue to your eyelids in the beauty of their translucence, and you envision me in all my reflections. An unbelievably clean-cut shaft of sunlight has broken through the clouds you complain about, and I could project either continuation or a gradual thinning. You are powerful, Michael; you light fires in my thirsty fibers; you destroy my reluctance; you spread a high gloss on the surface of my submissive threads. And all seems good, possessing the texture of wet sand. Now that I know you will always return, I can love you for small moments that constitute forever, or for small moments that stay discrete and only dapple time. Really, my dears, there's no difference.

—Temporarily, Eve

Good, Brother

WE USED TO take the fish we'd catch out of this dirty river that runs through this dirty river town and we used to cut off their still-glistening-with-silver-scales heads and we used to nail them, those heads, to the creosoted pole out back behind our yard. We'd hammer nails into those cold-water-eyed heads and make for ourselves what my brother and me used to call our back yard fishing pole. We did not stop fishing for and catching and nailing those fishes' heads into wood until the day our father came home from work and told us we were leaving. When our father told us we were leaving, he meant it, we were leaving for good: this dirty river, this dirty town. We did not want to leave, my brother and me. We did not want to leave behind the town or the river or the fish-headed telephone pole the two of us brothers turned into a back-of-the-yard fishing pole out back behind the wood tool shed where our father kept his hammers and his saws and his cigar boxes full of rusty, bent-back nails and his nuts and bolts and screws and those bottles half filled with whiskey.

At night, from our bedroom's window, my brother and me could look outside and see those fishes' marbly-looking eyes looking back all walleyed out from the sides of their chopped-off heads. The biggest of the big-lipped fish looked like they might leap out and bite the hand left dangling over the side of a boat. Each of the fish heads, us brothers, we gave each one a name. In the end there were exactly a hundred and fifty fish heads named, each with its own name. Not one was called Jimmy or John.

Jimmy and John was my brother's and my real name. We called each other Brother.

Our father call us brothers Son. When our father hollered out Son, the both of us brothers would turn back boy our heads. Us brothers, we both knew, we were crossing this river together.

Our mother called us brothers her dirty little boys. Us brothers boys were made, our mother liked to say, in the muddy image of our father. We did not like it much when our mother made us wash the mud from off the bottoms of our muddy boots. We liked mud and those dirty river smells that smelled of fishing and worms. We did not like it when our mother made us wash our hands to rid ourselves of those fishy river smells. We liked the way the fishes' silver fish scales stuck to and glittered sparkly in our hands. At night, we liked to hold our hands up to the moonlight shining into our bedroom window. It looked like our hands had been dipped in stars.

But our mother and our father both were sick and tired living in a town with a dirty river running through it and with river winds that always smelled of fish. Our mother said she wanted to go somewhere, *anywhere* is the word she used, so long as anywhere was west of here. West where? was what our father wanted to know. And what our mother said to this was, West of all this muddy water. Somewhere, our mother said, where there's not so much mud and rusted steel. There's a bigger sky, our mother wanted us brothers to know. There's a sky, our mother told us. There's a sky not stunted by smokestacks and smoke.

We couldn't picture a sky bigger than the sky outside our back yard. We did not want to imagine a town without a dirty river running through it where we could run down to it to fish. Us brothers, we did not want to run or be moved away from all this smoke and water and mud.

We didn't know what we were going to do, or how we were going to stay, until we looked outside and saw our fish. The fish heads were looking back at us, open-eyed, open-mouthed, and it was like they were singing to us brothers. Us brothers, we climbed outside through our bedroom's window. Only the moon and stars were watching us as we walked out back to our father's tool shed and dug out his hammers and a box of rusty, bent-back nails. We each of us brothers grabbed a handful of nails and a hammer in each of our hands and walked over to our fish-headed fishing pole.

Brother, I said to Brother, you can go first.

Give me your hand, I told him. Hold your hand up against this wood.

Brother did like I told.

We were brothers. We were each other's voice inside our own heads.

This might sting, I warned, and then I raised back that hammer. I drove that rusty nail right through Brother's hand.

Brother didn't even wince, or flinch with his body, or make with his boy mouth the sound of a brother crying out.

Good, Brother, I said.

I was hammering in another nail into Brother's other hand when our father stepped out into the yard.

Son, our father called out.

Us, our father's sons, we turned back our heads toward the sound of our father.

We waited to hear what it was that our father was going to say to us brothers next.

It was a long few seconds.

The sky above the river where the steel mill stood like some sort of a shipwreck, it was dark and quiet. Somewhere, I was sure, the sun was shining.

You boys remember to clean up before you come back in, our father said.

Our father turned back his back.

Us brothers turned back to face each other.

I raised back the hammer.

I lined up that rusted nail.

Reply All

To: Poetry Association of the Western Suburbs Listserve
  <7/17>
From: Lisa Drago-Harse
Subject: Next Meeting

Hi all,

I wanted to confirm that our next meeting will be held in the Sir Francis Drake Room at the Bensonville Hampton Inn on August 3rd. Minutes from our last meeting and an agenda for the next meeting will follow shortly.

Peace and Poetry,
Lisa Drago-Harse
Secretary/PAWS

To: Poetry Association of the Western Suburbs Listserve
  <7/17>

From: Michael Stroud
Re: Re: Next Meeting

Dearest Lisa,

First of all, I LOVE your mole and don't find it unsightly
in the least! There is absolutely no reason for you to be
ashamed of it (though it might be a good idea to have it
checked out). But please don't remove it! Heaven forbid,
my darling! As I recall, I gave you considerable pleasure
when I sucked and licked it like a nipple. A nipple it is, in
size and shape, if not placement. That no one else knows
your mole's position on your body (other than your
benighted husband, poor limp Richard, that Son(net) of a
Bitch as you call him) is more the pity (if Marvell had
known such a mole, he undoubtedly would have added
an extra stanza to his poem). But my coy mistress is not
SO terribly coy as all that. When you started massaging
my crotch with your foot underneath the table in the
Sir Francis Drake Room, I was at first shocked. I thought
perhaps the unseen massager was none other than our
esteemed president, the redoubtable Darcy McFee (makeup
and wardrobe courtesy of Yoda). Is that terrible of me? I
have nothing personal against her, really, except for her
execrable taste in poetry, and the fact that you should be
president, not she. And her breath. And that habit of pulling
her nose when she speaks and that absolutely horrific expression of hers, Twee. As in, "I find his poetry just so twee."
What does twee mean and why does she keep inflicting it
upon us! So imagine my horror when I felt this foot in my
crotch and I stared across the table at the two of you—she
twitching like a slug that's had salt poured on it and you

immobile except for your Mont Blanc pen taking down the minutes. Ah, to think that the taking down of minutes could be such an erotic activity, but in your capable hands, it is. To think that mere hours later, it would be my Mont Blanc you'd grasp so firmly, guiding me into the lyrical book of your body. But initially, I thought the worst, that it was Darcy, not you. My only consolation was the idea that at least I had her on a sexual harassment suit, her being my boss after all at Roosevelt. Another reason I thought it was her and not you was because I know you're married and she isn't and I knew that Richard is a member of our esteemed organization, too (and he was in the room, seated beside you no less!). It was only that sly smile in your eyes that tipped me off. I, too, love the danger that illicit public sex brings, as long as it's kept under the table, so to speak. And yes, maybe someday we can make love on that very same table in the Sir Francis Drake Room, my darling. Thinking of you now makes me so hot. I want to nibble you. I want to live in your panties. I want to make metaphors of your muscles, of your thighs, of the fecund wetness bursting with your being and effulgence.

With undying love and erotic daydreams,
Mikey

To: PAWS Listserve <7/17>
From: Darcy McFee
Re: Re: Re: Next Meeting

I am traveling now and will not be answering e-mails until I return on July 21st.

Thanks!

Darcy

To: PAWS Listserve <7/17>
From: Sam Fulgram, Jr.
Re: Re: Re: Re: Next Meeting

Whoa boy! Do you realize you just sent out your love note to the entire Poetry Association of the Western Suburbs listserve?

Cheers,
Sam

P.S.—That mole? You've got my imagination running wild. As long as the entire organization knows about it now, would you mind divulging its location? I'd sleep better at night knowing it.

To: PAWS Listserve <7/17>
From: Betsy Midchester
Re: Re: Re: Re: Re: Next Meeting

Hi all,

Well! That last message from "Mikey" Stroud certainly made my day. I thought at first the message was addressed to me. As I had no memory of placing my foot in Mike's crotch, I naturally assumed that I needed an adjustment of my medication so that I wouldn't forget such episodes in the future. Now I see it's simply Michael ("Down Boy") Stroud and our esteemed Secretary of the Galloping Mont Blaaaaanc who need the medication adjustments. Thanks, in any case, for a much needed lift in an otherwise humdrum day.

Betsy Midchester
Treasurer/PAWS

To: PAWS Listserve <7/17>
From: Lisa Drago-Harse
Re: Re: Re: Re: Re: Re: Next Meeting

This is a nightmare. I'm not quite sure what to say except that life is unpredictable and often irreversible. While I do not wish to go into details or make excuses for the above e-mail from Michael Stroud, I would like to clarify one thing: that was not my foot in your crotch, Michael. But your belief that it was my foot in your crotch explains a few things concerning your subsequent behavior towards me that were up until this moment a mystery.

LDH

To: PAWS Listserve <7/17>
From: Michael Stroud
Re: Re: Re: Re: Re: Re: Re: Next Meeting

I'm

To: PAWS Listserve <7/17>
From: Michael Stroud
Re: Re: Re: Re: Re: Re: Re: Re: Next Meeting

I hit the send button by mistake before I was ready. This isn't my day, to say the least! I'm sorry!!!! I'd like to apologize to the entire PAWS community, and also to Lisa's husband Richard and to Darcy. And to you, Lisa. I don't mean to make excuses for myself, but I would like to say that I've been under a tremendous amount of pressure of late, at school, at home, and I am nothing if not vulnerable and flawed. All I can say is that in poetry I find some solace for the petty actions of others and the sometimes monstrous actions of which I'm all too capable. I ask you all to blame me, not Lisa, for what has happened.

But if not your foot, Lisa, then whose?

Michael Stroud

To: PAWS Listserve <7/17>
From: Greg Rudolfsky
Re: Re: Re: Re: Re: Re: Re: Re: Re: RESPECT

Just a little bit, Just a little bit.
Sock it to me, sock it to me, sock it to me, sock it to me, sock it to me, sock it to me, sock it to me, sock it to me, RESPECT, Just a little bit, just a little bit . . .

To: PAWS Listserve <7/17>
From: Samantha M. Poulsen, RN
Subject: Fecund Poets

I do not care whose foot is in whose crotch, but I think it's insulting and idiotic that so-called educated people would use such phrases as, "the fecund wetness bursting with your being and effulgence." And officers of the PAWS at that!

To: PAWS Listserve <7/17>
From: Richard Harse
Re: Fecund Poets

I would like to tender my resignation in the Poets of the Western Suburbs, as I will be tendering my resignation in several other areas of my life. I only belonged to PAWS in any case because of my wife's interest in poetry. I wanted to share her interests, but clearly not all of them.

To: PAWS Listserve <7/22>
From: Darcy McFee
Re: Fecund Poets

Well, it seems that our little organization has been busy in my absence. I have over 300 new messages in my e-mail account, all, it seems, from my fellow poetry lovers! I haven't yet had a chance to read your exchanges, but I will soon. In the meantime, I wanted to convey some exciting news. This weekend, while attending a workshop at Wright State in Dayton, I ran into the former Poet Laureate, Billy Collins, who has agreed to be our special guest at our annual Poetry Bash in Oak Park. He said he's heard quite a lot about our organization in recent days and that our board had achieved near legendary status in the poetry community. I knew this would make you as proud as it makes me.

To: PAWS Listserve <7/24>
From: Darcy McFee
Subject: Twee

So this is how it is. Upon reading the 300 e-mails that collected in my inbox over the weekend, my mind is a riot of emotions. I have not slept for nearly 48 hours. Never before have I been so insulted. Yet, I also know that I am, at least in part, to blame. Had I not stuck my foot in Michael Stroud's crotch, none of this would have happened. Twitching like a slug that's had salt poured on it? That hurts, Michael. It really does. I didn't realize you were so shallow. But in reading your collective e-mails, I see that at least half our membership has a decidedly sadistic bent. In any case, it was not your crotch I aimed for, Michael, but the crotch of our Vice-President, Amir Bathshiri, with whom I have long been intimately acquainted, both of us having lost our spouses several years ago. If the seating arrangements in the Sir Francis Drake Room were any less cramped, none of these misunderstandings would have occurred. Of course, I never would have tried to fondle you, Michael. In the first place, you are the most boring, tedious person I have met in my life, and believe me, as Chair of the English Dept. at Roosevelt, I have met my share of boring, tedious people. You recite poetry with all the grace of a highway sign that cautions one to beware of falling rocks. But enough! I know that it is my errant foot to blame. Amir and I have talked this over and have decided to withdraw from PAWS as well as from academia. Early retirement calls, Michael and Lisa, and I will give neither of you a thought as I walk along the beach hand in hand with Amir in the months and years to come, listening to the mermaids singing each to each.

Yes, Michael, I find you and your crotch and your paramour the very essence of Twee.

To: PAWS Listserve <7/30>
From: Betsy Midchester/Treasurer
Subject: New Elections

Please note that the agenda for our next meeting has changed. We will spend most of the meeting on new elections to be held for the positions of President, Vice-President and Secretary of our organization. Note, too, that we will no longer be meeting in the Sir Francis Drake

Room of the Bensonville Hampton Inn. Instead, we will be meeting in the cafeteria of Enchanted Gardens Residence for Seniors in Glen Ellyn. The change in venue was planned well in advance of recent events, so members should not read anything into this (though if any organization's members are skilled at reading between the lines, it should be ours). Please think about whom you would like to nominate for these important positions in our organization. And in the meantime, please remember to always be conscious and considerate of your audience.

Peace and poetry,
Betsy Midchester
Treasurer and Acting President/PAWS

Escort

MY FIRST DAY as an escort, my first "date" had only one leg. He'd gone to a gay bathhouse, to get warm, he told me. Maybe for sex. And he'd fallen asleep in the steam room, too close to the heating element. He'd been unconscious for hours, until someone found him. Until the meat of his left thigh was completely and thoroughly cooked.

He couldn't walk, but his mother was coming from Wisconsin to see him, and the hospice needed someone to cart the two of them around to visit the local tourist sights. Go shopping downtown. See the beach. Multnomah Falls. This was all you could do as a volunteer if you weren't a nurse or a cook or doctor.

You were an escort, and this was the place where young people with no insurance went to die. The hospice name, I don't even remember. It wasn't on any signs anywhere, and they asked you to be discreet coming and going because the neighbors didn't know what was going on in the enormous old house on their street, a street with its share of crack houses

and drive-by shootings, still nobody wanted to live next door
to this: four people dying in the living room, two in the dining room. At least two people lay dying in each upstairs bedroom, and there were a lot of bedrooms. At least half these
people had AIDS, but the house didn't discriminate. You
could come here and die of anything.

The reason I was there was my job. This meant lying on my
back on a creeper with a two-hundred-pound class-8 diesel
truck driveline lying on my chest and running down between
my legs as far as my feet. My job is I had to roll under trucks
as they crept down an assembly line, and I installed these drivelines. Twenty-six drivelines every eight hours. Working fast as
each truck moved along, pulling me into the huge blazing-
hot paint ovens just a few feet down the line.

My degree in journalism couldn't get me more than five
dollars an hour. Other guys in the shop had the same degree,
and we joked how liberal arts degrees should include welding
skills so you'd at least pick up the extra two bucks an hour our
shop paid grunts who could weld. Someone invited me to
their church, and I was desperate enough to go, and at the
church they had a potted ficus they called a Giving Tree, decorated with paper ornaments, each ornament printed with a
good deed you could choose.

My ornament said: Take a hospice patient on a date.

That was their word, "date." And there was a phone number. I took the man with one leg, then him and his mother,
all over the area, to scenic viewpoints, to museums, his wheel-
chair folded up in the back of my fifteen-year-old Mercury
Bobcat. His mother smoking, silent. Her son was thirty years
old, and she had two weeks of vacation. At night, I'd take her
back to her Travelodge next to the freeway, and she'd smoke,
sitting on the hood of my car, talking about her son already

in the past tense. He could play the piano, she said. In school, he earned a degree in music, but ended up demonstrating electric organs in shopping-mall stores.

These were conversations after we had no emotions left.

I was twenty-five years old, and the next day I was back under trucks with maybe three or four hours sleep. Only now my own problems didn't seem very bad. Just looking at my hands and feet, marveling at the weight I could lift, the way I could shout against the pneumatic roar of the shop, my whole life felt like a miracle instead of a mistake.

In two weeks the mother was gone home. In another three months, her son was gone. Dead, gone. I drove people with cancer to see the ocean for their last time. I drove people with AIDS to the top of Mount Hood so they could see the whole world while there was still time.

I sat bedside while the nurse told me what to look for at the moment of death, the gasping and unconscious struggle of someone drowning in their sleep as renal failure filled their lungs with water. The monitor would beep every five or ten seconds as it injected morphine into the patient. The patient's eyes would roll back, bulging and entirely white. You held their cold hand for hours, until another escort came to the rescue, or until it didn't matter.

The mother in Wisconsin sent me an afghan she'd crocheted, purple and red. Another mother or grandmother I'd escorted sent me an afghan in blue, green, and white. Another came in red, white, and black. Granny squares, zigzag patterns. They piled up at one end of the couch until my housemates asked if we could store them in the attic.

Just before he'd died, the woman's son, the man with one leg, just before he'd lost consciousness, he'd begged me to go into his old apartment. There was a closet full of sex toys.

Magazines. Dildos. Leatherwear. It was nothing he wanted his mother to find, so I promised to throw it all out.

So I went there, to the little studio apartment, sealed and stale after months empty. Like a crypt, I'd say, but that's not the right word. It sounds too dramatic. Like cheesy organ music. But in fact, just sad.

The sex toys and anal whatnots were just sadder. Orphaned. That's not the right word either, but it's the first word that comes to mind.

The afghans are still boxed and in my attic. Every Christmas a housemate will go look for ornaments and find the afghans, red and black, green and purple, each one a dead person, a son or daughter or grandchild, and whoever finds them will ask if we can use them on our beds or give them to Goodwill.

And every Christmas I'll say no. I can't say what scares me more, throwing away all these dead children or sleeping with them.

Don't ask me why, I tell people. I refuse to even talk about it. That was all ten years ago. I sold the Bobcat in 1989. I quit being an escort.

Maybe because after the man with one leg, after he died, after his sex toys were all garbage-bagged, after they were buried in the Dumpster, after the apartment windows were open and the smell of leather and latex and shit was gone, the apartment looked good. The sofa bed was a tasteful mauve, the walls and carpet, cream. The little kitchen had butcher-block countertops. The bathroom was all white and clean.

I sat there in the tasteful silence. I could've lived there.

Anyone could've lived there.

RON CARLSON

The Gold Lunch

As the lights go up, a man standing on a small platform facing stage right (an imaginary audience there) waves one more time at those people and turns and steps down toward us. He is dressed in an impeccably casual way: slacks and a sport coat, tie optional. Around his neck on a ribbon is a gold medal.

MAN *(takes the medal in his hand, looks at it, looks up at us, and begins):*

T HIS BITTERSWEET VICTORY represents a lot of work; as everyone knows it was close, real close, but I know the reasons the judges gave me the 9.999.

First, I want to say, we were very happy when the committee saw the challenges in such an event and Lunching was made an Olympic sport. People told us it was easy, and we knew it was not easy. When you go to lunch with your ex-wife, or your ex-husband, it is not easy. The luge is easy, if you want to know: lie down and all downhill. Lunching your Ex is sit up and all uphill. Now the world knows Lunching is a complicated, full-blown contact sport, loaded with punishing ambiguity and emotional twists and turns that dwarf the Grand Slalom.

What I brought to the Olympiad this year was my experience at so many lunches with my ex-wife, sure, but what I came with was a willingness to try some utterly new strategies that had never been seen before, and I am deeply gratified that they have paid off with this beautiful award.

MY EX-WIFE, DANA, is as formidable an opponent as has appeared in this event. She is tall. She looks good and knows how to dress. She's noted for creating differing effects with her hair, both offensive and defensive, and she has smart and effective table manners. As everyone now knows, lunching is best of seven for the Gold, and I'd only survived to the final round by sympathy, luck, and gravity. I took the Second Lunch because of Dana's Ravioli Drop. And in Lunch Five, Dana had me hands down, but her napkin dropped, and as she picked it up, she looked away. Going into the final round yesterday, I was bracing for a real contest. I'd lost to her at lunch so many times before.

I DREW THE Down Position, sitting at the table first, waiting for her. I had already decided to go with the Standard American Greeting, and when Dana made her entrance I judged her speed and rose to meet her. In the Standard American Greeting, you touch your Ex-Spouse on the outside of the elbow or upper arm, and my variation was to hold on just a moment and couple it with a nod and a closed-mouth smile; it was a bit of a giveaway, but I was determined to go a new way this time, even with the Gold at stake.

The mistake I'd made before was always using the Overt Opening immediately after we were seated. I mean, I would double my smile, lean forward, look at her, et cetera, et cetera. I behaved like hope itself, and there's only one answer to that kind of hope. So, what I did yesterday was crucial to my entire plan, and you can say what you want, but it isn't easy. What I did was: I picked up the menu. I'd never done it before, because I'd been a little excited seeing Dana to think about food. I went right for the menu and held it between us for another second before I lowered it—still reading. This made her pick her menu up, and I knew I was taking a point for that.

WITH THE BALL in my court that way I just pressed it with a volley. Instead of my meaningful "How Have You Been?" which only means one thing, *I love you so much still and do you love me even a little?*, and which pretty much just gets clobbered, I went with the "I, Too, Have a Life" overture and said, "Say, I'm getting the garlic chicken. One of my friends has been working with garlic, and I have to say, she's done some wonderful things."

Immediately, Dana tried her Knowing Smile, which I had anticipated. She knows I don't have any friends. Everybody saw the smile, and it is a killer smile, which is always good for half a point, but I think her timing was off, or I sensed it was, because I didn't let it faze me. I parried with, "And the pinot grigio. My Wine Club is halfway through the whites." Wine Club was a big fat lie; I haven't been out of my apartment for seven months, but I pronounced it with a certain gusto. I wanted this because I had never ordered wine before, because it's a challenge to sit there and sip wine like a normal person when the only thing you've been drinking for months on end is Old Milwaukee in your ratty apartment watching *When*

Animals Attack. Look, understand, behind the wine order I was heartsick, but I had my game plan, and I stayed with it.

THE BANTER WAS next, and I made a bold decision. I decided: no banter. Banter can get you points when you're on top, but with me, it all comes out like I'm begging the waiter to tell Dana, *I still love her; please tell her I love her, please, please, please;* so yesterday when the waiter appeared I told him directly what I wanted, and I did so with the glancing eye contact and my quarter smile which I'd practiced for two months. The judges, I know, gave me points for not pointing with my finger at the selections in the menu.

In Lunch Six the menu was written in French, and I pointed. It was a rout. This was a huge moment for Dana, and I knew she could harvest points big-time. It gives her a chance to lift her chin, smile, and sit up. What she did was clever. She looked up and gave the waiter her order, and then she pulled her shoulders back. She was wearing a green silk blouse that I'd never seen before, and her shoulder move tensed the buttons down the front, and when her shirt is moving like that and the little gaps open and close between the buttons, it has cost dearly. If you get caught with your eyeballs on the breast gap, you might as well call for the check; you're finished.

What I did was keep my eyes up, on the waiter, in a move I patented, called Friendly Attention, as if he were still speaking to me.

The Body of the Lunch was tough, as always. I knew it would be. I was pretty exhausted from not looking down her shirt and from the lying about having a life, and I could feel my heart rate up and my breathing quickening. This is where

I had flushed so many times before, and if your face reddens or one small line of sweat blooms on your hairline, you get the quadruple-penalty from which it is hard to recover. In fact, no one ever has.

I was looking at her, because you've got to stay in the ring. Eye contact. Every time you look away, there go the points. She's looking at me as if she's interested, smiling as if she still had one iota of affection for me or for the four years we lived together in the same house, sleeping together every night, cooking together, and making each other's bag lunches including small surprises, notes, drawings, and neither of us could draw, unembarrassed in all things, we had been in love.

I mean, I remember some lunches. We were in love, and lunch was like everything else, an accessory to love, a way of bringing food into the deal. We'd had a year of bed picnics sitting there cross-legged in the ruined sheets eating brie and crackers, naked as people get, except for maybe crumbs everywhere in the hair, as we pinched morsels from each other like monkeys, drinking ice cold white wine right from the bottle. Such is the very purpose of food. We had two-hour lunches in the bath, that old tub too small for such things, really, but not for us! She'd unwrap a Reuben sandwich, a four-layer deal thick as a book, and laughing she'd thrust it into my mouth while I kept both my hands on her knees. Listen: we made eye contact those days. We put food in each other's mouths.

"My intention," she said as we sat tangled in that hot water eating pickle spears and sharing a can of Dr. Brown's Celery Tonic, "is to love you through every meal of my life."

My mouth was full, and tears flooded my eyes. What did I do: Sitting there naked a long time ago, I lifted my hands from her sweet naked knees, and I showed her my palms as my perfect promise.

Well, a bath with a girl long ago is what they call history, her twin peninsulas floating before you—history, her washing your hair with her feet—history, her eating potato chips from your hand—history. And if you want a chance in the Olympics, you leave history behind, and you play to win.

NOW, THE FACE-TO-FACE of a Lunch is by far the hardest part. You wait for a while, making small talk, and then the food comes, some garlic chicken, and you've got to pretend to enjoy choking it down, sipping some hideous white wine along with it, as if the nasty stuff were the very nectar of life itself.

As I set down my silverware yesterday in the Lunch, I figured it was real close. I knew for a fact it was my best effort to date. I'd been as cryptic as I'd ever been, but Dana was right there every step, and so, as the waiter cleared the plates, I decided to try a Combination Gambit, and I knew it was all or nothing. We're not dessert eaters, and the clock was ticking.

I dropped my smile from half to quarter and held her gaze. It was key to hold my head still while I lifted my hand on the table. This was all neutral; I knew I was close to penalty points, but still neutral.

It all happened then in ten seconds. It's on the tape.

I don't feel like commenting on the tear controversy. Fake tears, they said in the papers. I'll just say: what would that be? A fake tear? Listen. Let me tell you what the judges already know: a tear is a tear. They are generated in each eyelid, and they are a saline solution, which serves several purposes. They served my purposes yesterday. A tear burned across the surface of my eyes, and when I saw Dana's beautiful face blur in the water, I turned my hand open, in a move they'll be imitating

in the Olympics for years, and I showed Dana my palm, the most intimate thing you can reveal at lunch, and I knew the risks. I could feel the air on my naked palm, and then I felt the next thing: her hand.

When Dana reached and took my hand yesterday, it felt cool and dry and perfect. She recoiled immediately, of course, realizing her mistake. But her hand, so smooth.

It felt a lot like what it was. Gold. Pure gold.

Doughnut Shops and Doormen

HAVE TO HAVE him. Have him for real someday, not just in my fantasies. I'm not so far gone yet that I can't tell the difference. Chris Cornell, former lead singer of Soundgarden. The god of my life with the leather-lunged wail. My Gilgamesh, my Valentino, my Elvis, my Clark Gable and Yul Brynner altogether. He is the one crush I've never gotten over. For ten years, I've adored him. That might be why I have no one. No man, no friends, no rapport with family. He is more real to me, more necessarily a part of me, than the people I know. I've never met him, but he is all I need. I have long conversations with him, speaking his parts. I put words in his mouth and thoughts in his head. He understands me deeply, completely. We share the same interests. When I touch myself, it is him touching me.

I'm the kind of woman no one pays attention to. I want to pay for things in exact change, but I am intimidated by the impatient looks of cashiers, so I have heavy purses with broken straps, and ashtrays full of coins. When the people I work with have get-togethers, I am often not asked along. It's not because they don't like me. I don't think they have any feelings toward me at all. It's because they forget about me. I am unnoticeable, just as I intend. There's no room in my life for reality, only for Chris.

I live off a busy intersection and there are always vagrants at the corner where I catch the bus to work. They loiter the nearby strip mall, congregating mostly in front of Winchell's doughnut shop. There's some kind of cosmic trilogy between doughnuts, coffee, and hobos. Today, Winchell's has a doorman. It's a bum, begging change. In my fist, I have exactly 72 cents. The price of an old-fashioned. This is one of the few ways I can dispense with my abundance of change, when I know exactly what something costs. I approach the shop, my body language shouting "Leave me alone." The bum pulls the door open for me. How much is that worth? What does it cost? I'm sure he would patiently wait for me to count out change. Upon thinking this, I break the cardinal rule and make eye contact with him.

My world wobbles. The same aquamarine eyes, the long, curly black hair. The same finely painted mouth. The same nose. Tall, slender. Beautiful hands with long, dirty fingernails. His unwashed body smells sharp, unpleasant, like runny French cheese. There is a familiar quality to his smile when I drop the 72 cents into his upraised palm.

"Thank you," he says. A rich timbre. I feel as though someone has punched me in the head: fuzzy, shocked, adrenalined. I move so slowly past him, the closing door almost hits me in the ass. I order my doughnut like an automaton, pay with a dollar and receive my 28 cents in change. He opens the door on my way out. I give over my change and offer him the greasy-bagged old-fashioned as well. He beams me a smile through a scruffy beard and I am afloat on wings that span my wildest dreams. I am suddenly emboldened.

"Come home with me," I say.

"One hour, ten dollars," he says, seemingly unsurprised. I nod my acquiescence and motion him to follow me. He walks a couple of steps behind me, munching on his doughnut, but I can still smell him. We are halfway to my apartment before I speak again.

"Can I call you Chris?"

He shrugs. "Whatever."

In the elevator, his presence and his stink are overwhelming. I let us into my apartment. "You're going to have to take a shower," I say.

"Great. I'm dying for one." He kicks off his sneakers, which are so filthy I can't distinguish the brand. He's not wearing socks. I point him toward the bathroom. "There's a brand-new toothbrush and clean towels in the closet behind the door." I follow him into the hallway and stare at his back as he pulls off his hooded sweatshirt. His back is smooth-skinned and lithely muscled.

At the bathroom doorway, he turns to find me staring. I glance away. "Throw your clothes out and I'll wash them if you like."

"We only got an hour."

"I'll pay you."

"Okay." He pauses. "What do you want me to call you?"

"Amy." I chip polish off my nails.

"That really your name?"

"Of course," I say, looking up at him. His eyes seem lighter in the dim hallway, and they stab me straight to the groin. He enters the bathroom.

While I'm on the phone, telling my manager that I think I

have the stomach flu, I unwind my hair from its tight bun and rub my scalp. The toilet flushes.

The bathroom door is ajar. I find his clothes heaped in the hallway. Sweatshirt and jeans, both soiled almost black. I pick them up with the very tips of my fingers and carry them to the stacked washer-dryer in the hallway. I dump in two scoops of soap and a third of a bottle of Lysol disinfectant. The washer fills with hot water and I turn it off to soak.

The shower is running. I walk past again heading for the kitchen. It's not even nine o'clock in the morning, but I mix myself a Stoli and ginger ale on the rocks. Standing over the sink, I gulp it down. My throat spasms from the cold. I fix myself another.

I sit down in the living room and sip my drink. When it's gone, I get up and fix another. I sit back down and wait.

The shower stops. Five minutes later, he's still in there. I put down my empty glass and propel myself back down the hallway. "Everything okay in there?" I call through the small space of open door. He yanks it open and I jump back. He stands there, a towel wrapped around his midsection. His body is beautiful, both lanky and chiseled. His long hair spirals over his shoulders to his nipples. The ends drip water.

"Sure," he says. "I was just getting ready to shave."

"Can you leave a neat mustache and goatee?" I ask, almost panicking at the thought of him shaving his face clean.

"Why not?" He soaps his face looking at me in the mirror. "You look nice with your hair down."

"Thank you." I stand there and watch him shave, just to make sure he does it right. I notice the nail clipper on the countertop. His fingernails and toenails are short and clean. He smells like apple shampoo and Dove soap.

He rinses and turns to face me. "How's that?"

"Perfect," I sigh, my heart thundering away.

He smiles, then takes me in his arms. "You know, since you've been so nice, I've decided to cut you a deal. The hour starts now." He kisses me. Fantasies come so cheaply and they taste like mint and insanity.

Chris stayed for five days. He was a great lover, did everything I told him to. When he left, he took with him a pillowcase half filled with coins. My ashtrays are empty. I haven't seen him again. Bums have migratory patterns known only to them. I am one of the few people I know who have fulfilled a fantasy. It might have been a fantasy of a fantasy, but I am grateful. I count out exact change now, unafraid. My new purse swings lightly in the crook of my elbow. People notice me now, and I let them.

RONALD FRAME

A Piece of Sky

2004's WAS THE wettest August since 1912.

"We'll cheer ourselves up," Gavin said. In a good old-fashioned stationer's shop in Carnbeg he'd bought a five-hundred-piece jigsaw. A view of Princes Street in Edinburgh.

"Take it back!" Suzanne told him. "They'll give your money back, won't they?"

She hadn't tackled a jigsaw since she was child. She was thinking, the man who's asked me to relocate my job and move in with him likes *jigsaws*! How come I never guessed?

"Too late!" Gavin laughed.

He'd opened the box, and with a flourish he tipped out the contents onto a big table in the hotel's winter garden.

Somehow, they both instinctively felt, this was a pursuit for a public place. Sure enough, in the course of the afternoon other guests stopped to look and offer encouragement.

Suzanne didn't stop reminding him how ridiculous this was as they sat side-by-side making sense out of chaos. An activity for two grownups? Jigsaws just devoured your time. But gradually *she* was the one who became engrossed by it.

She pored over the accumulating panorama of Edinburgh on the table-top, continually referring back to the lid of the box. Edinburgh was her city and London was his. In her imagination she was walking along Princes Street, or off it and up to the Royal Mile and on to the Castle Esplanade.

She liked to be orderly, and worked in turn on the spiky Scott Monument, then the bandstand and the trim Gardens, and then the Castle sprawling on its forbidding crag.

"You thought I'd get nostalgic?" she asked him. "So you bought this one?"

"Well, I didn't think you'd want a couple of Bugattis."

"True," she conceded.

"Or Beachy Head Lighthouse either. It was the best of a bad bunch really."

No, that wasn't the reply she'd been anticipating. She felt her mouth settling, in spite of herself, to a prim straight line.

SHE LEFT THE sky till last.

In London you were hardly aware of the sky. Edinburgh's sky was its true crowning glory, she felt. Clouds scudded briskly no-nonsense across it; you could almost *see* the wind.

The sky was the most difficult part of the puzzle. Every so often she would glance up and see Gavin smirking at her concentration. He obviously thought he'd managed to have her succumb.

After however long it had taken them, the end was in sight. She wanted to finish the job before it got dark. An idiotic way to spend an interminable wet afternoon, yes. Suddenly, another forty years on in time, she was hearing him say "D'you remember that first jigsaw we did? Beachy Head Lighthouse."

"No, it wasn't. It was Edinburgh."

"Was it?"

"Princes Street Gardens."

"*Was* it?"

"Don't you believe me, then?"

Did she have a premonition as she was thinking it? Was this really an omen?

The sky had been taking shape under their hands for half-an-hour. She had been telling him what went where. These were the final remaining pieces. A dozen. Six. Four. Two.

Then one, the very last piece.

But two blanks of sky in the picture still left to fill. "There's one missing," she told him.

They looked everywhere. They couldn't find it.

"There must've been one short," he said.

She showed him the peel-off sticker on the box. CHECKED BY B42.

"Then B42 wasn't up to the job."

"Don't blame B42," she said.

"You're taking his side?"

"No, I'm not."

"*Her* side, then?"

Something about the tone of his voice. She was riled.

"Why does it have to be human error?" she asked him. "Human mischief, more like."

"Meaning—?"

"What d'you think I mean, Gavin?"

She went on to say quite a lot of other things—to-the-point, personal, hard-hitting. She was conscious as she was doing so that she might regret them later, but persisted nevertheless. A dam seemed to have burst.

As she got up to leave, to walk out, she caught a final glimpse of Edinburgh—and the missing blank of sky—all that wasted, cheated labor. It was as if that one small absence on the table-top swallowed up all the rest of the picture, and nothing else mattered.

"You've got this all out of proportion," Gavin was saying.

Maybe I have, she was thinking. But she couldn't allow him to win such a big point.

She'd had no intention as she walked off through the winter garden of making this the do-or-die showdown it almost immediately became. But he didn't come running after her, and it was that fact which altered the situation for her. She was changing her mind even as she got into the lift, and up in the bedroom—as the minutes passed, with no apologetic knock on the door—she decided.

It was over.

HE SLOWLY BROKE up the jigsaw, and returned the pieces to the box.

He'd realized what she was implying. That he'd kept one of the pieces back, hidden it. Why the hell would he do that? Understandable that she'd be pissed off because that one last piece was missing, to finish the sky and the whole picture. But was that good enough reason to go flying off?

He didn't see her leave the hotel with her luggage and get into a taxi. He was in the bar. After a couple of strongish drinks up on a stool at the counter, he felt a mite unsteady and moved to one of the low sofas, in a darker corner. He sank into the cushions, spilling a little of drink number three. Shit! It had splashed onto the calves of his trousers, onto the cuffs. He was adjusting the turn-ups when his fingers fidgeted with the cloth at one point. From inside the fold he extracted . . .

A piece of jigsaw! He flipped it over, turned it this way and that to see better. The missing portion of sky, the final one-five-hundreth of the whole. It must have fallen in. Some fluke. Now he could go and find Suzanne and tell her.

He tried to get up, but straightaway fell back. On second (woozy) thoughts . . . What was he going to say? And what was *she* going to say? "Oh, *what* a surprise, you've found it after all!" She would call *him* a "rotter," that damning put-down she used for others. She would assume he'd deliberately hidden it from her, and that finding it was no happy accident. "In the turn-up of your trousers? Seriously?"

"Yes."

"I've only got *your* word."

"Yes."

"Look, Gavin, what d'you take me for?"

From his sofa in the tartan-dressed cocktail bar he didn't hear the Edinburgh train whistling its way into Carnbeg and then out again. He couldn't foresee that a friend of a friend of hers would meet Suzanne at Haymarket station, and they'd go off for a late meal, and hey, that would be the start of something romantic and very special in her life and Ronan's. From Carnbeg he would hear her mobile ringing in her bag, and the phone in the flat, and he would leave quite garbled messages for her on both and not sense that, in the words he'd used at the beginning of the afternoon, it was too late now.

Much too late.

He sat with the fragment of jigsaw in his hand, turning it over and over. It was just a piece of sky. To Suzanne, unbeknown to him, it had been blue (*sensibly* blue), breezy, brac-

ing Edinburgh sky, with traces of high fleecy cloud blown
Fifewards: a one-and-only kind of sky, and oh how she was
pining for it.

HE WOULD HOLD on to that one piece when he'd thrown
out the box with the other four hundred and ninety-nine in
it. He would carry it around in his pocket for many months,
until the card began fraying at its edges and the picture started
to fade.

Suzanne would only ever tell Ronan she had a phobia
about jigsaws, laughing about it, and she would wonder to
herself—once in every long while—what could possibly have
got into her that wet afternoon in Carnbeg.

Gavin would learn to recognize and catch glimpses of that
precise chilly blueness of sky from an aircraft window, or look
up through the car windscreen for it once he was safely married and driving home, with his past very nearly put behind
him.

Stolen Chocolates

M Y FIRST LOVE has tripled in size. I didn't recognize him, though I noticed him when he entered the Greek restaurant, because the waiter replaced his armchair with a piano bench before he let him sit down. He was with a woman who wore apple-green silk and was heavy too, though not nearly his weight.

"Vera," he called out across the restaurant, and hoisted himself from the piano bench. His bulk drifted toward me as if carried by the scent of the exotic spices, surprisingly agile, fleshy hands leading.

I glanced behind me, searching for an escape or some other woman named Vera, though I know it's not a common name. All through school, I was the only Vera in my class.

"Vera, sweetie, it's me—Eddie," he said as if accustomed to identifying himself to people he hadn't seen in a long time. His suit looked expensive, made to order, and in the amber glow of the fringed ceiling lamps, his hair was blond and curly as ever.

"Eddie," I said, trying to reconcile this man with the image of the wiry boy I'd followed around the neighborhood at fourteen. I would wait at the end of his street for hours, heart pounding, just to get a glimpse of him, and when he finally started noticing me, he blotted all the questions and uncertainties I'd felt up to that day about my future. Whenever he helped me with my chores in my grandparents' grocery store, I rewarded him with stolen chocolates that we ate until we both felt as though we were about to explode.

"We will always be together," we said the afternoon he kissed me. "We will always be together," we promised each other in our letters for nearly half a year after his family moved to Cleveland.

"You look good, Vera. Real good." The voice was the same, though the fat had changed his features and stretched his skin so tightly that there wasn't space for a single wrinkle. "How long has it been?"

"Almost thirty years, Eddie."

"How's the food here?"

I felt ill at the thought of him squeezing anything else into that body. "I sold them the restaurant."

"It was yours?"

"No, no. I'm selling real estate now. The new owner, Mr. Fariopoulos, gave me a bonus—two hundred dollars' worth of meals."

"I hear their buffet is famous. All you can eat for twelve ninety-five."

"I usually just order a vegetarian dish."

"My first wife died seven years ago." He said it as if her death had been the result of being a vegetarian. He motioned to his table. "Bonnie over there—we got married the year after."

"Sorry about your first wife. And congratulations on—"

"I don't like weddings."

"Okay."

"But that's what we're in Albany for. Another wedding. My cousin's boy. Come, sit with us."

I hesitated.

"You're probably waiting for someone."

"Not really."

"No argument, then." One hand on my elbow, the other balancing my plate and wineglass, he led me toward his table like a trophy, his hips brushing dangerously close to other tables.

Certain that everyone was staring at us, I felt ashamed of my embarrassment to be seen with him.

He introduced me to his wife, Bonnie. "This is Vera." He beamed. "You know, the Vera of my youth." He made me sound mysterious and glamorous, and I wondered what he'd told his wife about me.

She tucked her handbag under her arm and greeted me with the cautious smile of heavy women who don't trust thin women. Her face had the natural look you can only achieve with skillful makeup.

Eddie sat down, his knees spread to accommodate his enormous thighs. "My cousin says you married a dentist."

"That was finished a long time ago."

"Sorry to hear that."

"Don't. I was ready."

"Any kids?"

"A daughter. She's at the University of New Hampshire."

"Good for you. Bonnie and I, we have our own pharmacy. In a mall. She handles the cosmetics and over-the-counter stuff, I get to count the pills." He laughed. "Amazing . . .

Remember how I used to hate math?" He leaned over to his wife, one hand across his tie to keep it from falling into my glass. "Vera let me copy her homework."

"And you helped me in the store."

But he didn't hear me. He was frowning at my plate of eggplant and rice. "I think I'll go for the buffet, Bonnie."

"Me too."

His enormous backside blocked out half the buffet table as he loaded up his plate. Oh, Eddie, I thought, Eddie, unable to continue my meal as I watched him eat silently, shoveling his food into his mouth at an alarming speed, giving shape to my deepest fears. To think I used to eat like that as a girl. To think I sometimes still longed to eat like that.

"How long are you staying in Albany, Eddie?" I asked, wishing he hadn't come back at all.

"Hold that question, Vera, I'll be right back." His breath had taken on the rich aroma of the food. Pushing the piano bench back, he headed for the buffet.

Bonnie only kept up with him for three trips, and then she sank into her chair, tiny beads of moisture between her perfect eyebrows; but Eddie kept returning for more, and with each bite he swallowed, I felt my stomach distend, harden.

It was on Eddie's fifth approach to the buffet that the owner of the restaurant, Mr. Fariopoulos, stepped into his way. He was nearly a head shorter than Eddie, and he raised one lean hand and held it up in front of Eddie's chest to stop him. Without lowering his voice, he informed Eddie that he had eaten enough. "More than enough," Mr. Fariopoulos said.

His face purple-red, Eddie stood there like a boy caught stealing chocolates, and I felt his humiliation as though it were my own. Nearly everyone in the restaurant was watching him, except Bonnie, who was staring at the white tablecloth, her face rigid. Eddie opened his mouth—not to say something, but to breathe easier. He did not move—neither toward the buffet nor toward our table.

I had no idea what I was about to say when I got up and walked toward Eddie and Mr. Fariopoulos. My stomach was aching as if I'd eaten far too much, and my heart was beating as fiercely as all those times I'd waited for Eddie to appear in the door of his house.

I linked my arm through his and gave a nod to Mr. Fariopoulos. "I'm glad you've had a chance to meet my friend Eddie."

"Vera—" Mr. Fariopoulos started.

"The menu," I asked, "what do you have printed next to the word 'buffet'? Is it 'all you can eat'? Or 'all we let you eat'?"

"You and your friends are always welcome here."

"All we let you eat?"

"All you can eat. You know that. But we can't afford to keep this place open if everyone eats like him."

"Then I'll be glad to put it back on the market for you."

"Vera," Eddie said, "you don't have to—"

"But I do," I said, and turned to Mr. Fariopoulos. "Tell me"—now I was going—"how many of your customers stop after the first trip to the buffet? Do you give them a discount? A doggie bag?"

It ended up with Mr. Fariopoulos apologizing to Eddie and telling him there would be no bill at all. In the parking lot, Eddie was rather quiet, and his hands felt cold when I grasped them to say goodbye, but Bonnie told me to visit them if I ever got to Cleveland. What I didn't expect was the dream I had that night, a wonderfully erotic dream about Eddie—not the way he used to look as a boy, when I'd suffered that first, glorious crush on him, but the way he was now. He drew me into his huge embrace, sheltered me against his solid chest. We were lying in the meadow behind my grandparents' store, and spread in front of us were all the pastries and cakes I had ever denied myself. We ate together passionately, joyfully—letting each other taste the most satisfying delicacies without remorse. Eddie's breath was sweet as he consumed me with his hungry mouth, replenished me with his hungry mouth. My arms were long enough to reach around him. His body felt light as he enveloped me into his soft vastness, so light that he took us all the way up to the sky.

Juan the Cell Phone Salesman

IT WAS A holiday which means the woman in question went home. And this included an encounter with the mother of the woman in question, and the mother's questioning of the woman upon her arrival. The woman questioned waited for her special box on the go-round and endured.

That same evening, over chicken and lemonade, the mother made a strange statement: She had pinpointed on this earth the Perfect Man for the woman in question. Actually she had found two. But one perfect man was out of town so luckily there was another.

The second Perfect Man had a name and a career and those were Juan and cellular phone salesman respectively. The mother and the little sister showed the woman the phone he had touched and sold them and explained how its presence had transformed them into a super-efficient mother/daughter tag team. Team of two, that is, until today, happily, now three, if only momentarily, now that she, older sister, woman in question, was home.

A cell phone salesman, said the woman. This is who you want your daughter to plan her future with.

How, said the mother, did my daughter come to be such a snob.

The woman questioned was slipping through thin fingers as she phoned Juan the cellular phone salesman on mother's cellular phone, phone to phone, phoned because when the woman at first refused, mother said that she was deliberately ruining Christmas for everyone.

Several hours if not a whole day had elapsed by this time. And then there were several more hours, if not a whole day, while the woman and mother and sister waited for Juan to pick up his cellular and phone their home. Which he didn't. The mother carried the cellular phone from room to room, set it next to her as she pinned balls to the tree, and said, Where is he? Where could he be? Maybe she should call again. How did she know he'd even gotten the message, those cell phones are so unreliable and she should call again.

Obediently, foolishly, the woman in question did call again, while meeting eyes with the younger sister and noting a note of sympathy in them because everyone knows that according to the social rules and regulations we have agreed on, to leave two messages for a stranger is a bit untoward. But she left it, then retreated to her bedroom like the old days.

Sure enough, he still didn't call, and sure enough, the mother was like a bride left at the altar. How dare he not call. She walked through the house, checking the phones one by one. He had said he'd like to take her out and she had shown him the nicest picture and now why would he lie, the bastard. Slowly, slowly, the mother circled around and around with the cellular phone. She tried to be casual, the mother, tapping on the door, Hey let's call Juan! like it was a forgotten invitation to a party. But the woman—woman, yes, not a little girl of nine—would not be fooled and even the sister agreed that three times was two times too many but when the mother began to get the swirled crazy eyes, the woman grabbed the phone and phoned again. This time though she lost all patience and dignity and said onto his voice mail the devastating: Hello Juan, my mother would like to go out with you.

What happened next happened fast, which is why the mistake about the off button was made. When mother grabbed the phone from the woman, she screamed a word that wasn't very nice, about the woman in question, screamed it before she realized about the off button, that nobody had pressed it, and everybody stood horrified for one long moment before mother ran from the room.

That afternoon the sister and the woman in question had fun with the phone, shouting desperately into the cellular, *Juan, we miss you, Juan!* or sternly, *Juan, you're ruining Christmas for everyone,* or sadly, *Juan, please call us, Juan, and leave us a little message,* or angrily, *It's over for good this time, Juan. Don't ever call us again!* And the woman in question felt, well, pleased with her sister, but also a bit unwomanly as she stuck herself under her thin blanket that evening.

This part is miraculous: Juan phoned the next day. He phoned while the woman was showering.

He phoned and I nearly dropped the receiver, said the sister, which would not have been good. These little phones are delicate creatures.

He phoned and he spoke charmingly, said the sister. He, as always, asked many interesting questions.

Which is impossible, of course, to even say such a thing

because how long is always if you've only spoken to him twice?

It's the kind of man he is, insisted the sister. The kind who asks questions and listens and asks more questions.

Like a talk show host, said the woman. What a treat. Still she will go out with him on this very night. And for the next several hours the three, they are a three, yes. Look at them, they sew and unclutter, they pin hair and dresses. How womanly they are, how sisterly, how motherly, daughterly.

And now here is the climax. Look how they stand in the mirror, the three, and joke and apply lipstick for the Coming Juan, the cell phone salesman. The sister says she almost wishes she could go in her place and the woman in question says she doesn't see why she shouldn't, who cares if she's only sixteen, the sister and she could simply swap names. Or better yet they could both go and say they have the same name and are, in fact, doubles. And the sister and the woman practice in the mirror saying her name over and over, in unison and separately, and the mother joins in like a song. This is a nice moment.

The next moment is not so nice. It will be a few hours later and Juan will be very drunk and unable to drive the woman in question home. She will also be drunk and having an unpleasant time with Juan who can be a little mean. And she will—by this time she is in his apartment, an unsavory detail—phone mother on Juan's cellular phone at three in the morning, and mother and sister will come to retrieve her, minus one shoe which she will never recover, and it will be at this moment that Juan will utter the only statement anyone anywhere will ever remember him making, and he will roar it as he lifts his head from between two couch cushions: "Get your drunk sister out of here!" he will say and that will be his great contribution. Thank you, Juan.

The very last part is this: We are in the front seat without any lipstick on, me and mother and sister. It is dark and late. We aren't talking about Juan.

TOM FRANKLIN

Nap Time

THE BABY WAS finally down, so the parents took a nap, too. But they couldn't sleep.

Her husband said, "Listen how quiet."

They listened. It was late in the evening and the walls of the room were colored red by the sun through the red drapes, drapes she hated but hadn't yet replaced. The landlord had told them they could make any cosmetic changes they wanted. But nothing came off the rent, he'd said.

"How long does it normally last?" her husband asked.

"Two or three months, according to the book. Didn't you read it?"

"Not yet." He rubbed his eyes with the heels of his hands. Except for their socks, both were naked, thinking they might have sex before their nap. Until now, they'd mostly been too tired to try, and when they had, she'd been too sore.

Then she said, "When he's screaming like that and you've been carrying him all night, swinging him till you can't feel your arms, do you ever think about, like, dropping him? Just letting him fall out of your hands?"

Her husband didn't answer, and she thought she'd said the wrong thing. But he took a breath. "Yeah," he said. "Sometimes I do. Sometimes I think about dropping him on the porch." Which was concrete.

She propped up on an elbow. "Really? God, I'm relieved to hear you say that. I've been thinking I'm the worst mother imaginable."

For a while, neither said anything.

Then, "Sometimes," he said, "I go farther with it."

"Farther? How?"

"I'll be driving, like on the interstate, and he'll be screaming, and I'll think, what if I were to sling him out the window. Car seat and all."

She didn't say anything. She wished it were darker in the room.

He looked at her. "You must think I'm terrible."

She leaned and kissed his shoulder blankly. "No, of course not." She sat up, her elbows orange in the light, Band-Aids on her nipples, and reached for her cigarettes and shook one out of the package. "The other day I thought—" She lit the cigarette.

"Tell me."

"I was carrying him, I'd been lugging him around in that colic hold for two hours and he was crying, crying, crying. Nothing would make him stop, and I was so exhausted. I'd walked around the house so many times I'd started doing it with my eyes closed, counting my steps, and he still kept crying." She drew on her cigarette. "I went through the kitchen for like the thousandth time, and I thought, god, of putting him in the microwave."

He moved his feet under the sheets. "We did that to a hamster when I was a kid."

"Really?"

"Yeah. My brother was at school and I was home sick. I wasn't really sick. I'd pretended to have a stomachache. Me and my little sister took his hamster out of its cage and I held it under the faucet. We wanted to see what it looked like wet. But when we did it, we realized mostly all it was was hair, the little body was only as big around as your finger. We thought, he'll know we did this. So I put the hamster in the microwave." He hesitated.

She could feel him breathing. "What happened?"

"It started steaming, so we took it out. It seemed fine at first. Then, about two weeks later, it grew this huge tumor on its neck. It kept crawling in a circle in the cage until it finally stopped under the little Ferris wheel and lay there breathing hard. In the morning it was dead."

"God," she said. She looked at her cigarette and dropped it in the Diet Coke can on the table beside the baby book. She'd quit smoking when she learned she was pregnant, and except for New Year's Eve and Mardi Gras and two or three other nights she'd been vigilant. With drinking too. But when the baby came she'd had problems breastfeeding, her milk ducts infected, oozing thick green pus, the baby almost malnourished, screaming so loud in the doctor's office the nurses had to yell to hear each other. So she'd been forced to use bottles and thought, Why not smoke? But she didn't enjoy it anymore.

"Did your brother ever find out?" she asked, lying back.

"No. I told my sister if she ever blabbed, I'd put her in the microwave. To this day she won't use one." He gave a dry laugh.

She looked over at him for a long time, taste of nicotine in her mouth and nose. Then she said, "Okay. I've got one." She put her arms under the covers, felt his foot brush against hers. "Growing up, I knew this girl who was murdered. Somebody grabbed her off the street while she was walking home from the pharmacy where she worked after school. It was almost dark. They found her body in the woods half a mile from this dirt road she'd never been on in her life. She'd been hit in the forehead with some kind of hammer. She was dead. My best friend's older sister."

"You never told me that," he said. "Did they find out who did it?"

"The police went crazy looking. They were interviewing everybody they could find. They stopped people on the street and went door to door, but all they ever got was that somebody might've seen a pickup. Then one night, it was a week after the funeral, I had this dream. I dreamed I was her, and I was walking home from the pharmacy. Wearing the same green pastel dress she'd had on. I knew it was me, but I was her, too, somehow. And I knew what was going to happen, but I couldn't stop it. I turned around and this truck had pulled up beside me, a blue pickup truck. The door opened and this guy I sort of knew was driving it. He was our preacher's son's friend, who'd been kicked out of the marines. I knew not to get in the truck with him, but he showed me that he had a joint, and so I got in anyway. We drove without saying anything. His radio was playing Dylan, but I can't remember what song. He turned on a county road and kept driving. I couldn't remember his name but he had cute side-burns and a cute little chin. I liked the way his Adam's apple bobbed and the way he smoked his cigarette. The way it looked in his fingers. Then he turned onto the dirt road."

Her husband had rolled to face her. He put his hand on her stomach, which was softer than before, the skin loose and cool.

"He stopped the truck right where all the police cars and the ambulances would be later," she said. "We got out and he took my hand and led me into the woods. On a path I hadn't even seen. We walked for a long time, holding hands, till you couldn't hear any cars anywhere. You couldn't hear anything. We smoked the joint and he started unbuttoning my dress. I let him. I was buzzing all over. I let him do whatever he wanted—"

"What'd he do?" He was moving his hand on her stomach, going lower. She could feel him getting hard against her leg.

"I let him, you know."

"Did you like it?"

She shifted her hips. "Yes," she said. "I liked it."

He said, "Then what happened," as his hand opened her thighs. "He took this hammer out of his pocket," she said, "and I shut my eyes, and he hit me right here—" She touched herself at the bridge of her nose. "And I woke up panicked, with this splitting pain in my forehead."

He moved his hand gently into place. "Was it him? Was it the preacher's son's friend?"

"I don't know. Nobody was ever arrested."

He began to rub her with the pad of his thumb, the way she liked. "Did you tell anybody?"

"No," she said, her eyes closed, "I never told anybody . . ."

He whipped the sheet up and in the tented air rolled on top of her. When the sheet had floated back down around them he was already edging in in his familiar way. He went slowly and she stretched her legs so exquisitely her hips popped and when he murmured against her neck did it feel good she could only nod and raise her knees. She was climbing in the truck again and there he was, holding his cigarette in his fingers. He offered it to her across the long bench seat which had a quilt over it, and she took the cigarette and put it to her lips and sucked in the good-tasting hot smoke. Drive, she told him.

But something was wrong. She opened her eyes.

"Listen," she said.

In his room, across the hall, behind the closed door, the baby was silent.

Audio Tour

HELLO, AND WELCOME to the rent-stabilized apartment of Todd Niesle. I'm Debby, a specialist in Todd Niesle, and I'm going to be your guide. Before you begin your journey through the World of Todd Niesle and His Stuff, may I ask you to reduce the volume on your Acoustiguide player to a polite level? Todd Niesle does not know that you are here. Moreover, the woman in 12-A has had a bee in her bonnet about me ever since I, Debby, while, O.K., yes, a tiny bit drunk, mistook her door for Todd Niesle's late one night and jimmied it open. But that's another Acousti-story.

You are standing in Todd Niesle's foyer. The faux faux-marble table on your right is attributed to Todd Niesle's mother, circa last Christmas. It's a fine example of a piece that I, Debby, do not like. Take a moment to look through the mail on the faux faux-marble table. There should be a lot of it, because Todd Niesle is away, skiing in Vermont with his brother. Is there a letter postmarked Milwaukee? Just curious.

Proceed through the foyer and into the living room. In this room, we can see the influence of early Michelle. Notice how Michelle seems to like making bold statements with splashes of color, especially in upholstery. You can tell by the excess of passementerie on the throw pillows what an incorrigible bitch Michelle is. If you care to pause to look at some of the art and other knickknacks, simply press the red button on your Acoustiguide. We will continue at the medicine cabinet in the bathroom off the master bedroom.

To reach the master bedroom, you must traverse the cavernous room on your left. The sole function of that room is to provide a way to the next room. It doesn't seem fair that Todd Niesle pays only eleven hundred dollars a month for this spacious two-bedroom with a dining room, when I, Debby, happen to know that his income far exceeds the maximum allowed for a tenant in a rent-stabilized apartment. Furthermore, I, Debby, have heard Todd Niesle say on more than one occasion, "There's tons more closet space here than I know what to do with." And yet I, Debby, was never offered more than half a drawer, and even that humiliating amount I had to demand. The phone number for the Rent Info Hotline is 718-739-6400 (ask for Eligibility Violations).

Examine the objects in the master bedroom. Here is the famous jar of pennies and the original green shag rug from Todd Niesle's college days. Pay close attention to the black lace brassiere in the bottom drawer of Todd Niesle's bureau. The brassiere (36D) is not typical of the underwear of Todd Niesle. Or of mine (32B). You may be wondering what the brassiere is doing in this exhibit of the World of Todd Niesle and His Stuff. As Todd Niesle's quondam girlfriend, I, Debby, am wondering this, too.

Now we're in the bathroom. Actually, don't bother looking through the medicine cabinet. Todd Niesle must have taken all of the incriminating artifacts with him to Vermont.

Our next stop is the kitchen. Open the refrigerator. The carton of milk dates from the twelfth century A.D. See the Krups espresso maker? I, Debby, gave him that. It cost two hundred and forty-nine dollars, not including tax. You know what his gift to me, Debby, for my birthday was? A colander. You will observe that Todd Niesle's apartment has no gift shop. Correction: You are standing in the gift shop. Take the espresso maker.

As you help yourself to the professional-grade milk frother that I, Debby, also gave to Todd Niesle, be careful not to step on the creaky floorboard, as it will alert the neighbor down-stairs, who also has it in for me. She's insane. Besides, I, Debby, wouldn't even know how to poison a dog.

We are now in the commodious coat closet in Todd Niesle's foyer. Our eyes are drawn immediately to the strik-ing composition of the skis and the parka against the back wall. This is a stunning visual statement about a man who is on vacation, skiing with his brother, isn't it? Once again, Todd Niesle proves himself to be a master at creating a scenario that elicits powerful emotions, such as hatred and disgust.

After you have scrolled through the caller-I.D. log on the phone in the study, looking for Todd Niesle's brother's num-ber to see if Todd Niesle really went to Vermont, place a prank call to Sue Ann Kraftsow. She lives in Milwaukee and she's in the book.

Please turn to your right. Just past the doorway, you'll see a framed photograph. The subject of this photograph has not been identified with certainty, but Todd Niesle scholars like me, Debby, believe that it depicts Sue Ann Kraftsow.

Now go back to the gift shop and get a knife from the drawer next to the sink. When you pry the backing from the picture frame, a photograph of me, Debby, will be revealed. In the art world, this is called "pentimento." In the real world, this is called failure to commit and to recognize undying love when you have the luck to get it.

Compare the two images. Can you discern from the vulgar contours of Sue Ann Kraftsow's face, the lifeless pallor, and the vague gaze that she is unworthy of even as base a miscreant as Todd Niesle? She's also fat. The second image, of me, Debby, on the other hand, shows a woman blessed with keen intelligence and generosity of spirit. It would be unscholarly of me, Debby, to point out the obvious aesthetic differences, but you, the viewer, can draw your own conclusions.

We have come to the end of our retrospective of the World of Todd Niesle and His Shit. You can return your Acoustiguide in the foyer. There is no charge for this tour, but, if you enjoyed yourself, call Todd Niesle and tell him so. His number is 212-399-4838 and he can be reached at 3 A.M. He likes pizza, ten pies at a time, and Rizzo's delivers. I, Debby, care not what you do with the key.

Paper Slippers

Y OU GET PREGNANT on October 22nd although you
don't realize it until well into November. Your body
starts changing; your breasts swell a little and become more
sensitive to touch and you start to get an obsessive enjoyment
out of food for the first time in your life. You feel good and
happy just because you're enjoying all the newness.

You go to a doctor, nevertheless, to make sure. You urinate
into a small plastic cup, being careful not to let anything run
out over the side, and take it to the woman at the desk. She
has café-au-lait-colored skin, and her nose is long and thin, its
nostrils bending over her front lip as though trying to peer
into her mouth. You wonder if the skin behind her fingernails
is white because of a lack of pigment like in her palms, or
because of the pressure of the nails on the skin. She looks at
your face studiously, her eyes slightly squinted behind their
spectacles, as though trying to figure out what you're feeling:
fear, hope, excitement, embarrassment. You imagine you look
very young to her. But you don't really feel anything except

a sort of strange smugness, and she looks disappointed that she can derive nothing from your expression.

The result is positive, as you knew it would be. The woman at the desk once again seems unsatisfied with your lack of a reaction.

"And how would you like to proceed from here?" she asks.

"Excuse me?" you reply.

"Well, would you like to follow through with the pregnancy or should I schedule you for a D&C?"

"A D&C?" you ask, obviously unclear as to what it means, and too distracted to try to deduce it.

"An abortion," she replies with her head slightly cocked downwards as though she is speaking into her pencil sharpener.

"Oh, no thank you," you say, "nothing for the moment." You take your coat from the closet and leave without putting it on. "Good-bye," you say. You don't hear her return your farewell before the door is completely shut, although she may have. You come home, eat an entire cold roasted chicken with bread and mayonnaise, put on sweat pants and a T-shirt, and crawl into bed with a book of stories by Hemingway. You turn first to your favorite story, to where the book naturally opens, and read the beginning as you always do before turning to anything unfamiliar. "MADRID is full of boys named Paco," it begins, "which is the diminutive of the name Francisco, and there is a Madrid joke about a father who came to Madrid and inserted an advertisement in the personal columns of El Liberal which said: PACO MEET ME AT HOTEL MONTANA NOON TUESDAY ALL IS FORGIVEN PAPA and how a squadron of Guardia Civil had to be called out to disperse the eight hundred young men who answered the advertisement." Every time you read this passage you get a kind of weak feeling in your stomach (just because it is so beautiful), like on the few occasions when you would watch blood being drawn from the middle of your arm. After about two hours, you shut off the light, lie on your back, arrange the blankets using your arms and legs, rest your hands on your belly, and close your eyes for the night.

And your belly grows. You don't really encourage it to, but you don't do anything to stop it, and it takes off, as though of its own will. At first it is just a little lump in the usual flatness, until finally it becomes something big and unevenly round, the dent of the belly button having disappeared, and the skin pulled to a bluish tightness. You find you're running to the bathroom far more than you used to, and when you ask why you are told your kidneys are now working for two. Your hair becomes thicker and grows quickly and wildly. You become cautious at sidewalk steps and revolving doors.

Finally, the day arrives. It is the third week of July, and it is so hot and humid you expect fish to pass by the windows. Labor is difficult, but not unbearable. You try to be cooperative, and constantly remind yourself that it isn't going to last forever. You accept the epidural when it is offered, even though you vowed you wouldn't. When you first see him, in your delirium, you think he looks strange like someone else's child. You decide he should be called Alex.

The first months are the most difficult because he can't speak. You leave school and take a job as an assistant at a publishing company. You bring him to day care every morning and pick him up after work. Most of the children there are from black or Hispanic families, as are the ladies hired to take care of them. Alex is white as soap, like you, and you wonder if you are being racist toward them by wondering if they will be toward him. You read articles about children who are drugged by their caretakers to keep them from crying, or not given any human contact for hours on end. And because he is unable to tell you what happens to him when you are not around, you lead a very restless life for what seems like a very long time.

His early years pass slowly, but not without the usual milestones: when he can hold his head up; the first sounds resembling words; the first movements resembling crawls; the first real steps. Still, you don't get much sleep and you worry about the future: whether you'll have enough time and money to raise a secure child; how you are supposed to explain the fact that he has no apparent father.

When the time comes and the questions arise you tell him that his father is a journalist and that he travels to many different countries, sometimes putting himself in great danger. You say that although you haven't heard from him in a long time, you are certain that if he is well he will contact you one day. You try to look sincere. The truth is that last you heard he *had* become a journalist, but somehow you don't doubt his safety. You also don't believe he has any intention of seeing either you or his son ever again, nor do you expect him to. He was strongly against your having the child.

And so Alex grows, bringing less hardship than you had expected. In kindergarten, he is the first to learn to read, and by the first grade he has mastered the grip of the pencil so that he can not only write, but can draw beautifully as well. He makes little plasticine figures that both he and you take great pride in, and soon they decorate every corner of your apartment. And you become friends. You read him postcards that come from far away. You take him food shopping and quietly gossip about people in line with funny toes or hats or mustaches that have been twirled into a second smile. You take him camping and horseback riding, things you used to do with his father. And once in a while, even late on a school night, you turn up the volume on the radio, and dance until you're both silly with exhaustion.

And soon you are celebrating his first decade, just the two of you (he is too old for birthday parties now, you are told), first at home with a small cake barely able to contain its eleven candles, and then in the bicycle shop where you tell him he can choose any one he wants, within reason. You have been promoted in your job, which you now call a career, and living conditions are better although your time is still pressed. You aren't seeing anyone romantically because you have neither the time nor the desire, but the thought of marrying crosses your mind on occasion. Alex becomes silently convinced of his father's death.

And so life passes. You conform to the parenthood role into which you still don't completely fit. You enforce ridiculous rules concerning table manners and chores and maximum hours of television. But you also give him books to read and movies to see, and he soon learns to trust your judgment. In junior high he takes up playing the guitar as a hobby, and sometimes when you are in bed at night, you don't allow yourself to sleep in order to hear him and his Fender from underneath your door.

AND THAT'S WHEN you decide to go back.

Perhaps he doesn't do well in school at all, and his teachers merely let him get by, thinking he's just another boy from a broken home. And maybe in junior high he becomes close friends with "Stretch," a skinny, irreverent kid with yellow teeth, and starts skipping school and smoking pot and not car-ing anymore about the books you so carefully choose for him. And perhaps one day, when you angrily pick him and Stretch up from the police station after they've been caught shoplifting, he decides that you aren't his friend after all, you are his mother, no better or worse than any other mother. And maybe that day, on your way home, he asks you softly, from the passenger seat, if you really think you've been such a good role model with your lonely life and your crappy job, while Stretch broadcasts a condescending yellow grin into your rear-view mirror.

And then you go back further and wonder if *he* is really a he at all, or if you should be adding that crucial *a* to the end of the name you are now so comfortable with. And you slowly proceed to forget how to gently clean between the many fine creases of baby testicles.

And then you take the final step and call the lady at the desk and tell her. And a half a month later, you put on a little blue paper robe with little blue paper slippers and watch your knees strapped to cold metal lest they betray you. And you cry and feel like a hypocrite for crying, and you leave the room empty. And the father of your emptiness waits for you, and hugs you when he sees you, as if he loves you. But you feel hatred for him that his love is so paltry, so incomplete, that it lets him sleep so peacefully at night.

Crossroad

Two weeks it had been now, and still no show. She'd seen it twice: this young-but-not-so-young couple pausing at the crossroad, her car and his pickup, to enact their odd drama, smack in the middle of the highway, there where Gophertown Road met Interstate 5.

Tonight it'll happen, she told Piper, her neighbor, who'd joined them—he sat between Viv and her on the porch in her dead husband's chair. The roadside anise was strong this evening, intermixed with auto exhaust.

Just watch, she told him.

I'm watching, he said, bald head glowing in the gold light.

He'd been over a number of afternoon-evenings this week, quaffing iced tea, crunching El's Waverly Wafers. And had seen nothing—nothing besides the usual light traffic of cats, tractors and trucks, the UPS van, the corn patch across the way and garden of melons, the occasional jackrabbit. But Vivian had seen the thing too—the second manifestation, to use

Eleanor's phrase—so he was obliged to believe it was true. Two against one.

This'll fix Piper, El said, pouring more tea. Piper the unbeliever.

Piper the skeptic, Viv said. She'd lived upstairs ten months, had known El since high school, read readers' club books, and never married. She'd worked at Value City thirty-eight years; retail, clothing. She rented the top half of El's house.

Piper the cynic, said El.

Piper the piper, Viv said.

You two're prone to visions, I fear, said Piper. Alone or together.

Eleanor laughed, said Pooh, glanced over.

He looked good for his age—he kept his back straight despite his belly and had a fine face, never mind the avocado nose (he'd given up booze), the wattles starting to show at his throat. He wasn't really a cynic but a docile, agreeable, if faintly bitter ex-plumber, raised three miles away, fond of TV and yet bookish, unlike Hank, her slumpy imported departed. Piper'd lost his spouse also, though long ago, i.e., the late '70s. And not, by the way, to the Maker, but to a man from West Mead, a Catholic. A man who raised chickens.

I'm patient, Piper said, grinning.

So are we, Viv said, raising her cup. She herself was well kept, permed and attractive, if frail, and no virgin, old maid or not. She'd warmed up to Piper as well.

Well? he asked.

Hold your horses, Eleanor said, trotting out the cliché.

Have a cracker, said Viv.

The first time El saw it herself. A sultry evening it was, not unlike this one, and about this hour, when the sky, sighing, went Winchester blue. She'd stared up from her newspaper crossword as a truck and a car, first the one, then the other, rolled toward the stop sign. A man leaped from the pickup (red, snazzy with pinstripes), ran back, knelt beside the sedan (cream-white in that light, the color of brides) and handed the woman a package. She took it, exclaimed, tore the thing open, squealed. Then all but yanked the man through the window, knocking his cap off, his baseball cap, which landed belly-up on the road.

Piper finished his cracker and chased it with tea. None of them spoke. A feed truck rattled up on Gophertown Road, signaled, made a wide left onto the highway.

The next time El saw it with Viv. Same thing, except this time the man fed her a peach, or nectarine, and wiped her mouth for her—of course with his tongue. After the smooching and cap tumbling off he danced her around on the asphalt, something between a waltz and a polka, then bowed, bending down, one leg sticking out stiff, doffing the cap (which he'd retrieved from its place by her tire) with a circular motion like some Renaissance fop, all codpiece and tights. Then *she* jumped into the pickup, he into the sedan, and off they went.

The thing was, despite El's assurances, chances were it wouldn't happen again. Twice might've been all they were in for. People who fall in love with such fervor fall out just as easy, she knew. The love stuff between her and Hank died long, long before he did, which is to say in the first five years. Often she wondered—lately, especially, now that his ghost had stopped hovering, occupying the chair in which Piper now sat, stopped breathing chill breath on her cheek in bed in the wee hours of morning, murmuring Ellie, Ellie, why did we, can't we . . . never completing his sentence—now, that is, that he'd released her at last, she wondered what might have happened if it'd all happened differently.

If they'd started as friends, say. Porch jokers, drinkers of tea. Idle, unhurried, mindful. Minus the idiocy, the romance, the lunacy no one can maintain. No wonder every couple you saw at the market, or most, had that death-in-life look, dead sad, so many. Sleepwalking through the bad dreams they became.

Viv stepped inside to visit the toilet, excusing herself. A state trooper cruised past on the interstate, white letters on dusty dark green. Piper grinned over at Eleanor, head gleaming.

Sweet night, he noted.

Ah, she agreed. Beats TV.

Beats lots of things, he said, sighing.

Dusk was beginning to clot—the sky'd opened up with all its wet stars. Across the road fat melons shone on their stems, refulgent, like unmoving buoys. It was no show again, no refund on tickets. Hard not to feel shortchanged, in a way. But so what? El was out here for Piper, as Viv was, the mobile love drama merely the ostensible reason. In his humorous backwater courtly manner, too, he seemed to favor her, Eleanor, in spite of Viv's superior looks. El *was* a homeowner, after all. Unlike good, impecunious Viv.

Then it began. She'd given up, resigned herself altogether to twilight: that's when it started. They came blasting in, the woman in the lead for a change, the man behind honking, flashing the emergency flashers, off- and on-ing his headlights. Out he leaped in his cap as she stopped at the stop sign. He dashed up to rap on her window—lavender, her car looked, in the fading light.

Her door jerked open. Son of a bitch! she screamed.

He backed up in his boots, pleading as she advanced. Son of a bitch! she kept screaming. He stood two heads taller than she, albeit deflated—much more gawky and skinny, less TV-idyllic, El noticed, than last time. The woman seemed a bit dumpy, for that matter, with her overblown butt and stumpy legs.

Viv had returned and hung at the door, barely breathing. She appeared shaken, abashed. She'd had few serious dealings in love; she'd told El so herself.

Wait, listen, the man howled.

No, yelled the woman and began to climb into the car.

He'd been clutching her fingers and clutched harder now, hoping to delay her escape. She lunged, punched him square in the stomach. Over he went, bent double, like a pump in the no-pump position. The cap fluttered off.

El glanced at Piper. Piper gazed at the pair—the woman glowered, the man held his gut—beaming, elbows on knees, leaning toward the porch railing. It was as if this were the show he'd expected. Made to order. Precisely in the evolution of things. He looked delighted, prepared to applaud.

She understood then that she would marry this man. Her friend, this plumber, ex-plumber, Piper. She loved his purple nose, his battered knuckles and bandaged smile, the sweet way he'd snort when he laughed—loved him, yes, and not just because Viv did, or seemed to. He made her laugh; he made her feel lighter. He had nice teeth, thought before he spoke, caught cracker crumbs in his palm to toss past the railing. He didn't let hard luck take his good fortune hostage either, or not often, and would say, Hey, Jesus, life's life, why be unhappy?

Eleanor reached for the pitcher. Viv eased into her chair.

Piper pressed index finger to lip, twinkling. El poured out the last of the tea. The anise scent rose, riding the breeze, accented by carbon dioxide. The couple continued, did their dance in the dark at the crossroad, long after twilight, with no light left to see.

Determinants

SHE IS, LIKE Jimmy, in her fifties. Her hair, pulled back in a bun, is like his, graying. They both need glasses. She is as black as Jimmy is white. Her figure is compact for her age, or well corseted. Do women still wear corsets?

She leads him into the fitting room. She does not smile. She has always seemed to like him the least of any of the staff who fill his orders for prescription anti-embolism stockings—a sort of super-strength, super-expensive, custom-made support hose that one wears if one has been hospitalized for blood clots in the lungs. She is the only one who insists he leave a hundred-buck deposit when reordering. She was not happy when he kept calling to see if the last pair, delayed three months, were ever going to arrive.

He sits on the edge of the padded fitting table and pulls off the pair he is replacing, which have lost, as they do within two or three months, a great deal of their elasticity. "I think I need tighter ones next time," he says.

She stares at the wrinkles in the pair he is removing: "Have you lost weight?"

"I've lost about twenty pounds, I guess, since I was measured for these."

"You should get re-measured at least once a year when you're losing weight or gaining weight."

"Next time," he says, reflecting on the extra fifteen bucks a leg that will push the cost of a single pair over two hundred dollars. Non-durable prosthetics are the one thing his insurance does not cover.

She has removed the new pair from their plastic wrappings and is rolling one of them into the proper fold for donning. She alights on a wooden chair across from Jimmy and gestures to her lap, her skirt pulled tight a few inches above her shiny, nylon-stockinged knees: "Right-foot first."

A bit surprised, Jimmy complies, his right heel coming to rest atop her firm lower thighs. She struggles to ease the stockings over his heel without tearing the stiff reinforced fabric, a fraction of an inch at a time. "This is the tricky part," she says.

"I know," Jimmy says. He would not have been so gentle, but that is no doubt why his stockings also wear through and wear out sooner than they should.

"They have to be tight to do any good," she says.

"I know."

"There we go," she says, as the stocking heel conforms to Jimmy's. It is easier to tug the top of the stocking gently up his calf. "Over the hills and through the woods. . ." he says . . .

". . . to grandmother's house we go," she finishes.

"We were raised on the same rhymes," he says. "I wonder if the kids today grow up on that one."

She shakes her head: "I don't know what their parents pass on to them today. Maybe nothing. I read every night to my babies, just as my mother read to us."

"My mother read to me," Jimmy says, "and then she had me reading to her. She was a schoolteacher." First grade, he remembers. At an all-Negro school. "I teach," he says, "and I find I can't take anything for granted anymore—can't assume that my younger students will have grown up on any of the staples I did."

She smooths the stocking up his calf, removing a wrinkle or two. He does not have to wear the style that go above the knee, or, thank God, the panty-hose. "Other one," she says, as one of his aunts might have, and he removes his right foot and settles his left on her tight-kneed lap, taking pleasure in the businesslike quasi-intimacy of their contact. "I doubt the young ones grow up on any of the songs and rhymes that I did," she says. "Of course they have their own music, if you can call it that."

"They certainly have more social life than we did," Jimmy says.

"Social life!" she laughs. "Church was our social life."

"A young teacher at one of the high schools (a young black woman, he thinks) told me if her students' parents are younger than thirty she tells the kids to have their grandparents come to see her because the parents will have as many problems as their kids, or worse."

"I believe that," she says. "I don't even want to think about the drugs."

"I know that I don't have the answer," Jimmy says.

"The answer is the family," she says, "but what's the answer for the family?"

"I don't have that one either," Jimmy says.

"Well," she says, smoothing the stocking up his left calf, "these fit fine for now, but you make an appointment for re-measuring before we order the next pair."

"I'll do that," he says, removing his foot from her firm lap with some reluctance. "I guess I'll just wear these new ones."

"Might as well," she says, wrapping the old pair for him. He follows her out to the cashier, observing the pull of her skirt against her hips. Handsome, he thinks; a handsome woman is how we would have referred to someone still attractive at her age. Probably, he thinks, the business of my foot on her lap and rubbing my calves meant nothing to her. Maybe she's been a nurse. Maybe she's just tired of the whole business of bodies.

He writes a check for the balance owed and makes a point of checking her name-tag: "Goodbye, Lareice," he says. "See you in a couple of months.

She glances at the check: "Goodbye, Mr. Abbey." She comes close to smiling, almost lets a hint of friendliness creep into her voice.

Back in the car, he thinks, It would certainly be under-standable if she just has a blanket resentment of whites. Who knows what treatment she's had to put up with in her life. Maybe she's learned to hate men also. Race matters, gender matters, there is no denying that. It's just that he's sure they have a lot of things in common that matter also: children, middle-age, the way that their generation was brought up, a subtler code of sexuality—markers that traverse boundaries of sex and color. Maybe these are the denominators that, against all reason, have kept his wife and him together. He turns the key in the ignition, late for a meeting on campus. Hemingway said, at about Jimmy's age, that people were dying who had never died before. It seems to Jimmy that, all of a sudden, he is learning things he never learned before.

SHERRIE FLICK

How I Left Ned

I KNEW FROM THE start the men who sold me the corn
were not farmers. They didn't have the right look or peace-
ful demeanor. They did not *look like* farmers. Their clothes for
instance and their hair.

Now their location was okay: Dirt road. Fields. They had a
pickup, big blue sky—but gold chains and razor stubble. Soft
curly perms like poodles. Big black poodles dressed like
Italian men, selling corn. Cologne. Hell, I'm no fool. A real
farmer would shave before he struck out to sell some produce. Especially corn. Especially in Nebraska. And I know
farmers, in general—with the public at least—are kind and
gentle and generous. This has been my experience. It was
clear these guys were going for pure profit, and there I was
with my car idling, just expecting fairness.

I said I wanted four. Four ears, just so there was no confusion.
One of them said, "I'll sell you six for two dollars."

I know as well as the next person that two dollars is too

high a price for anything less than a dozen of anything grown and sold alongside the highway. I said, "Four."

He said, "I'll throw in an extra, make it seven."

I said, "Four."

He looked at me, smiled and shrugged. He said, "We only deal in bulk," as he turned his back on me. The other one looked way off into the patch of sky beyond my head as if he expected me to float away and eventually make it into his line of vision.

By now I'm wanting the corn. *Wanting* it. I can see the sample ear. It looks fresh and young and perky the way a young farmer would look waiting at church on Sunday to shake the preacher's wife's hand. Young. Perky. I wanted it. I did not, however, want these faux farmers messing with me—ripping me off. Right in the middle of the Midwest.

I said, "Six. Okay. I'll make some friends, have a cookout. It'll be good for me to expand my social circle beyond me and Ned and the cat." These two fake farmers looked at each other like they had a secret, and then one picked up a bag and put eight ears in.

"Bulk," he said. He said it like he was saying, "Pussy." A threat.

I said, "Three dozen." Folded my arms across my chest.

The other one who before this had been staring at my chest—the one without the bag—raised his eyebrows real nonchalantly—like three dozen was like two—like it was nothing really—three dozen ears.

I said, "That would be thirty-six ears. A whole lot of corn." He looked at me like he had a whole crop of corn back by his farm—corn beside cows and a silo and some pigs. But I knew. No way. He lived in a seedy tenement building. He knew what a cockroach looked like. I bet he couldn't start a lawn mower let alone a John Deere to save his life. I knew. The corn was hot.

The guy with the bag said, "Three dozen. Why not make it four? Why stop at thirty-six when you could have forty-eight? Why not make a whole lot of friends while you're at this socializing?" He was implying I couldn't socialize if somebody paid me. I was getting pissed.

The bag was full-up. He was putting ears of corn in willy-nilly now, like he'd never stop. The bag was full. A big grocery bag full of corn there in the late-afternoon sun. A big grocery bag sitting on the gate of the faded red pickup. The sun shifted. The wind blew. And suddenly, like a brick in the head, I understood bulk food. The beauty of a silo of wheat. The immensity of thirty pounds of soy beans. The numbers. The quantity. The bulk.

I thought about Ned, about his organic lentils and his rice cakes. About his fat content and antioxidant obsession, about his juicer. I thought about Ned spooning exactly one level teaspoon of nonfat sour cream onto his microwaved baked potato every Wednesday night as a special treat. I thought about Ned tying his condom into a little knot when he was done, pulling a Kleenex from the box beside the bed—dabbing himself and pecking me on the cheek.

I thought then about pounds of butter, gallons of whole milk—ears of corn. I thought about ears and ears and ears. Then I thought about divorce.

The fake farmer still sitting in the lawn chair—the one with the Catholic-looking medallion sitting on his hairy exposed chest—had lit up a cigarette. He inhaled slowly, squinting his eyes. Looking me over he said, "Hell, hon. We'll give you a deal on this whole truckload if you want. Think about the possibilities," he said.

He smiled like he was making a joke. Then he was laughing like the joke he was making was funny.

I said, "You know. Confidentially. Ned is an asshole."

The two fake farmers looked at each other with sly grins, "This Ned," one said with a wink, "we could take care of him, you know. Teach him to appreciate corn if necessary."

Crickets made noises all around. Cars zoomed from up on the Interstate. I heard the whirring of big bugs off in the distance—the kind I don't like to think about.

I knew they had found some farmer somewhere, stolen his truck, his corn, probably shot his dog.

I smiled. I said softly, "Did anyone see?"

One thrust the full sack toward me. The other stood up and coughed, smoothed the crease running along the front of his pants.

"We better be going," he said.

I said, "Okay," heading toward the passenger door of their truck.

He said, "No *we* better be going. We've got some corn to eat. Things to do."

I smiled. I said, "I *like* corn. I like to eat it. I like to look at it. I like to sell it." Slowly, I said, "I don't mind quality produce one bit."

This was the way we came into an understanding.

I left my car right there, engine running. I hopped in, holding onto my bulging bag.

Down the road a few miles the one behind the wheel said, "Just to be fair. That'll be five-fifty."

After I handed over the money, he said, "Much obliged."

It was then I noticed his Italian loafers. I put my hand on one fake farmer knee, then another. I looked straight ahead. I asked about dinner, about the possibilities of building a small stand where we could settle down for a while. They both nodded. I turned up the country music on the radio. I thanked my lucky stars.

Moscow

S HE TOLD HIM: "I am completely naked."

These were the first words she spoke and they tumbled from her mouth, beautifully shaped, smoothed by an accent which sounded French, but was from farther east, Moscow, so that what he heard was: *Ah im compledly neggid.* Her voice rose slightly, placed emphasis on the third word, as if her nakedness were a gift meant entirely for him, presented without forethought, without the least awareness of the rougher ends to which such declarations can be put.

They were on a thin, hissing phone line. She might have been speaking from fifty years ago. He closed his eyes. And as he did, she slipped into a new kind of nakedness, a nakedness untainted by the body's awful math, restored to classical grace. He saw white breasts, plucked from the white of her chest, her high bottom, the soft furrows of her rib cage. He saw her on tiptoe. He saw her lips make the words in wide, red bands.

He understood that what she said was not intended as titillation, even coy provocation. It was merely a happy coincidence. The phone rang and, in her urgent hope that it be him, she picked the receiver up, forgetting to cover herself, forgetting that she stood, in her apartment, in Moscow, without a stitch of clothing. It was an act of forgetting, then. And her statement to him, an act of delighted remembrance.

He desired in her this wondrous capacity, no hint of which she had shown him previously, that she would someday grow so accustomed to him, so unembarrassed by her own physicality, that she would forget, and then remember, her own nakedness, that just such a cycle might mark their days together. Hearing her words, he felt transported above shame, above lust and privation. If the moment could be clung to, sustained like a perfect note. Perhaps Moscow was such a place. Perhaps there, such possibilities existed.

He had never visited, had only seen photos: grim, towering statues, wide streets, open squares, and, on the horizon, church spires of the oddest shape, like clumps of wet chocolate drawn to a point. Perhaps Moscow was banked in snow, and perhaps the heat of her pale body, standing beside a window, caused the pane to fog.

But even as this image formed, a second image took shape, of him below her window, outside, staring up. And here, from this vantage point, she grew blurry, obscured not by some trick of condensation, or light or distance, but his own insistent longing.

Hardly any time had passed since she spoke, but now he could not see her at all, not as she had existed before. He felt the hard knock of need, stiffened against himself. He might have reached out, tried to explain to her what was happening, but he didn't understand himself. A singular vision of love was perfecting itself in the singular shape of her. And yet that shape, by its very recognition, was now receding, dissolving, and reemerging as something else, a myth of his own illusive want, a creature with a thatch of glistening pubic hair, a crude mouth, nipples the color of bruises.

Years later he toured the factory in Hershey, Pennsylvania. It was late and he was the only visitor, and the guide—a young woman in a severe suit—walked him briskly through each cavernous room. Workers in surgical scrubs scurried to and fro. Steel machines hissed and banged and choked. He watched one dip down and release through invisible apertures a thousand coins of chocolate, then pull away so violently as to bring these to a sharp, liquid point. The process was repeated time and again, a mass production of the inimitable, which seemed to him, in that moment, terribly wrong.

He hadn't loved her in the beginning. He was sure of that. He may never have loved her for more than that one, long-ago moment.

But now, as he watched the spires of Moscow reproduced in miniature, as the guide hustled him along toward a bin with free chocolates, urging him to select one-just-one-now-is-the-moment-sir-*please*, coldly appraising his dazed expression; now, as he staggered toward the bin and obediently removed a piece, as he exited into the frigid parking lot, as he tore at the foil, as the chocolate fell into his mouth through a puff of steamy breath and began at once to seep away; now he recognized that he would never rid himself of the moment. It was insoluble.

He had suffered, without a doubt, one perfect memory which, though misplaced, had never been forgotten. It lived inside him and would continue to do so for the rest of his life, to be reawakened again and again. And so he got into his car and drove on the turnpike and exited and turned into a field and stopped the car and stepped outside and removed each piece of his clothing and lay down in the banked snow and waited for Moscow—the cold lips of that distant city—to brush his skin.

ABOUT THE AUTHORS

Steve Almond is the author of two story collections, *My Life in Heavy Metal* and *The Evil B.B. Chow*, and the nonfiction book *Candyfreak*. His new novel, *Which Brings Me to You* (written with Julianna Baggott), came out in 2006. He lives in Somerville, Massachusetts, and teaches at Boston College. More of his work can be found at www.bbchow.com.

Steve Amick is the author of the novel *The Lake, the River & the Other Lake* (Pantheon). His short fiction has appeared in *McSweeney's*, the *Southern Review*, the *New England Review*, *Playboy*, *Story*, the anthology *The Sound of Writing*, and on National Public Radio; his nonfiction, in the *New York Times* and the *Washington Post*. He has been a college instructor, playwright, copywriter, songwriter, and musician. He was born in Ann Arbor in 1964 and lives there now. Though he has never been afflicted with Pica, it is, for some, a potentially dangerous medical condition. See more at www.steve-amick.com.

Larissa Amir grew up in Livermore, California. She and her husband live in Seattle, where she works as a stockbroker. Her stories have appeared in the *Portland Review* and *eye~rhyme*. She is currently writing a short novel and story collection.

Jorge Luis Arzola is a member of the National Union of Writers and Artists of Cuba. With his book *Prisionero en el círculo del hori-*

zonte, Arzola became nationally known; among his award-winning works are *Los últimos serán los primeros* (The Last Will Be The First, Havana, 1994), *The Voice of the Turtle* (London, 1997), and *La bandada infinita* (The Infinite Bandana, Havana, 2000).

Aimee Bender is the author of the short story collections *Willful Creatures* and *The Girl in the Flammable Skirt,* which was a *New York Times* Notable Book and a *Los Angeles Times* selection of the year, as was her novel, *Invisible Sign of My Own.* Her short stories have appeared in *Granta, Harper's,* the *Paris Review, GQ, Fence,* and *McSweeney's,* and have been broadcast on National Public Radio's *This American Life.* She won a Pushcart Prize in 2002. Her web site is www.flammableskirt.com.

Elizabeth Berg is the author of several novels, including the *New York Times* best sellers *True to Form, Never Change,* and *Open House,* which was an Oprah's Book Club selection; *Joy School* and *Durable Goods* were both selected as American Library Association Best Book of the Year; her novels also won a New England Booksellers' Award. *The Year of Pleasures* was published in 2005. A former nurse, she lives in Chicago.

Tessa Brown grew up and still lives in Chicago. Her fiction has appeared in *Harper's,* and she also writes book reviews for the *Forward.* She is a junior at Princeton University, where she is studying religion.

Robert Olen Butler has won many awards for his fiction, including a Pulitzer Prize in 1993, two National Magazine Awards in Fiction, and the Richard and Hinda Rosenthal Award from the American Academy of Arts and Letters. He is the author of ten novels and four story collections, the most recent of which is a volume of sudden fiction, *Severance.* Another book of sudden fiction, based on the photographs of Weegee, will be published in 2007.

He teaches creative writing at Florida State University. The author's web page is www.fsu.edu/butler.

Ron Carlson is the author of eight books of fiction, including his selected stories, *A Kind of Flying*. His work has appeared in many magazines such as *Esquire*, *Harper's*, *The New Yorker*, *Gentlemen's Quarterly*, *Tin House*, and the *North American Review*, and in dozens of anthologies such as *The Best American Short Stories*, *The O'Henry Prize Stories*, and *The Norton Anthology of Short Fiction*. Among his awards are the Cohen Prize from *Ploughshares* and a National Endowment for the Arts fellowship. His novel *Five Skies* will be published in 2007.

Lan Samantha Chang is the author of a collection of stories, *Hunger*, and a novel, *Inheritance*. She was on the faculty at Harvard, has taught at numerous writers' conferences and workshops, and is now the director of the University of Iowa Writers' Workshop. Her work has appeared in the *Atlantic Monthly*, *Ploughshares*, and *The Best American Short Stories*, has won many awards, and has been translated into more than a half dozen languages.

Margaret Jull Costa has translated many Portuguese, Spanish, and Latin American writers, including Eça de Queiroz, Mário de Sá-Carneiro, José Régio, Bernardo Atxaga, Ramón del Valle-Inclán, Carmen Martín Gaite, and Juan José Saer. She was joint winner of the Portuguese Translation Prize in 1992 for her version of *The Book of Disquiet* by Fernando Pessoa, and won the translator's portion of the 1997 International IMPAC Dublin Literary Award for Javier Marías's *A Heart So White*, as well as the 2000 Weidenfeld Translation Prize for *All the Names* by José Saramago.

Ronald F. Currie Jr. is a native of Waterville, Maine. His fiction has appeared in *Glimmer Train*, the *Alaska Quarterly Review*, the *Cincinnati Review*, *The Sun*, *Swink*, the *Southeast Review*, and elsewhere. His first novel, *God is Dead*, will be published in 2007 by Viking. His web site is www.roncurrie.com.

Pia Z. Ehrhardt lives in New Orleans with her husband and son. Her stories have appeared in *McSweeney's*, the *Mississippi Review*, *Quick Fiction*, and *Narrative Magazine*; her short story collection, *Famous Fathers* (2007), and her novel, *Speeding in the Driveway* (2008), will be published by MacAdam/Cage. She is the recipient of the 2005 Narrative Prize. Her web site is www.piaze.com.

Zdravka Evtimova has published four short story collections and three novels in her native Bulgaria. Her stories have been published in literary magazines throughout Europe and the United States, Canada, Argentina, and India; her novella collection *Bitter Sky* was published in Great Britain, and her novel *God of Traitors* was published as an e-book by Buck Publications. Evtimova works as a literary translator for the Bulgarian Ministry of Culture and has translated many novels from English and German into Bulgarian. She lives with her husband, two sons, and daughter in Pernik. Her story "Blood" was originally published under the title "Blood of a Mole."

Sherrie Flick is the author of the award-winning flash fiction chapbook *I Call This Flirting* (Flume Press, 2004). Many literary journals have published her work, including *Mānoa*, the *North American Review*, *Prairie Schooner*, *Puerto del Sol*, and *Quarterly West*. Anthologies in which her work has appeared include *Flash Fiction Forward* (W. W. Norton, 2006) and *Sudden Fiction: The Mammoth Book of Minuscule Fiction* (Mammoth Press, 2003). She lives in Pittsburgh, where she is the cofounder and artistic director of the Gist Street Reading Series. Find out more about her at www.gist street.org.

Geoffrey Forsyth's fiction has appeared or is forthcoming in the *New Orleans Review*, *Other Voices*, *CutBank*, the *River Oak Review*, the *Newport Review, Oyez Review, Rhino, Karamu*, and the *Gihon River Review.* He lives in LaGrange Park, Illinois.

Ronald Frame was born in 1953 in Glasgow, Scotland, and educated there and at Oxford University. A previous winner of the Samuel Beckett Prize among other awards, he has produced thirteen works of fiction, five of which have been published in the United States. He also writes for radio and television. His novel *The Lantern Bearers* (U.S. edition, Counterpoint, 2001) is being developed for the screen. Eleven of his Scottish-set short stories have appeared recently in American journals. Others have been read on national BBC radio in Great Britain.

Tom Franklin is from Dickinson, Alabama. His collection of stories, *Poachers*, was named Best First Book of Fiction by *Esquire.* The title story of the book also won an Edgar Award. He is the author of two novels, *Hell at the Breach* and *Smonk*. He lives in Oxford, Mississippi, with his wife, poet Beth Ann Fennelly, and their two young children, Claire and Thomas.

Ian Frazier's books include *On the Rez, Great Plains, Coyote v. Acme, Fish's Eye, Dating Your Mom*, and *Nobody Better, Better Than Nobody.* He wrote for the *Lampoon* at Harvard, was a staff writer for *The New Yorker*, and edited the *Best American Travel Writing* anthology in 2003. Frazier's work has also appeared in the *Atlantic*, the *Washington Post Magazine*, and other publications. He grew up in Ohio and now lives in Montclair, New Jersey.

Lynn Freed was born and grew up in Durban, South Africa, and moved to New York to take graduate degrees at Columbia University. She is the author of five novels, including *Heart Change*, which was republished as *Friends of the Family* by Story Line Press in 2000; a collection of short stories, *The Curse of the Appropriate Man*, which was a *New York Times* Notable Book of the Year in

2004; and a collection of essays, *Reading, Writing & Leaving Home.* Her work has appeared in many magazines, such as *The New Yorker, Harper's,* the *Atlantic Monthly,* the *Southwest Review,* the *Santa Monica Review,* the *New York Times,* the *Washington Post, Mirabella, House Beautiful,* and *Vogue.* See more at www.lynnfreed.com.

George Garrett is the author of the novels *Death of the Fox* and *The King of Babylon Shall Not Come Against You.* He has written thirty books of fiction, poetry, drama, and criticism and has edited twenty-five more. Among his many honors are the Rome Prize, an Award in Literature from the American Academy and Institute of Arts and Letters, the T. S. Eliot Award, and the PEN/Malamud Award for Short Fiction. He is Henry Hoyns Professor Emeritus of Creative Writing at the University of Virginia and lives in Charlottesville with his wife of fifty-four years, Susan.

Teolinda Gersão has been a lecturer in Portuguese at the Technical University of Berlin, a professor at the New University of Lisbon, and recently a resident writer at the University of California at Berkeley. A central theme in her novels and other works is the concept of time within various periods of Portuguese history: the Salazar dictatorship (*Paisagem com mulher e mar ao fundo* [Landscape with Woman and the Sea]), the twenties (*O cavalo de sol* [The Sun Horse]), the nineteenth century (*A casa da cabeça de cavalo* [The House of the Horse's Head]), and the fifties and sixties in Portuguese colonial Mozambique (*A árvore das palavras* [The Word Tree]). Her web site is www.teolinda-gersao.com.

Barry Gifford's *Night People* was awarded the Premio Brancati in Italy, and he has received awards from PEN, the National Endowment for the Arts, the American Library Association, the Writers Guild of America, and the Christopher Isherwood Foundation. David Lynch's film *Wild at Heart,* which was based on Gifford's novel, won the Palme d'Or at the Cannes Film Festival in

1990, and his novel *Perdita Durango* was made into a feature film by Spanish director Alex de la Iglesia in 1997. Barry Gifford co-wrote the film *Lost Highway* (1997); he also co-wrote the film *City of Ghosts* (2003), as well as the libretto for Ichiro Nodaira's opera *Madrugada* (2005). He lives in the San Francisco Bay Area. For more information please visit www.barrygifford.com.

Nadine Gordimer was born and raised in South Africa. She has been politically active most of her life, and has often written about the relationships among white radicals, liberals, and blacks in South Africa. Her collection *Loot and Other Stories* (2003) is her first since she won the Nobel Prize in Literature in 1991. Her latest novels are *Pickup* (2002) and *Get a Life* (2005).

John Gould is the author of *Kilter: 55 Fictions*—which was short-listed for the Giller Prize in Canada—and *The Kingdom of Heaven: Eighty-Eight Palm-of-the-Hand Stories*. He teaches in the Department of Writing at the University of Victoria and serves on the editorial board of the *Malahat Review*. He lives in Victoria, with his wife and stepchildren.

Ron Hansen is the author of the novel *Isn't It Romantic?* (2003) and a book of essays called *A Stay Against Confusion: Essays on Faith and Fiction* (2001). Among his other books are *Desperadoes: The Assassination of Jesse James by the Coward Robert Ford*, *Nebraska* (a collection of stories that won an award in literature from the American Academy and Institute of Arts and Letters), *Mariette in Ecstasy*, *Atticus* (a finalist for the National Book Award), and a children's book, *The Shadowmaker* (Trophy Press). A native of Omaha, he is Gerard Manley Hopkins, S.J., Professor of the Arts and Humanities at Santa Clara University.

Tobias Hecht is the author of *After Life: An Ethnographic Novel*, from Duke University Press. His first book, *At Home in the Street*, from Cambridge University Press, won the 2002 Margaret Mead Award. He has translated several works of fiction, including a collection of short stories, *The Museum of Useless Efforts*, by Cristina Peri Rossi. He also writes in Spanish, and his story "La sexta columna" won second prize in the Hucha de Oro, Spain's most important prize in the category of the short story.

Ursula Hegi grew up in a small German town and moved to the United States when she was eighteen. At twenty-eight, with two sons under five years old, she enrolled as an undergraduate at the University of New Hampshire. She won many awards for her writing, including five PEN Syndicated Fiction Awards, became a professor of creative writing at Eastern Washington University, and lived in the Pacific Northwest for many years. She now lives in New York State. Her novel *Stones from the River* was an Oprah's Book Club selection. Her latest novel is *Sacred Time*, and she is also the author of a children's book, *Trudi & Pia*.

Robin Hemley is the author of seven books of fiction and nonfiction. He has published his stories and essays in the *New York Times*, *New York Magazine*, the *Chicago Tribune*, *Southern Review*, *Prairie Schooner*, *Creative Nonfiction*, *Fourth Genre*, *Ploughshares*, *Shenandoah*, and many other literary magazines and anthologies. He has won two Pushcart Prizes, among many other awards, and his work has been published in Great Britain, Germany, the Philippines, Sweden, and Japan. He is Director of the Nonfiction Writing Program at the University of Iowa and writes a bimonthly column for *The Believer* on defunct literary journals. See more at www.english.uiowa.edu/faculty/hemley.

Jenny Hollowell was a Henry Hoyns Fellow in Fiction at the University of Virginia and the recipient of the 2002 Balch Short Story Award. She lives in Brooklyn, where she is at work on her first novel. "A History of Everything, Including You" is her first published story.

Ha Jin served from the age of fourteen until he was twenty in the People's Liberation Army in China. Upon his release he taught himself English, working the night shift as a railroad telegrapher, and came to the United States in 1985 to pursue graduate work at Brandeis University. After the Tiananmen massacre in 1989, he decided to stay. His poetry and fiction have won numerous awards, including the PEN/Hemingway. His novel *Waiting*, the story of an army doctor in Communist China in the late 1960s, received the National Book Award. In 2005 his novel *War Trash*, about a Chinese soldier taken prisoner during the Korean War, earned him his second PEN/Faulkner Award.

Roy Kesey was born in California and currently lives in Beijing with his wife and children. His fiction and creative nonfiction have appeared in more than forty magazines, including the *Georgia Review*, *Other Voices*, *Quarterly West*, and *Maisonneuve*. His novella *Nothing in the World* won the 2005 Bullfight Review Little Book Prize, and was published in 2006. His dispatches from China appear regularly on the *McSweeney's* web site, and his "Little-Known Corners" meta-column appears monthly in *That's Beijing*. See more about him and his work at www.myspace.com/roykesey.

Robert King's stories have appeared recently in the *Cream City Review*, the *Potomac Review*, the *Crab Creek Review*, and the *Baltimore Review*. His poems have appeared in *Poetry*, the *Missouri Review*, *Northeast*, the *Atlanta Review*, and many other literary magazines. A poetry chapbook, *What It Was Like*, appeared in 2003, and a creative nonfiction volume, *Stepping Twice into the River*, in 2005; and a volume of poems, *Old Man Laughing*, is due out in 2007. A professor emeritus at the University of North Dakota, he now lives in Greeley, where he teaches part-time at the University of Northern Colorado.

Chrissy Kolaya is a poet and fiction writer from Chicago now living in rural Minnesota. Her poems have appeared in *Salt Hill* and the *North American Review*, and her fiction in *Iron Horse* and *Crazyhorse*. She is currently at work on a novel.

Andrew Lam was born in Vietnam and now lives in San Francisco, where he works as an editor for New America Media. He is the author of *Perfume Dreams: Reflections on The Vietnamese Diaspora*, which won the 2006 PEN-Beyond the Margins Award, and is a commentator on National Public Radio's *All Things Considered*. Lam is working on his first collection of stories. His essays can be read at http://news.pacificnews.org.

Romulus Linney's recent plays include adaptations of Ernest L. Gaines' novel *A Lesson Before Dying* and an adaptation of Tim O'Brien's novel *Going After Cacciato*. The winner of two Obie Awards, two National Book Critics Circle Awards, and three DramaLogue Awards, he is the founding playwright of the Signature Theatre Company, and was recently inducted into the American Academy of Arts and Letters. His fiction has appeared in *Pushcart Prize Stories* and *New Stories from the South: The Year's Best* (2001 and 2002). His latest novel is *Slowly, by Thy Hand Unfurled*. He has taught at Columbia, Princeton, the University of Pennsylvania, and the New School University. His daughter is the Emmy-winning actress Laura Linney.

Gerald Locklin has taught English at California State University at Long Beach since 1965. His numerous books of poetry, fiction, and criticism include *The Case of the Missing Blue Volkswagen*, *Charles Bukowski: A Sure Bet*, *The Firebird Poems*, *Down and Out*, *Go West, Young Toad*, *Candy Bars: Selected Stories*, *The Life Force Poems*, and *The Pocket Book*. His magazine publications include the *Wormwood Review*, *Poetry/LA*, *Ambit*, *Tears in the Fence*, *5 AM*, the *New York Quarterly*, *Slipstream*, *Nerve Cowboy*, and the *American Scholar*. See more at www.geraldlocklin.com.

Peter Markus has written three books of short-short fiction: *Good, Brother, The Moon Is a Lighthouse,* and *The Singing Fish.* His short-short stories have appeared in the *Black Warrior Review,* the *Massachusetts Review, Quarterly West, Northwest Review,* the *New Orleans Review, Third Coast,* the *Seattle Review,* and other publications. He has taught at the Interlochen Center for the Arts, has served as poet-in-the-schools in the public schools of Detroit, and now divides his time between Michigan and New York, where he is on the faculty of the Gotham Writers' Workshop. You can also find his work at www.calamaripress.com.

Yann Martel is the author of *The Facts Behind the Helsinki Roccamatios,* a collection of short stories, and *Self,* a novel. His novel *Life of Pi* won the 2002 Booker Prize for fiction and the 2003 edition of CBC Radio's Canada Reads, both the English and French competitions. He spent six months in India preparing to write *Life of Pi,* and a year in Saskatoon, Saskatchewan, as the public library's writer-in-residence; recently he collaborated with composer Omar Daniel on a piece of music based on his writing. Martel lives in Montreal, where he frequently volunteers in a palliative care unit.

Patricia Marx was the first girl on the *Harvard Lampoon.* She writes books and magazine pieces as well as comedy for film and television. Her television credits include *Saturday Night Live* and *Rugrats.* Among her books are *How to Regain Your Virginity, Blockbuster,* and several children's books illustrated by cartoonist Roz Chast, including *Now Everybody Really Hates Me* and *Meet My Staff,* winner of the Friedrich Medal (an award made up by Patricia Marx and named after her air conditioner). Her magazine pieces have appeared in *The New Yorker,* the *New York Times, Vogue,* and the *Atlantic Monthly.* She teaches sketch comedy at New York University.

Elizabeth McBride lives in Marfa, Texas. She writes an arts and culture column for *The Desert-Mountain Times*, an independent weekly newspaper in far west Texas. She has published fiction, poetry, essays, and art criticism in various places, including the literary magazine *Chelsea*. Find out more about her at www.eliza bethmcbride.com.

John McNally is the author of *America's Report Card*, *The Book of Ralph*, and *Troublemakers*, which won the John Simmons Short Fiction Award and the Nebraska Book Award. He was a 2005 National Magazine Award finalist for a short story that appeared in the *Virginia Quarterly Review*. He is the editor of five anthologies, most recently *When I Was a Loser*, a collection of original essays about high school loserdom. He is also a screenwriter—the recipient of a Chesterfield Writers' Film Project fellowship sponsored by Paramount Pictures. A native of Chicago's Southwest Side, he and his wife, Amy, live in Winston-Salem, North Carolina, where he is an associate professor of English at Wake Forest University. His web site is www.bookofralph.com.

Juan José Millás is a contemporary Spanish novelist and the author of short stories that have been translated into a dozen languages. He has won a number of Spain's most important literary prizes for fiction; his recent works include *Todo son preguntas* (Everything Is Questions), *Hay algo que no es como me dicen* (There's Something That's Not as They Tell Me) and *Cuentos de adúlteros desorientados* (Stories of Disoriented Adulterers). He has worked on a series of short films, *10 trenes 10* (10 Trains 10), and as a journalist has covered political campaigns for the newspaper *El País*. His web page is www.juanjose-millas.com.

Kirk Nesset is the author of *Mr. Agreeable*, a book of short stories, and a nonfiction study, *The Stories of Raymond Carver*. His stories, poems, and translations have appeared in the *Paris Review*,

Ploughshares, *Raritan*, the *Kenyon Review*, the *Boston Review*, the *Southern Review*, the *Iowa Review*, the *Carolina Quarterly*, and *Prairie Schooner*, and in anthologies such as *Flash Fiction Forward*. His story "Mr. Agreeable," originally published in *Fiction*, appeared in *The Pushcart Prize XXIII*. He teaches at Allegheny College, is a gothic rock DJ, and sings and plays guitar in a rock group called Unkle John's Band. See more about his work at merlin2.alleg.edu/employee/k/knesset/links.html.

Katherin Nolte's fiction has appeared or is forthcoming in *Glimmer Train*, *Confrontation*, *Fence*, the *Blue Mesa Review*, *Natural Bridge*, the *Beloit Fiction Journal*, *Quick Fiction*, and elsewhere. The story "Before the Train and After" won first place in the *Writer's Digest* fourth annual Short Short Story Competition in 2004. She was Truman Capote Fellow at the University of Iowa Writers' Workshop in 2003–4.

Joyce Carol Oates is the author of more than seventy books. Among her awards are the National Book Award, the Richard and Hinda Rosenthal Award from the American Academy of Arts and Letters, the O'Henry Prize for Continued Achievement in the Short Story, the Elmer Holmes Bobst Lifetime Achievement Award in Fiction, the Rea Award for the Short Story, and membership in the American Academy of Arts and Letters. Oates' fiction includes *American Appetites*; *Because It Is Bitter, and Because It Is My Heart*; *The Rise of Life on Earth*; *Heat and Other Stories*; and *Foxfire: Confessions of a Girl Gang*. In 2006 *High Lonesome: Selected Stories 1966–2006* was published. Find her author web site at www.harpercollins.com.

Peter Orner was born in Chicago in 1968. He is the author of the novel *The Second Coming of Mavala Shikongo* and the story collection *Esther Stories*, which received the Rome Prize from the American Academy of Arts and Letters and was a finalist for the PEN/Hemingway Award. His work has appeared in the *Atlantic*

Monthly, the *Paris Review*, *The Best American Short Stories*, and *The Pushcart Prize XXV*. Orner teaches in the graduate writing program at San Francisco State University.

Charles Michael "Chuck" Palahniuk is a satirical novelist and freelance journalist living in Portland, Oregon. He is best known for the award-winning novel *Fight Club*, which was later made into a film directed by David Fincher. His most recent novels include *Haunted* and *Rant*.

Frederick Adolf Paola is the medical director of and an associate professor in the Nova Southeastern University Physician Assistant Program in Naples, Florida. He is an associate professor of medicine in the Division of Medical Ethics and Humanities at the University of South Florida College of Medicine in Tampa, Florida. His short stories have appeared in the *Journal of the American Medical Association* (*JAMA*), the *Canadian Medical Association Journal*, the *Bellevue Literary Review*, and *Tatlin's Tower*. He is the father of three and husband of one.

Dean Paschal, an emergency room physician in New Orleans, has three completed, as yet unpublished, novels. His collection of stories, *By the Light of the Jukebox*, was published in 2002 by Ontario Review Press. He has been published in *The Best American Short Stories* of 2003 and received a Pushcart Prize in 2004 for his story "Sautéing the Platygast."

Leslie Pietrzyk is the author of two novels, *Pears on a Willow Tree* and *A Year and a Day*. Her short fiction has appeared in many literary magazines, including the *Iowa Review*, the *Gettysburg Review*, *TriQuarterly*, and the *New England Review*, and her work has won a number of writing awards, including *Shenandoah*'s Jean Charpiot Goodheart Prize for Fiction. For more information, go to www.lesliepietrzyk.com.

Stacey Richter is the author of *My Date with Satan,* a collection of stories. Her work has won many prizes, including the National Magazine Award for fiction. Her new collection of stories will be published in 2007 by Counterpoint Books. Visit her web site at www.staceyrichter.com.

Benjamin Alire Sáenz was born in a small town in New Mexico. He grew up writing and painting, and continues to do both. He has published four books of poems, four novels, a collection of short stories, and two books for children. His most recent novel, *In Perfect Light,* was published by Rayo/HarperCollins, and his most recent book of poems, *Dreaming the End of War,* was published by Copper Canyon Press. Sáenz teaches creative writing at the University of Texas at El Paso. His web site is www.benjaminaliresaenz.com.

Sam Shepard is the Pulitzer Prize-winning author of over forty-five plays, as well as numerous short stories and essays. Eleven of his plays have won Obie Awards, including *Buried Child, The Late Henry Moss, Simpatico, Curse of the Starving Class, True West, Fool for Love, The God of Hell,* and *A Lie of the Mind,* which won a New York Drama Desk Award. As an actor he has appeared in more than thirty films, and he received an Oscar nomination in 1984 for his performance in *The Right Stuff.* Shepard was inducted into the Theatre Hall of Fame in 1994. He lives in Minnesota.

Claudia Smith lives in Austin, Texas, with her husband, Nathen Hinson, and her son, William. Before becoming a mother, she worked as a librarian. Her fiction has appeared in online and print journals; she also guest-edited the November 2005 web issue of *Hobart* magazine. Her stories may be found online at www.claudiaweb.net.

Leelila Strogov is the editor of the literary magazine *Swink.* Her fiction and essays have been published in *Before & After: Stories from New York, Other Voices,* and the *Barcelona Review.*

Touré is a novelist and contributing editor for *Rolling Stone.* He has also hosted *Spoke N' Heard* on MTV2. He is the author of *Portable Promised Land: Stories* (2002). Over the past ten years Touré (who, like many of the music stars he interviews, goes by only one name) has created an impressive body of work that has appeared in *The New Yorker, The Source, Rolling Stone,* and *Playboy.* Having interviewed the likes of Lauryn Hill, Prince, DMX, Jay-Z, Notorious B.I.G., and Tupac Shakur, he is one of music journalism's most in-demand writers. He also holds the distinction of being *Rolling Stone's* first African-American staff writer. See www.toure.com.

Kimberly Kepa'a Tubania lives and writes in Pearl City, near Honolulu. "Doughnut Shops and Doormen," her first published story, appeared in the *Hawai'i Review.*

Deb Olin Unferth's stories have appeared in the *Boston Review, Harper's, Conjunctions, McSweeney's, Fence, Noon, StoryQuarterly,* the Pushcart Prize anthologies, and other publications.

David Foster Wallace is the author of *Girl with Curious Hair, Infinite Jest, A Supposedly Fun Thing I'll Never Do Again: Essays and Arguments, Brief Interviews with Hideous Men, Oblivion: Stories,* and *Everything and More: A Compact History of Infinity.* His essays and stories have appeared in *The New Yorker, Harper's, Playboy,* the *Paris Review, Conjunctions, Premiere, Tennis,* the *Missouri Review,* and the *Review of Contemporary Fiction.* His awards include a MacArthur Foundation "genius grant," a Whiting Award, a Lannan Award for Fiction, the Paris Review Prize for humor, and the QPB Joe Savago New Voices Award. He teaches creative writing and English at Pomona College.

Stephanie Waxman is the author of the internationally published *What Is a Girl? What Is a Boy?* and *Growing Up Feeling Good.* Her *A Helping Handbook—When a Loved One Is Critically Ill* was published in 2000. Waxman has worked extensively in the theater and has lectured throughout the world. Her fiction has appeared in the *Missouri Review*, *Bitter Oleander*, the *North Dakota Quarterly*, *The Distillery*, *Meridian*, *Oregon East*, *RE:AL*, *Epicenter*, *RiverSedge*, *Fox Cry Review*, and *Bridges*. See www.stephaniewaxman.com.

Tobias Wolff's books include two novels, *The Barracks Thief* and *Old School*; two memoirs, *This Boy's Life* and *In Pharaoh's Army*; and three collections of short stories, *In the Garden of the North American Martyrs*, *Back in the World*, and *The Night in Question*. He has also been the editor of *The Best American Short Stories*, *The Vintage Book of Contemporary American Short Stories*, and *A Doctor's Visit: The Short Stories of Anton Chekhov*. His work appears regularly in *The New Yorker*, the *Atlantic*, *Harper's*, and other magazines. He is currently Ward W. and Priscilla B. Woods Professor in the School of Humanities and Sciences at Stanford, where he lives with his wife, Catherine. They have three children.

CREDITS